WONDERFUL LOVE

MAGGIE MARR

BOOKS BY MAGGIE MARR

The Hollywood Girls Club Series

Hollywood Girls Club

Secrets of the Hollywood Girls Club

Hollywood Hit

Hollywood Girls Club, the Series

The Eligible Billionaires Series

Can't Buy Me Love

One Night for Love

A Christmas Billionaire

Last Call for Love

Running from Love

Eligible Billionaires Books 1–5

Eligible Billionaires: The Travati Brothers

A Forever Love

A Billionaire for Christmas

A Convenient Arrangement

A Forbidden Love

Eligible Billionaires Books 6-9

The Powder Springs Series

Courting Trouble

The Christmas Wish

Candy Cane Lane

The Glamour Series

Hard Glamour

Broken Glamour

Fast Glamour

Easy Glamour

Luxe Glamour

Impossible Glamour

Coming Soon: Vicious Glamour

The Hollywood Hitmen Series

Beck

Coming Soon: Jax

The Wonderful Love Duet

Wonder F*ck

Mister WonderFULL

Wonderful Love

This book is dedicated to
Maria Connor
You are brilliant and dedicated beyond measure.
Thank you, for everything you do.

PART I

CHAPTER 1

"HOW DID YOU FIND ME?"

"A friend." Her voice cracks and her gaze drops. She stands on the far side of my hotel suite like a doe in the crosshairs. Her words are a lie. I see this in how she brushes her hand over her hair and tilts her head.

Keep in mind *she* called me. They always call me.

I stay still. I don't move. I'm draped across a chair on my side of the room. All pent-up sexual energy and alpha male, restrained and waiting for her command. My suit coat is slung over the couch. I've untucked my dress shirt and unbuttoned two buttons. The sleeves are rolled up just enough to show my forearms. I am the fantasy.

My gaze remains locked with hers. I keep my eyes up. Now is not the time to let my gaze drift over her body, although I know every inch already. I watched her come in. I watched her spot me across the room as though she'd just seen a panther. I watched the muscles in her body tighten and her pupils dilate with desire, combined with the type of internal conflict I often inspire in women.

I remain still. I never move toward women, not in the beginning. She needs to know she's safe. That I'm safe. Meeting a stranger alone in a hotel room is a risk for a woman. A big enough risk, that I know when a woman calls my number, when she shows up here, that she *needs* this. She needs what I can give her with every fiber of her being. She needs the Wonderfuck.

She's stunned by her own brazenness, and yet compelled to stay.

She's not young, but she's not old either. No wedding ring, but that means nothing. I don't ask, I never ask. She's ash blonde with blue eyes. A solid B cup, and I'd guess about ten pound more than she thinks she should weigh. Which is utter bullshit. She's gorgeous. All women are gorgeous, each of them in their own unique way. My fucking God, I wish every woman I met could get it straight in her mind that she's fucking beautiful no matter what some fashion magazine tells her.

"What should I call you?" My voice rasps out. I'm hard. Her mere presence makes me hard.

Panic races through her eyes. I can practically hear her fluttering hummingbird heartbeat all the way across the room. "You said no names."

"Exactly." My voice a deep rumble. My cock responds to her femininity, her beauty, even with her standing fearful on the far side of the suite. "No names, but what do you want me to *call* you?" I lift my eyebrow. "When we're together." Always interesting to see if a woman gives me her real name or a false one. I can tell based on their shoulders.

She places her fingertip to her lips. One tap. Two taps. Three taps. A thought brightens her gaze. "Natasha," she says, her voice taking on a silky, sexy, deeper sound, laced with a thread of desire.

My lip twitches upward. A lie. But a lie with a purpose. Something about this name, Natasha, this persona she'll inhabit when we're together, will allow her to feel what she wants. To be who she's always wanted to be. This name, this alias, will enable "Natasha" to embrace her sexuality.

A concept I completely understand.

"Natasha." I let the name roll over my tongue. The word comes out of my mouth like a long languid caress. On the syllables I place an unspoken promise of all the pleasure my mouth will give every inch of her body.

She shudders. Her breathing is shallow, but not from fear. The hand that clutches her purse drops and her breasts press forward. Her hips tilt a bit toward me as her nipples pebble against the fabric of her dress.

"I love the name Natasha," I say. I remain seated in the chair. My body is open, one arm laid along the back of the chair and my legs spread. I own this chair. I am all male. Sexy alpha in the domesticated position. All sexy beast simply waiting for her command.

Any command.

My cock is hard. I want this woman. I want to make her come. I want to make her feel. I want her to know when she walks out of this room that she is the all-powerful and beautiful woman I see standing in front of me.

My gaze meets hers and I smolder. I smolder for her. For the physical. Because this is all physical for me.

Heat sears between us.

Her gaze drops to my crotch. My cock is tough to miss when it's erect, and it's definitely hard and ready. Her mouth, with those pretty rosebud lips, drops open. A blush starts on her chest and rises over her neck to her cheeks. Her tongue darts out of her mouth and licks her lips. She bites her bottom lip and her eyes lift to meet mine again.

Natasha is nearly ready, but she needs permission, she needs a command, she needs me to tell her what to do. In this moment, she needs me to make this okay for her.

"Natasha come to me. I want to touch you."

She swallows. She has every bit of control. She doesn't know it yet, wouldn't believe it yet if I told her, but she'll have all the control the entire time we're together. Every time we're together. I'll tell her what I want to do to her, I'll even command her to do things, but she won't ever have to comply. This meeting, and any others we have after today, will always be about what she wants. For *her* pleasure.

She drops her purse onto the nearby table, and as though another woman takes over, *Natasha* pulls her hand through her hair and swaggers toward me. Her hips sway with a sexual confidence that she may be faking but is most definitely being conveyed. She stops in front of me. Her pulse pounds in her neck. Her shortened breath telegraphs both her anxiety and her excitement. Natasha is scared, she's uncomfortable, but she's also turned on as hell.

She leans forward over me and places a hand on each arm of my chair. Her hair falls along the side of her face. Her breath smells of mint. I recognize the citrus and floral notes of Chanel No. 5. The lines of her face are deeper than I thought, and her eyes are more green than blue.

"May I touch you, Natasha?" I ask, my voice low.

She takes a halting breath. She nods. But a nod isn't enough, not now, not this first time. I need to hear her. I need to hear her say yes or no, and know that she is getting exactly what she wants. I raise my face, my gaze still locked to hers, not moving, waiting. Finally, she answers.

"Yes."

I reach out and my hand clasps her waist, just above her hip. I stroke up the side of her body. Her face is near mine, her body bent over me. Her eyes are closed. "May I touch you here?" I ask. She nods.

"Tell me, Natasha."

"Yes," she whispers. My thumb strokes over the hard nipple beneath the fabric of her dress.

I'm completely engorged. Her face is flushed with desire. I want her and she wants me, but this first meeting is meant to be slow. Needs to be slow. My focus is to unleash the sexuality that remains hidden within her.

"You are incredibly sexy, Natasha. Do you know that?"

She licks her lips. Her energy shifts and her eyes remain closed. She doesn't know she's sexy. My hand glides over her body to her hip.

Her eyes open and drop to my cock, which presses against my pants.

"Do you want to touch me, Natasha?"

She nods.

"Tell me," I whisper. My fingertips circle her hip.

"Yes, I want to touch you."

"I'm yours. My body is yours."

Her gaze widens. She glances at my face as though this thought, this idea, is more than she can comprehend.

Natasha reaches forward, and through the fabric she grasps my engorged cock. My breath hitches in my chest and she tightens her grasp. A moan comes from my lips as my eyes close. Because yeah, a hot sexy woman has my cock in her hands.

"You're . . . ," she pants. "You're so big."

I open my eyes and smile. "I am. And every inch can give you pleasure."

She takes a deep breath. Her hand grabs my belt and she unzips my pants. She grasps my flesh.

"Your cock . . . your cock is beautiful."

So I've been told.

"Can I take off your dress, Natasha?"

She nods and turns. I reach up, slide the zipper down, and let the dress fall from her shoulders. "I want to kiss you here." My fingertips skim the small of her back.

"Yes," she whispers, and I press my lips to her skin. I unsnap her bra and pull her panties down over her hips. She turns to me, naked. Her body is perfect, beautiful. She has a small four-leaf clover tattoo over her right hip.

How many people have seen that tattoo? What prompted

that image, something that seems so far from Natasha's character?

Her pussy is front of my face and the scent of desire comes from her, the scent of want. "I want to kiss you here," I say, looking at her sex. "May I?'

"Yes," she gasps. What I really want to do is pick her up and take her to the bed. To spread her legs and suck her clit until she comes, but that is for later, that is for when Natasha is ready and wants to be ravished. Now, this moment, this time, is for the slow methodical process of getting to know her sexual triggers.

I lean forward and place a kiss on the edge of her sex. Then I spread her with my fingertips and I kiss her. I let my tongue lick up over her clit. A moan splits the silence. Her fingernails bite the flesh of my shoulders.

"My God, that feels so good." Her body trembles. I know, in this instant I know, that Natasha has never experienced oral sex.

"I want to put you on the bed and I want to eat your pussy. Can I do that? I want your pussy."

Her mouth drops open and her eyes meet mine. Her breath is short. She can barely form words. "You want my . . . you want . . ."

"I want your pussy, Natasha. Your pussy, the taste, the smell —all of it turns me on."

It's like I've told her that aliens have invaded earth.

"But men don't like pussy. They think—"

"I do. Men do. I want your pussy. May I take you to the bed?"

"Yes, oh my God, yes." Tears form in her eyes and she presses her hand to her mouth. I stand. I lift her. I carry her to the bed. I silently condemn to hell whichever asshole taught this gorgeous woman that "men don't like pussy." Then I proceed to give Natasha the best afternoon of her life.

❦

"WHY DO YOU DO THIS?" NATASHA LAYS BESIDE ME, naked and gorgeous. Her eyes are bright, and a smile dances on her lips. She's beautiful, pleased, sated, no longer sad or afraid or quivering, and unable to acknowledge her own sexual power.

"Why?" I smile. "I'm a man with a penis and this is the best vocation ever."

"So that's what this is? A vocation?"

I lift my hand to her cheek.

"It's not a job—there's no monetary transaction. Besides, that would be illegal and it's truthfully not how I feel about this . . . our time together. Vocation seems to be the word. It fits how I feel about what I do and how I do it."

My explanation seems to satisfy her need to understand. Most of the women I sleep with don't dig too deeply for details. They're here for their own reasons, which they often don't share. Some women need to know things about me, others don't.

"What about you?" I ask. Natasha's gaze flits to mine. "Why are you here?"

She looks away. Her body is molded to mine, with my arm draped over her waist.

"I . . ." She sighs. Her eyes glisten. "I . . . uh . . . He . . . he's having an affair. Or he was. Maybe he still is." She starts to roll away from me, but I pull her closer. She rests her head on my arm. "He said the affair was my fault. That I'm frigid, that I . . . that he couldn't get hard because I wasn't attractive anymore."

The last words are whispers on a breath filled with shame. Her bottom lip quivers as though she's just admitted the worst secret any woman could carry.

"We both know that isn't true."

She looks up at me, and her smile bursts through her tears, like sun after a thunderstorm. "I do now." She sighs. "You . . . you're amazing. I feel more myself now, after these few hours, than I have in the last twelve years."

And those words, spoken by a satisfied happy woman, are all I need to hear.

"May I see you again?"

"That's entirely up to you."

"Well if it's up to me—" She pushes me onto my back and swings a leg over to straddle me. "Let's start now."

CHAPTER 2

"UNCLE JAKE, will you come visit this weekend?"

"You know it." The elevator stops on the thirty-second floor and the doors slide open. I shift the Chinese take-out bag into my other hand. I'm freshly showered, but exhausted and hungry. I want to be alone with my food and the soon-to-open Asian stock markets, but I *always* have the time and the energy to talk to my niece.

"Will you bring me doughnuts? The ones with the sprinkles." This kid has my number. One hundred percent, her wish is my command.

"Is your mom there?" I whisper. I stop in front of my condo door.

Lily drops her voice. "She's in the kitchen."

"Don't tell her, but yes," I whisper back. I pull my keys from my pocket. "Doughnuts with chocolate icing and rainbow sprinkles." An uncle's job is to bring his niece doughnuts and toys and any other thing that a precious bundle of freckles and pigtails wants. "Okay? Don't tell Mommy, but—"

"Don't tell Mommy what?"

Ruh-ro. I immediately stand at attention and clear my throat. My older, authoritative sister has liberated her phone from her daughter. My sister is also freckled, but without pigtails. "That . . . that I'm eating two entrees from Mr. Chow's for dinner," I offer up, knowing Rachel will see through my lie.

"Uh huh. Just like when you snuck out of the house at sixteen to visit *Nana?*"

"Nana confirmed the story."

"Nana was an easy alibi, plus a sucker for your big blue eyes. *I* know you went to see Carolyn Dombrowski. She told me."

"You need proof to convict." I smile. I'll let my big sister bust my balls as long as I can bring Lily doughnuts this weekend. "Kind of an important concept for a judge to forget."

"And yet more than some of the attorneys who appear in my courtroom seem to know. So, you're coming over this weekend?"

"Thinking about it. Does that work for you?"

"Yes." Rachel pauses and takes a deep breath. "But I'd really love it if you'd go visit Mom."

What's left of my heart cracks. I open my mouth to respond, but before I utter a word, big sis continues.

"She's been asking about you. She wants to see you, she misses you, and—"

"Rach, she doesn't even know who I am when I'm there."

"That's not true."

"It is."

"Not always."

"When I visit, Mom thinks I'm Dad."

Rachel sighs. My assessment is accurate, whether Rachel wants to admit it or not. Mom, when she asks about me, is really asking about twelve-year-old me, because that's where her Alzheimer's-addled mind has landed. For Mom, based on whatever neurons still fire, I'm forever gap-toothed, gangly, and twelve. So while I want to see Mom, it's pretty dammed painful, and I've already had my fair share of pain for this lifetime. I'm all about the pleasure now.

"Plus, when I go, because she thinks I'm Dad, she asks me about Susie."

Rachel gasps.

"But I'll go," I offer up. knowing its been ten days since I've seen Mom, and that's longer than I usually go without seeing her, even if it is painful. Beside, big sis sees Mom almost every day, and she's got a courtroom to run and a kid to raise. How big of a selfish slacker can I be?

"We'll *all* go," Rachel offers. "The three of us. It's fun. Mom calls Lily 'Rachel' and thinks I'm her mean nurse. Maybe that'll take the heat off, so she won't bring up—"

Rachel pauses. She can't even say her name. I don't blame her. It was only this year that I could finally say Susie's name without putting a fist through a wall or having my throat close up.

"Sunday? Meet you there around two?" Rachel asks.

"You got a date, but I'll be by your house on Saturday morning. I promised Lily—"

"Doughnuts. I know."

"She ratted me out?"

"I'm her mother"—I hear the smile in Rachel's voice—"I can read her mind. But yeah, she totally caved while we were on the phone. Firstborn. Not a good liar. Usually it's the youngest who can twist the truth."

I smile. My big sis, always with the digs, even when they're accurate. I say good-bye and finally slide my key into the lock of my front door. The Tokyo Stock Exchange opens in a couple of hours, so I've got time to eat before I play.

Today was a good day.

I'm exhausted—but the kind of tired you feel after you do something you enjoy. The spicy sweet and sour scent of my two favorite Chinese dishes, plus two appetizers, wafts up from the bag. I'm hungry and I'm home. My happy place. My silent refuge where I can—

"Hey, neighbor."

I glance over my shoulder. Tara, my neighbor, who I know in a friendly acquaintance sort of way, stands across the hall. A soft

13

crooked smile decorates her face. The smile is a lie. Her eyes and her makeup and everything on her face looks a little cattywampus, like she's been crying. Her dark hair is up in a haphazard ponytail. She hoists a giant white hanging bag and holds it high over her right shoulder while she struggles to get her key into the lock.

No. Go. Her keys fall to the ground. I'm hungry, I'm exhausted, and I'm ready to disappear inside my place and gorge myself on Chinese food, but Tara has been my neighbor for going on three years. She's a good neighbor. Brings in my mail if I'm out of town. Gives me baked goods at Christmas. Invites me to her parties. Smiles. Even has a pretty decent-looking dog. If not for the asshole fiancé she's had for two of the three years she's lived across the hall, Tara'd be downright perfect. I hitch my Chinese take-out bag onto my arm, turn, and in three steps and one slick move pick up her keys and unlock her front door.

"Thanks." A blush curls across her face. She shifts the giant hanging bag a little higher.

"Dress?"

She nods.

Wait . . . A thought percolates through my head. White envelope. Crisp black calligraphy. Gold lining. RSVP.

"*The* dress?"

A sickeningly sad-ass attempt at a smile crosses Tara's face.

"Congratulations," I say and smile back. I know what's important to women, and bringing home her wedding dress is definitely a big moment for a lady. "Dinner plans with George?"

"Greg, it's Greg," she says for probably the millionth time.

I know his fucking name. I simply refuse to say it.

"Right, right. *Greg*." I overemphasize, as though I'm an idiot and I really am trying to remember Douchebucket's name. Nope. I'm not. Greg will forever be "douche-something" in my head. "You two going out to celebrate the dress?" I ask with a nod toward the gown now draped over her arm.

She shakes her head and looks at the floor. "He has a work

thing tonight." Tara tries to mask her sadness. Maybe I'd believe her if we hadn't been neighbors for nearly three years.

Greg's choice of career as big-shot commercial real estate salesman ups his quotient on my douchebaggery scale. In my mind, he's one paved parking lot away from being a used-car salesman.

"Ah, got it." I drop her keys into her hand and turn back to my own door, with way too much Chinese takeout in the bag on my arm. Again I glance over my shoulder. "I have Kung Pao Scallops and Moo Goo Gai Pan," I say. "Care to join me?"

Tara is . . . well, she's beautiful. All women are beautiful, but Tara has this kindness that starts in her eyes and hovers around the curve of her mouth. She's the type of woman any man worth his salt would worship, because Tara's smart, kind, and—dammit, I'm not sure how Greg has managed it after all the shit he's pulled—loyal.

She pauses. One eyebrow lifts. We've been to parties at neighbors', but we've never had a meal together alone . . . have we? No, not hardly. I moved into my condo long before Tara moved into hers and back then I was still involved with . . . with . . . well, I was still involved. Then I was gone for a while. Then I was back. Then there was Tara's douchepickle. So no, while we're friendly the way neighbors are friendly, Tara and I haven't really had a meal together, or hung out alone, ever.

"Let me hang this up"—she nods toward the dress—"and change."

My glance takes in her clothes. Suit. Heels. Silk blouse that hints at her cleavage. I'd take her whether she changed or not.

"Fifteen minutes?"

"Deal." She walks into her place and closes the door.

Nothing wrong with being neighborly.

CHAPTER 3

My condo is quintessentially male. I don't entertain often. Okay, once, in all the years I've lived here. Not for me, but for Rachel. Big sis was dumped, preggers, and on her way to divorce court, while my morally bankrupt brother-in-law Dalton was on his way to Costa Rica to start a new life with his secretary. In my mind, Dalton and Greg were cut from the same cloth.

Actually, to be fair, ladies, we all are. Men. We're all a variation of Greg or Dalton. All card-carrying penis holders, harbor these douchey, cheating traits. It's simply that some of us discover our own proclivity to douchebaggery and fix it or corral it or contain it . . . we do whatever the hell we have to do to make our cocks behave. Or if we don't, we act like assholes and take off for Central America with our twenty-something secretary, leaving our pregnant soon-to-be-ex-wife behind.

I close my front door and like iron to a magnet, my eyes are drawn to my unused balcony. Thirty-two stories up, it's got a helluva view. That's the main reason I bought the place. On a clear day I can see all the way to the ocean. If I actually went outside onto the balcony. Which I don't. Not now. Closing in on six years.

I pull my eyes from the balcony and the view. I put the bag of

Chinese food on the counter and head to my bedroom. I pull on jeans and a T-shirt. If the neighbor is going to be comfy, I might as well be too. I head back to the kitchen and get out plates and utensils. Do a quick sweep to make certain the place is clean. Which it is. I sleep. I eat. I work. I don't have pets, children, or a girlfriend—the place looks like a high-end furniture catalogue.

I like my space. I dig my privacy.

The doorbell rings.

My heart jumps.

What the hell? I shake my head and smile. Wow, seriously? My heart jumps because of my engaged neighbor? The one I've lived across the hall from for three years? I open the door.

My heart jumps again.

Yeah. This neighbor. Her hair is still up in a ponytail, and I can't tell if she has on makeup or not, but she smells like some fresh flowery scent and that smile hovers around her lips.

"I brought champagne." She lifts a bottle of Veuve.

"What're we celebrating?"

Her smile falters and something cracks behind her eyes, but she recovers quickly and her smile brightens again. "A bright future."

"I'm down with that. I've got beer and Chinese food, a bottle of great champagne and a pretty cool neighbor to have dinner with, so my future already looks good."

Tara walks into my place. Gone are the high heels and skirt and silk blouse. Instead, she wears a comfy shirt and leggings with pictures of—"Are those bears on your pants?"

She glances back at me and smiles. "Grizzlies."

Leggings with grizzly bears. The woman does comfort clothing well. I'm pleased.

I uncork the champagne and pour two glasses. She walks toward the view.

"I always wondered if the extra price was worth it, but standing here, I think it might be."

She's referring to the nearly fifty percent more that condos on my side of the building go for than the ones on her side. She takes the champagne flute I offer her from my hand.

"To good neighbors with great views," she says, tapping the crystal glass to mine.

"To neighbors, I say." She has a gleam in her eye. A mischievous look, as though she's a woman with a secret. That is power for a woman, when they look like they know more than you, because they usually do, and men know it. Plus, they are killer with the details.

"You work at home, don't you?"

I take a sip of champagne and nod.

"So you get this view all day, every day."

"Not all day every day." I don't mention that there are some days, like today, where I'm at The Four Seasons in Beverly Hills or the Westin Bonaventure downtown or The London in West Hollywood for entire mornings, afternoons, or nights. I walk to the kitchen and pull out two platters from the cabinet above the stove. I know I own these two platters only because Rachel borrows them every year at Thanksgiving. I dump the two entrees onto the platters and walk to the dining room table, which I'm uncertain I've ever actually sat down and eaten at.

"This view, I can't get over it."

A knot lodges in my throat. I don't follow her gaze. Instead, I pull out Tara's chair and then sit at the head of the table.

I serve Tara and then I serve myself. She finishes her glass of champagne and pours another.

"You two planning on living here after the wedding?" I ask, knowing that I don't want Douchebucket on my floor but that I also don't want to lose Tara as a neighbor. I enjoy seeing her smile on the elevator and in the hall—plus the baked goods she gives me at the holidays.

She frowns. "I don't know." Her voice drifts away with uncertainty. Her jaw is tight and her lips are pursed. Is it Douchey-McDouche-Face that causes Tara's normally soft features to harden, or is it the idea of moving? Not my rodeo. Not my place to state an opinion. So instead of asking, I take a bite of my dinner.

"So what is it you do, again?" Tara asks. I notice she's changing the subject but don't comment.

"For money?"

She creases her eyebrows and smiles, a questioning expression on her face.

"I help new businesses."

"Help?"

"Venture capital."

She probably *thinks* that she knows what that means. She's smart and inquisitive. Goes with her job. "You still with the *LA Post*?" I ask. One of the few things I know about my neighbor is that she has a gig as a reporter for an online news service. I can neither confirm nor deny that I provided a big chunk of change to help the *LA Post* cover start-up costs for the company that is now her employer.

"For now." She sips her champagne. "I'm . . . I'm not sure I'll stay. Kind of depends on what happens."

I lean back in my chair. I never really thought of Tara as a marriage-ends-my-career type of woman.

"You keep the strangest hours."

I pause mid-bite. I tilt my head.

"I've been working from home the last three weeks, and I noticed you're in and out at the weirdest times."

Discomfort worms through my belly. I keep things clean and tight. Private and discreet, for obvious reasons. Not even my sister knows the details of my life. What to think? My egress and entrance is interesting to my journalist-neighbor?

"I mean, I'm not stalking you." She smiles and shakes her head, her glass nearly empty again. "This all sounds very weird. Okay, so when you open and close your front door, my bed shakes."

"Excuse me?"

"Look, I don't know how or why or what exactly causes it,

but I noticed it about a year ago. For the longest time I thought it had something to do with the elevator shaft, but then I realized that—"

"When I shut my front door your—"

"Bed shakes."

"I really don't know what to say to that."

"Right. Well, since I haven't been going into the office I sit on my bed to work with my computer on my lap, and I know when you're coming and going."

"I'm not certain the correlation is accurate. How can you be sure that when your bed shakes it's actually me who's leaving?"

That blush. The one that starts in the v-neck of her T-shirt and then rolls up that long neck and floods her cheeks. "Because"—she swallows—"once I'd formed my hypothesis I needed to prove it. So for the last two weeks, any time my bed shakes I dash to my front door to see if you're walking down the hall."

"And?"

"And half the time you are and half the time you aren't."

"Which leads you to believe—"

"That half the time you're entering your apartment, and half the time you're exiting." She pours more champagne into her glass. Discussing her hypothesis finally brings a true Tara-smile to her face. "I'm kind of embarrassed to admit that I've been running from my bedroom to my peephole to track you."

"Just borderline stalker-ish."

"I needed to prove my theory."

"So proving your theory has more value than not looking like a stalker?"

She presses her lips together and her gaze lasers on me. "For me, proving a theory has more meaning than nearly anything. I'm an investigative journalist, so yeah, if I have a theory, I need to prove it. Don't I? No matter what it takes to get the proof. My job is my life, it's what I live for . . . it's my vocation."

I glance up from my beer. I nearly choke on the word.

Vocation.

I understand vocation. What a person is willing to do to pursue a calling that is greater than himself. Or herself. I understand the complete and utter compulsion a vocation causes.

"I'm still not convinced." I lean back in my chair and cross my arms. Lift an eyebrow and send her a dare with my eyes. A dare, that I'm pretty certain a woman who has spent her life taking risks to prove every hypothesis she's ever had, is willing to take. "Prove it."

She sets down her glass with a seriousness that I know means "game on."

Like a flash of lightning to my cock, I'm aroused. Wow. Not the usual reaction I get unless I'm in a hotel room with a semi-anonymous woman, but the look on Tara's face, the need to prove her case, the idea that she will not be derailed by my cocky bullshit makes me hard as hell in an instant. Fight. Chutzpah. Balls. Tara, as cute and adorable as she is, has all of them times ten.

"Not a problem." She stands. A pretty graceful move. I barely notice she's tipsy until she grabs for the table edge. "You" —she points at me—"will sit on my bed and I"—she taps her palm on her chest—"will open and close your door."

"Done," I say and follow my cute, sexy, but very engaged neighbor to my front door.

❧

ADORBS. I THINK THAT'S WHAT THE KIDS ARE SAYING these days. Or that's what some of the mothers I sleep with tell me the kids are saying. Tara's place is adorbs in that kind of thrown-together girly way, with overstuffed chairs and silver and comfy rugs and framed pictures of friends and family and—

"Jango!" I yell as her shepherd-retriever mix jumps up and plants his paws on my legs.

"Jango, down," Tara says and pets the pup on the head. He

looks at her, looks at me, gives my hand a lick, and gets down. But he sits right beside me, tail swishing back and forth on the floor.

"How funny." She scrunches her eyebrows and shakes her head. "Jango usually doesn't like men. Never liked Greg." She turns toward the back of her condo.

I eye Jango. "Smart boy," I mouth and stroke the top of his head. He wags his tail like he completely agrees. We're both dudes. We know a douchesalad when we see one. I trail after Tara toward her bedroom.

"Okay, sit here."

Holy hell. Tara's bedroom is way different than the cozy-cutesy living room. The entire room is blood red and mahogany. Not at all what I expected. The bed is gargantuan, taking up nearly the whole room, with four giant posts that reach toward the ceiling. So easy to tie you up, to . . .

Down boy. My cock, which usually only responds in hotel rooms with near strangers, is suddenly quite aware that Tara's room is somehow . . . somehow out of character and yet enticing.

A blush unfurls over her swanlike neck and toward her cheeks.

"Greg hates my room," Tara says.

"It's different than the rest of your place."

"He says it looks like a bordello."

The thought . . . well, yeah, it had crossed my mind. "Red's a powerful color."

"I love red. The bed set was my grandparents' and they left it to me. Been in the family for generations. And I like red."

Enough of an explanation. A family heirloom. But it's obvious from the look on her face she's fought some kind of fight about this bed and these colors for a long time.

"Sit here." She points at the left-hand side, where two pillows are propped up against the headboard. Her side. Where she sleeps.

Heat unfurls in my belly. A vision of Tara lying in bed naked flashes through my mind. My turn to feel weird. Jango eyes me as I sit on the edge of the bed with my feet still on the floor.

"No, no, no. You have to sit like you would if you were me. Put your feet up." She grabs my feet and sets them on the comforter, then puts her palm on my chest and pushes me back against the pillows.

Hot fierce desire coils through me. She leans over me, two-thirds of her body above me. Her shirt hangs down, revealing her bra and her breasts, those gorgeous breasts, in it, to me. My incredibly disciplined eyes roam, as they never do, to the glorious sight of those breasts, her neck, her jaw.

Our gazes meet. She jerks back from the live wire of desire that pulses between us.

"Like this?" I feign nonchalance. I engage the skills I utilize in my vocation. Tara's mouth is an O shape, her pupils dilated with a hint of fear combined with shock and surprise. I'm hoping she doesn't notice that my cock is hard as a rock. Jango stands beside Tara, tail wagging.

She takes my cue and pretends she doesn't feel this heat smoldering between us.

"Just like that." She runs a hand over her hair, pulling stray wisps from her face. "Okay, now stay here." Jango eyes her, looks at me, and then jumps onto the bed to curl up beside me.

"Jango?" She tilts her head, obviously not used to Jango cozying up to menfolk who come to her place. By menfolk, I mean Sir Douche-A-Lot.

She turns and walks out of the room. "Okay," she calls from the front of her condo. "Wait for it."

I lean back, put one hand on Jango's head to pet him, and close my eyes. I'm exhausted. So very exhausted. Truly exhausted to the core.

Life is weird. I sit here, on Tara's bed, eyes closed, petting her dog, and this feels oddly normal. Then the bed shakes. I open my eyes. No . . . I wait . . . the bed shakes again. No way. A few seconds later, Tara's front door opens.

"Did you feel it?" she yells.

"Maybe."

"I'm going to do it again," she calls back.

What part of the building goes from my front door to Tara's —hell, there it is again. Her bed shakes. Not a lot. Not enough to be that noticeable, unless you were sitting here working or sleeping or basically minding your own business and then—there.

"Jango, that's weird." I stay where I am, waiting for Tara to return with a satisfied smile. But instead, Jango issues a deep and throaty bark. He jumps over me and tears across the room, headed to the front door. I follow him. Voices grow louder the closer I get to Tara's front door.

Jango stands at the door, sniffing the edge near the floor. Low growls come from his throat.

Through the peephole I see McDouche and Tara. She stands in my open front door and he's gesticulating with his arms. Does me coming out of her place after sitting on her bed make this better or worse for her? If he were a good guy, a guy who was on the up and up, then this wouldn't matter. Unless he actually caught me jackhammering his beloved, he'd believe her. But he's not, from what I can tell, a good guy. He's suspicious and jealous as hell. Which is crazy, because it's pretty damn obvious that Tara is not the type to fuck around.

Now Douchey? I have him pegged as a serial cheater. Just my guy sense.

I keep my eye pressed to the peephole.

I can hear their tone, and a bit of language. He points to her door and turns toward my front door. An asshole like this guy, he sees her coming out of my place, then me coming out of her place, and he's the type who won't believe the truth. Doesn't believe what Tara is telling him—that we had dinner, and her bed shakes when I open my door, and she was simply trying to prove her theory to me. He doesn't believe that what Tara tells him is the truth, because he's never told the truth to her.

I know that Douchey lies.

All men lie.

Greg lies, and he's still so fucking deep in his lies and unable to see the goodness in Tara, that he is nearly convinced Tara lies too.

She walks toward her front door. He crosses his arms. Rolls his eyes toward the ceiling, mouths "whatever," and is off down the hall toward the elevator. She stands alone in the hallway, watching him, then turns to her front door and takes a deep breath. Steadies herself. There are only two inches of door between us, and barely one step. Her face is so close to mine.

Through the peephole I see it.

I feel it.

Tara is miserable.

Heartbroken.

My heart jolts. My breath stops. Was this how . . . Oh my God, was this how . . . I can't breathe. Tara looks straight at the door, and the pain on her face stabs my core. My God. She is so tragically sad and yet . . . She glances down the hall toward the elevator, where the guy she's engaged to just went, and there's this longing in the curve of her mouth. She swallows and wipes her fingertips across her eyes. She turns back. I watch her psyche herself up and summon a small smile to her lips. Forcing herself to look happy . . . for me . . . for me, the neighbor she never sees, who always forgets to give out holiday cards, and who has weird hours and never invites her to dinner until tonight. Tara forces a smile to her face, because that's the type of woman she is.

I take four long steps back as her hand finds the doorknob. The door opens. "Did you feel it?"

Again, her mouth has that bit of a smile and her voice sounds halfway happy, but deep in those blue eyes lurks a hint of pain.

"I did. You're right, your bed shakes when my front door opens."

The pain is banished, and I see satisfaction mixed with happiness. She's won. She's vanquished my doubt and proved her hypothesis. I return her smile. I only wish the doubt she feels for her fiancé and her upcoming marriage could be banished from her eyes just as easily.

§

HOT ANGRY NOISE AND UGLY WORDS PULL ME FROM MY sleep. My phone tells me the time is 2:22 a.m. I squint and lift my head. In the hallway. I hear them, someone. A man, a woman, a tone . . . from both. Suddenly the thought that my door-shutting rattles Tara's bed doesn't seem nearly as far-fetched as it did before. Not when words all the way in the hallway have pulled me from the dream. That same fucking dream I've dreamt nearly every damn night.

Susie.

Still.

Susie.

I wash the fucking "what if" questions from my mind. I roll from my bed and my feet hit the floor. Cool feel of the cement actually helps me when I'm conflicted. I stand and pad out of my room down the hall to my front door. I look out of the peephole and see that McDouche is back. He stands in Tara's doorway with his arm braced against the door jamb. He looks like a beast standing beside Tara, who is in the doorway, arms crossed. This asshole, the douchebucket, leans down and attempts to kiss her. With his jerky movements, I can practically smell the booze from here.

Nice. Not a move I'm innocent of. Pulled more than a couple in my day. Long night. Drunk. Show up at the girlfriend's house —this case, the fiancée's—looking to score. Right. There isn't a guy alive who hasn't pulled that trick. And most women, if you're dating and if you're on their good side, are okay with this bad-boy behavior if it only happens once in a while. But Douchenugget pulls this scene often.

I must have thin walls, because I hear this guy pounding on her door at least twice a week, usually around 2:30 or 3 a.m. But tonight? Huh? Tonight it appears Tara wants nothing to do with Greg and his piss-drunk bad behavior, because not only is she holding her position at her front door, but she actually pushed his smelly-alcohol mouth-breathing face away with her palm.

A low whistle comes from my lips. Yeah, Douchenugget is getting nothing but cold shoulder tonight.

She holds up her left hand and points at the rock. And granted, I have to say that even from this distance I'm impressed, because it's a big rock. "This is what you think gives you the right to be an utter asshole?"

Greg says nothing, just continues to stand in the doorway with the smug look of a high school kid being scolded.

"Well this? You can have it back." Tara takes the ring off her finger.

Smug look gone. Greg's eyes widen. "Babe, don't be ridiculous."

"After what I saw tonight?"

Shit. What did she see?

The ring is off. Tara holds it with her fingertips. Does Greg have any semblance of reason in that drunken brain? He's about to lose the best thing he ever had.

I would've begged.

I did beg. Fell to my knees and pled my case when the woman I loved wanted to all it off.

It worked.

For a while.

The rock glitters in the palm of Douchey's hand.

My heart fills.

Nice job, Tara. Save yourself, save your life, tell that asshole good-bye.

CHAPTER 4

"UNCLE JAKE, I LOVE YOU."

Kill me now. This kid owns me. I'm her bitch. She plants her sticky little chocolate-covered lips on my cheek and her dirty little crumb-covered fingers on my starched white shirt, which now is chocolate-covered and wrecked and I don't give two shits. I don't even care that this open affection is under the influence of extreme sugar overdose, because this kid, with her curly pigtails and freckles and still-pudgy little arms, makes my head spin with everything that is beautiful in the world.

"Would you get me some water, please?"

"Of course." I pick her up and plant her on the chair where she's been sitting on my lap, then gleefully watch her shove more doughnut into her mouth. My sister disappeared the moment she heard me open the door. How often do single mothers actually get part of a Saturday morning to themselves? Uh, never. Especially one who's a single mother with a slacker little brother and whose own mother is losing her mind. Maybe Rachel is upstairs with a hot book and a vibrator—bad scenario. Where's the bleach for my brain? Whatever the fuck she's been doing for the last half hour, I hope it was good.

I pour water into a Sleeping Beauty cup, add ice cubes, and

set it on the table next to Lily, the princess of my heart. I sit down beside her.

"Uncle Jake, you know my birthday is soon."

"Soon?" I've come to understand that time for a five-year-old runs on a different clock. "Sweetie, your birthday is in six months. That's a way off. That's—"

"Soon," she finishes for me. Sure, okay. Like most wise men, I've discovered you don't argue with a woman. Without batting an eye, the tiny despot lifts a second doughnut from the box. Rachel would kill me. There is a strict one-doughnut policy in this house, of which Lily is completely aware, and I know the little pirate can count.

Whatever, I'm the cool uncle.

"Okay. I'm guessing you know what you want for your birthday, which is *soon*?"

She smiles her chocolate smile, the smile that makes my brain scream tell-me-what-you-want-princess-and-it's-yours, the smile that will send me to my knees, or to the nearest Target with my credit card at the ready. Because really, she could say she wanted the *Mona Lisa* and I'd be on the next jet to France. "What is it, Lily?"

She glances toward the door behind me and I jerk my head around. No Rachel. I turn back. Lily's gaze is deadly serious for a five-year-old. "Mommy won't like it. She already said no."

Oooo, this present gets better by the minute. "Okay. Well, what is it that Mommy said no to?"

Her lips press tight and her eyes widen. Such a sweet choco-late-cherub look. How my sister ever says no to this face is beyond me. The woman clearly has a heart of steel.

"I want a puppy."

"Of course you do. That's a great idea. Every little girl should have a puppy."

"Jake!"

Lily's eyes widen like flying monkeys are streaming through the kitchen window. Or that she's just gotten caught sneaking a second doughnut, which she totally has. Except there is an adult on duty who is meant to act like an adult and follow the one-doughnut, we-don't-say-yes-to-the-things-Mommy-says-no-to rules. That adult, who has now just broken not one, but two very important rules, is me. Bad boy, but very cool uncle, me. Big sis, standing in the kitchen doorway with her hands on her hips might not agree on my coolness level at this moment.

I grab a doughnut, knowing that while my sister is on a low-carb/no-refined-sugar diet, she has a weak spot for doughnuts, especially doughnuts with chocolate icing and rainbow sprinkles (the apple doesn't fall too far from the tree). Rachel licks her lips.

"We were simply discussing pets," I say. "Every child should have a pet." Her eyes are focused on the doughnut while I speak. Big sis wants this doughnut, my sister would nearly die for this doughnut, she might even let a felon roam the streets of Los Angeles for this doughnut right now. "You remember Matilda." Her eyes snap away from the lovely sugar confection and latch onto mine.

"Don't."

"You loved her."

"I did. I can't, it's too—"

"But you're glad she was in our life."

"Jake, stop."

"Who is Matilda?" Lily asks.

"Now do you see why?" Rachel mutters under her breath, grabs the doughnut from me, and takes a bite. I realize that my fond memories of Matilda, much like most memories in my life, are laced with pain.

The doorbell rings and saves me.

"Expecting someone?" Rachel is a homebody on weekends.

"Uh, no"—her guilty gaze flashes toward the front door and she takes a final jumbo bite of doughnut—"just a friend of mine."

I know guilt. I also know when my sister is hiding, lying, or simply trying to be conniving, none of which she does well. Nope. I inherited all those abilities, not her. Rachel heads down the hall.

"Hi!" I hear her say at the front door. I follow. When I turn the corner, I see a woman who looks vaguely familiar.

"Jake, do you remember my friend Cassidy?"

I reach out my hand. Do I remember Cassidy? I'm not sure. I have some sort of vague memory of a woman . . . with long black hair and dark brown eyes, tall, looking a little bit like a dominatrix. Also, the first time we met, Cassidy started talking about her baggage too fast. Ex-husband. Desire for kids. Wackadoo mom. Not the topics I like before a few toss-away conversations starting with; "Hey, so how about those Lakers?"

"She was at Lily's birthday party last year."

"Right. Of course." We have a winner. She also cornered me in the pantry and eye-fucked me all afternoon.

"I thought maybe we could go grab lunch," Rachel says. She runs her hand over her hair. Then I notice that Rachel is dressed. Not like Saturday schlubby-mommy dressed, but like Saturday I-have-a-brunch-date dressed.

"Sure. You guys want me to watch Lily while you hang out?"

Cassidy gives big sis a look. I'm obviously not playing the role as they intended. I know how women communicate without words. I've spent my life studying women.

"Is Lily in the kitchen?" Cassidy asks, wading through the tension that laps between Rachel and me. "I'm going to say hi." She slips by. Her guns look good, and she's pretty and perfectly polished. If I remember right she's a litigator and a partner at a big law firm. I glance at big sis.

"Are you a lesbian? Because as good-looking as Cassidy is, I think she likes guys."

"Ha, very funny. I wish. If I didn't like cock so much, it'd be easier."

"TMI, sis. But really, if you're not a lesbian then what's up with the random brunch date that I'm obviously intended to go on with you and Cassidy?" I lift an eyebrow. Rachel crosses her arms. "Oh, no." I over-pretend, like Rachel's whole charade wasn't completely obvious. "You want me to go out with her? You're trying to set me up."

Rachel is not a good liar. When she's caught, she crumbles like a week-old cookie. Her blush looks like an alcoholic Irishman's, not nearly as cute as my neighbor Tara's. Her nose even turns red.

"Not interested."

"She's perfect. She's smart. She's successful—"

"And she's beautiful. And while I appreciate each of those traits singularly in a woman, or in Cassidy's case, in a woman who is the whole package, I'm not ready to date."

"It's been almost six years."

My heart lurches. I careen from pain to near rage. I take a deep breath.

"It could be fifty and I won't be ready."

"You can't spend your entire life in mourning."

"And you don't get to spend your entire life being the big sister who tells me what to do."

Her lips thin and her eyes hold pain.

Damn. Damn. Damn. I'm an asshole. I scrub my fingers through my hair, take a deep breath, and turn back to Rachel. "Sorry for that. Look, I'm not willing to chance a repeat performance. Okay? Did that once, not doing it again."

"That won't happen again."

"Says the woman who still hasn't gone out with a man in five years."

"Not true. I . . . date."

"You? Date?

"I do date. I don't tell you, and I definitely don't tell Lily, but I date on occasion." She leans forward and tilts her chin. Her voice is a whisper. "There are men who take care of *things* for women, without dating."

"Those are illegal and you're a judge."

"They aren't all illegal. There's one in particular I've heard of that is very legal, very discreet, and very selective. No money involved. He calls it his *vocation*."

My chest tightens. My sister is talking about . . .

"Oh, really?" I ask, playing it cool because I'm the youngest and I can lie. I'm an excellent liar. Had years of practice. I'm telling you ladies, honesty comes on that extra bit of DNA that *you* get. Not us. Not ever. We have to learn to be honest. "Sounds dangerous to me. I'm thinking anything like that, has to be a sting operation by an overactive vice squad. Or maybe that TV show, you know, *Dateline Undercover*?

Color drains from Rachel's face. The only thing big sis loves nearly as much as her family is being a judge. I'm hopeful I've just scared Rachel enough that she will *never* call any number that could be related to any rumor she's heard about a man who has sex with women as a vocation. Especially one with a very special name. "Do you need me to watch Lily?" I ask. "While you and Cassidy go to lunch?"

Rachel shakes her head. "You leaving?"

I nod. Yes, it's the only thing to do. Cut it. End it before it even starts. Make it clear that I have no interest. Lunch would send the wrong message, maybe even create hope. "I can excuse myself, I can even explain why. I don't want you to feel exposed."

"Go." Rachel smiles. She shakes her head and pulls me in for a hug. I surrender. She's my sister. I love her. I love Lily. I love Mom. I even, still, love Susie. I'm at seventy-five percent with females I love still being alive, so I guess the odds are okay. I'd give anything to have the stat be at one hundred percent.

"You have to let this go at some point," Rachel whispers in my ear. "She'd want you to."

Would she? I'm not certain. With the rage and the pain, I'm not certain exactly what Susie would want for me right now. Or ever. My sister, "the Judge," might render a far different verdict about what Susie would want for me with regards to my happiness if she had all the facts. But this idea is more than I'm willing to wrestle with on a Saturday morning.

Lily runs from the kitchen and grabs my leg at the knee. "You're leaving!"

She always knows. A sixth sense with this one.

"I'll see you at Nana's." I bend down and lift Lily. Cassidy has washed up my sticky-chocolatey niece. Good woman. Attractive woman. Just not the woman for me. "There may be cake involved," I whisper in Lily's ear, planting a kiss on her cheek.

Her smile tells me this is an acceptable token of my affection. She kisses me back. I put her on the floor, hug my sister, nod to Cassidy—who stands just inside the doorway from the kitchen with a slight smile on her face—and make my escape.

As I always do.

ॐ

LOS ANGELES IS A SMALL TOWN. I KNOW IT SEEMS impossible to believe unless you live here, but it's true. L.A. is pockets of small communities nestled beside each other. My parents were raised here, I've lived my entire life here except during college, my sister is a judge here, and at this stage there's one degree of separation between everyone—including celebrities.

I suppose it's inevitable.

I stand in Gelson's. I grasp a tomato. Which one is firm and round and needs to be grilled this afternoon? I hear a cart before I see her. I glance up.

Her face turns red. A pinkish blush. She swallows. She's not nearly as "done up" as she was when we were together. It's not Natasha, or Shelly or Carolyn or Leslie, or my personal longest vocation, Cheryl. This woman was many many women back—six or seven.

Jennifer.

This woman gave me the name Jennifer. I don't flinch. I don't give her any hint I recognize her. I don't let on as though I've caressed every inch of skin. Pulled the nipples of her perky breasts, now hidden behind a sweatshirt with Stanford emblazoned across the front, into my mouth. I don't let on that I remember she has a special penchant for fucking in the bathtub, or that she likes to be blindfolded while having sex. No. I push all of the sexual specifics, every last lovely detail, from my mind. I compartmentalize—as men are so very able to do—and I simply smile and say, "Hello."

Her head jerks back and the skin between her eyebrows creases. One quick breath, as though she considers whether she's lost her mind.

"Never able to pick a good tomato," I continue. "They're always mealy when I get them home."

Now she's uncertain I'm the man she thinks I am. It's been over a year, and while her memory of our time together is so vivid she can feel every touch, every thrust—in fact, I'd bet her panties are wet right now—she's unsure. I mean, people do look substantially different when they're fucking.

"You want to go with firm." She lifts a tomato and presses the round red fruit to her nose. Her gaze meets mine. No, no, she knows it's me. Her tongue flicks out over her lips. "This one is the one you want." She holds the juicy flesh out toward me.

I take it. Our fingers touch. A zing pulses through me, and I'm hard. Simple as that. Hard as a rock.

"Thank you." I lift an eyebrow, incline my head, and walk away from the produce section, toward checkout.

I don't sleep with every woman who calls. Nor is every number with Wonderfuck scrawled above it mine. I'm selective. Careful. Detailed. One can't be too careful when meeting women to fuck away their insecurities and heartbreak.

As for the other men who share my name and my vocation, I haven't met them. Perhaps we should form a club.

CHAPTER 5

THE ELEVATOR DOORS slide open and there, standing on my floor in my hallway, is Douchey-McDouche-Face. I want to jab him in the nose. In my opinion, Greg's getting close to stalker territory, since Tara has made it pretty clear to him that their relationship is over. I walk out of the elevator and he gives me the head jerk. No hello. Nothing.

What. A. Dick.

The elevator doors slide closed, which is lucky for me, because a couple of minutes more and I might've said something or thrust myself into a situation that has nothing to do with me. I walk down the hall, but instead of veering to my left to open my door, I veer to the right. I get really close to Tara's door.

What the fuck am I doing?

Am I trying to listen? Am I checking on her? Why do I care? A week ago, I wouldn't have thought twice about Tara, or Douchebucket, or how she's feeling.

What the hell is my problem?

I shake my head and turn toward my door when Jango barks. Once, twice, three times. Jango is barking, not in that get-away bark that dogs use to protect their pack, but in that oh-my-God-I-love-you-open-the-door-and-pet-me bark.

I stop, kind of frozen. I'm never frozen, but now I'm frozen in front of Tara's door when it opens and Jango bolts out and pummels me with his paws.

"Jango, down!" Tara says with a coiled leash in her hand. She smiles at me, but there's sadness in her eyes. She's obviously just had some kind of conversation with her ex-fiancé, which doesn't necessarily breed a happy state of mind.

"Hey," I say. "Walk?"

"Three times a day," she smiles. "I have a walker that helps, but since I've been working from home . . . it's a great break in my day." She leans down and clips the leash to Jango's collar. He sits in front of me, his tail wagging back and forth across the floor, staring at me as though begging me to come too. Okay, buddy, I get it.

"Want some company?" I offer up.

Tara seems surprised.

"I mean if you want to be alone, I get it—"

"No, I'd love the company. Yes. Yes, please. Come with us. Jango will love it."

❦

AND HE DOES. JANGO LOVES HIS WALK. I DISCOVER HE also loves people (the ones who aren't Greg), children, squirrels, flowers, and bicycles, but not skateboards. Definitely *not* skateboards.

"He's a funny dog. Where'd you get him?"

"Well, I've been meaning to tell you"—Tara leans in close to me—"Jango is a girl."

"What?"

Tara nods.

"I guess I never checked Jango's bits. Fair enough. Where'd you get *her*?"

"Westside German Shepherd Rescue downtown. I love her."

37

Tara stops and leans down to stroke Jango. "She makes everything better."

"I agree. My niece wants a dog."

"Lily?"

"Wow, that's good, I'm impressed." I walk to a cart and spring for two ice creams.

"Your sister stops by sometimes. We've chatted in the elevator."

I nod. How strange. I never even considered that Rachel might know my neighbor.

"But I haven't seen Lily since she was really little."

"Rachel doesn't want a dog."

"Rachel doesn't like dogs?" It's as though I've told Tara that instead of putting criminals in prison, big sis drowns puppies for a living.

"No, no, no. The problem is Rachel *loves* dogs. She never got over the death of our family dog. So I think she's a little afraid to fall in love again."

Tara sighs. Whoops. Bad timing to mention "falling in love again," even if it is with a pet.

"What're you working on?" I change the subject, then take a lick of my chocolate cone.

"I have this idea for an investigative piece. I'm still trying to figure out whether it works or not. Right now I'm researching."

"Can you talk about it?"

"Not really. So far it feels more like an urban legend than anything real." Her tongue skirts around the edge of her ice cream, and I've never in my life so badly wanted to be a scoop of mint chocolate chip. "And you? Any great businesses you're thinking of giving money to?"

I smile. I can tell her some details, but not many. "There's one I like, met with the founders twice. We might end up with a deal."

"When you say deal can I ask . . ."

"How much?

She nods.

"They want two hundred million."

She coughs. Actually, she nearly chokes. I pat her on the back and she looks at me. Jango turns back and sits on Tara's feet. "Uh . . . wow. That's a lot of money. Is it your money?"

"Not all of it."

"But a lot."

I say nothing. Discussing my financial value is tiresome. I don't like to, so I don't. Big sis doesn't even know the investments that I've made for her and Lily, which are in a trust making more money each month than Rachel makes in a year.

"Do you like what you do?" Tara asks.

What an odd question. I don't think anyone has ever asked me if I like what I do.

"I like finding people with great ideas and then helping them make those ideas become real things. We live in a capitalist society, and it's nearly impossible to make something work in business without capital."

"But two hundred million."

"They've earned the right to ask for that much." I smile. "They're not just two guys straight out of Cal Tech in a garage somewhere. Although one of the best businesses I gave VC to was just that. Only it was two women."

"Do you keep these businesses?"

"Sometimes. Sometimes the creators buy back my part. Sometimes they fail. Sometimes I stay invested."

"But you don't manage them. You don't get emotionally invested in these businesses."

I stop and turn toward Tara. She has no idea how insightful her statement is, or how her words apply to every part of my life.

"Emotionally invested? No. I don't allow myself get emotionally invested."

"I get emotionally invested in television commercials." She bites her cone. Tara has a smear of chocolate on the corner of her

39

mouth. I reach out and dab it with my napkin. Those bright blue eyes lock onto me.

We're standing close to each other. I take in the scent of her body, the warmth of her nearness, Jango laying on the grass, and the fading sunlight. Her lips are close to mine.

This is a moment.

I know moments. I spend my life as Wonderfuck cultivating these types of moments so that the women I wonderfuck have these memories to hold onto. This is the moment where, if I was attracted to Tara, which I am, I'd kiss her.

My desire for her is thick in the air and trails along my skin like a living thing. There is more than simple physical desire here. I like Tara. But to kiss her, to allow myself to start something with her, would be to untie a part of me that I've knotted up so tight that with one loose strand, all of me might unravel.

I step back, away from the moment, away from Tara's sexy mouth and the potential kiss. The risk of real intimacy is too great. I ball up the napkin that I used to wipe the chocolate from the corner of her mouth and do the absolute most obtuse guy thing possible—I take my shot at the trash can.

I make my two-pointer, but lose the moment.

Sadness lingers in Tara's eyes. Women recognize a moment. Some women even create moments to give men opportunities. Tara's energy shifts. She was hopeful I'd take the moment, with the sun warming both of us and the soft breeze of afternoon air.

I didn't.

Instead of taking it, I let the moment fade away.

CHAPTER 6

AFTER MY WALK with Tara and Jango, I toss my Saturday mail onto the counter and pull my Wonderfuck phone from my pocket. It's like the Batphone, only for women and for fucking. My vocation saves my soul from the abyss that threatens to swallow me and prove my nothingness.

Cheryl.

Cheryl is special. My connection with Cheryl is . . . deeper. Not love, no, not that, but she somehow sees beyond her own needs and beyond my Wonderfuck façade, seems to see me.

Yes, me.

She was my first Wonderfuck.

I listen to her message. My cock is hard. Her voice, with its hint of southern dialect, coos in my ear. The curve of her hip. Her breasts. The rounded, lush swell of her belly. She's a gorgeous woman. All of her walks through my mind.

Her outrageous power is both sexual and real.

I glance at my other phone as I listen to her ask if we can meet tonight. We can. I pull the Wonderfuck phone from my ear and text her. That's all it does, receive calls and send texts. No apps. Nothing. It's an old-school flip phone. A burner. Disposable. This phone, like wonderfucking, is good for one thing and one thing only—physical connection.

🐾

"Darlin', there is nothing on this planet that makes me feel as good as you. I've tried Pilates, yoga, meditation, and every drug known to man, but nothing compares to a Wonderfuck."

Cheryl's words please me. I stretch out on the king-sized bed. The sheet drapes at an angle across my thigh. Her gaze rakes over my body. I love being good at my vocation. She traces a fingernail between my pecs, down my chest, and across the ripple of my abs. I grasp Cheryl's hand and pull the palm to my lips. She's the closest thing I have to a regular. I've lost count of number of times and places we've wonderfucked.

"You sure you don't want to come to Kauai next week? Just you, me, the sun, the sand? I won't even make you leave the house if you don't want to."

"Too much going on."

"Your mom?"

I say nothing. Cheryl knows more about my life than I'm comfortable admitting, but over time we've both collected details about each other's lives.

"That disease is some kind of bitch." Cheryl shakes her head. "Watched my aunt go through it when my kids were little. Tore our family up." She stands from the bed. Her body is marked by life, with scars from her two kids, a car accident, stretch marks. Cheryl isn't young, taut, and thin, but she is sexy as hell. She inhabits each mark on her body as though it were a fucking award. That—her shameless unapologetic comfort with her body —makes her sexier than the women I wonderfuck who are half her age.

My cock is hard.

"Look at you, finding this old broad so sexy," she purrs, a

ghost of her old-south accent coming through even after decades of living an upper-crust lifestyle in Los Angeles. "Darlin', I wish I had more time," she turns toward the bathroom, "but I've got a gala to save something, I don't even know what. One of those things I have to do with those stuffed shirts that run my husband's company while he's off in Malaysia or New Zealand or some damned place."

I hear water gush from the showerhead and hit the marble tile. Usually I'd join her, but I know where that will lead, and she's in a hurry. Cheryl is happy to stay and play for days if we're both available, but when she's busy, she has to go. I know this about her. I also know her kids' names and where they each live and what they do, just like she knows about my mom. Funny what she knows, when she doesn't even know my name.

I get up and look out the window at Beverly Hills. Cheryl may be the closest thing to a *relationship* I've had since Susie.

"What are you thinkin' about?" Cheryl walks from the bathroom with a towel around her body. She drops it to the floor and again, my cock is instantly hard. "If I got that kind of reaction from my husband we'd still be sleeping on the same continent," she says, taking her panties and bra from the chair. "But it's been close to twenty years since his cock got hard for me."

"What'd you do for the other fifteen?"

She lifts an eyebrow and sends me a teasing smile, but says not a word. She proceeds to put on her Chanel skirt. I leave her, sitting at the dressing table in her bra about to apply her makeup, and head to the shower.

"DARLIN' WE'VE BEEN DOING THIS FOR WHAT? FIVE years now?"

I pull the towel from my hair. Cheryl is perfectly coiffed, looking like the billionaire businesswoman she is, not like she just spent the last three hours rolling around getting wonderfucked.

"Five years in two months."

"Which means . . ." Her words drift away. My lips thin. She's asking me about Susie's death. The anniversary. "This still workin' for you?"

I pull on my jeans and don't answer. Every year around this time, Cheryl asks me a similar question. I don't know if it's her way of assuaging some guilt about never asking about my mental well-being at any other time, or if she really cares about me and my life.

"Doesn't it seem like it's working for me?" I quip. A way for me to avoid her obvious question.

"I mean, it always seems to work for you," she walks over to me. Her hand grasps my cock through the denim of my jeans. Damn, she can make me hard fast. "But darlin', there's more to life than fucking, even I know that. You're young, and there are women who would be very pleased to have you as their full-time man."

"You don't want me part time anymore?"

"Oh, I'd take you full time if I could get away with it."

I press my lips to Cheryl's. She's perfect for me in many ways. Sexy. Self-confident. Successful. And aside from this question every year, she's as uninterested in a committed relationship as I.

"I'm good," I whisper. I care about Cheryl. Not a romantic, knock-you-on-your-knees love, like the kind I had for Susie, but a genuine caring from companionship, shared unapologetic sexual chemistry, and physical compatibility.

The concern in her eyes makes me uncomfortable. Do I believe my own words? Wonderfucking has worked for me. It's been my salvation and my sanctuary. A way I can feel without feeling. I can't be emotionally vulnerable. I don't have enough in my heart to give to another person, not in the way I gave all my heart, all my love, to one woman once upon a time.

"Got you a little something." She nods toward the nightstand.

A tight feeling works my ribs. Gifts? This isn't our style.

"Open it."

I lift the lid. The face of a blue Patek Philippe nestled on velvet. A gift with a statement. I've never worn a watch, but if I did, this would be the one any man would want to wear.

"They call it grand complications." Cheryl says.

She refers to the ability for this watch to show month, and day and seconds and even phases of the moon. This watch. . . this watch is worth more than my car and I have a fantastic car. I look into her eyes. I want to ask why, but that would be rude, instead I say words that every polite person is trained to say, "Thank you."

Cheryl smiles and kisses my cheek. She steps back and picks up her bag.

"See you in a couple weeks, darlin'," she says. Then she's out the door and out of my life until the next time she makes my Wonderfuck phone buzz.

CHAPTER 7

THE NEXT DAY my muscles are sore and my need is sated. I sit in the home I grew up in, next to Mom. Sun streams through the back slider. My sister sits on the couch near my niece. Lily has three dolls, a teddy bear, and six tea cups set up on the floor.

"Richard, when will Jakey be home from soccer?"

Rachel's lips thin into a line. My mother grasps my hand. Her blue eyes are so focused and honest in her question, wondering when my twelve-year-old self will return from soccer. I wish I were that kid. Life was easier when my biggest question was whether to play my Nintendo or watch hours of Saturday morning TV.

Life was good at twelve.

I sigh. I smile. I clasp Mom's hand a little tighter. Really, why not? Why can't I be Richard, my dad, for a little bit?

"Anna, I think he'll be home around three."

"Oh good." She smiles and nods.

Rachel shoots me a grateful smile. We don't argue with Mom anymore, trying to get her to remember. No point. Her mind is a hodgepodge of facts. Some memories from years ago sharp and in focus, while others, like who Rachel is, seem to have faded into a distant ether. They bounce around like a bucket of ping pong balls dumped onto a cement floor, with little attachment to this time and place where the rest of us remain. We talk to her and we bring her everything she needs and she watches Lily play with dolls and sometimes she plays with Lily, but we definitely don't tell Mom that I'm not Dad and that Rachel is her daughter and that Su—

"When will Susie get here?"

Shards of glass knife through my chest and into my belly.

I clear my throat and swallow. "Mom, Susi—"

"Mom? Did you see Lily's new doll?" Rachel nods toward my niece. "Lily? Show Nana your new doll."

Mom is mesmerized by Lily, but she often thinks my little niece is my sister Rachel. I breathe. I stand. I scrub my hands down the front of my jeans and head out the back slider while Mom and Lily talk about Lily's latest doll, who is named Mackenzie.

Sunlight cuts through the branches that rise up above the backyard. In the quiet, I can almost convince myself I'm anywhere but Los Angeles. A place other than with my Alzheimer's-riddled mother in my childhood home.

The pool is crisp and blue. A light breeze ripples the surface. Deep breath in and deep breath out. Susie loved this pool. She loved Mom. I have fond memories of being in this pool with Susie. That long lush blonde hair, white bikini, sun-kissed skin.

My eyes sting. Too early for fires in the hills. What could possibly be in the Los Angeles air to make my eyes water? Smog? Maybe. Or maybe it's simply that the woman I loved is dead.

"You okay?"

I turn toward Rachel. She crosses her arms over her chest. Concern laces her tone and touches her eyes.

"Never better," I say. "It's been almost six years." My words aren't to Rachel, not even to me. Really, to no one in particular. Just to state the fact, to reconfirm to my heart what my head already knows.

"It wasn't your fault."

"Fuck if it wasn't." I'm Rachel's little brother, and she wants to believe that I wasn't the asshole that caused Susie to die. But she's wrong. Just as wrong as Mom is about my identity. Neither one of them *really* knows who I am. Can't. Because I won't let them. Nor do they really know how hard I pushed Susie to get what I wanted.

"How was brunch?"

"Good." Rachel sits on a chaise lounge beside the pool. "What'd you do all day?"

Fucked. "Had ice cream with my neighbor," I say.

"Tracey?"

"Tara."

"Isn't she getting married soon?"

"It would seem not," I say. "Watched her give back the ring the other night."

"Wow." Rachel's tone conveys more than simple surprise. "How'd that happen?"

"Heard the arguing, looked out the door, she said 'sayonara, sucker' and handed him the rock."

"Should've kept it for her trouble." Rachel looks at her left hand. Her fingers are ringless and slim. She squints. "Did you know?"

What is big sis *really* asking? I feel like her question is loaded with innuendo.

"I mean, you said you went for ice cream . . . were you two . . ."

"No Rachel, I wasn't *fucking* my engaged neighbor."

"Right. Right." She sighs. "Of course not. I mean she's cute." Rachel smiles, attempting to make her words into a joke. "Not sure if I'd be mad at you or happy."

But they're not a joke.

I replay my self-righteous tone in my head and I realize that my ability to compartmentalize is nearing sociopathic levels, because while I haven't been fucking my engaged neighbor, I don't have the moral high ground as far as fiancée-fucking is concerned. No. Not at all. Because I fuck. I fuck a lot. I don't ask questions.

Some women come alone.

Some women come with engagement rings.

Some with divorce stories.

And some with bands of gold.

I don't care. We fuck. No hearts involved. No emotions except for those traded in the room. That's the beauty of the encounter. The physical connection, the endorphins, the serotonin boost to my brain—not enough to engage my heart. Not enough to engage any part of me but my cock. We fuck and then we're finished, because I no longer have a heart, or the desire to be slapped around by that bitch named Love. Nope. Never. I gave Love my all, and she tore me to shreds when my heart, my love, my Susie jumped from the thirty-second floor.

CHAPTER 8

LIQUOR IS A SALVE. Or it can be. Right after Susie, I climbed into a bottle for a while. Until I discovered an addiction of a different kind.

Wonderfucking.

I sip my whiskey and look up at the Dodgers game. I'm in a bar around the corner from my building. A dive. A place I used to frequent, but don't come to often anymore.

I kept this seat warm for a couple months when I couldn't bear to go home. I glance out the window just in time to see a flash of brown hair go by. I know that profile. I know that hair. The bell above the door jingles, and in walks Tara.

She looks way too good for shithole like this. She wears a tank top and jean shorts. Every pair of eyes in this place latches onto her, including the women's. She's curved and round and really beautiful. It's obvious this can't be her normal watering hole. Her eyes adjust to the darkness and she scouts the bar. I lift an eyebrow when her gaze lands on me.

She smiles.

I smile back. Why not? I'm a guy, and a beautiful woman that every guy in this place wants to bang just smiled at me. I'm not interested in Tara, but I'm not an idiot. She walks past the barflies, and their necks swivel to tag her ass with their eyes. Go ahead fellas, take a look.

"Hey, neighbor." She's a little bit breathless. Her cheeks are flushed.

My cock grows hard.

A breathless woman with dilated pupils turns a man on. It makes us think of fucking.

"Hey. Wouldn't have pegged you for a Taggert's type of woman."

She sits on the barstool beside me. Joey, the bartender, arms covered with eagle tattoos from the Vietnam War, ambles over and graces Tara with his smile.

"Haven't seen you in a while, Tara. Want a martini?"

"Yes, please." She turns to me. She lifts a corner of her mouth. "What exactly is a 'Taggert's type of woman'?"

Obviously my neighbor comes to Taggert's often enough for Joey to know her and what she drinks. But then again, what man in this place wouldn't remember Tara's name if she told it to them? She's top shelf where Taggert's is concerned.

She doesn't wait for me to answer. "My old boss at the *Post* used to come here," she says, as if by way of explanation. "Besides, I like dive bars. I especially like knowing about places and things other people don't."

"It's convenient." I glance at her hand. Still no rock. Huh. Wonder if that will stick.

Joey drops off her martini. I notice it's dirty, with an olive.

She takes a long pull on her drink. When she sets her glass back on the bar, the damn thing is half gone. Tara means business. Her eyes sparkle. There is a fire.

"Did you see your Mom today?"

I nod. Tara and I had talked a little about Mom over ice cream on our walk in the park. Lily and Rachel had also come up. I know there were uncomfortable questions about me that she didn't ask, and right now I wonder if I'm meant to return the favor, or if she wants to discuss the absence of a giant diamond on her left hand.

"He's fucking his co-worker," she says and takes another drink. "I walked in on them Friday. On my way home from the office."

"With the dress?"

"With the dress."

Ouch. "That sucks."

"Yeah." Tara finishes her drink and waves to Joey, who starts another martini for her. "The no-fucking-other-people rule applies even before the wedding, don't you think?"

"I think every couple makes an agreement, and if monogamy was part of your agreement, then he fucked up."

"He absolutely fucked up." There is venom in her voice.

I sip my whiskey. She's pissed. I get it. Guys fuck and fuck up. It's what we do. It's who we are. Trying to end the pussy patrol after being a single man is like kicking an addiction. Hardcore habits are fucking hard to break. You try. You fail. You try. You succeed. You fall off the wagon. It sucks. I know. You can fucking destroy people when you fail.

Destroyed me.

I don't say any of that, because it's not what Tara wants to hear. No woman wants to hear or know or accept that even though, yes, men choose whether to actually fuck a woman, our dicks, man, our cocks, wow, they're like weathervanes in a storm, homing devices set to find, fucking drones loaded to explode.

I could go on.

"We're done."

It's been less than forty-eight hours. They were engaged to be married. They're not done.

I take a deep breath. "Sucks about the dress."

"Yeah. I put it on eBay."

"Maybe a trip to Hawaii."

"With that dress? Maybe a trip to Paris." She rolls her gaze toward the ceiling. "My parents are pissed."

"I bet."

"Not the way you think." She flattens her palm onto the bar. "My mother actually asked me if I was sure. If. I. Was. Sure. This is *after* I told her I caught him with his penis in another woman's vagina."

There's nothing for me to say. I can't defend Mom. I also can't bag on Mom either, because then I'm the asshole who says shitty things about Tara's mother. Nope. Best to sit still and enjoy the scenery. And there is some excellent scenery. The swell of Tara's breasts peek out the top of her shirt.

She leans forward.

She notices me noticing.

Oh, yeah, Tara is DTRF: Down To Revenge Fuck. She throws back martini number two and waves for her third. Tara is tall, but she's not a starting lineman for the Rams. Three martinis in less than thirty minutes? Another half hour and she'll be praying to the porcelain god.

"Did you hear us?" She rips tiny pieces of her cocktail napkin from the edge. "Arguing?"

I nod.

"Did you watch?"

"I did."

That seems to sit well with her. I don't know if it's the watching or the honesty, but she obviously likes what I just said.

"My sister thinks you should've kept the ring, for your inconvenience."

"She's a judge, right?"

"Good memory. She's also the recipient of a similar gift, courtesy of her ex-husband. She didn't walk in on him. He left her a note and took a permanent vacation to Costa Rica with his secretary, sans family."

"Bastard."

"She was five months pregnant with Lily. So in her opinion, she thinks you got lucky."

"Maybe. But she has Lily."

"Yeah, but Lily has an asshole for a father who she never sees. She wouldn't trade Lily, but I think Rachel thinks that finding out about his affair five years into her marriage means it might not have been the first time. We tend to be repeat offenders. Recidivism rate is pretty fucking high when it comes to our dicks."

She laughs. "That's funny."

I smile. "Glad I could help."

The smile softens and so does her gaze. "It does help. Thanks."

I nod. I know. I remember. When you lose the person you love, no matter how it happens, every laugh helps.

Her gaze remains locked to mine. She's examining me with that half smile on her face. I know what she wants. I'm a port in a storm. I'm her neighbor. I'm good-looking. She doesn't know what I could do for her because she has no idea who I really am, but she does know I'm an alternative. I'm an alternative to feeling like a piece of shit, an unattractive woman who's been duped and betrayed by the man she loves. She's afraid, and she wants to feel attractive and sought after and wanted. Most of all, she wants me to want her.

And I do.

But I can't.

I could if I was Wonderfuck. But I can't as Jake. I won't as Jake. I don't ever as Jake. Not anymore. Not in five years. Not since Susie. No. No more.

The heat is intense, but I don't make a move. She breaks her gaze from mine. She spins on her bar stool and stands. "What about pool? Know how to play?"

"Of course." I leave cash on the bar for Joey and head toward the back of Taggert's. As if I'd miss the opportunity to watch Tara bend over a pool table in a tank top and jean shorts?

"Wager?"

"Name it." I walk toward the table, stop, and lift a pool stick from the rack.

"Twenty a game."

"The lady is flush."

"Naw"—her gaze locks to mine with heat and desire and need—"the lady feels reckless."

I could use those feelings, if I were inclined. I could totally use what she's feeling right now toward her ex, Mr. Douchediaper: the pain, the anger, the betrayal. I could use every ounce of that and be in her bed, with those perky tits bouncing above me and my hard cock in that blazing wet heat, within the hour.

They're fucking awesome tits.

I could have her after this martini and one game of pool. Hell, I could have her now. She's so angry. So hot. So down to fuck. I could, but I won't.

Will I?

CHAPTER 9

THE SUN IS GONE and a warm wind rushes down the street. The ocean is miles away, and yet the scent carries to us on the wind. Tara is drunk. Not drunk in a wasted-can't-walk way, but drunk in a tipsy, everything-is-funny sort of way. She's a good drunk. A happy drunk, the kind that gets a little loud and laughs. I can hang with that kind of tipsy person. I've never understood the morose or aggressive or teary drunk. What's the fucking point? Life is depressing enough. If you're going to get gloomy or sad or fight when you're drunk, then save yourself the money and the hangover and stay sober.

She cleaned me out of sixty dollars at the pool table. She's a fucking shark with a smile.

"See you've been getting your grocery money at Taggert's."

She bumps her hip against mine and laughs. "My grandfather used to say a good pool player was the sign of a wasted youth."

"Grew up in pool halls and dive bars, did you?"

She smiles and lifts an eyebrow. "I've seen my share."

There's a story here. One that piques my interest. I want details, and yet I don't ask, because I can't. Details lead to interest, interest leads to expectations, expectations mean there's a relationship, and I don't want that. We turn the corner to our building.

There is a wall.

A wall in the form of a man.

A man who could be me five years ago.

McDouche.

"We need to talk." Rings under his eyes, his skin the pallor of death, hair a wreck. The scent of desperation rolls off him, and desperation isn't a good smell on any man. The clothes he wears are possibly the ones he wore to work two days ago. Bad call, dude. That only brings back the memory of what she walked in on. His gaze rolls from her to me.

He recognizes me. Guesses that I know. Assesses whether I'm moving in for the rebound. The muscle in his jaw flinches and my core tenses. He may have twenty pounds on me, but damn, I'm certain I can drop him like a rock.

Tara's face is ashen. Her mouth opens, and the sparkle in her eyes goes out. I stop. I wait. Not moving until I get the okay, because as of now Tara hasn't said a damn word about what she wants.

"I don't have anything to say." Her head tilts higher and her chin takes on an angle that any man with half a brain recognizes. When he sees that chin angle? He'd best call for a retreat. There is no forward advancement possible when a woman's jaw takes on that tilt. Tara steps forward to get past her ex, and I move with her. His hand juts out and grabs her arm.

I stop.

Tara stops.

I look at her. She looks at me. Her eyes close briefly with resignation and defeat. This I-don't-know-what-the-fuck-to-do look. She glances down at his hand and back up at his eyes. "Let go of me." She starts to pull away. His grip tightens.

"Not until we talk."

I stand still as stone. Except for my fists. My fingertips curl up and into my palm. There's a tingle in my toes as adrenaline starts to pound through my body. My gut tightens.

"Let go," Tara says one more time and pulls her arm from Greg's grip. She starts to walk by, and his hand reaches out a second time.

There won't be a third.

"She said no."

Both of them turn to me. I'd become nearly invisible in this emotional tug-of-war they're waging. Greg's gaze snaps to me. He's fucking thrilled. I get it. He's angry, he's scared, he has completely fucked up and lost what he now realizes is the best thing he will ever have, and he's pissed at himself but now . . . now . . . there's a guy in the mix and McDouchey has a place to direct all his rage.

Bring it, asshole.

He takes a step toward me. I said twenty pounds more? Maybe more like thirty-five. "This isn't any of your business."

Oh yeah. He says it low and mean and with a dare behind the words, because the unspoken part I hear, the unspoken part every guy with adrenaline pounding through his body and standing beside a woman that he feels he needs to protect hears, is: *What are you going to do about it, asshole?*

"Really?" I've got absolutely nothing to fear and not much to live for. "Because I think right now, tonight, it *is* my business."

I stare at this motherfucker, knowing we are two beats away from throwing down. Tara is like a fucking doe in the sniper's crosshairs. Suddenly she's out of her trance. "Hey, Greg, this is ridiculous, I don't want to talk now, please just go—" She grabs his arm, but he rips it free, yanking hard enough that she falls back and stumbles to the ground.

I smile. Oh yeah. This asshole is going down.

My fist smashes his jaw. The flash of pain through my hand is like a hot starburst. Fuck. Yes. For a split second he takes it like maybe he deserves it and wants the pain, because we're all fuckers undeserving of the women we love and he's just let his cock do some stupid-ass shit. Really, he wants me to beat the shit out of him, he needs me to beat the shit out of him, he will actually *enjoy* me beating the shit out of him, and I'm happy to comply. Because as much as Greg hates himself right now and thinks he's a piece of shit for what he's done, well, I've been wallowing in my own grief, my own misdeeds, my own loss for nearly six fucking years, and I know how good this shit is going to feel.

His hand pulls back and I see it, like fucking slow motion, I see the punch coming and I step into that motherfucker because I'm going to let this asshole land one punch and then I'm going to beat the ever-loving shit out of him. That one fucking punch, as it connects with my jaw and my head jerks back like a tetherball on a rope, makes me fucking mad. That mad feeling digs deep into my soul and grabs onto the rage that lives just below the surface. The rage from Susie, the rage for every bad fucking thing I've done or had done to me—that beast rises up and takes over and is there like a living breathing thing. As I swear to fucking God, once Greg hits me I breathe fucking fire and see red.

My fists are hammers and I start pounding. One. Two. Three. He drops and is up. One. Two Three. In the distance I hear a scream and a yell and then a siren. I hit Greg again and I'm on top of this motherfucker when I feel hands grab me from behind and lift and spin me. My chin meets metal, my wrists meet cuffs, and my ass meets—not for the first time—the backseat of a police car.

§.

L.A. COUNTY JAIL SMELLS LIKE FORTY MEN TOOK A PISS on a two-foot shag rug, put the rug in a car in a July, and then wet that rug down and rubbed that fucker along every inch of the wall in lockup.

I sit in a corner and wait.

"Reynolds, you're up." A cop pulls open the bars and I hop to my feet. Two other guys eye me from the far side of lockup. They've been in here a while.

I roll out of the cell and the cop eyes me. "Could've told me your sister's a judge in criminal."

"Like I want to be that asshole," I say, walking beside him. He nods, maybe thinking at least I have standards, even if I am rolling out of lockup after a street fight.

Rachel stands just past the door to lockup. She wears a long coat over her clothes, her hands shoved deep in the pockets. She stands beside a cop who's obviously important, based on the way the other cops look at him. He nods at me and the officer who just brought me out.

"Good night, Judge Reynolds."

"Thank you," she says.

He turns and walks down the hall. Damn. Most of these cops probably appear in Rachel's courtroom on a regular basis. My need to beat the crap out of Douchey has put her in an embarrassing position.

She reaches her hand out and touches the bottom of my chin. "I hope the other guy looks worse."

We silently walk down the hall to the property window, where they hand me a giant envelope with my stuff. I dump it onto the counter.

"Since when do you have a flip phone?" She picks up my Wonderfuck phone. I pluck it from her fingertips and shove it into my front pocket, put my iPhone into my back pocket, and grab my wallet. "And a Patek Philippe?" Her eyes widen at the watch that cost more than her entire salary for a year. "Investments must be good," she mumbles and we walk toward the lobby and out the front door. Before we reach the stairs down to the sidewalk, Rachel stops and turns to me.

"I have a five-year-old, a mother with Alzheimer's, and a full-time job. I have a docket that starts at eight a.m. tomorrow. I just burned through a dozen favors to get your ass out." She crosses her arms over her chest. "Would you please tell me if we're heading back to the abyss that we visited five and a half years ago? Because if we are, I need to line up child care."

"No," I sigh. "I . . . honestly . . . I was protecting a woman."

"So I hear. Why do you think I came?" She glances down the front steps and across the walkway. I follow her gaze.

Tara stands on the sidewalk. Her arms crossed. Wearing a jacket. Her hair still in that messy ponytail. That's how Rachel found out. That's who called my sister.

Tara.

Fuck.

The tiny pieces of my heart that refuse to die vibrate with warmth.

Then my brain kicks in.

Fuck.

"She wanted to come too. She told me what happened." Rachel takes a deep breath. "I . . . I would've wanted someone to do that for me when . . . when that happened." She dug the toe of her shoe against the pavement. "I get it. I do. But does she?"

"No."

"Then you've got to decide. Do you want her to understand or not?"

My eyes meet Rachel's, and I know she's sad for me. Her lips do that thin line thing they do when she isn't happy about something I've said or done, or when another neuron in Mom's mind has obviously shut down. No, Rachel's not happy with me, but that's okay. She's got Lily and a career, and some day when she's ready she'll have a man. But tonight she's worried about me, her fucked-up little brother who hides an entire life from his big sis. While she doesn't know the details, my sister is smart enough to know that I'm hiding something. She just hopes I'm not a drug runner, a serial killer, or something worse.

And I'm not. Because Wonderfuck isn't any of those things. Wonderfuck is simply the alter ego I need to skirt the edges of the black hole that threatens to suck away all that remains of my soul.

Tara stands beside a palm tree, waiting for me. Her presence here tells me that I don't have to go to my place and be alone. I'm the knight in shining armor who beat the shit out of the asshole who broke her heart. I can tell by the look on Tara's face that she thinks I'm her prince charming.

I'm not. I won't let Tara get close to the edge I walk. I've given up on love. Wonderfuck is the only thing that saves me and makes me feel whole. I can't let go of Wonderfuck, and I can't be Wonderfuck and have a lover as Jake.

I can't.

I won't.

But I will ride home.

"You okay?" I ask Rachel.

"I got an entire building full of cops and I'm parked right there." She points to her car, which has the premiere spot next to the front door. "There are perks to being a judge. You two want a ride?"

"No. We'll uber."

"She—" Rachel nods her head toward where Tara stands. "I like her. She's smart. You know that, right? But it's too soon . . . for her. You know that too."

I nod. I know it all.

Rachel pulls me in for a hug. "I love you, dumbass," she whispers in my ear. Her voice cracks, and she pulls me even closer.

When you've lost people you love, you realize just how fragile the connections are, just how quickly they can disappear.

"I love you too. Thank you," I say. "I didn't want to pull you into this, I know it's my—"

"Shut up," she says, shaking her head. She smiles that big sis smile, the one that says my problems will always be her problems because she's my older sister. She backs toward her car. "Call me tomorrow. Don't forget dinner on Wednesday."

I nod. I watch while she climbs into her car. Just to be sure. Probably the safest place in all of Los Angeles at two a.m., but still, I love her. "Text me when you get home," I call after her. She waves.

I turn away as she pulls from the parking lot.

Tara.

She stands with her arms crossed, rolling forward and back on the balls of her feet. What to do about a problem like Tara? And she is a problem. Obviously.

"You have my sister's number?"

"Gave it to me the first time you asked me to pick up your mail." The sparkly tipsy buzz is gone. Understandably. It's been hours since my street fight.

She leans in and stares at my chin.

"How's it look?"

"Not too bad. Broke the skin and you've got a bruise." She steps back and her blue eyes meet mine. "I'm sorry," she says. "I wish I'd handled that better. I should've just talked to him, I should've—"

"Stop. There's nothing you could've done."

Tara squints at me and says nothing.

"He was past reason. I was past reason. This isn't your fault," I add. I pull out my phone and order an Uber.

"Okay," she says, not really buying what I'm telling her. "But if I'd just talked to him—"

"Maybe," I say, "but I think he wanted the fight." I glance at my phone. "Three minutes." I look up. She has her head tilted like she's waiting for me to explain.

"Look he just fucked up the best thing he'll ever have, okay? And he knows it. He may be an idiot, but he's not so stupid that he doesn't realize he fucked up. He knows. And now, what he did is sinking in . . . what he actually did and how badly he's fucked up his life. He's pissed at himself. And when a guy gets pissed at himself, most guys anyway, they want to fuck or fight."

"Fuck or fight?"

"Kind of flight or fight, only with more rage."

"So the only way I could've stopped the fight is if I fucked him?"

"No, but if you would've talked to him, then he still would've had the hope of eventually fucking. But you didn't talk to him, so he knew there wasn't going to be any fucking, and there I was—"

"So there was the potential for fighting," she finishes my sentence. She seems interested in what I'm saying, curious, as though a specific thought is forming in her mind.

"Right. So he got a fight." I don't add how I was down to fight as well because I'd already decided there wouldn't be any fucking, at least not with Tara, and even though it was my decision, it kind of made me mad at myself.

"And what about you? You seemed eager to fight, does that mean—"

The Uber BLACK glides to a stop in front of us. "Here's our car," I say, avoiding Tara's question. I've got the answer, but based on how close she's standing and how she's looking at me, my answer isn't the answer she wants to hear. Not now and, most likely, not ever.

CHAPTER 10

"Do you want to come in for a drink or something to eat?"

Yes, I want to go to Tara's. I want to run my hands down her body and press my lips to her mouth. I want to have her lying beneath me, whispering my name as I slowly slide into her. I want to fuck away any insecurity she might feel because of Douchey-McDouche-Face. I want it all.

But I can't have any of it. To walk into Tara's home, to put my lips on hers and make love to her, is to involve her in my madness.

Two identities, one man.

One version of my life feels good physically and soothes my soul after the pain of Susie, and the other is a guy who lives across the hall from Tara.

"Sorry." My gaze locks to Tara's blue eyes. "I'm beat. I . . ." I want to kiss you and fuck you and maybe even hang out with you . . . "I need to shower and get some sleep."

The corners of her lush mouth twitch downward and disappointment flickers in her eyes, but only for a millisecond. Then it vanishes. I guess telegraphing your emotions isn't helpful when you're an investigative journalist.

"No problem." She doesn't turn toward her door or shift

away from me. She just remains in the hallway, looking into my eyes and waiting.

I want Tara as much as she wants me.

"Good night," I step forward and press my lips to her forehead. The clean scent of lavender.

She gasps.

I pull back. Her eyes are closed and the pulse in her neck flutters. I feel the desire too. The heat only makes me want to pull her into my arms and kiss her. A whine from the other side of the door and then a bark.

"She knows we're home." Tara steps away from me.

"Thank you for the help tonight," I say.

"Thanks for protecting me."

I turn toward my door and walk inside. I look through my apartment to the view. The magnificent view. The balcony . . . that balcony.

My heart spasms. I drop my gaze and walk down the hall to my bedroom and the comfort of sleep.

"DOES ANYONE KNOW WHO YOU ARE?"

I run my hand over Celia's bare hip and press my lips to her belly. I don't answer. She doesn't want me to. Not really.

"Do you know who you are?"

I pause. I pull my lips from her skin and glance across her naked flesh toward her eyes. I spread open her legs, her thighs, and look up at her, my eyes just above her glorious mound.

"I know I'm the man who can make you come."

Her scent fills me and my cock is hard, so fucking hard. I press my tongue to her clit. Her eyes close. Her mouth stops asking questions and forms an O.

"Oh yes," she moans. I pull her into my mouth. The glorious taste of pussy. Sharp and earthy and female. My tongue circles out letters on her clit. Her hips buck up and roll beneath me. I clasp her hip with my hand. God yes. Fucking amazing pussy.

My eyes close and the face, that face, enters my mind. The face isn't Celia's. I don't see Cheryl or Natasha or Leslie or Debbie or Peggy or Caitlyn or Pamela or Maria or any of the women I've made feel sexual and sensual and amazing.

The face isn't even Susie's.

There is one face that bursts into my mind like a bullet through hot butter. Her hair lush and deep brown, her eyes blue, her breasts full and round. Hips that flare and legs that go on forever, with a full ass a man can grab onto.

Celia shrieks. She grasps my head and sits up, her body shaking. She pulls my mind back to now, to her, to this instant where she orgasms.

CHAPTER 11

I SUCCESSFULLY AVOID Tara for over a week. Or maybe she avoids me. I pull my mail from my box in the lobby of our building and wave to Del, our concierge, as I walk to the elevator. I rifle through the stack of ads and bills. I pause at the envelope with my name in handwritten calligraphy on it and tear it open.

The cancellation notice for Tara's wedding. Does she know these will hit guests' mailboxes today? Has she heard from friends and family and everyone else she invited, or is there silence? Deafening silence, like after a horrible loss or tragedy? That silence is worse than the all the initial noise. With Susie, the first seven days were cacophonous, but then I came home to complete and total silence.

I get off the elevator, but instead of turning to my door, I stop in front of Tara's. I lift my hand to knock. I pause. I stop.

What am I doing? My life is exactly the same as it was the night I declined her invitation to come in. Nothing's changed. What can I say to Tara? Why would I complicate feelings that already seem complicated enough by actually going to her door the day I receive notice her wedding's been cancelled? My hand drops to my side and I start to turn toward my own door when Jango barks.

The door opens. Tara's face is beautiful despite her puffy red eyes. She forces a smile my direction. She's fighting back tears. By the look on her face, she's fought them all day.

"Hey, I just wanted to stop by—"

Her gaze drops to the pile of mail in my hand, with the opened wedding cancellation notice on top. She plucks it from my hand.

"I haven't seen them. My mother took care of it." She reads the postcard-sized correspondence, then turns it over and examines the back. "I'm surprised she sprang for the expensive paper." Her attempt at a joke falls flat.

"Sucky day," I say, because I can't really think of much more than that.

"Sucky day," she whispers. I glance at Jango, who nudges Tara's hand with her snout. She, too, must realize what a horrible day Tara is having. The corner of the right side of Tara's mouth lifts as she strokes Jango's head. "Haven't seen you around lately."

My chest tightens. I clear my throat. "Busy with work."

She nods. "Okay, well I've got to take Jango for her walk—"

"I'm going to watch my niece later, want to come?" The words blurt from my mouth before the idea hits my brain. Funny how I know just exactly what to say to heartbroken women. Damn. The offer is out now, can't retract it. "Might be better than hanging out alone. I know Lily would love to meet Jango." I squat down and put a hand on either side of Jango's face. We both look up at Tara as though begging for permission.

"How can I say no to those two faces?" She nearly smiles . . . nearly, but not quite. That's okay, because I know the combo of Lily and Jango and, yes, even me will get Tara out of this funk. How could it not?

※

"YOU BROUGHT MY DAUGHTER A DOG." MY SISTER hisses under her breath. She's all decked out in a blue dress and high heels and makeup and jewelry.

"I didn't get Lily a dog. I brought Tara, and she brought her dog."

"This doesn't help me, okay? Lily is after me for a dog and—"

"And I think she's right, every kid should have a dog."

"I don't have time for a dog. I barely have time to shave my legs."

I get it. Big sis's life is full to the top. Seriously, if I had all her responsibilities my head would explode. Nope. I'll simply keep my life to sex and no commitments.

"Then let Lily enjoy Tara's." Rachel's gaze slides toward the living room, where Tara is showing Lily all Jango's tricks.

"What's going on there?"

"Nothing. Friends."

"Really?"

"I have no desire to get involved."

"Fair enough, but do you have any desire to—"

I hold up my hand. "I know we're close, and sometimes you forget I'm not one of your girlfriends that you discuss every bit of their sex life with, but I'm *not* one of your girlfriends, so even if I was having a physical relationship with Tara, which I'm not, I wouldn't tell you. Not interested."

"Bullshit. You're interested.

I take a long breath. "Okay, who wouldn't be interested? She's smart and beautiful and engaging, but from a personal standpoint, the one that involves what happened to my fiancée, I'm absolutely not interested. Can't be. We're friends."

"Friends?" My sister laughs as though I've just told her the best joke ever. "Men and women can't be friends. Especially if they're attracted to each other."

She might be right, but I'm not ready to admit that yet. Besides, Rachel is too used to always being right.

"She'd be perfect for you, in about six months. She needs time to get past the asshole."

"That's why I invited her. The wedding cancellation card arrived today."

My sister's teasing face crumples, replaced by a sincere look of sadness for Tara. "That sucks. Is there anything I can do?"

"I think we're doing it."

In the other room, Tara laughs. Lily tells Jango to roll over, and she does. Lily claps with glee.

"You're a good man, Jake Reynolds." My sister squeezes my arm for an instant. "Look at you, killing it with the ladies. Making all four of us women happy."

Again the warmth in my chest. Because, yeah, big sis is right. By babysitting Lily and bringing Tara over, I've made both my niece and big sis happy. I know Jango's over the moon, and Tara? I focus on her face. Her eyes aren't swollen anymore, and the blotchy red patches on her cheeks and nose are gone. Her I'm-about-to-cry face has been replaced with a smile and even a laugh as she chats with Lily about Jango.

Tara's gaze darts toward me and her smile grows bigger.

Heat bursts through my chest. Tara is my friend and my neighbor. Any good neighbor would do what I did, right? You help out your neighbor when you know they're sad or upset or in need. That's what I did. I helped out my neighbor.

Fuck. Then why does my chest pulse with this fucking joy and a hint of need?

I redirect my attention and the conversation back to my sister. "Are you going with *Alan*?"

"Shh." Rachel does a quick head check toward the living room. According to big sis, Lily isn't supposed to know about Alan, the guy she's had a couple dates with—at least, not until Lily's left for college. "We're meeting there," she says under her breath. She reaches for a glass of white wine and drains it.

"What's the award?"

"Jurist of the year," she says. She puts the wineglass in the dishwasher. "Really, I think it's because they needed to give it to a woman, not because I'm any great judge." She turns to me. I know this isn't true. My sister *is* a great judge. She takes her work, her career, her decisions very seriously.

"I'm going now." Rachel throws a shawl over her shoulders, picks up her clutch, and walks toward the living room. "Lily, be good for Uncle Jake and Tara."

Lily walks to Rachel and gives her a kiss. "You look beautiful, Mama."

My tough big sis almost crumbles into tears. "Have fun this afternoon." She turns to me. "The birthday gift is on the dining room table. Seriously, just one hour. They know you're doing me a favor by bringing her by and won't be offended."

One of Lily's little friends from preschool is turning five, and we're required to attend the late-afternoon party. Part of the babysitting gig. What single guy doesn't want to spend an afternoon with twenty five-year-old kids?

❧

"Do I know you?" A voice coos in my ear as I take off Lily's shoe so she can join her best buddy Ava in the bouncy house. I turn toward the voice. Yes, yes, you do know me. I've slipped those nipples pressing against your cotton top between my lips.

"Afraid we haven't met. I'm just the uncle."

I stand and glance past the woman who I wonderfucked about three times two years ago. Lily bounces with Ava. Tara wanted a soda and had headed toward the stand on the far side of the yard. Without a glance toward the woman—whose name I can no longer recall—I walk toward the soda fountain. I glance back at Lily, who is smiling and bouncing.

"I got you a water." Tara hands me a bottle and I take a long pull. I finally glance back at the spot where . . . was her name Kendall? Or Candy? I can't remember a name, but a face and a rack? Those are indelibly marked in my brain—Kendall, her name was Kendall, and she no longer stands beside the bouncy house. Maybe she decided I wasn't the right guy, maybe she thinks I have a doppelganger, maybe she can't remember after two years. Maybe . . . maybe . . . she doesn't want to relive the past. I don't.

I survey the giant yard that is made up to look like a carnival, including a ferris wheel, an elephant, a monkey, a bouncy house, and a magician.

"I don't mind the five-year-olds," I tell Tara. "It's the parents that scare me."

Tara smiles, one of a handful of real smiles today. Together we walk toward the bouncy house, where Lily and her BFF Ava are giggling and shrieking.

"It makes me happy to see them laugh." Tara slides her gaze toward me. "Thanks for bringing me too."

"Can't imagine a better companion for a birthday party." I look toward the clown, who's turning a long skinny balloon into a dog. Kendall stands beside a boy who looks just like her, only younger. Her son, I'd guess. On the other side of the boy is a guy. His legs are spread and his arms crossed. He wears aviator shades and has kind of an I'm-king-of-the-world asshole stance to him.

Hmmm . . . some of Kendall's story is coming back. Separated. Nearly divorced. Husband had an affair. Wonder if this is the same guy? Or if she just has the ability to pick assholes. Some women do. Asshole is simply their preferred type.

"Do you know her?"

"She looks like someone I knew a couple years ago." Not completely true and not completely a lie. I glance into Tara's eyes. There's that pain again, the sadness that Douchenugget caused.

Ava and Lily slip out of the bouncy house.

"We want to go on the ferris wheel!"

Tara and I follow the two happy giggle-boxes toward the line.

"I'm getting another water, anything for you?" I ask.

"I'll monitor the troops." I flash her a thank-you smile. I need to make a detour to the restroom, so I head toward the back door into the enormous house and walk down the far hall, where our hostess had directed us earlier when Lily had to go. No line. I head into the bathroom and do my deal. I've washed my hands and move to open the door when the lights go off.

"What the fuck?"

"It is you."

A hand slides around my waist, drifts to the front of my jeans, and grabs for my cock. I'm hard in an instant.

"I've missed your cock."

She pulls at my shirt. Her hand glides over the muscles of my belly to my chest.

My head swoons. Physical touch. Want. Need. Sex. All of it a drug, an elixir that sinks me fast.

"Still amazing." Her hands move to my belt, and that motion rips me from the pleasure of touch. I grab her hand.

"We can't do this."

"Oh yes we can," she says, trying for my belt again.

"No," I say, my voice firm but not cold. I understand desire and the need for a physical connection. "I won't do this now." I flip on the bathroom light.

Her shoulders drop and she stares at the floor, as though my words have destroyed her. Slowly she raises her head and her brown eyes meet mine.

"I went back to him . . . I thought we could fix it, that he wanted to fix it, but it's the same." Her expression is flat, life-less, defeated. "So much of the same."

"I'm sorry."

She nods, covering her mouth with her hand as though forcing herself not to cry, but to remain stoic. Panic in her eyes, as though she is a woman drowning. A woman nearing the edge. A woman without hope.

"I just . . . I don't know what to do."

I nod. This is deeper than something sex can fix. This is pain and heartbreak and a trade people make with themselves when they decide to stay with a person they no longer love for the sake of money, or stability, or children. For whatever reason they think is better than their own happiness. And those reasons aren't better or more noble, because sometimes the decision to pursue your own happiness is the most noble pursuit of all.

Tears roll down her cheeks and I pluck two tissues from the box on the counter.

"Thank you." She takes one of the tissues from me and turns toward the mirror. "You're the only bright spot I've had in the last two years." She attempts to fix her makeup. She glances in the reflection at me. "Are you here with your wife?" Her tone is suddenly icy, and her face looks hard.

"Not married." Her sudden anger melts away. "My niece and a friend." I fix her gaze with mine. My cover has been blown. Completely blown. She could seriously mess up my life right now if she wanted. "Do you think we could—"

She smiles and tosses the used tissue into the trash can. "Your secret is safe with me." There's an edge to her smile, though, a desperation and a sadness that make little alarms go off in my head.

"Thank you, Kendall," I say, leaning in to kiss her cheek.

She sighs. A flash of our time together. She is a soft woman filled with need, who liked to be made love to in a gentle way. There was something sad in her bottomless want that I, through physical intimacy, would never be able to fill.

"You go first," she says.

I pull open the door. There is no one in the hall, and I slip away from Kendall and from the possibility of my two lives colliding.

CHAPTER 12

"DID SHE HAVE FUN?" My sister whispers to me as she exits Lily's bedroom.

"I think so. She bounced forever. There was a ferris wheel and pony rides and—"

"They had a ferris wheel?" My sister raises an eyebrow. "Unbelievable, those people." She walks down the hallway toward the stairs. She pauses on the landing. In the living room Tara sits with Jango's head on her lap. Tara stares into the distance, stroking her pup's head. "How'd that go?" Big sis whispers and I know she's not discussing the dog or Lily.

"I hate seeing her sad," I finally say, which is lame in comparison to everything I'm thinking when it comes to Tara. But I don't have the luxury of always saying what I think. Sometimes I don't say anything at all.

"Such an asshole, to have an affair while he's engaged."

"It wasn't an affair. He was fucking a colleague."

My sister whips her face toward me. Her eyes filled with fire. "How is that not an affair?"

I sigh. I know that by the female definition, banging a hot piece of ass on your desk is an affair, but by the male standard, that's simply rubbing one out. It's a tough transition for a man, and some can never cross over to the female definition. Some men really don't ever understand how fucking a piece of strange is cheating. I won't win this disagreement, nor do I want to. I understand the definition. I understand how any sex with a woman other than the one you've committed to is a betrayal. I get how when a man fucks a woman other than the one he's made a commitment to and she finds out, that his decision strikes at the very core of a woman's identity.

But truly, women shouldn't give our cocks that much power over their self-worth because, well, our cocks? Not so smart. Bad choices. No brain involved.

"You're right. She seemed happy today."

Rachel walks down the stairs and Tara glances up. She replaces her thoughtful look with a smile as we enter the room. She stands up and picks up her jacket and her purse, holding Jango's leash in one hand.

"You survived a five-year-old birthday party."

"I did." Tara says. "It was fun. Lily was so good. Jake even knew a couple of people there."

Ice drips through my belly. My gaze shifts from Tara to Rachel.

"You did? Who?" Big sis asks, now obviously curious. The parent set is not my group, and I don't hang out at Lily's school enough to *know* anyone.

"I . . . I'm not sure." I shake my head. "I mean, maybe I know—"

"The blonde."

"Which blonde? Sheila Martin or Janelle, or Carol, or Kendall or—my God, we're in Southern California. I think all of Lily's classmates have moms with blonde hair except me."

"She has brown eyes, and I think a little boy," Tara says.

"That must be Kendall Prescott. Her husband is some hedge fund manager."

Tara looks at me and so does big sis, both of them seeking confirmation that I understand which woman they're discussing.

And I do. I know exactly which woman they've identified. I even know how Kendall shrieks when she comes.

"She was wearing white jeans," Tara continues. "She spoke to me later in the day, and I thought she said—" My look must convey my discomfort, because Tara suddenly stops talking. For a second her eyebrows lift, and then she says, "My mistake." Tara shifts her purse strap up higher on her shoulder. "I probably just assumed he knew everyone because he's Lily's uncle and always speaks to people." She turns to Rachel and pushes a smile onto her face. "I'm much shyer by nature."

My sister crinkles her eyebrows and glances from Tara to me, but says nothing. She puts a hand against the wall and slips her feet from her high heels. A look of relief floods her face.

"I suppose Lily ate nothing but junk." Big sis gives me the side-eye.

"That's what uncles are for, but she did have a turkey hot dog halfway through the party. *After* the bouncy house."

"Smart man. Thank you." Rachel places a kiss on my cheek and we all walk to the front door. "Don't forget you're with Mom next Friday." She thanks both of us, and then Tara and I are on the front steps, headed for home. I breathe in the cool evening air. I dodged a bullet tonight. Next time, I might not be so lucky. Next time, it might not miss.

❧

"I NEED TO GIVE JANGO A WALK BEFORE I HEAD UP FOR the night." Tara quickly cuts across the parking garage toward the locked gate and I hustle up behind her. She stops and turns to me. "You don't need to come with me. I walk her every evening."

I pause. Tara is irritable. I don't know what I've done or said or failed to do. She may not want me to come with her to walk Jango, but I'm a good guy and I'm not ditching her in a parking garage after dark to walk her dog alone.

"I'll come too. I want the fresh air."

We exit onto the sidewalk and turn the corner to the park. We walk in silence. Joggers run by and other dog walkers pass us on the path. Tara lets Jango sniff and walk and sniff and walk.

"Did you have a good time today?" I finally ask, pretty certain at this point Tara is angry.

"I . . . I . . . don't like lying," she finally says. She stops and turns to me, lifting her gaze to meet my eyes. "What happened to me taught me that there's no place for lying in my life." She stares at me, almost daring me to confront what I'm pretending not to know or understand.

And she's right. I'm completely pretending that I don't get what she's saying, because I can't cop to Wonderfuck. Not to Tara. Not to Rachel. Not to anyone. Wonderfuck is me, and he was created for my sanity.

"Look." She shifts and crosses her arms over her chest. "I know you know that woman. The blonde with the brown eyes?"

I raise an eyebrow.

"I saw the two of you coming out of the bathroom."

"Spying?"

"Needed to pee, actually. Plus, she spoke to me later. Told me I must be enjoying myself."

Heat floods my face. Shit. Shit. Shit.

"Look, we each have different rules we live by, but that woman is married and after what happened to me I can't . . . I can't be around a person who doesn't think marriage is important."

"Marriage is important. I do know her. But I never knew she was married. She wanted something from me today that I can't give her."

Tara's processing what I've said. All of my words are true . . . technically. Please don't ask any questions . . . If Tara asks the obvious question, I don't know how I can sidestep without actually telling her a lie. A bold-faced lie.

And for some reason, it's important to me not to lie to Tara.

"It's really none of my business." With a small tug of Jango's leash, she turns and leads the way back to our building.

It isn't Tara's business, but part of me wants my business to be Tara's business. I can picture a woman like Tara being part of my life, and that is fucking terrifying.

CHAPTER 13

"THIS IS OUR THIRD TIME TOGETHER."

"It is."

Natasha's happier than the first time we met. More confident. Less likely to take the bullshit that was being served to her on a daily basis. She can orgasm, and she's not frigid. She burns with a bright intensity when she comes, and now she knows that she can.

"Can I ask you a question?"

"You can ask me as many questions as you want." I roll toward her. She's exquisite. Her body is lush and full and the sexual glow that emanates from within her has grown brighter and brighter with each moment we're together. I bask in this glow. My heart aches less because of her joy. She's stronger, and won't be as willing to accept scraps of affection from a man.

"Can men change?"

"Their underwear?" I ask, making a joke out of a tough question.

Natasha doesn't smile at my response. She rolls away from me, onto her back. She stares at the ceiling. Her full round breasts peek from beneath the sheet. The urge to lean forward and pull one taut nipple into my mouth flows through me. My cock is hard.

"That's what I thought." She breathes out. She turns her head to me. "He wants to try again."

I nod. This often happens. When a man loses a woman and discovers she's actually doing better without him . . . well, that's when he wants her back. We're like that. The bottom line has improved, we made a bad deal, a mistake, and now we want what we've lost.

Or do we?

That's the kicker. Do we want what we've lost, or do we simply want what we can't have?

"If he wants that because he just wants what he can't have, then he'll start being an asshole again. Revert back to the shit that broke your heart. Now, if it's because he realizes what he lost and he's changed?" I sigh. "Well, you let me know when you meet a man that's changed."

I tell it like it is from my vantage point, but only if a woman asks. Natasha asked.

"So in your opinion . . ."

"We don't change."

She nods. I'm merely confirming what she suspected, but hoped wasn't true.

"Our edges get smoothed and we get better at empathizing because, well, that muscle barely exists for us until we've gotten our heart busted a couple of times. But no, it's been my experience that if a guy is an asshole and the relationship doesn't work the first time, then it won't work the second or the third."

Natasha closes her eyes. She takes a deep breath and covers her face with her hands. Oh shit. Here come the tears. I'm prepared. I've wiped away gallons. I scoot forward, knowing she'll need to be held. The tears, the emotional baggage, this is part of my vocation, my redemption, my penance.

A sound comes from her mouth, soft at first. I lean in closer and put one hand on her belly. I'm ready to give her whatever she needs to get through this pain. Her belly twitches. Here come the wails, the crying—but instead, I hear a laugh. Not one, not two, but many.

Starting small and building from her belly, all the way up until her gorgeous body is shaking. Her laughter is deep and her breasts tremble with her joy. The sheet falls away from her. I smile and laugh in response, because when someone is laughing, you can't help but laugh too. She pulls her hands from her face and sweeps her fingertips beneath her eyes, wiping away tears, a smile still on her lips.

"Oh thank God." Her laughter subsides. "I really didn't want to take that asshole back."

Now I laugh. I really laugh. Because this is the best-case scenario for 99.9 percent of the women who come to me because a man cheated.

Don't take the bastard back.

He had his shot. He failed. Don't give him the opportunity to fail again. Just my thoughts on the subject.

She turns to me and presses a kiss to my lips. "Thank you."

One of the torn-up bits in my chest that used to be a heart responds with warmth.

"You . . . being with you . . . I couldn't have gotten through all this without our time together."

I say nothing. Natasha would've gotten through this. Most definitely could've gotten through this. All you women can, and do. You're strong. Much stronger than you realize. Stronger than any man you'll ever meet. The well of strength that Natasha has tapped into, that maybe she thinks I've given her? That strength was always there. Maybe I guided her to it, helped her, because I reflected back to her the beauty, the strength, the courage that was already present by fucking the living shit out of her. This desire, her sexuality, allows her to tap into this river of strength that she'd either forgotten or didn't even know existed deep inside of her.

Natasha doesn't say anything more. I can tell our time

together is nearly finished. Her hand slides down my belly and grasps my cock, which is hard and thick and pulsing with the need to fuck her one final time. Because this is what happens when I'm with a woman. We go from her needing me, to me needing her. I can only be with a woman a few times, because after Susie, I can't need a woman like I needed her ever again.

&.

"RICHARD, WILL SUSIE BE ABLE TO JOIN US FOR LUNCH today?" I stop. I was in the midst of pushing in Mom's dining room chair. "Maybe we should go out to meet her?"

"I . . . uh . . . I don't think today," I say. I walk to the chair beside Mom. Her caregiver had a doctor's appointment today, and big sis had a docket of cases, and since I run my own company, well, I'm the guy who gets to pinch-hit in these scenarios. I pull a to-go box from a bag. I stopped on my way over and picked up Mom's favorite salad from La Scala. I always hope that foods that she loves, favorite smells, familiar sounds, some of it will jog her brain and bring her back to me, at least for an afternoon.

"I love it when Susie has lunch with me. You know, she was over here just last week. We had salads then too."

And no such luck. My fiancée has been dead for over five years, so while Susie probably did stop by for lunch on occasion with Mom, she certainly didn't stop here last week.

I pour the salad from the to-go box onto Mom's plate and set it before her.

"It's La Scala chopped salad, Mom, you love this salad."

"I do?"

I nod as I pour my salad onto my plate, then put both containers in the bag and take it into the kitchen. Mom is Mom, no matter what piece of time she exists in. Who knows? Einstein said the passage of time in a linear fashion was a construct of the brain. Maybe Mom is right about Susie.

I sit down. I'm thankful she can still feed herself. That she can still bathe herself. That she remembers all kinds of things and how to do them. Because we don't know how long those abilities will last.

"Richard." Mom reaches out and clasps my hand. She has a serious look on her face, as though there is something very important she must tell me. I'm conflicted in these moments. Some specialists say not to tell the patient that they're confused, let them go, let them believe their own reality. Other doctors tell you to gently redirect them. I'm torn because Richard was my father, and there was a special intimacy between Mom and Dad. When Mom confuses me with Dad, I feel like I'm eavesdropping on my mother's most private and innermost thoughts. Things she would've only said to her husband.

"Mo—"

"No, Richard, please listen, this is important. I need to share this with you." Her face is serious, so instead of correcting her, I simply nod and wait for whatever words my mother needs to say to my father.

"Susie was here, and Richard, I need you to speak to Jake."

My heart drops from my chest. My belly tightens.

"I . . . I don't know how to say this, but Susie seems to think . . . she's concerned about"—Mother closes her eyes and presses her lips into a tight line—"She's concerned about fidelity within their relationship."

My breath is shallow. A cold clammy sweat crawls across my skin. My mouth drops open. What do I say, how do I say—

"I know that this could be a particularly difficult topic considering our own marriage, but perhaps you could share with him how you overcame your challenges to monogamy."

"Mom, it's me." I hear my own voice. It's loud and abrasive and I can't stop myself.

Mom's eyes snap out of her haze for an instant. "Jakey," she says, and her hand clasps mine. "You brought me La Scala? For lunch? Oh, Jakey, thank you, that's my favorite! Could I get a sparkling water too?"

My mother. My gorgeous, beautiful mother is here and lucid. I don't get up for a moment. I simply stare into those beautiful blue eyes that recognize me as she eats. I don't need her to say anything to me, I simply bask in the knowledge that she's present, that she's here with me. That I'm not my dead father and for this instant, however brief it may be, Mom is with me, here in this moment, eating La Scala salad.

"My sparkling water?" she asks with a smile.

I kneel beside her and give her a hug, because I don't know how long Mom's lucidity will last.

"I love you, Mom." I kiss her cheek.

"I love you too, honey," she says as though her life is normal. She touches her fingertip to my forehead and slides a wisp of hair back. A movement from my childhood. "Want me to get the water?" She starts to rise.

"No, no, no." I rush into the kitchen and get the bottle of Pellegrino and two glasses filled with ice. I return to the dining room.

"Mom, I'm so excited to have lunch with you. Man, Lily is amazing. Did you know that she can read now and—"

I set the bottle and the glass in front of my mother and she tilts her face up to me.

She's gone.

Her smile remains, but the sharpness, the focus, the consciousness in her eyes has been replaced with a fogged-over look.

"Richard, I wondered where you went."

My heart hurts. I pour the Pellegrino. I sit in the chair beside Mom and I surrender to the heartbreak that is this horrid disease.

❧

"Did Mom ever mention her and Susie talking . . . before she died?"

My sister removes her judicial robe and hangs it on a coatrack. I'm in her chambers downtown, a week after my lunch with Mom. We're meant to go together to see Mom and have dinner.

"I think Susie used to go see Mom a couple times a month." Rachel pauses, and in that pause is discomfort. "She'd bring over lunch. Sometimes they'd go shop. I mean, she knew Mom almost as long as you knew Mom."

Susie's family lives in our neighborhood. We were neighbors, and our parents were friends. Our engagement seemed like the perfect union of two families that had known each other for decades.

"They were a natural fit, Susie and Mom." My sister does a good job of nearly hiding any tinge of jealousy in her words. Where Mom was all Waterford crystal and etiquette, my sister was all feminism and Wellesley. They hadn't been a natural mother-daughter pair. There was love between them, but little understanding.

Susie was cut from Mom's cloth.

A textile designer with a penchant for interior decorating, Susie was the modern-day version of Mom. They spent hours looking through catalogues together for just the right shade of green, while my sister would rather pay someone to pick out her clothes.

"Why?" Rachel lifts her purse.

"Mom had some lucidity last week and she mentioned—" I stop here. Rachel knows everything because she always did, even when we were kids. Even if she didn't always discuss the details of what she knew, she did know it all. "Mom mentioned that Susie had concerns during our engagement."

Color drains from Rachel's face. She turns toward her office door. Fleeing? My sister is trying to flee a confrontation.

"Rachel?"

"What can I say, Jake? It was a long time ago. We all had concerns."

The muscles in my face tighten.

"No one doubted that you loved Susie. I don't even think Susie doubted that you loved her, it's just that"—Rachel glances away—"her *problems* made us think that it wasn't the right time for marriage."

Problems.

"So yeah, I do remember that Susie went and talked to Mom. Tried to get her advice, and then I think Mom talked to Dad." Rachel narrows her eyes. "Did Dad talk to you?"

I shake my head.

We both stare into space. We know. We both know what that means. Susie talked to Mom, and Dad never had time to talk to me.

Would it have mattered?

I don't know. I guess I won't ever know.

CHAPTER 14

THE NEAR-MISS with Kendall spooks me. I shove my Wonder-fuck phone into the top drawer of my nightstand. For over a week, I don't check new messages or texts or calls. This is the beauty of no commitment, no names. I don't owe anyone any explanations.

But I have an itch.

An itch I want to scratch. I sit down on my bed and slowly open the drawer. I flip open my phone and—

Knock. Knock. Knock.

Flip the phone closed, set the phone in the drawer, close the drawer, and head through the apartment to the front door.

"I come bearing gifts."

Tara stands in my hallway with Jango by her side. She carries some sort of cookware and a bottle of wine, with a bag of groceries slung over her shoulder. I lean against the doorframe and cross my arms over my chest. This isn't a good idea. It's a very bad idea.

"For who?" One corner of my lip quirks upward.

"For you."

I angle my body to let her in. I want her in my place, I simply don't trust myself with her here. She squeezes by me and her body skims mine. Yes, much too dangerous with the two of us alone in my apartment. She goes straight for the kitchen, where she starts the oven and slides the pot in. Then she sets her bag on the counter.

"I thought about inviting you to my place, but you have the better view." She nods toward my balcony, where the sun sets in a pink and orange sky.

I do have the better view. It's one I try not to look at very often, but it is better.

She hands me the bottle of wine. "Please?"

I get a wine key while Tara commandeers my kitchen and chatters about her day, her life, and her career. "I never got a chance to thank you properly. Plus, I've been cooped up working on a new story for nearly two weeks, so I absolutely needed to get out tonight."

The cork pops. "*Out* is coming to my house? Across the hall?" I pour two glasses of wine.

She turns to me and gives me her wide-faced smile that could drop me to my knees. "*Out*, for me, is anywhere not in my house. At this point, *out* is the park with Jango."

Jango perks up her ears from the spot on my couch that she's claimed as her own. "Besides you've been busy, too. Or so it seems. I haven't seen you since we babysat Lily."

She puts a skillet on the top of the stove, pours in a bit of olive oil, and tosses in some garlic. The scent fills the kitchen and my stomach growls, but my mind wanders back to when I would come home and find Susie in my kitchen. Oftentimes nearly naked, perhaps just wearing one of my work shirts, and cooking dinner. Some of my favorite memories. I'd nuzzle her and we'd have dinner and then sex.

Always the sex.

"What's the new story you're working on?" I don't want to think about Susie.

"It's kind of a secret. It's about a guy. With a very unique job."

"This is L.A. There are thousands of people with unique jobs."

Tara takes a wooden spoon and crushes the garlic. She takes a long sip of her wine. "True that. But this one? This one might be the strangest. If it's true. Still trying to figure it out. Could be total hype."

"Hype, eh? Must be entertainment related."

The timer dings. Tara grabs an oven mitt and checks her dish in the oven. "Ten more minutes." She stands and puts asparagus into the skillet on the stove. "You do like asparagus, right?"

"Who doesn't?" I look into the bag on the counter. "Want me to start the salad?"

"Oh, yes."

I pour the already-washed lettuce into a bowl, adding cheese, candied pecans, cherry tomatoes, and a tiny bit of chopped onion. When Tara pronounces the cooking done, we head to the table and sit down to eat.

❧

"I DON'T THINK I DID ANYTHING TO DESERVE THAT meal." I haul the final dish into the kitchen. I rinse it and load it into the dishwasher. Tara insisted on washing and drying the skillet. We've swapped childhood stories while completely cleaning the kitchen.

"You've been a great neighbor and a good friend." Tara empties the final bit of wine into her glass. "I've been over here a couple times. You check on me. Don't think I haven't noticed the notes sliding under my door."

A blush climbs onto my cheeks. "Everyone needs a little pick-me-up sometimes."

"Well, you've been my big pick-me-up for a while. So thank you."

We're close now. Physically close. She stands just opposite me. Her shirt is a regular tissue T-shirt, nothing sexy, nothing erotic, but beneath the fabric her nipples are tiny peaks. I want to touch them and lick them and suck them deep into my mouth.

I want Tara to call my name, my real name, from the pleasure I give her.

She steps toward me. Wine on her breath and heat between us. We both know where the other stands—she with a nearly broken heart and a barely over engagement, me with a penchant for non-commitment and no relationship—and there can be no mistake that this, this moment, this time between us is just this, right now. We've had the conversations, we've become friends, we each know the other, except we don't know that one thing, the one thing every couple who's ever been attracted to each other in this way wants and needs to know.

What it's like to fuck.

She reaches up and sweeps a stray lock of hair away from my forehead. A deep intake of breath. Her body, the scent of her, the nearness of her . . .

In one motion, my arm sweeps around her waist and she steps forward. Her lips press to mine or my lips press to hers and we're a tangle of want and need and hot desire that has built for months, maybe even years.

Her lips, plump and thick and just what I want, open, an invitation to me. My tongue presses into her mouth, sweeping and seeking and wanting. My cock is furiously hard and I press into her. Her hips thrust up and back in an incredibly feminine rolling motion that taunts and teases and makes me want to strip her bare right here in my kitchen.

I press my hand to her ass, pulling her closer so the hardness of my cock makes no mistake of what I need and want from her.

A deep low moan escapes her mouth. The want inside me is a living breathing thing, nearly devouring my restraint. I pull my mouth from hers and put my lips on her neck. My hand cups her breast. The pad of my thumb strokes the sensitive flesh of her nipple.

"Oh yes," she moans.

I pull at her shirt—fuck it. I rip it from bottom to top. My impatience makes her kiss more impassioned. Because I want her. I fucking want her like a man possessed. A man denied. A man in need of a woman.

I slide my hands down the front of her belly. I unbutton her jeans and push them over her hips. They drop to the floor. Nothing but lace covers her nipples and her sex. I reach my hands behind her and unhook her bra, my lips once again on hers. I run my hands down the sides of her nearly naked body, letting my hands devour her curves. My fingers slip beneath the tiny bit of fabric over her hips and push her panties to the floor.

She is naked.

I am greedy.

There is need, and I have no responsibility but to satisfy my need and hers. I don't have to be slow or cautious because Tara knows me, she trusts me, or she wouldn't be standing here naked in my kitchen.

She reaches for my waistband and unbuttons it. Then she unzips and reaches deep into my jeans, gripping my cock. Her hand strokes down the shaft. I pull her bottom lip into my mouth and suck.

Yes. God yes.

Her firm even stroke on my shaft. A buzzing noise in my head. A near collapse of all thought. Fuck yes. I need to fuck her. I need to fuck her now.

I pull away, put one arm beneath the back of her legs, and carry her over my shoulder down the hallway to my bedroom. I push open the door and set her on my bed.

She stretches out, a picture of fine flesh, lush curves, pure feminine beauty. Her hair spreads out behind her. I stand at the side of the bed, pull my shirt up and off. She sits up and pushes my already unbuttoned jeans down over my hips. Her gaze flicks from my cock up to my eyes. Never taking her eyes from mine, she leans forward and runs her tongue over the head of my cock.

No surprise here, ladies, but Wonderfuck rarely gets his dick sucked.

I nearly bend double. She grasps my shaft at the base and pulls me forward. Takes me deep into the languid wet warmth of her mouth.

Hot. Wet. Suction.

She follows her lips with her hand, igniting a trail of heat. I bend forward, my stomach muscles tightening with the pleasure.

Faster. Her mouth moves faster now. Heat builds in the soles of my feet. Like a trail of white lightning, energy tears up through my calves and my thighs and races to the small of my back. Every muscle in my body tightens and spasms. My balls draw close to my body. Come, hot and furious, is ready to push from my balls and shoot out of my shaft.

"Tara, baby, please." I start to press her back from my cock, but she latches on tighter, sucking even harder. I know what she's just agreed to. She wants me to come, she wants me to take this pleasure for myself. She wants to feel me let loose in her mouth.

Heat tears through me and shoots out of me with a huge fucking force.

"Tara!" Her name breaks from my lips and bounces around the walls of my room, the shout so thick, so guttural. I thrust into her mouth. I've lost control and she's taking me, she's swallowing my come, milking me with her hand and mouth. Taking every drop I have. She grasps my balls gently and squeezes. I fall forward with one hand on her shoulder. My legs barely support my weight, so complete is my orgasm.

"Fuck," I whisper. Her tongue takes one final swipe across the head of my cock as she pulls her mouth from my shaft.

My entire body shudders with the overload of pleasure. Tara glances up at me through those thick eyelashes. I cup her chin with my hands and tilt her face up toward me. The blue of her eyes nearly glows in the lights from the city shining through the window. A tiny smile plays on her lips, full and swollen from taking my cock deep into her mouth and sucking me off. She's pleased with the pleasure she's given me.

"I'm going to make you feel better than you've ever felt."

I press her back onto my bed.

Ready and able to fulfill every word of the promise I just made.

CHAPTER 15

I START WITH HER TOES. Each delectable toe. I take her foot in my hands and rub with my thumb, firmly enough not to tickle. Over the arch I massage deeply, letting the stress in the muscles unfold and relax. Then I squeeze her pinky toe. I gently caress and knead the muscles, working from the outside in, until I've gotten to her big toe. I slowly bend down. I lift her foot and pull her big toe into my mouth.

She watches.

She gasps.

Her body quivers.

Yes, her breath is short and her nipples are taut and tight. Her eyes can't look away from me.

My hand glides up over her calf, working those muscles as I kiss up along her flesh. I spread her legs. And kiss her thigh. Her hips roll upward in anticipation of the pleasure that my lips will give the spot between her legs. I move my lips up her thigh. I'm above her sex. The scent excites me. I spread her sex with my fingers. Her hands claw deep into the sheets.

"Oh my God, Jake, please," she groans.

I smile. No. Not yet. My tongue flicks once, twice, three times very lightly over her clit. Just enough to get her attention, just enough to make her want more, just enough to tease and promise all at once. I kiss her hip and trail my kisses up over her belly. My stiff cock nestles against her cleft. My shaft slides through the hot wetness without entering her. Teasing her with its hard length.

"Fuck, my God." Her eyes are closed as she rolls up and around, trying to get my cock inside her. She needs this. She wants this. I doubt there's been anyone since her engagement ended.

I hold my body above hers and gaze at her gorgeous flesh laid out beneath me. I dip my head and pull a nipple deep into my mouth, rolling the firm pink bud around my tongue. Her hips thrust up with a hard impatience.

I want her too. I want to shift my body and plunge my cock strong and fast and deep into her sex. I want to make her come over and over again, but the pleasure of this first time can be teased and tamed and brought to fruition in a way that will nurture every time we fuck again.

Again?

I chase the thought, the word, from my mind. I roll to the side, my mouth still locked to her nipple, while my hand drifts down over her belly and finds the hot wet spot between her legs. I tease her, and slide two fingers deep inside.

She tightens around me and her hips pulse up and back. Her head presses against the pillow. A wild need surges through her body and her hands claw the bed. I release her nipple and move lower. Between her legs, her scent is earthy and hot, making my cock grow harder. My fingers plunge in and out while my tongue laves up one side of her sex. I flick across her engorged clit.

A shriek tears through the room. Her body arches up.

My tongue sears down the other side of her sex. She is close now. The rhythm of her hips, the moans from her mouth, tell me she's about to tumble into ecstasy. I suck her clit between my lips.

The soft engorged piece of flesh that opens every gate of pleasure for a woman is in my mouth. My tongue begins to move. I spell. I spell out with my tongue, across that hot flesh, the nub of nerve endings, the gateway to bliss, I spell with my tongue what I am.

I spell Wonderfuck.

I get to the f.

Her body trembles. Her head thrashes against the pillow and her nails dig into my shoulders as she grabs me.

"Please, please, I want you in me. Fuck me. Please!"

I can't wait. I need to be in her. I take a condom from the drawer next to my bed, rip it open, and roll it over my cock. Her face is flushed and her eyes open. I thrust into her deep and hard. Her body tightens around me. Her hands are all over my chest and she pulls me down. I can't look away, I can't stop, I can't pause, I can't be anything other than who I am.

"Jake," she says, and that is who I am with her.

For the first time in almost six years, my name spills over a woman's lips.

"Jake. Jake. Jake!"

She wraps her legs around me, pushing me even deeper into her body. The tingle starts in my feet and surges like a tsunami up over every nerve ending, every muscle, every cell. It rolls up to my legs and tightens my back. My balls pull close to my body and the heat, the wave, I'm blinded by the pleasure. I stare into her eyes and the hot sharp come tears out of me. She clenches around me and together we plummet over the edge.

I AWAKEN TO DARKNESS. THE LIGHTS OF LOS ANGELES bathe my bedroom.

I can't be here.

I can't do this.

I can't—

Tara lays beside me. She's on her belly with one arm flung over my chest. Her hair long and lush. Her lips like a cupid's bow. Soft. Peaceful. Beautiful. The presence of her enticing, like a path leading home.

I can't do this to her or to me. I won't ruin another future. I'm not the man she needs me to be. I gently move her arm. I slide out of my own bed like a thief in the night. I pull open my nightstand drawer and grab my Wonderfuck phone. I pull on my jeans, a shirt, and I'm out of my bedroom.

I grab a jacket from the back of a chair in the living room. Jango lifts her head, her eyes peering through the darkness at me as if to ask, *What about her? The woman I love?* I pet Jango on the head. Leaving now is the best gift I can give Tara. Leaving now will save her and me.

I grab my keys and my wallet from the kitchen counter, slide them into my pocket, and out the door I go into the darkness of the Los Angeles night.

Alone.

⤜

DEEP IN THE DARKNESS, IN THE HOURS BETWEEN midnight and daybreak Los Angeles is a city that longs for fulfillment. In these hours, the despair we pretend doesn't exist because of the sunshine and the perfect weather catches a break and grabs those who dare to brave the night.

I walk to a diner I visit when memories of Susie, of my parents, of a life before what happened, haunt my brain and keep me from sleep. I pull open the door and slide into a booth beside the window. I'll order something to eat though I'm not hungry.

Late-night partiers still drunk from their evening share a booth and take pictures of each other. A shift worker going from day to night or night to day sits alone in another, sipping coffee with an empty stare on her face. Two cops eat a meal and speak in hushed tones near the back of the diner. I flip my coffee cup over.

I slip my Wonderfuck phone from my pocket. This is the longest I've ever gone without listening to the women who need Wonderfuck. There are lots of messages. Some I delete, some I save. In the final message, the voice is tentative and uncertain and mentions a woman I remember. That woman referred the caller to me because something bad has happened to her. Something that has broken her heart.

I pause.

My thumb hovers over the "9" to delete the message. But I don't. Instead, I flip the phone closed as I greet my waitress and give her my order. Then I stare out into the darkness of the night.

�ઢ

"YOU'RE BACK."

I close the door. Tara sits at my dining room table with a steaming mug of coffee. Morning sunlight streams through the windows.

I'm a coward. I'd hoped that she'd be gone, but I knew she'd be waiting. She's stronger and better than I am. She's more than I'll ever be.

"I couldn't sleep." I walk into the kitchen and pour a cup of coffee. She looks at me from her perch beside the table. Her face, her expression, is . . . well, expressionless.

I realize I've done her no favors. I've fucked her and ditched her and that is exactly what she doesn't need. But she also doesn't need me fucking up her life. She needs a nice solid guy with no baggage or bullshit or alter egos dragging him down. Or she needs a Wonderfuck. I can't tell her about what she needs. I can't be Jake and Wonderfuck at the same time. It's one or the other. They're mutually exclusive identities, and I can't be both to her.

"I guessed as much." She stands and turns to me. "I waited because I need to tell you something." She walks to the breakfast bar and stops. A wide piece of granite now separates us, but it's close enough that I can't miss the beauty of her face, the vivid blue eyes, the tiny freckles that decorate her nose.

"Okay." I sip my coffee.

"We live too close to each other for this to be weird."

I say nothing. I peer at her over my coffee cup and wait for her to continue.

"I enjoyed last night," she continues. "But I'm loaded with baggage right now, and you've got your stuff that you're dealing with."

I raise an eyebrow. My stuff? Not that she's wrong, but I wonder just exactly how much of my stuff she knows about. Mom? Susie?

Wonderfuck?

"I know this isn't going anywhere, and I knew that last night. I wanted to let you off whatever hook you've hung yourself on." She walks around the counter and into the kitchen. She dumps her remaining coffee into the sink. "I will say, though, in my opinion, it's kind of shitty to ditch a woman in your own house. Just for future reference."

Fair enough. A gentleman I'm not.

She picks up the bag of clean dishware from last night.

"Try not to be weird about this, okay?" Her tone is softer. In her eyes I see disappointment, and I get it, I'm disappointed too. Tara is exactly the type of woman I could fall for if I allowed myself to fall.

She turns toward the front door and Jango pads to her side.

"Tara," I call. She turns back and glances at me, hope in her eyes.

"Yeah?"

"You forgot your spatula." I hand her the utensil. She cocks an eyebrow, her expression screaming *such an asshole*, and tosses it into her bag.

"Thanks." She and Jango exit my condo. The door slams closed.

I'm alone. She's absolutely right. I am an asshole.

CHAPTER 16

YOU CAN FUCK AWAY your pain. I've done it. Fucking is a form of exercise, and it releases ten times the endorphins of running a marathon. Fucking cures depression.

Fucking has worked for me for almost six years, but fucking isn't working now. In three weeks, I wonderfuck my way through a barrage of women. Then I stop. I stop cold turkey. The calls keep coming and I delete them all, except the one.

I stand at Hollywood Forevermore Cemetery. Across the rolling hills interspersed with plot markers is a hearse and a phalanx of people.

I turn back to the grave marker in front of me. Susan Marie Carson. My Susie. She died six weeks before our wedding date. Forty-two days. Today is the sixth anniversary of her death.

I lean forward and lay the bouquet of peonies on her grave. She liked peonies.

"Why are you here?"

The voice cuts a chill down my spine. I don't want this confrontation. I don't want to cause any more pain than I already have.

"Mother, please." A second all-too-familiar voice.

I turn and I see Susie's mother and sister. Both older than the last time I saw them. The grim expression on Mrs. Carson's face tells me she's not any more forgiving than she was six years ago.

"Get away from her. Get away from my daughter." Mrs. Carson is hauling ass up the small incline from where her car and mine are parked bumper to bumper. Jane, Susie's sister, trails her mother.

"Mom, please, stop. Jake misses her too."

"Misses her? He killed her. He killed my girl with his lies and his cheating and his behavior. He had no right to a woman like Susie then, and he definitely has no right to stand by her grave now." Mrs. Carson turns to me. Her face is a twisted mass of pain, her lips a red scar of anger that cuts across the sags of her face.

I take it. I take it and accept it. I didn't deserve Susie, her love, her life, her goodwill, her commitment. I didn't deserve her saying yes to my proposal. I didn't deserve shit.

What I do deserve, right now, this moment, is Mrs. Carson's anger, her hate, her loathing, because there is nothing Mrs. Carson can say that I haven't already said to myself.

Jane glances at her mother and then at me. We grew up together. Jane and Rachel were besties all through high school. So were our mothers.

I ruined all of it.

I ruined Rachel's friendship with Jane, Mom's friendship with Mrs. Carson, and Susie's life.

My need for Susie to be mine ruined it all.

Mrs. Carson slowly bends over and picks up the flowers I've laid on Susie's grave. "Peonies? You brought her peonies? You're still such a self-involved asshole. She hated peonies."

My heart cracks and chest constricts. Somehow, these words are worse than any other words that Mrs. Carson could say to me. I look to Jane for confirmation.

No. No, no, no, no. Peonies were Susie's favorite flower. Peonies were *our* flower. The flower I got Susie for her birthday, for special occasions, just to tell her I loved her.

Pink peonies were the flower I always got for Susie.

"Tell him," Mrs. Carson says. "Tell him how much your sister hated these damn flowers. Never liked peonies, never wanted peonies, only took them because *he* was so self-absorbed he didn't know better." She throws them aside.

I watch Jane. She's a fit version of Susie. More athletic, not as slight. Stronger, more resilient.

"Go on, tell him." Mrs. Carson kneels beside Susie's grave and places a bouquet of roses in a vase.

"Is it true?" I ask, my voice barely above a whisper. This . . . this thing with the flowers . . . why the fuck is it cracking my soul, shredding me?

Jane looks at me. We've known each other a lifetime. This moment was not what anyone expected, with Susie in the ground and me to blame. No. There were supposed to be grandchildren and holidays and celebrations. Not funerals. Not peonies on a somber April day.

"She hated the peonies," Jane says. "But she loved that they came from you."

An oily feeling churns my gut, and I fight the urge to vomit. Instead I walk to where Mrs. Carson has tossed my bouquet. I lean over, pick up the pink peonies, and walk away from Susie's grave.

She hated my fucking flowers for years and never told me. Never said a word. Susie simply kept taking them from me and smiling. Unhappy with my selection, unhappy with my choice, but never telling me. Never.

How long was she unhappy?

I will never know the answer to that question.

I sit in my car. My heart pounds and a roar rushes through my brain. I pull my Wonderfuck phone from my pocket and dash off a text. I usually don't send except to set up a requested meeting, but in this moment, I need. I need the mind-numbing effect of a physical boost, so I text the one person I'm physically connected to that I'm comfortable enough to text. I text Cheryl.

I wait. Up the hill, Jane and Mrs. Carson still linger beside Susie's grave. Jane glances over her shoulder toward my car. They both want me to leave. I start the car and slowly drive away, passing the hearse and the cluster of mourners not far from the road standing near an open grave with the casket still above it.

The day we buried Susie is a blur. Bits of memories weave through my mind like dark tendrils, from the moment of her death to her burial. Then there's a blank spot. Months of unaccounted-for time. Until Dad and big sis finally yanked me back from the abyss and into reality, a reality that sucked much worse than the abyss into which I'd fallen. But I was determined to stay, here, with them, and that's exactly why Wonderfuck was created.

My phone buzzes. I pull to the side of the road, still inside the cemetery, and glance at Cheryl's response.

Come by.

I put my car in drive and head toward the one thing that will take the pain from my mind.

❧

"WHAT'S GOIN' ON WITH YOU, DARLIN'?"

Cheryl hands me a bourbon neat, then tips her champagne glass toward her lips. She leans against a carved stone railing high in the hills of Bel Air. Her home is an enormous testament to her wealth, room after luxurious room appointed in finery. But the silence in this giant building is deafening.

The bourbon slides down my throat and warms my chest. I don't know how to answer or what to say. I don't want to talk. I want to fuck. "Do I seem unwell?"

"You seem"—she purses her lips, as though searching for the right words—"on edge."

"Maybe." I rest both my forearms on the railing and stare out from this elite vantage point toward the expanse of Los Angeles. "It's that time of year."

"Indeed it is." Cheryl upends her glass. She walks through the French doors into the living room to get more champagne. She has people to do such things for her—cook, clean, refill her glass, walk her dogs—but when I visit her home, only the cook remains. I follow her inside the house.

"Darlin', you ever think about changing this existence of yours?" Her gaze drops from my eyes to my wrist, where her gift to me resides.

I sit beside her on the couch. If anything, today at the cemetery proved I can't ever stop being Wonderfuck. To stop might kill me.

"It makes life bearable." I finish my bourbon and she is up and across the room with my glass, pouring me another.

"I understand how you need what you do." She turns back to me. "I even understand *why* you need it. I'm not suggesting you stop being who you are. I'm simply asking if you'd be willing to be who you are for just one woman."

She hands the glass to me and our fingertips touch. Heat zips through me.

My chest tightens at Cheryl's suggestion.

"Exclusive?" I take a long drink of my bourbon. Commitment is the very thing that terrifies me. The need for exclusivity was the very thing that destroyed Susie.

"Not the marital definition of it, maybe not even what one would call monogamous." Cheryl sits beside me. "But more of an agreement about who we are to each other. Something more permanent." She glances around the gargantuan living room. "Maybe you live here?" These aren't easy words for Cheryl to say. She's as independent as I am. For different reasons, but still, she's not a woman who wants to need anyone. "I mean, the house is huge. I'm gone half the year. You'd continue to do what you do . . . your *vocation*, as you call it. But I'd also have a companion when I'm here in L.A."

A vise squeezes my temples and pain shoots through my head. I press my hand to my forehead. "Why?"

"It's not working for me anymore." Cheryl leans forward, puts her hand on my thigh, and runs it up my leg. "Darlin', I know who you are and I know what you need." Her words are sweet and thick like honey. "I don't want you to be anyone you're not. I love that you have a vocation, and I won't ever ask you to change that about yourself. All I'm asking for is that I get more of you. More of the Wonderfuck that I need." Her hand drifts up and over my chest, and she unbuttons my shirt.

Fuck yes. Physical pleasure. I slide down on the couch. She untucks my shirt. Her lips place hot kisses on my chest and she sucks on my nipple. She unfastens my belt, then unbuttons my jeans.

She pulls down the zipper and slides her hand into my pants to grasp my cock. Sex clouds my thoughts as she slides her hand up and down my shaft.

"I leave for Asia tomorrow. You think on what I want. What we can give each other, what I can give you."

I lean back against the couch. Cheryl bends over me. Her red lips open and she takes my cock deep into her mouth. The heat, the pleasure—we are on our Wonderfucking way.

CHAPTER 17

EACH OF US has one of the coloring books and a box of colored pencils. Except Lily—Lily has crayons. Mom's geriatrician suggested that we color as a family. This supposedly keeps Mom's fine motor skills up longer and also has a meditative quality.

Rachel and Lily and Mom think it's great.

I think it's stupid.

I wanted a coloring book with swear words and Rachel said no, so now, instead, I color rainbows and fairies and some other bullshit, all of which I have no desire to do.

"Jane told me she saw you last week," Rachel says, so quietly that Mom and Lily, who are at the far end of the dining room table, can't hear.

"I didn't know you still spoke to Jane."

"Just because Susie was nuts doesn't mean we stopped being friends."

My heart kajolts against my ribs. "She wasn't nuts."

"Oh, okay." Rachel rolls her eyes. "Right." Sarcasm drips from her voice. She carefully puts her purple pencil back into her pencil box and takes out the green.

"I made her crazy."

"You most certainly did not." Rachel pauses mid-scribble and looks at me. "Is that what you think? That *you* made Susie crazy? That you caused what happened?"

I don't respond. And really, how has it taken Rachel six years to sort that out? Yes. Yes to all of it.

"You two weren't an ideal match, what with each of your own respective *issues.*"

I pause and drop my brown pencil onto the table, then pull the purple from my own box. Rachel reaches for the brown pencil I've just abandoned and starts to put it back in my box. "Don't."

She glances at me.

"Don't put my pencil away."

"It doesn't go on the table."

"It's mine and I want it out. You don't need to put every pencil away every time you use it."

"It keeps things neat," she says, continuing to slide the brown pencil into place.

"I don't want neat. And you're keeping yours neat, I don't need you keeping mine neat too." I pick up my box and dump all the pencils onto the table.

Rachel gives me "the look." The look my superior older sister has always given me, her little brother, whenever I've done anything that she's thinks is wrong or childish or ill-advised.

"Does that make you feel better, Jakey?" she asks in a tone I loathe, one she's been using since I was born. "Have you proved you're a grown-up by dumping all your pencils onto the table?"

"I don't know. Have you proved that you can control everything that goes wrong in life by putting every damned pencil into a box each time you're done using them?"

I've gone too far.

"Come on, Lily, let's go. You have ballet. Mom, you want to come with us?"

"Oh yes." Mom stands. "Will I be dancing too? You know, I'm quite a good dancer." She grasps the back of her chair and points her foot. Lily giggles and puts all her crayons in her box. She skips to me and kisses me on the cheek.

"Mommy likes things neat," Lily whispers in my ear.

I nod.

Don't we all.

I EXIT THE ELEVATOR ONTO MY FLOOR. I LOOK TOWARD Tara's door. I can't stop myself. I walk slowly down the hall, hopeful that maybe this time I'll be walking down the hall at the exact moment she's leaving to walk Jango, or go to dinner, or go work out, or go to the grocery store. I want to see Tara. I want to be with Tara. Tara is the type of woman I could fall for, and that's exactly why I can't be with her again.

I pause in the center spot halfway between my front door and hers.

I hear crying. No loud wails. No angry sobs. Nothing that obvious. No, it's soft muffled tears. A quiet crying, as though someone is trying to hide their pain, their sadness. I leave the middle spot in the no-man's-land of the hall that separates my life from Tara's. I walk to her side of the world. Did I give up the right to check on her and be a friend the night I ditched her in my bed? I lift my hand to knock, but I don't. I pause. I take a deep breath.

I can't do it.

I can't do this to her. I can't do this to me.

I can't let myself be involved in Tara's life. I don't want her to feel sad. I wish I could wipe her tears and make her pain go away. Help her to see that Douchey-McDouche-Face isn't worth her tears. But instead of fixing things, I've made them worse, haven't I? Because I rejected her too.

Sure, she can say she understands. She can say that she didn't want a relationship either, but there was real heat between us. Not one-night-stand heat, not even Wonderfuck heat, but the kind of heat you only get when there's something real behind it.

The realness scared the living shit out of me.

I can't do real. Not emotional real.

I did emotional real once. Or I thought I did. Only one out of two people survived. 50/50. I don't like those odds. Don't want to play those odds again. I drop my hand to my side. The muffled crying continues.

I'm an emotional coward. I turn to my side of the hallway, to my front door, to my life. I turn back to what I know and what I can survive. I turn back to being the Wonderfuck that I am.

❧

THE VOICE ON THE VOICEMAIL SITS WITH ME. I'VE kept that message for weeks. I haven't met with a new woman in a long time. I get other calls from referrals, but I delete them all, except for this one. This one voice. Each and every time I listen, my fingertip hovers over "9" to delete the message. Longing, need, pain—all of those emotions weave through her voice. A quality that in the past inspired me to respond, asking the woman to meet me at one of the luxury hotels I like. Some would say yes and some would never respond.

When do you want to meet? I text.

I wait.

My Wonderfuck phone buzzes. For the first time in a long time, my belly tightens with excitement, a kind of longing toward this person who wants me, needs me, has called me to provide her with the physical release and emotional satisfaction she desires.

Saturday.

I can do Saturday. I type the name of a hotel.

Yes.

The day after tomorrow. I haven't been excited since the night I was with Tara, but I'm definitely excited now.

CHAPTER 18

MY FAVORITE HOTEL in Los Angeles is The London. There isn't an ocean view, but there is quiet and discretion, a feeling of being tucked away where no one can find you. I love the luxury of anonymity and yet having an identity that makes a woman feel better than she's ever felt. Redemption is mine through Wonderfuck.

I ride the elevator up to the sixth floor and exit. I open the door to my room. The concierge here knows what I like and what I need. The room is well prepped, and he's well paid.

I walk across the room. Today's been another brilliant blue-sky day. Out the window, orange and fuchsia flame from the setting sun as day shifts to night. I'm ready. Tonight is what I want and what I need. I slide my jacket from my shoulders and hang it in the closet. My routine is the same when I meet with a new woman. I get here early, I prepare myself, I sit and I wait. I've texted her the number of this room. She'll show.

I sit in the chair opposite the door. I glance at the clock across the room and I wait. I wait for her. I am the Wonderfuck, and I'm waiting to rock her world.

I close my eyes. I hear Tara's muffled tears. I see Tara's face. I see her face as it looked when she came, when she called my name, when she rolled her hips and made me come. A card slides into the door. A beep. I open my eyes. The room is dark except for one last bit of sunlight that angles just short of the hotel room door. She's in shadow. I'm in shadow.

My cock hardens. A slight shift of her hip, the tilt of her head, the rhythm of her walk. Slowly she releases the door. She wears expensive black leather heels. She steps forward, and the light travels up over her calves to the hem of her skirt. I am in shadows, or I would never let my eyes roam over her this way; too soon, too familiar, too much for this moment. But she can't see my eyes, my face, my body. Not yet. The light travels up over her hips and then her silk shirt, the neckline outlining the curve of her full breasts. Fair skin. Soft, curved, plump lips. I reach out to turn on the light beside me. I glance away and flip the switch. Bright light bathes us both.

My cock hardens to steel. My belly tightens. She's beautiful. She's mine, and I already know exactly how to make this woman come.

CHAPTER 19

HER MOUTH DROPS OPEN, but there's no surprise in her eyes. Did she know? Has she known all along? Is this a game she's played with me? These questions all involve a completely separate identity I refuse to bring into this room. Here I'm Wonderfuck, and that is the only identity that exists.

"I was supposed to get married today," Tara says.

My heart tightens, and sadness mixed with anger plows through my body. I feel. I'm emotionally invested in her, and not in the way I invest when I'm Wonderfuck. Wonderfuck feels empathy for a woman's pain, her sadness, her broken heart, but those feelings are never personal, no deeper than the physical connection we share.

Right now, my feelings are personal. They're linked to Tara. They're linked to the feelings for Tara that I've tried to ignore, tried to pretend don't exist.

Wonderfuck wants to make her feel better by unlocking her sexuality, her strength, her beauty, and her sensuality.

My heart, Jake's heart, hurts for her. I want to stand and wrap my arms around her, pull her to me and kiss her and hold her tight. Make her feel safe and cared for and whole and loved. I want to emotionally fix the wound that's cut her heart. I want to give her my heart, my warmth, my love.

But I'm not Jake. Not now. Not here.

"Maybe it was a mistake," I say. "Maybe you'll be better off than you would've been." These are words I've spoken before tonight, to other women in similar circumstances.

Tara's gaze sharpens. She walks toward me and sits on the couch perpendicular to me. Her skirt rides up her thigh. My usually disciplined gaze travels over the soft flesh of her leg.

"I know that. I believe that. I'm thankful for what I found out, but I'm still hurt by what he did."

My breathing shortens. I loathe hypocrisy, and yet I continue to wallow in it every time I'm Wonderfuck.

"How did you find me?"

Her head tilts and the muscle in her jaw twitches. An internal debate as to what to tell me.

"A referral," she says, crossing her legs. "From a friend."

She's a good liar. She meets my gaze without flinching, her eyes don't drop away from mine, her body language doesn't give away her lie, but I know she's lying. I know based on her hands. Her pointer finger strokes her thumb. She did the same thing when she sat in my apartment telling me how she didn't care that I'd left. Didn't care that I'd walked out that morning, leaving her alone in my bed. Didn't want to be involved with me.

All of it lies.

Now she's lying again.

Or so I think.

"What's your name?"

She smiles at this question. She cocks her head and really looks at me, and for the first time in all the times I've been Wonderfuck, I feel uncomfortable. Tara sees through me. She sees all of me. She's the first woman to know Jake and experience Wonderfuck.

Ever.

I feel naked, exposed, vulnerable. What could she do with

this knowledge? What will she do? For the first time, I realize how much I'll have to trust her, believe in her. Allowing Tara to have this much control over me and my life is terrifying, and yet the risk of her disclosing my identity to the world is oddly thrilling. My cock is hard. Her nipples press against her bra and the silk of her shirt.

She wants me.

I want her.

"My name is Tara," she says. "And you?" She nods toward me, she stands, she pulls her silk shirt from the waistband of her skirt. "You're the Wonderfuck." She slowly unbuttons her shirt before me until it's open and her black lace bra peeks out. She takes off her shirt and drops it onto the floor. The ripe flesh of her breasts spills over the top of her bra. Her breathing is short. I remain seated. I don't move. I want to jump to my feet, grab her in my arms, and fuck her. Fuck her and make her mine. Claim her for my own, as Jake, as Wonderfuck, as whoever the hell I need to be so this woman is mine now and forever.

She slides the zipper down the side of her skirt and the fabric drops to the floor. Her full, curvy body is now nearly naked in front of me.

"Why don't you show me what you've got, Wonderfuck? Fuck away my pain, my fears, all the sad things in my brain, because I was supposed to wear a beautiful white dress and get married today."

Her bottom lip quivers with the final word. And I know how much sadness courses through her and I can feel her pain, because she's more than just another woman, another stranger who uses me to fuck away feelings they don't want the same way I use them to stay out of the abyss of pain that threatens to swallow me whole. I know, because this is Tara. She's the woman I've slept with as Jake, the woman I've spent time with, the woman I've heard crying softly behind a closed door. She's the woman I see when I close my eyes and the first person I think of when I awake each day.

I stand. When I do, I realize how much bigger I am than she is. Somehow, this never crossed my mind before. How small she appears next to my body. This body that can both protect her and give her pleasure.

And I will. I will give her the Wonderfuck of her life.

Then we'll be finished. We won't be together again. But I don't tell her that, not now, not today, not in this moment. Because I can't. All I can do today is make her forget that this was going to be her wedding day.

I clasp her chin, tilt her head up, and press my lips to hers. A soft and gentle kiss. I put one hand at the small of her back and pull her toward me. I take off her bra. Her body fits against my sex. She feels the hunger of my hard cock, pressed against her cleft.

She knows this cock. She's felt this cock before.

Her mouth opens and I slide my tongue into it. My hand trails down her arm. Goosebumps on her skin. I pause at her hip. The tiniest string of fabric keeps her panties on. With one twist and a swift flick of my wrist, the bit of string snaps.

She gasps.

I smile.

Her panties drop to the floor.

My hand travels across her sex, down into her cleft. I pause just over her clit, and her hips shift forward, seeking my finger, seeking pleasure. I pull my lips from her mouth and my gaze locks with hers. Huge pupils surrounded by a thin ring of blue, her mouth open, breathing shallow. I press my finger to her clit and a tiny note comes from her mouth.

"Oh my God, Jake."

I pull my finger away. "Wonderfuck."

"No, no, no," she begs, not wanting to lose the blissful sensation flooding her body.

"Wonderfuck," I say again. This can go on all night. She'll call me Wonderfuck in this room. She'll forget I'm Jake.

"Wonderfuck," she pants. My finger resumes circling her clit and her hips press against me. "Please, oh my God, Wonderfuck."

I kneel, bring my lips to her right breast and pull the nipple deep into my mouth. My tongue circles her taut flesh at the same tempo as my finger circling her clit. Yes, yes, her body responds as she rocks forward and back. Her fingers clasp my shoulder and dig into the fabric of my shirt. I plunge a finger deep into her sex and stroke her clit again.

"I'm going to . . . oh my God, I'm going to come!" She pants out.

I pull her closer, I suck harder, I caress her clit.

She yells. Her body vibrates and tenses with pleasure. I take her over the edge, and her body becomes limp in my arms. Her eyes are heavy-lidded. I will fuck her senseless. Tonight, I will make her come over and over again. I will give her more pleasure on this, the night she thought would be her wedding night, than she ever could have imagined.

Tonight she will be my bride.

I lift her and carry her to the bed. She fits in my arms. She is beautiful and perfect, everything a woman should be. She deserves to be worshipped and adored. I lay her on the bed, naked in front of me. I undress and her eyes roam my bare skin. As my pants drop to the floor, her hips twitch upward. I'm not even touching her.

Damn.

A tingle begins in the bottoms of my feet and the back of my legs tighten. My cock throbs at the thought of driving deep into Tara's heat. My own desire thrums through me, and I fight to remain Wonderfuck. I fight to not become Jake, not succumb to my knowledge of Tara and the emotions that are barreling through me.

She licks her bottom lip. Her hips continue to rise and fall, and the wetness of her sex glistens. I climb onto the bed. I move above her. She puts her hands on my chest, and our lips lock together. This kiss is fire.

I pull my lips from her mouth, shifting down to her left nipple. Her hips move up and back, up and back. She wants my cock inside her.

"Please, I want you! Please."

I fight the urge to give in to her plea, to forego the pleasure I know I can give her. I stop myself from thrusting deep and hard into her. No. I wait. My lips drag along her body. Over her belly and to her mound. I am between her parted legs now. The sweet scent of her sex arouses me. I press my mouth to her slick clit and her hips thrust up. I can barely stand to continue. My balls pull tight to my body.

I'm about to come.

How is that fucking possible? I'm about to lose it. I never lose it as Wonderfuck. I'm invincible as Wonderfuck. I control my release when I'm Wonderfuck. I pull her clit deep between my lips. My tongue strokes out the words I can't say, the thoughts I have for Tara. She keeps rolling up and back with the pleasure. I press two fingers deep into her sex and she clenches around me. She is shattering with her orgasm.

"Fuck, oh my God, Wonderfuck!" she yells. Her head arches back into the pillow and her hands clasp my shoulder as I continue to tongue the words on her clit. Her body shakes and shakes. Then I hear her tiny moan, a whimper, and I realize she's ridden her orgasm to the end.

"Please," she whispers, "please, I want you inside me."

I reach for a condom from the well-stocked nightstand and glide it onto my cock. I can barely contain myself.

Heat builds in my legs. I don't have long. I won't be able to give her the ride she deserves now, but we have all night. We have as long as it takes.

Her gaze focuses on my face. I fix my eyes on hers as the head of my cock nudges slowly and gently into the tight muscles of her sex. She gasps, and so do I.

Sweet pleasure. Beautiful pleasure that I want and she wants. Her hips remain still. I slowly, so very slowly, press into her and her sex gives way, the soft hot flesh slowly parting for my cock and tightening around my shaft. I'm inside her. Sheathed by her heat.

"Yes," she whispers.

I pull back, all the way out, except for the tip of my cock. Slowly, slowly I slide back into her. She tightens around me with the contraction of a woman about to come. She grinds her fingernails into the muscles of my ass.

"Please, oh my God, please, faster!"

Her words rip away my disciplined, slow movement. I thrust deep and hard into her body. Ferocious heat climbs through my legs and tightens my lower back. I'm about to explode. Our eyes never leave each other's. I thrust again. Heat jets through me and out my cock as she pulls me closer, her body climaxing and tightening. I thrust one final time. My body turns to stone. I careen over the edge, filled with pleasure.

CHAPTER 20

THIS TIME WHEN I WAKE, I don't leave. I don't need to leave. I'm not Jake, a man filled with fear and anxiety and the belief that I'll wreck Tara's life and mine by caring for her, getting involved with her. No, I'm Wonderfuck. I'm safe in the knowledge that this interaction is finite.

No names.

I shove the knowledge that Tara knows my name, my true identity, from my mind. I push away the real possibility that she always knew who I was. I don't want to consider that thought, so I shove it deep into my brain and lock it up with the memories I so desperately try to ignore. I am Wonderfuck. Wonderfuck has rules, and Tara will follow the rules.

I look over at her. She's awake. Her blue eyes peer through the darkness.

"Hey." It's nearing midnight. Soon this day, the one meant to be her wedding day, will be over, and hopefully she can rebuild. Her pain will lift and eventually reside in the past.

"You're awake." I press my lips to her forehead. Not too familiar, not anything I haven't done with a myriad of other women I've wonderfucked.

"And shockingly hungry." A smile curls up over her face.

"Hunger requires sustenance. What do you want to eat?" I lift the phone receiver.

"What do they have?"

"They have an excellent concierge, who can get us anything you want. What'll it be?"

"Chinese," she says. "You know what I like."

And I do. I let what Tara just said go by. The slight allusion to Jake, to my other life, to her knowledge of who I am and where I live and the things I know about her and me and us. I make the call and place the order. Then I turn to her. I pull Tara into my arms. I kiss her slowly and I wonderfuck her again as we wait for our food.

§.

"I DIDN'T REALIZE HOW PAINFUL TODAY WOULD BE."

We stand at the window, a blanket draped around us. The sky grows lighter as we watch. We've wonderfucked on the bed, the couch, the chair, the floor, even standing by the wall. I'm nearing my limit, but each time I think that I can't, Tara turns to me with that sweet mouth and those lush lips and her eyes that see through me and I can't stop myself from reaching out and kissing her. Kissing Tara turns into my cock getting hard, and her getting wet, and us wonderfucking again and again and again.

"Was it like this for you too?" she asks.

My blood chills and my muscles tighten. She stands in front of me, her ass pressed against my cock.

"On the day you were supposed to get married?"

She doesn't turn her head when she asks. Maybe she notices how her words affect my body. How I pause, as still as stone.

"I . . ." I'm torn. Never has anyone asked me about my wedding day, the day I was meant to wed Susie. No one has asked me as Jake, and most definitely not as Wonderfuck.

My worlds collide. Pain mixed with fear mixed with want and desire churn in a cocktail that is too sweet, too bitter, simply too much for me to swallow. The walls I've created are crumbling and I don't know how to stop the destruction, so I do what I do best.

I press my lips to the back of her neck. I slide my hand down the front of her belly and my fingertip slips between the hot folds of her sex.

"Oh yes," she moans.

Yes, there it is, my cock, my cock hardens and wedges underneath her. No words. No answers. No thoughts. She opens her legs to me. Conversation is gone. Pleasure replaces questions. My other hand reaches to her taut nipple. I pinch it between two fingers, giving her pleasure just on the cusp of pain.

Her hips, her ass, shift back to me. I turn from her and grab a condom. A moment later, my finger strokes her clit again. She bends forward ever so slightly and I press my cock deep into her.

"Oh, Jake."

I'm deep inside her. Bindings of pleasure tighten around me. I don't know who I am anymore. I weave my fingers through her hair and tilt her head back, my lips beside her ear.

"I. Am. Wonderfuck," I say, one word with each thrust. And with each thrust, a gasp escapes her lips.

I will her to say it. I will make her forget Jake. I will fuck her until she knows this name, my only name when I am with her.

"Say it."

"Wonderfuck."

I brace my palm against the cold glass of the window, and heat shoots from me and out of my cock as the new-day sun bathes us both in the early morning light.

WE DON'T RIDE HOME TOGETHER. WE CAN'T. I DON'T want to. I get her a car. I watch her leave. I turn and walk away from the hotel. A weariness gathers deep in my bones. I'm exhausted.

I don't want to go home and chance running into Tara in the building. My heart is a gaping hole—a wound. Instead I walk. Where I'm going, I have no clue. Nobody walks in L.A. This is never more evident than early on a Sunday afternoon. Cars whiz by me. Finally I pull out my phone, type in an address, and order an Uber.

꙳

"RICHARD, DID YOU GOLF THIS MORNING?"

I realize when I walk into my childhood home that I've made a mistake. I wanted to go home, but the home I wanted disappeared with Mom's memory. I surrender to the role that Mom's brain needs me to play.

"It's beautiful outside," I say and lean down and kiss her cheek. I say hello to Sylvia, her weekend nurse.

"Uncle Jake!" The sound of my niece's brilliant crystal voice pummels me from the backyard.

"Rachel is swimming with some other children." Mom looks toward the backyard. "And that woman is here. The one I don't like, who's always ordering me around. I tried to go for a walk earlier and she wouldn't let me." Mom grasps my hand. "Will you talk to her, please?"

I know from experience that when Mom says "Rachel," she means Lily, and "that woman" is my sister, who Mom can't seem to remember either.

Lily leaps into my arms. She's wet from the pool, but I don't care. This is the kind of salvation I need. Simple love and pure joy. The kind that only kids can make and adults spend a lifetime trying to manufacture. She hugs me tight and gives me a big wet kiss on the cheek. "I'm swimming!" She slides down from my grasp, leaving a giant wet mark on my shirt. "Come watch me."

"Sure thing." I follow her to the lanai. Four kids swim and Rachel sits beside the pool with two women. Hmm . . . this is really the last thing I wanted, but I'll do my brotherly duty and say hello. Then I may slide into my childhood bedroom and snooze.

I walk over. The moms are looking pretty good, and they're eyeing me. I flip down my shades so I don't feel exposed.

"Didn't expect to see you here today," Rachel says.

"I was over this way. Thought I'd stop in and say hello."

Rachel introduces me to the moms. One of them mentions she remembers seeing me at the birthday party. I do the honorable little brother thing and chat for five minutes. Then Rachel hooks her arm through mine, tells them she'll be right back, and walks me inside.

"You look like shit," she whispers.

I pull up my sunglasses and give big sis my version of her evil eye.

"What'd you do? Were you out all night? You look like you haven't slept in days."

"Work stuff," I lie. "I needed to get out. A quiet place away from my computer."

"Go upstairs, grab a nap. We won't bother you. Want me to wake you before Lily and I go?"

I nod. The need for sleep scrapes my insides. I turn and head up the staircase with the pictures on the wall that lead me back through time, all the way to when I was a preschooler. Handsome boy even then. I turn the corner, walk into my childhood bedroom, and fall onto my bed. I'm asleep before I hit the mattress.

❧

TARA'S HAND GLIDES UP OVER MY JEANS AND RUBS against my cock. I'm rock hard. I want nothing but to fuck her over and over again. She smiles at me and unzips my fly. She grasps my cock and pulls it free from my jeans, a mischievous gleam in her eyes. Thrilled with the size. The look every man wants to see on the face of the woman he wants to fuck. Tara is that woman for me.

She bends forward, opens those plump lips, and slides my cock into her sweet mouth.

"Fuck yes," I mumble.

The heat of her mouth is followed by the long stroke of her hand over my shaft. My hips slide up and back with the pleasure of her mouth around my cock.

"Yes," I whisper. I won't last long. My hands grasp the comforter and my eyelids blink open. I'm . . . not in my place . . . or Tara's . . . or a hotel. I am . . . my eyes land on the Foo Fighters poster, circa 1996.

My room.

I am in my room at my parents'. I look down.

The woman sucking my cock isn't Tara.

A head bobs up and down, up and down on my cock. My God that hair is blonde, and who the fuck is sucking my dick?

I grasp her shoulders. As good as it feels, and as much as I could totally wait two more strokes and come . . . who is sucking my cock?

She looks up at me, her eyes filled with surprise.

It's her. Kendall.

The mom from the party.

The one who knows me as Wonderfuck.

"Hey," she says, a smile on her face. When did she get here? She holds my hard cock in one hand, just to the right of her mouth. "Let me finish." She leans down to start sucking, but I stop her.

"I . . . I can't." I pull away from her. I slide back up the bed.

"Come on," she says, her voice playful.

I don't feel playful. I feel dirty. And violated. And now I'm starting to feel pissed.

"You liked it last time." She caresses my thigh. "I thought you'd like it today."

"I . . ." I put my cock in my pants and stand. I zip up my pants. "I don't—"

"It's that woman, isn't it? You're involved with her."

She stands too. Her smile slides from her face and is replaced with a smirk. Anger filters through her eyes.

"No," I say. "I . . . I . . ." I rub my hands through my hair, back away from her. I don't know if it's my composure slipping or my sanity, but the crack inside is growing into a crevasse, and I feel myself falling into it.

"Really? I texted you, I called. I tried to do what you want, but I didn't get an answer. You're the Wonderfuck. You're supposed to answer when I call."

"That's not how this works." Any emotion, any vulnerability I felt upon waking up with a woman sucking my cock is gone. Placed behind a hard exterior of uncaring. "I don't *have* to return any calls or texts."

Her face changes, shifting from anger. In the blink of an eye she's gone from rage to attempted seductress. She walks toward me slowly, throwing out all the sexual vibes and power she can, trying to make herself alluring to me. Her attempt at seduction would work on most men, probably any man but me. But I've had her. I didn't give her any part of my heart, and I don't want any part of her at all now.

"Come on," she whispers, "Just this once. We were really good together, weren't we?"

"We were." I will give her this, though I can't remember many details of our time together. She strokes me, and while I know my body won't respond now, I grasp her wrist and pull her hand away from my sex. "We were very good, but now we're finished."

"Does your sister know?"

My face is stone. I can't let on what my sister does or doesn't know. This woman, who is married and has a kid, has much more to lose than I do.

"What about your *girlfriend*? Wonder how much she'd like to know about Wonderfuck." She practically hisses the word. I pull her close and stare straight into her eyes.

"Let me give you her number, and you can find out her thoughts yourself."

She yanks her hand from my grasp and turns to the bedroom door.

"Your loss," she says, tossing her hair. "I give good head." She opens the door and exits my boyhood room.

I collapse on the bed. I've never before been more thankful for an interrupted blow job.

CHAPTER 21

MY WONDERFUCK PHONE RINGS, but it's not the number I want to see on the screen so I don't pick up. There's only one number I'm interested in answering, and she hasn't called in nearly ten days. I haven't bumped into her in the hall or the elevator or on our block. I almost knocked on her door yesterday, but wondered if it was an intrusion. Was I meant to be Jake or Wonderfuck?

I stare at my view, at the balcony I never go out on. My cleaning lady goes out there, and guests went out there at the one party I had for Rachel at my place, but I don't. Or I can't.

Not since that night.

The phone vibrates in my pocket. The number I wanted to see.

How about Wednesday?

Yes, I text back.

Is she across the hall now? Is she laying on her bed working? Is her hair in that messy ponytail that makes her look sexy as hell? Does she have on her grizzly bear leggings?

Does she want Wonderfuck, or does she want me?

Fuck.

I finish my drink. I stare at the skyline. I'm in deep, and for the first time in what feels like forever, I'm uncertain how I'll escape. I pour myself another bourbon.

What the hell would Wonderfuck do?

≈

SCHOOL IS FINISHED IN TWO DAYS. TODAY IS LILY'S end-of-year school presentation. I squeeze past the parents already sitting on elfin chairs designed for preschool bodies. Rachel, sitting beside Mom, pats the seat she saved me.

"Glad you could make it." Rachel lifts an eyebrow.

Technically I'm three minutes late, but they haven't started. Family members tardier than I scurry into Lily's classroom.

"Was it busy in court today, Richard?" Mom lays a hand on my arm. I smile and nod. Mom leans close to my ear. "I have no idea who this rude woman is to my left, but I think she's helps take care of Rachel in class. Rachel seems to like her." I fight the urge to laugh. Of course the "rude woman" my mother refers to is my sister.

"I'm sorry she scolded you, darling," Mom whispers in my ear.

"It's okay." I pat her hand. I shoot Rachel a look indicating that I realize I'm Mom's favorite and always have been. Rachel rolls her eyes toward the ceiling in response.

Lily's teacher walks to the front of the room, and the adults squished into tiny chairs stop their yammering. She welcomes us. Then, from behind a curtain, a passel of five-year-olds file out and onto the risers at the front of the pre-K classroom.

There is no greater proof of God than watching five-year-old children sing "Catch a Falling Star" *with* hand gestures. Lily's cherubic smile beams toward Mom, Rachel, and me. She's too cute with her braids, bright yellow dress with pink flowers, and tiny smattering of freckles. Her giant smile is infectious, and she waves to me, her eyes twinkling. She belts out the words. I swear I can discern her voice from the crowd of angelic warblers.

I peek at Rachel. My hard-ass criminal court judge sister presses a tissue to the corner of each eye and I get it. I understand. This moment is perfect. Beautiful. Life doesn't get much better than this. Despite Lily having a no-show of a dad, and Mom's mind being MIA, sitting here watching Lily sing makes each and every pain in life worth it. The pain is worth bearing because of this moment.

The kids finish their first song and start the second. Lily's told me there are three total. I sweep the room with my gaze. Two rows in front of us sits Kendall, a.k.a. Madame Cocksucker. She's beside the guy I saw her with at the birthday party, which confirms he must be the Mr. to her Mrs.

The door isn't too far. I make a mental note to escape quickly after congratulating Lily on her performance.

The final song is "Rainbow Connection." A tear-jerking showstopper. Not a dry eye in the house, including my own. Except Mom. Mom isn't crying. She's sitting there with that beatific smile that makes me believe she's passed into a Zen state from her disease. She doesn't get emotionally ruffled much anymore. She's reached this calm that she seems to exist in as long as neither Rachel nor I argue with her about our identities or what year it is.

The final note ends, and all the family members burst into applause.

"Well, that was . . ." Rachel tries to smile, but her face crumples. She dabs at her eyes with the wilted tissue in her hand then forces a smile. "It's just going way too fast."

It is. She's right. Next year Lily will be in "big girl" school and she'll go all day. None of this half-day stuff anymore. I remember holding her right after she was born. A red-faced bundle of cries until those big blue eyes latched onto me and she smiled. I don't give a fuck what anyone says about gas, Lily saw me and she smiled, and that smile saved my life. I knew . . . I knew that I would survive. I might not be okay or normal or involved in a romantic relationship with a woman, but I would be here for Lily, no matter how heartsick or broken or barely able to cope with life I was. I would live for Lily.

"Mama!" Lily rushes over. She holds two fresh pink gerbera daisies. One for Rachel and for Mom.

"Rachel, you did a brilliant job! Didn't she, Richard?" Mom turns to me and she smiles.

I nod. Big sis presses a finger across her lips in the universal "shhh" symbol to remind Lily that yes, she is in on the big-person secret that Grandma thinks Lily is her mother, and we don't say anything because Grandma is just confused.

"Grandma, I want you to meet my teacher."

"Okay, darling," Mom says, not missing a beat on the Grandma bit because that's how it is. No rhyme, no reason, no logic involved with this asshole disease, because logic has flown south for the rest of Mom's life.

"I think I need to be in on this," Rachel whispers in my ear. She takes Mom's hand while Lily leads them both across the room. I glance toward Kendall, who stands with her little boy and the man in a suit. He glances at his phone and scrolls. He's checked out. Not paying attention to his son or his wife. He gives her a quick peck, nods toward the boy, and puts his phone to his ear as he heads out the door. The boy rushes toward his friends and Kendall's face falls flat. Sad. She is absolutely despondent, at a complete loss with regard to this life she chose.

As pissed as I am over being violated while I slept, I know that Wonderfuck might be the only hint of pleasure she's had since her son was born, or even before her son was born, and I understand. I get it. I get my pleasure from Wonderfuck too, and it's easier. Less mess.

She glances toward me. Her eyes go cold. The sadness disappears. She's projecting her disillusionment over her life, her horrible relationship with her husband, her failure, her sadness, her frustration, she's projecting every bit of her negative feelings onto me, because I gave her hope and then snatched it away.

And maybe I did.

Maybe the pleasure Wonderfuck provided just put into stark contrast how bereft of desire her real life is. Instead of making her life better, Wonderfuck made it worse.

"I'm ready to go." Mom stands beside me. Her voice is chilly. "Richard, did you hear me? I wish to leave."

Rachel lifts both shoulders and shakes her head, both of us uncertain what happened to Mom's happy mood.

"Are you sure, Mom?" Rachel asks. "They've got cake, and Lily wants to play a bit with her friends."

"Richard and I are going home. Bring Rachel when she's finished, please."

Rachel leans toward me. "Got this?"

I nod. No problem. I trail Mom out of the room, glancing back at Kendall one final time. When I turn back to Mom, she stands just outside the doorway, watching me and waiting. Frigid stare, pursed lips. I've only seen that look a couple times on Mom's face. I take her elbow, walk her to my car. I buckle her into the passenger seat and we head for home.

"Why must you always humiliate me?"

I press my turn signal and wait at the light on Sunset Boulevard. "Mo—"

"Every time we go somewhere, you leer at other women. Richard, I thought we agreed when I let you come back home, that business was finished. That part of your life was over."

My stomach rolls. I'm trapped in a turn lane with my mother who thinks I'm her philandering husband—who also happens to be my deceased father. I don't want to have this conversation or hear this conversation or—

"That blonde, the woman in Rachel's classroom, I saw you ogling her. Was she . . . is she . . . one of your . . . one of your women?" Mom's voice is hard-edged. She clasps her hands together on her lap so tightly that I think her nails will break the skin.

"I . . . Mom . . . I don't know—"

"Richard, please, don't patronize me. We discussed this. I

know all about your suite at The Beverly Wilshire. I found the receipts, or don't you remember? I simply cannot live like this. Do you understand? I *won't* live like this anymore. Not even for the children. This was part of our agreement. I let you come home and you . . . you stop fucking around."

"Mom!"

"Stop calling me that! I'm not just the children's mother, and I'm tired of the man I'm married to calling me 'Mom' all the time."

I breathe. I breathe deep. The light changes. I press the accelerator and gun the car. We whip through the left turn and I'm speeding down the street. I can't get her home fast enough. I don't want to hear any of this conversation. I don't want to replay the memory of Dad moving out for six months. I don't want to know the details of my parents' marriage or his infidelity or how they dealt with their marital issues.

"How about some Mozart?" I ask and turn on the stereo, knowing that sometimes, *sometimes*, classical music soothes my mother and calms her addled mind. I offer a silent prayer that the strings will work their magic on her brain. The music swells in the car and Mom sits silent now. No words. She stares out the front window, her face an emotionless mask. Impenetrable. I don't know if she's left me for another memory, or if she's still reflecting on what she said. I turn onto her street and pull into the driveway.

"Ah, we're home." Mom smiles and turns to me. "Jake, want to come in for some tea? Maybe a sandwich before you head home?"

Jake. I'm Jake again. Thank you, God; I'm no longer the philandering man who nearly destroyed my mother and my sister and me and our life.

"Sure, Mom." I get out of the car and walk around to help her out and up the front steps. Hopeful that maybe we can have that sandwich and I'll remain Jake all the way through the meal.

CHAPTER 22

"HOW DID THIS START?"

Tara is naked in bed, her breasts halfway covered. Her left nipple peeks out from beneath the sheet. I twirl chopsticks into the noodles in the Thai take-out box and extend them toward her mouth. Her lips open. How can simply looking at Tara's mouth make my cock hard? Especially since we've already had sex three times.

"You texted me, remember?"

"I don't mean that." She smiles around her bite of noodles. "I mean this. The Wonderfuck thing, how did it start? I have theories, but I want to know how."

Alarm bells sound in my brain. She's veering dangerously close to Jake territory, not with her question, but with her comment on "having a theory." I've been asked this question before by other women I wonderfuck. We take a break from sex, we eat, we talk. They ask questions. I have responses that don't venture too close to the truth.

Because I'm Wonderfuck, I create whatever backstory I want for these women. Sometimes, I even tailor the backstory to fit what I think a particular woman might need to hear.

Tara knows too much about me and both my identities for

too much falsification to work. She's pushing. She's digging. She's like a Jack Russell Terrier scavenging for a bone. I have to answer her, or she'll simply ask the same question a half dozen different ways until she gets a response that satisfies her curiosity. She's a journalist. She seeks the truth, needs to prove her hypothesis.

"I needed a release," I say. She listens, her blue eyes are intense. "I needed this to survive."

Empathy softens her gaze. Of course she understands, or thinks she understands, because she needed the same type of connection to survive the loss of her wedding day. "Why did *you* call?" I ask, turning the tables, getting the story refocused on her instead of me.

"You know why I called." Her gaze drops to her hands. "It was my wedding day." Her voice is close to a whisper.

"I know it was your wedding day, but *why* did you call?" Now I'm digging, trying to get at the emotion beneath the reason, because, ultimately the answers are the same. She called because she didn't want to be alone. She wanted to be wanted. She needed to feel the physical pleasure of being in another person's arms.

"I . . ." She pauses. Her eyes look at me. There are tears. Her lips tremble. "I didn't want to be alone. I . . . wanted to feel alive and be with"—desire filters into her words—"be with you." A tear rolls down her cheek. I reach out and pull her close. I wrap my arms around her.

I can understand her pain and her vulnerability, even her need to be desired, because I have it too, but I can't give into my emotions. I move the remnants of our meal off the bed. I press my lips to her trembling mouth. Then I pull back and look into her eyes.

"I'm here. I want to be here, and I want to be with you." I say it as Wonderfuck, but I mean it as Jake. I want to be with Tara in a way that I can hardly admit.

I press my lips to hers again. I cup her breast, sliding the pad of my thumb over her nipple.

"Oh yes."

I need to fuck away her doubts, my doubts, her fears, my fears. I want to fuck away this reality and sink into pleasure. I want to wonderfuck.

We slide down the bed. I know her body now. I know what she likes. I know what she wants. I've paid attention each time we've been together. I press my lips to her nipple and her hips arch.

Me sucking her tits is a trigger for her.

I know she's wet now. I know the motion of her hips will continue until she's satisfied.

Which will be a while.

I intend to make her come over and over and over again. I intend to erase her tears, her doubt, her pain. I intend to imprint myself and our time together upon her soul so that after we're finished, no matter who she's with, she'll never forget her Wonderfuck.

I won't forget her.

I roll the taut nipple around in my mouth and my fingertips skim over her belly to her sex. I brush over her clit with my fingertip. She grasps my hair in her hands.

"Please." She bucks her hips up to my hand. I pulse two fingers deep into her sex, and her muscles clamp around me.

"Please, oh yes, please!"

I want her. I want her now. I want her the way that *I* want to take her.

I pull out my fingers and flip her onto her stomach. I need this. I want this. I pull her up onto her knees. My fingertips return to her sex, circling her clit. I bend over her back and she tips her round ass toward me, inviting me to fuck her. Fuck her fast and hard.

And I want this.

I want to pound deep into her over and over again. To make her mine, to prove she's mine to fuck. I grab a condom and unroll it onto my shaft. Heat pulses in my legs and climbs up to my balls. My back muscles tighten as my cock strains to plunge deep into her sex.

She looks around at me. Her eyes are liquid lust. Besotted with desire. There's a beast deep inside me, one that I don't let out when I'm wonderfucking, one I haven't let out in years. A gluttonous creature that takes what he wants. A beast who doesn't give like Wonderfuck gives. A part of my sexuality that I thought died with Susie, but the beast awakens now. Awakens with the curve of Tara's ass pressing against my cock, with the gleam in her eyes, with the hint of her tantalizing smile. I rub the flat of my hand on her ass.

So beautiful.

So round.

Smack.

Tara moans.

The tiniest red mark outlined on the fair skin of her ass. My cock throbs. I bite down hard on my bottom lip. I reach forward and intertwine my fingers in Tara's lush brown hair. I grasp it tightly and I pull. She looks back at me.

"Is this okay?" I'm barely able to speak. My words, my voice, are thick with lust, with heat, with the desire I've contained for nearly six years.

"I want you," she says. "It turns me on."

Her words are all I need. I press the head of my cock to her entrance and tug her hair. Her head lifts up and back. With one hand on her hip, I thrust hard and deep into her. I'm hip deep into Tara. I stroke back out and plunge deep into her sex again. Heat rockets through me. I won't last. Can't last.

My breath is hot quick pants as I pulse in and out. I lean forward and kiss the corner of her mouth. I'm above her, and I pull harder on her hair.

"Please, God, yes, please!" she wails.

Her sex clamps around me and her ass presses toward me.

Oh. So. Deep.

Come jets from my balls and through my shaft, and I turn to stone above her with one hard thrust. She tightens around me.

"Oh my God, Jake, oh my God."

We both come, and I'm so lost that I can't even tell her that I'm not Jake, that I'm the Wonderfuck.

&

"ARE WE ALLOWED TO GO OUT TOGETHER?" SHE ASKS. "I mean as Wonderfuck?"

I lay in bed beside her, both my arms are wrapped around her. Her ass is toward me so I can't see her face. Want laces the question she's asked. Not sexual want, but a desire to get what she asked for.

"I know the rules about anonymity, but is there a rule about going and doing something while we're together?"

I know it's not a good idea, but it's what I want too. I press my lips to the back of her neck. Her body responds. Her body always responds to my kiss.

"What did you have in mind?"

She rolls over in my arms and faces me. Her beautiful face with those sharp, focused sky-blue eyes. Her soft smooth skin and the sparkling smile that makes me smile in return.

"There's an opening at The Legend Gallery in Venice. I like the artist. Thought maybe we could go."

I kiss the tip of her nose. I want her to be happy. I want to please her in more ways than simply the physical.

"We can do that."

I don't think about the conflict, the possibilities, the damage that could happen to my two worlds. No, I don't stop to think at all, because this gorgeous woman, with a beautiful face that enchants me, is smiling at me. I've just made her happy, and that's all that matters in the world.

၆ၜ

WE FUCK IN THE SHOWER.

Two times.

Fucking her is the best experience of my life.

CHAPTER 23

THE LEGEND GALLERY sits on Venice Beach. It's a big open space two stories tall.

"They just remodeled." Tara holds my hand and pulls me inside. Hipsters and models and actors wander the gallery. My heart beats at an erratic pace.

Who am I while I'm here?

With Tara I'm meant to be Wonderfuck, but here, in this space, as I walk by the second person that looks familiar, my breathing grows shallow.

Is this a date?

What the fuck? I bring my hand to my forehead, and Tara turns to me.

"Are you okay? Should we leave?"

I'm processing her words. Thinking about what I need to do versus what I want to do when—

"Yo, Jake! Man, good to see you here!"

I turn. Andrew stands in front of us. Beside him is Ingrid, his wife, a former friend of Susie's and a hater of me. Andrew clasps my hand and pats me on the back. I meet Ingrid's gaze and she lifts a brow.

"Jake." Her tone is cool. I've known Ingrid since college.

Andrew and Ingrid started dating after Susie and I introduced them to each other.

They both look at Tara.

My throat tightens. They want an introduction, but I'm at a loss. I run my hand through my hair. This . . . my worlds are colliding . . . the woman I loved . . . the woman I destroyed. Ingrid loved her too. Loved us both, and now I'm standing in a public place as Wonderfuck with a woman I want to keep hidden in a separate compartment of my existence. The walls I've spent years building are crumbling, taking me and my identity down with them.

"This is . . ."

"Tara." She finishes my sentence when I stumble. Tara extends her hand first to Ingrid, who introduces herself, and then to Andrew. They don't mention Susie, although Ingrid continues to shoot sour looks my way.

"Are you a collector of Frederika's work?" Tara asks.

"Oh, no, no, no." Ingrid hooks her arm through Andrew's and glances up at him. "We're close friends of the gallery owner, but as for the artist?" She purses her lips and shakes her head no.

Ingrid's gazes runs up and down over Tara as though measuring her worth. Was Ingrid always this big of a snobbish bitch? Did I realize it when I dated Susie? Did Susie realize it? They were absolutely best friends. Ingrid was meant to be in our wedding, would have been if not for . . .

"We do have three Rengalis. That's the next show. We came by tonight to get a private viewing of our fourth." Ingrid squeezes Andrew's arm.

He looks green. From the rumor mill, I know Andrew's company isn't doing well. I glance from Andrew to Ingrid. Fuck. She has no idea what's going on with his business. Deceptive bullshit. Deceptive bullshit of which I want no part.

"We're going to grab some dinner. Do you two want to join us?" Ingrid asks in a honey-dripping voice.

"No," I blurt out much too fast. But I don't want to. I'm here as Wonderfuck, not as Jake, and I don't want to sink further into this quagmire.

"We just got here," Tara adds. "And we ate before we arrived. Nice to meet you though."

"You too," Ingrid purrs. They slide past us.

My head fucking hurts.

They're out the door. Tara's gaze gathers me up, as though she sees all my broken bits, and that sucks. I feel vulnerable, weak, and like she knows too well who I really am.

"Do you want to leave?"

She does know me. She knows me both too well and just well enough. While a part of me wants run off into the night, shove Tara into an Uber alone and go be Wonderfuck for the rest of my life, another part of me wants to stay with her, walk through the gallery and look at the amazing art by this artist Ingrid is much too pretentious to like, but which Tara loves, which makes me like the artist all the more.

"No." I shake my head. "I want to be here with you." I reach out and clasp Tara's hand with mine. We turn and walk together toward the paintings at the back of the gallery.

❧

WE'RE CLOSING IN ON FORTY-EIGHT HOURS. ASIDE from Cheryl, I've never stayed with a woman this long since I began wonderfucking. I need to leave. I need to tell Tara that we have to leave—

"I need to go," Tara says and stretches her arms over her head.

Wait . . . what? *She* wants to go? She wants to leave? She can just get out of this bed and walk away from what we're doing here?

Tara closes her computer and flips her glasses on top of her head. "Jango—my dog," she adds, as a nod toward my anonymity rule, "has been with the dog sitter for two days, and I have work to do."

We both have lives to return to, but the realization that this is the end of our second time together and that I'll soon be ending our Wonderfucking time together is nearly too heavy to bear.

I lift her computer from her lap and set it on the nightstand. I take her glasses from the top of her head.

"We can leave," I say. I press my lips to her cheek. I pull back and look into her eyes. "After we fuck one more time."

She smiles. A devilish gleam glows in her eye.

"You won't get any arguments from me." Her hands reach out to my cock. She strokes down and up with a firm grasp. Her gaze doesn't waver from mine. She presses her lips to my lips and pushes me back onto the bed. She leans over me now, her breasts against my chest. She lifts her leg and straddles my body. I grasp her hips and lift upward. I shift her body forward, positioning her sex above my mouth.

This is what I want. I want her hot glistening sex just above my lips. I hold her still. I reach out my tongue and lave up one side of her.

Tara's head falls back and she braces her palms on the headboard.

"Oh my fucking God," she says over pants of pleasure. I pull her clit into my mouth. My tongue strokes the letters of the words I will never say to her. She grasps one of her breasts and plays with her nipple.

Fuck.

So hot. So beautiful. I want her.

I suck hard on her clit and then let her flesh slide from my mouth. I reach up with my tongue and shift her body forward to pull her down onto it. I slide my tongue deep into her hot core. I probe deep and hard into her sex. Her juices come into my mouth. Her sex clasps around me.

She slides up and down on my tongue.

"Yes, yes, yes," she gasps.

I lift her hips and shift her back. I pull her clit into my mouth again. I spell out the words on her flesh.

"Please, oh my God, please, Jake, wonderfuck me."

I can't hold back. I roll a condom onto my shaft. She hovers above me, her eyes open.

"I love having you inside me."

She grasps my cock with both hands and slowly, ever so slowly, more slowly than I want, more slowly than I can take, more slowly that I can stand, she slides her hot sex down over me. She takes all of me. She's beyond beautiful. She's a fucking goddess. She's everything feminine and gorgeous, all that I could want or need, and she's sitting with my cock thrust deep inside of her.

Tara pulls her sex up along my shaft until all that remains inside her is the head of my cock.

My breath stalls in my chest. The only thing I want on this entire planet, this entire world, my entire universe, is for her hot body to thrust down.

And she does. Her breasts bounce. I take in her beauty, the tiny rosebud nipples and her belly and her lush brown hair, as she rolls forward and back above me. Tara's gaze never leaves my face. We're locked together. In this moment, she's in control, she's in command. She lifts her body. I press my fingertip to her clit. Her mouth drops open and she gasps.

She slams her body down onto me. Her rhythm grows faster. She moves up and down, up and down. My fingertip circles her clit. I don't have much time left. Her sex clenches tight around my shaft. She moans, and then a shriek rips from her lips.

Heat jets through me, to the base of my back, and down my shaft. Come explodes from me, and we both fall over the edge.

THE RIDE HOME SUCKS. THE RIDE HOME HAS NEVER

sucked like this before. Never. My body aches. My muscles are sore.

But my heart.

My heart is shredded.

Wonderfuck's heart doesn't hurt.

I am screwed.

So fucked.

I climb into the elevator. I've waited two hours. I even picked up food. I don't want to see Tara in the hall. The elevator doors open. I walk down my hall. I stop in the middle, no-man's land. As much as I don't want to see Tara, God, I fucking do. I will her to open her door. I think of Jango and will her to know that I am standing here. I will them both to have a sudden urge to go for a walk.

I wait.

I wait longer than I should.

What the fuck is wrong with me?

I turn toward my door. I unlock the lock. I go inside.

I wait.

I shut the door.

I'm Jake.

I'm alone.

Abso-fucking-lutely alone.

Just like I always need to be.

CHAPTER 24

THE BROAD ISN'T in my top ten places to take a five-year-old in Los Angeles, but Rachel is on an arts and culture kick this summer where Lily is concerned, and they invited me for this outing. Personally, I think Legoland is culturally enriching, or maybe the latest Pixar movie, but Rachel wouldn't be swayed. We walk to a Takashi Murakami painting trailing Lily, who carries a pad of paper and has a box of crayons in her Hello Kitty backpack.

She plops down in front of the painting. "Mommy, I want to draw this one," she says. I glance at the Murakami. How absolutely aspirational. My five-year-old niece, a world-class artist.

"Go for it!" Rachel smiles. She glances at me. "You okay?" she whispers.

A half dozen people wander through this gallery, but many are using indoor voices, not whispering.

"I guess. Why?"

"Just checking. We never really talked about your arrest, or that day at Mom's."

I flash on the blonde mom, her open mouth fellating my cock. Nope, won't be sharing that with Rachel.

"And you haven't said much about your neighbor."

"Tara."

Rachel nods.

"Not much to say." I turn to the giant painting. How long did he work on this piece?

"So you two aren't . . ."

Her words trail off. Irritation flashes in my chest. I may be her little brother, but do I have to share everything in my life with her?

"Fucking? Dating? What do you want to know, Rachel?"

"Touchy," she says. She wanders past me toward Lily and leans forward to examine her artwork.

Rachel's right. I'm damned irritable. Discussing what's going on between me and Tara with Rachel isn't an option. It's confusing and it breaks too many rules. I haven't heard from Tara in close to two weeks. I also haven't seen her. I'm beginning to wonder if she still lives across the hall from me.

"Hey." Rachel walks back to me. "You mentioned something happened between you and Mom? When you took her home from Lily's performance?"

A sick feeling slides through my belly, and my stomach folds in on itself. "Do you remember when Dad moved out?"

Color drains from Rachel's face. Those were dark days in the Reynolds household.

I lower my voice. "Mom started talking to me about . . . what happened." My gaze meets Rachel's. "She thought I was Dad."

"Oh shit." Rachel's eyes widen. "Did she think you were—"

"Still cheating on her. Ripped me for gawking at one of the moms in Lily's class."

"Were you gawking?"

"No. Besides, that isn't the uncomfortable part."

"Right." Rachel rakes her fingers through her hair. "Right, you're absolutely right. Wow, that sucks."

I turn away from Rachel and look at Lily's picture. Blue and pink fight for primacy on her page.

"I knew like six months before Mom did." It's a secret I've never shared.

"Wait? What?" Rachel turns to me.

I can't meet her gaze. This isn't a story I've ever told, not to Mom, not to Rachel, not even to Susie, and Susie and I knew *all* of each other's secrets.

"Sixth grade. Skipped fifth period with Jeff Wexler. Took our bikes to Brentwood to get a soda at—" I stop. Why am I telling Rachel this? Why am I even remembering this story?

"And?"

"And we were behind the store, you know, heading up that side street that led to the arcade."

Rachel nods.

"And I saw Dad."

"Behind the grocery store?"

"With a woman."

My heart races. I'm twelve again. Hopping on my bike. The sun beats against my scalp. One hand clutches a cool aluminum can, and the other, my handlebars. We zip around the corner.

Dad's Mercedes.

Shit. I'm screwed. I duck my head and pedal harder. I sneak a look at his car, to see if he's looking . . . but he's not. Through the windshield I see his mouth pressed tight to a woman's mouth. A *blonde* woman's mouth.

Mom isn't blonde.

My jaw drops.

I nearly steer my bike into his car, but instead I jerk the handlebars. I look back.

Dad's eyes lock on me.

I see him.

He sees me.

Shit.

"We never talked about it. That day." I shove my hands into my pockets. I lift a shoulder. "What the fuck? I lied. He lied. I

. . . I should've told Mom." The guilt. Maybe truth isn't a possibility with my DNA.

"*You* should've told Mom?" Rachel screws up her face. "What the fuck? *You* were twelve. *He* should've told Mom."

The knot in my chest loosens. If my Dudley Do-Right of a big sis doesn't think I should've raced home to tell Mom what I saw, maybe my moral compass isn't as damaged as I've always thought.

"Yeah, maybe."

"No, not maybe. You were a kid. He was the grown-up. Not fair to expect your twelve-year-old self to make that kind of choice. Shit, there're adults who can't make that kind of choice. I know them. You know them." Rachel leans closer. "How many of my friends knew Dalton was fucking his secretary? Come on. So many of them have crawled out of the woodwork since we split." She rolls her eyes toward the ceiling. "And I'm like, fuck you. What good does it do me now that you knew my husband was fucking around on me? Could've told me sooner. Saved me a shit ton of pain."

Is she right? For more than two decades, I assumed there's something fundamentally wrong with me because I didn't rush home and tell Mom about Dad. Something on the Y chromosome that prohibited me from being honest. Faithful. Truthful.

Then after what happened with Susie . . .

I press the heel of my hand to my forehead.

"Hey." Rachel stares into my eyes. "Not your fault. Okay?"

"Why do you think she let him come back?" I ask.

"For us." Rachel glances at Lily. "Once you have a kid, you totally get it."

"Would you—?" I nod toward Lily.

"Not now. It's been too long. It'd be confusing. But before? If he'd asked? Maybe. Probably." She nods, and her eyes grow sad. "Yeah. I would've. I'm not saying we would've worked, but I would've at least tried. Just to know. Because I want that for her. I want two parents and a 'normal' home and—"

"There are no normal homes."

"Okay, well normal-ish, or whatever passes as normal. I'd like for her to have a home with two parents in it."

"You can give that to her."

Rachel's cheeks flame red and her eyes inform me I've stepped onto an explosive path. What the heck. I just told her one of my biggest secrets and survived. I'm feeling reckless. "I mean there's Alan. He'd love to be a dad and—"

Rachel shoots her hand up. "Stop. Stop now. Not an option."

"But—"

"Mommy, do you like it?" Lily interrupts. Rachel steps closer to have a look and plasters a happy-mommy smile onto her face.

"I love it, sweetie. It's gorgeous."

Lily grabs a pink crayon and continues. Rachel grasps my arm and pulls me further away.

"I told you about Alan in confidence, and in a very weak moment, okay? No. Just no. I am not putting Lily through that again. Not now. Not ever. Alan and I . . . we . . . we just take care of each other's *needs*."

I put my fingers in my ears and shut my eyes. "You're my sister. Don't want to hear about needs."

"Whatever. We all have them. Even you." She jerks her chin towards me. "You're not Mr. Celibate. I know you're not. I'm certain in the past five years you've had needs as well." Rachel leans in. "Or at least that's what I hear." She lifts an eyebrow.

What the fuck does she hear? And how does she hear it?

I'm not taking her bait. Not now. Not today. Kendall? An assumption about Tara? Wonderfuck? I can't imagine by-the-book Rachel knowing about Wonderfuck and not raising holy hell about the idea of me having sex with strangers, even if it's an unpaid volunteer position.

"Mommy, look!" Lily jumps up, runs toward us, and reaches out her hand to Rachel. I look over her shoulder. Hmm. Yeah. My niece, the next Picasso.

CHAPTER 25

THE ALERT on my phone beeps. Tara's published a new story. I open my laptop and click on the bookmark for the *LA Post*, the site she writes for. I programmed the alerts after the first time we slept together. Not when I slept with her as Wonderfuck, but when I slept with her as Jake.

I scroll to her byline. I read. She's a good writer. Solid. They have her doing investigative stuff, but they also have her doing one piece a week called "Unseen Los Angeles." This week it's the artists around town. The work that goes unseen, on the periphery of the mainstream.

It clicks. The gallery. The other night. Was research. For this article. I continue to read. Tara references the showing at The Legend Gallery and talks about the redemptive nature of societal credibility.

My heart beats faster.

I keep reading.

Nope. Nothing. No mention of me, of Ingrid, of Andrew. Nada. Just her and the gallery and the artist and the opening.

I close my eyes.

I hear her voice.

I see her face.

I feel her touch.

I want to feel her touch again.

It's eleven at night. Easy. Convenient. I could get up out of this chair. Walk across the hall. Knock on her door.

Who knows if she's home?

I don't.

I know less about Tara's life now that I'm wonderfucking her than I did before, when we were neighbors who rarely spoke.

What's my problem? Why can't I accept that I care for her? I care for her as Jake. I care for her as Wonderfuck. I want more from her than I've wanted from a woman since Susie.

Because the idea of being attached to a woman scares the fuck out of me.

I push back my chair and walk into my half-empty closet. A testament to me living alone. Susie's clothes hung there for twenty-four months after she died, until one day I came home from wonderfucking and they were gone. Disappeared. Rachel packed up Susie's things. We never spoke of it, but I know she did it. I know because the sad look on her face the next Sunday at Mom's told me that she had.

Rachel left a few of Susie's things behind. Very few. But a few. I reach up to the top shelf in my closet and shove my hand to the back, where I find a rectangular box, bigger than a shoebox, but not much bigger. I pull down the box and turn toward the dressing table in the center of the closet.

Deep breath.

When was the last time I opened this box? I can't even fucking remember. I pull off the lid and look inside.

Like a steak knife into my heart.

The detritus of a life I was meant to lead. A life torn from me when Susie died. On the top of the pile, a testament to our joy, our love, our future, is our engagement picture. We did two days of shoots. This photo, at Echo Park, was Susie's favorite. I'm leaning against a tree and Susie is leaning against me. Her head beneath the angle of my chin. Behind us the lake and the bright blue sky.

We're happy.

I'm happy.

Susie smiles.

The sun shines.

Her diamond gleams.

I tilt the box to the side and metal rattles against cardboard. The diamond ring slides to the corner. I pick it up.

She took it off before she dove off the balcony.

Otherwise . . . thirty-two stories.

I retch.

I rush from the closet and into the bathroom. I heave.

Nothing.

Been here before.

Tons of fucking times.

There's a reason I don't get the box out very often. A reason I don't return to the memories of what was meant to be my perfect life. I sit on the floor and rest my elbow on the toilet. I open my left hand. The ring lays in my palm. Glittering with the promise of a future that will forever go unfulfilled.

Love will do that to you. That bitch.

CHAPTER 26

My Wonderfuck phone beeps.

I've been waiting weeks for this beep. I flip open my phone.

Ready? her text reads.

Always.

Three's the charm.

I don't respond.

This won't be our last time, will it?

Everything is different where Tara is concerned. My entire life is flipped with her. I do things . . . I say things . . . I think things I never thought possible again, or even before.

It's the last time, I finally type.

Her response is immediate. Friday at 5. She types in an address. It's not a hotel, but a private residence on the ocean in Malibu.

Normally I'd say no. I'd text right back and tell her impossible, it's not happening, but I don't because this is Tara, and this is the final time I'll hold her in my arms, kiss her, be with her. Pretend that she's mine. This is the last time, because for my sanity it has to be.

I don't even try to fool myself with the idea that we're simply wonderfucking. I know she makes me feel as good as I make her feel. This isn't *just* wonderfucking, this is more and that scares the fuck out of me, and only proves that this needs to end. The climb back from losing Susie was bloody and brutal, and I can't survive that crawl again.

I CAN'T CONTINUE SEEING TARA, BECAUSE IF I'M WITH her eventually I'll fall in love and this time, if something bad happens, I might lose not only my mind but also my soul. And I won't, not even to be with Tara.

໖

"HEY, SO DID YOU WANT TO COME TO DINNER tonight?" Rachel asks. I'm on the PCH, headed to Malibu and trying to beat the Friday traffic.

"I have some plans for the weekend."

"Plans?" Rachel doesn't even try to hide the surprise in her voice. "For the entire weekend? As in, laying-on-your-couch-eating-Chinese-food-and-having-a-marathon-session-watching-baseball plans or like real-plans-with-human-type-people plans?"

"Ha! You're so funny," I say, but don't answer her question. She hates that. She's a judge and I'm her little brother. Those two things mean that not only am I always supposed to answer Rachel's questions, so is everyone else in the world. I know she hates when I don't answer her questions, and even though we're grown-ups I still like jerking her chain, or at least letting her know that I *can* jerk her chain. I remain silent. I glance out the window toward the bright blue Pacific.

"Seriously? You're not going to answer me?"

I smile. "Oh? You wanted an answer?"

"Ha, ha. Of course I want an answer. I'm worried about you." Her voice is softer. "In the past this has been a rough weekend."

The realization hits me like a baseball bat to the head. This weekend. Tomorrow. Would've been my wedding anniversary. My six-year anniversary . . . with Susie.

Fuck.

I clear my throat.

"I forgot."

"Shit," Rachel says. "Wish I hadn't said anything."

But in the last six years, I've never forgotten the day that I was meant to marry Susie. The date is etched into my brain like a scar seared into flesh. The days leading up to it, I'm always morose, not very communicative. The past five years I've wonderfucked my brains out on this date. Endorphins help to minimize pain. I don't have to feel sadness, loss, desperation—or at least I don't feel them as deeply. It's hard to feel sad while you come.

"I think it's good. That you didn't remember," Rachel says.

Is it? I'm uncertain. Remembering Susie is kind of my thing. Trying to help women so they won't ever feel like Susie did is kind of my thing too.

"Where're you going?"

"Malibu."

"Ohhhh." The way she draws out the word makes her tone an unspoken question about my weekend plans.

I'm absolutely not responding to this inquiry. "I might not make it to Mom's on Sunday."

"Got it," Rachel says. "Can you do next Wednesday?"

"What's Wednesday?"

"Doctor's appointment. Assessment. Remember?"

I don't want to remember. I'm in complete denial about how poorly Mom is doing with the Alzheimer's. Her doctor is pushing for us to move her into an assisted care facility. The idea makes me sick. I pay for nurses and caregivers. Why put her in a facility?

"Mom loves being at home."

"It's not about her loving being at home, it's about safety and her not getting enough stimulation."

"There has to be a way that doesn't include shuffling her off to a facility."

I grudgingly agree to the doctor's appointment because Rachel is my big sister and she'll simply hammer away at me until I capitulate. She's good like that. I might not answer all her questions, but she can totally make me cave on doing things I don't want to do.

I turn into the Malibu Colony and pull to a stop at the guard gate. The guy opens his window.

What name? I squint. What name did Tara give him?

I roll down my window.

"Tara Jennings," I say.

"And your name?"

My name . . . what is my name . . .

"Mr. W," I say, hoping Tara knew that's what I'd use.

The guard scans his computer screen. Taps two keys. Smiles. "Thank you, sir. Sixth house on the left."

I nod, pull into the Colony, and realize that this is going to be a spectacular final time.

CHAPTER 27

THE SKY IS BLISSFULLY blue and waves caress the sand. Six steps lead from the lower deck to the beach. I stand and watch the infinity of the waves. The never-ending love affair between water and land. The constant give and take. I take a sip of my whiskey. I'm early.

The house is perfection.

Just exactly the type of home I'd want.

The perfect place to entertain. To have kids. To bring family. Lily would love this place. I imagine Jango would too.

Woof.

About to find out.

"Hello?"

A tremor rushes through my body. I smile. How can I not? Tara makes me happy. I love her voice, her words, her thoughts.

"You're here." She walks out onto the deck. Her arms open to me and I wrap mine around her. Standing with Tara in my arms feels like home.

A jolt rips through my belly

I don't fucking care. I pretend that my emotions don't alarm me. I lean into her, into the happiness and contentment that come from holding her in my arms. She smells of lemon and lavender and sunshine. Jango barks and wags her tail. Jango loves Jake and to Jango, that's who I am, no matter how I might try to explain that I'm Wonderfuck.

Reality hits me.

I'm a fool.

A complete and utter fool.

I'm not Wonderfuck. Have never been Wonderfuck. I'm Jake. Forever and always—Jake. I'm not my persona, my persona is me. I look into Tara's eyes. Her smile captures me. I shake the thoughts of identity from my head and press my lips to Tara's.

Heat zips through my cells. I'm hard, and I want her.

Tara pulls back from my hungry kiss. "That's better than nice."

Fuck. She's perfection. Beautiful and smart and lovely. Inspiring physical want but also the emotional contentment that hasn't been in my life for a very long time.

"I thought we'd eat in tonight," she says.

"Let me cook."

"You cook?"

"Of course I cook." I smile at her. "I have to eat."

"I guess . . . I just assumed that you had takeout most nights."

"I make a mean garlic cream sauce."

I pull her toward me and head into the kitchen, a big, open, chef's type of affair. There's a six-burner chef's stove and two sinks, plus a Sub-Zero refrigerator already fully stocked for the weekend.

"This has everything I need." I shut the refrigerator door. "Want to start now?"

She walks up behind me and slides her arms around my waist. "I kind of hoped we could eat a little bit later . . ."

I'm gone. Done. We can eat later, we can eat next week, we can eat never, as long as I now get to do to Tara all the fabulously sexy things I've been thinking about doing to her for the last two weeks. "I missed you," I whisper.

She tilts her face toward me. A hint of a question followed by sadness lurks in her eyes. The irony of my statement hits me. Yes, I've missed Tara and yet, according to me, we can't be together again after this weekend.

I don't want to talk about it.

I press my lips to hers.

The ocean roars. I pull her close.

Her body fits with mine.

I cup my hand around the back of her neck.

I want her.

I need her.

We will wonderfuck the questions away.

She grasps my hip with her hand and holds on to me. She lifts my shirt over my head, and I know that she is fucking me and we're fucking each other. Her hands rub my chest. Desire pulses through her fingertips. She traces the curve of my pec and down my arm. She touches her lips to my nipple and pulls it into her mouth.

Fuck, yes.

My fingertips drift over the smooth skin of her thigh, up and under her skirt, where I pull her panties over her hips and ass and the cloth drops to the floor. Her sex is naked beneath her skirt. I turn her toward the wall of windows, and she flattens both palms against the glass. I pull the skirt up over the curve of her beautiful ass. So lush and full. Her ass arches back to me. Her head turns and her gaze locks onto me. Yes. Oh yes. I stroke my hands over the curve of her ass and the rhythm of her hips grows more impatient.

"Fuck me," she says. "Fuck me now."

I pull a foil package from my wallet and unbutton my jeans. They drop to the floor. I'm naked behind her. She turns to me and takes the condom wrapper. Rips it open and unrolls the condom onto my cock.

"Now," she says, turning back to the glass. The ocean is before us both, but the better sight is her ass in front of me. I reach my fingers beneath her and stroke her clit. I slide one finger deep inside her.

She is wet.

She tightly clamps around my finger.

"I want your cock," she breaths out. Her voice rasps with a need for satisfaction.

I spread her legs with my knee and grasp a hip in each hand. With one strong thrust, I am deep inside her.

"God, yesssss," she moans.

"Yes."

I thrust in and out of her. Her palms press to the window and her ass presses back toward me. Heat starts in the soles of my feet and then rolls up and through my legs. Fuck yes. I am going to come. Her sex tightens and tightens again. Her breathing is shallow and heavy.

"Yes, oh God, yes, please, Jake, please!" She looks over her shoulder at me again and her eyes . . . I could fall into those eyes for the rest of my life. Live in her arms. Be satisfied with Tara for the rest of my life.

But could she?

I thrust deep and hard, and come jets from me.

"Yes!" Tara yells.

We fall into the pleasure together.

THE SWEET SMELL OF GARLIC IN BUTTER AND CREAM fills the kitchen. The prawns are nearly done, and angel hair pasta is already divided into two bowls. Tara spreads chopped tomato on the salad she made. The timer beeps.

"Garlic bread," she says to me.

I lean forward and pull the baguette wrapped in aluminum foil from the oven. We are ready. She fills two wineglasses from the bottle that is open and breathing. She hands me one and smiles.

"To us." She clinks her wineglass against mine and takes a sip of her cabernet.

I sip mine as well.

"That smells amazing." Tara stands beside me at the stove.

I grind a tiny bit more pepper into the sauce. "Now it's amazing," I say.

I pour the sauce onto the pasta. Oh yeah. The scents of butter and garlic and prawns. I glance at Tara. She smiles. She's living in the moment like I am. We're doing this. We're being together this weekend for our final time and ignoring the consequences of our feelings. And then . . .

And then we will say good-bye. This will end. Our Wonderfucking will be over. She'll go back to her life and I'll go back to my life . . . and . . .

My throat tightens. I put the saucepan into the sink and Tara sits. I serve her and myself and sit.

"This is amazing."

"Yeah?" I twirl my fork tines in my pasta. I take a bite. I look at the beautiful woman sitting beside me. "I haven't seen you for a while. Are you busy with work?"

Tara looks at me. Her jaw drops. At first, for a split second, it doesn't register what I've just done. I've just . . . I've bled this reality, my Wonderfuck reality, into my Jake reality, and I've done it without even noticing. As though I'm allowing us to cross over into that other part of my life, the one that I pretend doesn't exist. She raises an eyebrow, but she acts like she doesn't notice.

"I've got an article I'm working on. One that I really like."

I nod. I sip my wine. I'm uncertain I want to talk. I . . . I'm uncertain I want to do anything but have sex, because the sex takes away my confusion. We finish our meal in silence and clean up our dishes. The sun begins to set into the sea.

"Walk?" she asks. As much as I'd prefer to take her upstairs and fuck her instead, I take her hand in mine. Jango hears the magic "W" word and skips around at our ankles like a five-year-old going to Disneyland. Tara grabs a tennis ball from a basket filled with them by the back door, and Jango bolts out the sliders and across the sand toward the water. I smile, and Tara throws the ball into the surf.

Jango bounds into the water as though this moment is the best of her life. I smile, I can't help but smile, at her irrepressible joy. She swims, grabs the ball, and hurdles toward us as we slowly walk up the beach. She does us the courtesy of shaking off the water before she reaches us, and drops the ball at my feet.

"She'll do this all day," Tara says.

"Can you blame her?" I reach down, pick up the slobbery wet ball, and throw it toward the ocean. Not too far, but just far enough. Jango is off like a shot. Ball. Water. Her favorite people. She's is in dog nirvana.

Why can't life be this simple for humans?

A warm breeze lifts Tara's hair from her shoulders. A smile hovers on her face as we head north along the beach, enjoying the brilliant light show of the sun sinking into the sea.

"Nice place, where'd you find it?"

"It's my parents' place. They don't use it much since they retired, so it's open most of the time."

"I'd be here all the time." The sound of the waves coming to shore takes the edge off the thoughts in my mind. The metronomic continuity of the sound numbs all the chirping in my brain.

"I come out here to write. Especially if I'm working on something that's tough for me to figure out."

"Is this where you've been?"

"I needed to get away." She pulls a strand of hair behind her ear and glances down the beach. "To work on this story."

"Tough one?"

"Kind of personal."

She doesn't offer any more words, and though I have all kinds of questions, I don't ask them. Unfair, isn't it, for me to pepper her for answers to my questions when I don't really want to answer many questions from her.

I wonder if the story is about her engagement, or maybe some other part of her life, a part that I know nothing about. Unfortunate really, how badly I want to know what she's working on, to hear what has her bothered or worried. How I want to fix whatever problems she has. I want to take care of her. Fix her coffee and breakfast in the morning, make her lunch and dinner, sit with her and talk and take walks where Jango splashes into the waves over and over again.

I want to be here for her.

But I can't.

I tried that once. Tried to fix Susie's problems. Tried to love her through the challenge. Tried to help her, and I failed. I failed so badly that she died.

"Do you miss her?"

I stop walking. I turn to Tara. This is a complete violation of our agreement, of what I allow myself to talk about with women when I'm Wonderfuck. I bend down and pick up the tennis ball for an excited Jango, who waits ever-so-impatiently for me to throw it. This gives me a couple moments to consider if I'll answer Tara, and also to decide what I'll say.

"I used to think about her every day."

"And now?"

"Now it's not every day." I can't quantify it. I don't want to, but I realize that my thoughts of Susie aren't as insistent as they once were, nor are they as morbid. I've even started to think of funny things that she did, and when I think of the funny things, those thoughts aren't always tinged with grief. Sometimes I even smile. My thoughts of Tara are more numerous than my thoughts of Susie. It's a wholly new experience that I can barely admit to myself, so I'm definitely not telling Tara.

"Do you miss Garrison?"

She laughs. "I know you know his name." She turns away from me and we continue our walk up the beach. "But it's sweet that you still pretend you don't."

"Want to know what I really call him? In my brain?"

She shakes her head and wraps her arm through mine. She leans in. "But I appreciate the thought."

Jango drops the ball, and this time Tara throws the yellow-green orb into the waves. She looks at me. "The sad part is, I don't think about him much. I think more about what an idiot I was."

"You weren't an idiot."

"Yeah, I kind of was. I'm an investigative journalist and he was boning a co-worker. You'd think I would've sorted that out."

"Maybe it was the first time."

"Really?"

"Okay, definitely unlikely, but I wanted to give you an out."

She smiles at me, and a little laugh escapes from her mouth. "I know now, after a couple months, that what your sister said is right. Better to figure out now that he's a cheater than later. After a wedding and a couple kids. Then you're really stuck."

Did that cross Susie's mind? Is that what she was thinking?

"So yeah, I think my mother may have even forgiven me."

"Forgiven you?"

"It embarrassed her. The idea that her daughter called off a wedding. She's a very Bel Air Country Club sort of woman, you know. Substance isn't really something that matters so much. You hide things you dislike with a perfect smile, loads of money, closed doors, and scotch. Vats and vats of scotch." Tara stops and looks toward the ocean. "I think if she was me, she would've gone ahead and married him."

I stoop down and grab Jango's ball.

"I think a long time ago, maybe she did." Tara's eyes meet mine.

I lob the ball into the ocean. I don't have any judgment. It's a choice that a lot of women make. Some are content, some leave, some need a Wonderfuck and then stay in their faithless but cushy marriages. A number of couples create an entirely separate life, where the wife uses the husband's money and name without bothering about him.

"It's amazing what you sort out about your parents as you age," she says.

"No kidding."

Jango is back, but she's moving a little slower. She drops the ball at my feet and drops to the ground.

"No way! Jango? Did we wear you out?"

Her tongue lolls to the side and she pants, but she still seems to smile an entirely contented smile, as though this walk may have been the best walk of her doggy existence. Until the walk tomorrow, of course. She's a dog, they've got that live-in-the-moment thing down. Wish I did. Tara wraps her arms around herself. The wind has picked up and the sun set into the ocean long ago.

"Cold?"

She nods. I pull her into my arms. This is where she fits and where I want her to remain. We stare out toward the infinite sea. I lean back and look down at her. I press my lips to hers. A long warm luscious kiss. A kiss that says more than "I want to fuck." This kiss is meant to tell her that I care, and that if the facts of my life were different, if I wasn't so damaged and selfish and if all the pain that has brought me to this moment could dissolve, I would pick her. I try to put that all in one kiss.

I'm not sure if I succeed, but when we break apart, there's a look in her eyes that tells me she shares my feelings. If our lives were different, we might be able to spend a lifetime together making each other happy, walking on the beach, making prawns in garlic cream sauce and throwing a tennis ball into the Pacific Ocean as the sun fades.

I don't say all the things that cross through my mind, like "I don't want this to end," or "I wish things were different," or "I care for you, I really care for you" . . . I don't say any of it. Instead, I say, "We should get back."

"Yeah, we should."

I don't know for certain that the same thoughts go through

her mind in this moment, but her eyes seem to reflect my thoughts back to me.

We turn back toward the house and Jango trots beside us, no longer dancing at our feet and begging for one of us to throw her ball into the waves. No, we've worn her out. Now she's content to walk beside us and slowly plod her way home.

CHAPTER 28

THE AIR GROWS cool as the evening deepens. I start a fire in the fireplace in the bedroom. A wall of windows provides an ocean view from the bed, which is loaded with plush pillows and a fluffy duvet. I walk into the bathroom of white tile, silver faucets, and grey marble. Tara stands in front of the mirror, wearing only my shirt, unbuttoned.

"A shower," I say. My hands part the fabric of the shirt and I pull it down over her shoulders. My lips stroke down her neck. She reaches out and grasps my cock.

My God, yes.

I can fuck her over and over again. We just finished and napped, and now, I'm hard. I can't imagine my body growing tired of hers. Still kissing her, I reach into the shower and turn on the four shower heads. Steam rises around us. I pull my lips from her neck and look at her naked body. A flush hovers on her cheeks. Her nipples are erect.

Grasping her hand, I step into the shower and lead her in. The warm water flows down her body like art, accenting curves that already steal the breath from my lungs. I reach for the soap and I turn her back toward me. Gently, carefully, I begin at the nape of her neck and run the soap down the curve of her neck. My hands caress her shoulders.

Her breathing shifts, because we are close, we are naked, and we want nothing but each other. My smooth touch over her slick flesh that I know so well, after so many times together. I press my fingers into the dimples of her back, right above her ass and her hips. Like I've hit a button that commands arousal, she shifts forward, her ass arches back, and her head tilts ever so slightly toward me.

She is as responsive as she is beautiful. Water washes the bits of soap from her flesh and my lips press to the spot where her shoulder meets her neck.

"Oh, yes, yes," she whispers.

I take her hand, cup it with mine, and slowly move her fingertips to her sex. She gasps. I press her finger, beneath mine, to her clit.

"I want to watch you make yourself feel good."

She moans. She pulses her finger over her sex while my hand guides her.

My cock throbs. I look over her shoulder, her taut, tight nipples, and the soft curve of her belly to where our hands are connected as I guide her fingertips over her sex.

Her moans grow more insistent. I move my cock up between her legs, and while she touches herself, her ass presses back, seeking my cock.

Fuck yes. A deep need tears through my body. Her ass shifts back toward me. "Please," she whispers, "please fuck me."

I can't stand it. I can't stop myself—I don't want to stop myself. I thrust my cock up and into her sex. Her fingertips pull away from her clit, but I press them back into place.

"Oh, my God," she moans. If she keeps touching herself she won't last, can't last. I can't last either. All I want is to fuck this woman, fuck her for the rest of my life.

"Please, oh my God, Jake, I'm going to come, oh my God, I'm going to come!"

Heat flashes hard and tight through my body. My balls tighten. I pull back and thrust deep into her body.

"Yes," she shrieks. Her sex tightens around me. Fuck. this hasn't felt so good, I haven't . . .

"Fuck, Tara, fuck yes." I yell, and my throbbing cock spurts into her.

I fall forward, my hand against the wall of the shower, my legs barely able to support my weight.

The water rinses over us. I wrap Tara in my arms. I press my lips to hers. Through the water, I taste the salt of tears, and I'm unsure if they're hers or mine.

❧

THE PHONE RINGS AT 5:58 A.M. NOT MY WONDERFUCK phone, but my real phone. My stomach pitches forward. The people in my life that I love are few, and I desperately need every each of them.

Rachel.

There are a handful of reasons why Rachel would call me at six a.m. on a Saturday when she knows I'm out of town, and none of those reasons are good. I glance toward Tara, who appears to be sleeping. I slip from the bed and walk into the bathroom.

"What's up?" I say.

"It's Mom."

"Okay, what happened?"

"She's gone."

My heart plunges in my chest and I sag against the wall. "Wait, how? When? I don—"

"No . . . no . . . I don't mean gone as in 'dead' gone. I'm sorry . . ." Rachel sighs, and then I hear in her voice the tiniest hint that she's crying. "I mean gone as in 'we can't find her' gone."

"Wait? What? Since when?"

"Since I'm not sure. Sylvia isn't sure either. She . . . she turned off the alarm and she's gone. Her purse is here, and the car is here, but her shoes and a jacket are gone and—"

"And nobody knows what time?'

"Could've been as early as just after midnight or as late as five a.m. Sylvia put her in bed at nine. Checked on her at midnight and then went to bed."

"No ID?"

"No ID."

"Fuck." I circle the bathroom. "I'm on my way . . . I—"

"You don't have to come. The police are on their way, and I can—"

"Are you kidding? No way you go through this alone. I'll be there." I'm in Malibu. Mom's house is on the Westside. It's Saturday at six am. "I can be there in about forty-five minutes. Maybe less."

"Okay." Relief weaves through Rachel's voice. She was there for me with Susie, and I was there for her with Dickface, and we'll be there for each other with Mom. It's simply how this works. She and I and the family tragedies we endure.

I press off on my phone and scrub my hand through my hair. My face, rough with stubble, is reflected in the mirror. Through the open door, I can see Tara in the bedroom, illuminated with the light of dawn. She's nestled beneath blankets. Her skin soft and warm, her scent enough to harden my cock. I want to walk through the door, lift the covers, and slide into the sheets beside her. Awaken her with a kiss. Slide my cock deep into her body and let physical pleasure drive out the thoughts in my head and the reality waiting for me.

But I can't.

I turn on the shower. I close the bathroom door. I don't even trust myself to tell her that I have to leave until I'm ready to go, because her pull over me is that strong. If I walk into the bedroom and feel the warmth of her close to me, in minutes, I'll be back in bed fucking her.

❧

"OH MY GOD." TARA COVERS HER MOUTH WITH HER fingertips. Her eyes widen and she looks . . . well, she looks how I feel. She looks scared.

"Go," she says. "Go, and please let me know if there's anything that I can do or if I can help."

I pause. I want to say, yes, come with me. Be there. Help me look for my mom. If you're with me it'll make this easier. But I don't say any of it. Instead, I lean forward and I press my lips to her forehead. The wisest choice I've made in a long while is showering and dressing before telling Tara, because otherwise, I'm selfish enough that I'd be back in bed with her. I'm fighting the urge even now. I pull back and look into her eyes. Those bright blue eyes with flecks of gray. Those all-seeing eyes that gaze much deeper into me than I want anyone to see.

"I . . ." I can't find the right words. I don't know what to say to her. This . . . this is our final time together. Instead of speaking, I press my lips to hers. Soft. Warm. Perfect. I remain in that kiss for as long as I can, and then I pull away.

"I have to go," I say.

She nods. She pulls the blanket tighter around her body, up beneath her chin. I've already told her that I need to go on my own, and she's respecting my words, even though my words, what I've said to her, are different than how I feel and what I want.

CHAPTER 29

THERE ARE two cop cars parked in front of Mom's house. Judges get a response. I walk into the living room. Both cops stand across from my sister. They eye me, and she continues describing the layout of the house. Really, the only way Mom could've left is the front door. The back gate has a combination lock she doesn't know the code for, and the windows are too high off the ground.

"This is my brother, Jake." Worry etches Rachel's face. Both cops look at me the way cops do. Sizing me up.

The older one, with silver hair and a lean build, rolls forward on his feet and turns his gaze back to my sister. "We're going to start in the neighborhood and circle. Already contacted local fire departments and hospitals. We think she took off around four this morning."

"Why four?" I ask.

"She made coffee," Rachel says. "And that coffeemaker always shows when the pot brewed."

"What can we do?"

"One of you needs to stay here," says the red-headed younger cop, who barely looks older than twenty.

"Sylvia is already walking the neighborhood," Rachel says. "She feels awful."

Well, of course she does. She lost our mother.

"Anyplace she might want to go? Anything today she might want to see?"

"YOU TOLD THEM ABOUT THE ALZHEIMER'S?"

Rachel nods and rubs her hands together.

"We'll check back. If you find her, let us know." The older cop hands my sister a card. They leave. Rachel's mood has shifted. She turns her back to me and walks into the kitchen. I know better than to follow, but I follow anyway.

"Where's Lily?"

"Asleep upstairs." Rachel doesn't look at me. She dumps out the old coffee and starts to make fresh. Her actions are fast and concise, and I know just by how her gaze won't meet mine what she's thinking.

"This could've happened anywhere," I say.

"But it didn't," she says, "this happened here and it happened on our watch."

"Our watch?"

"What the hell, Jake? Who do you think is in charge of keeping Mom alive? It's not Sylvia."

I cross my arms over my chest.

"Oh wait, do you think it's me?" She taps her hand on her chest. "Alone? Do you think Mom is all my responsibility?" She slams the lid on the coffee tin and puts it on the shelf. "Because you sure as hell act like it is." She pushes the button on the coffeepot. "You get a pass on nearly everything, but I'm not giving you a pass on this one. She's your mom too."

Heat fires in my chest and unkind, unpleasant words form in my brain. "You're so used to making decisions about everyone's life you can't stand that I won't let you throw Mom in a home."

"Throw Mom in a home? What the fuck? Jake, she's missing.

Mom is out there, on the streets, and she doesn't even know her first name. This is Los Angeles. She could die."

I have nothing to say. If I'm really honest, the anger isn't just because Rachel is right. Fuck, I hate it when she's right. The anger is because I don't want Mom in a place like that. I can't stand the idea of Mom rotting away in some room. I turn and storm out of the kitchen. Rachel follows me, hot on my heels.

"Where are you going?"

"To find Mom." I slam the front door. On the front step, I pause and look at the neighborhood I grew up in. Birds chirp at the early daylight, flowers line driveways, green lawns stretch from home to street. This place wasn't perfect, but damn, it was close. And whatever shit my parents went through they mostly hid, because even when they were separated because Dad was fucking around, it mostly felt like he was only away on business.

I walk down the front steps to the street. Damn, Mom loved Dad. Loved him even when she must have hated him. I close my eyes for an instant and let the pain of what happened between me and Susie wash through me. To my right, three houses down, is where Susie grew up. I glance toward the house. Her parents are still there. Her mother blames me for Susie's death—she's laid that tragedy squarely at my feet. Does she take any pleasure in what's happening to me now?

I TURN ONTO VETERANS AND CRUISE ALONG SLOWLY, scanning the sidewalk for a woman, mid-sixties, who may or may not be wearing a jacket. Mom left her pajamas on her bed, neatly folded per her usual, but none of us are certain what she's wearing.

Would it be possible that Mom's neurons are firing on a level that she might remember . . . or somehow think . . . what the hell. I cut across Sunset and onto Stone Canyon. A few minutes later I pull to a stop and hand the valet my keys. I walk across the grounds of The Bel Air Hotel to the spot where Dad and Mom got married, the same place where Susie and I, this day six years ago, were meant to take our vows. Nothing. Not one person. I turn back to head across the grounds toward the front entrance and that's when I see Mom. She's wearing a dress and pants. An odd combination, but one that definitely kept her warm early this morning. No jacket, but a navy fleece-lined sweater that used to be Dad's.

My heart sinks with the knowledge that Rachel is right. Mom may need more care than she can get at home.

"Richard!" Her eyes light up. A smile curves over her face, and I love that even if I'm not Richard, the idea of seeing Dad gives Mom this much pleasure.

"Hi Mom." I walk to her and put my arm through hers. "Where are you off to? You know I like it best when we go together."

"But I didn't want to be late. The wedding is today, isn't it?"

I sink to the bench by her side. Some foggy misty place in her brain thinks I'm Dad, but also remembers that I was meant to get married, here and on this date, six years ago.

This fucking disease.

"It . . . it doesn't start until much later today," I say. My throat tightens, and it feels like an elephant sits on my chest.

That weight is the recognition that Mom will never be okay and that I can't avoid this place, or this day that I pretend is a non-day, because Mom, who is losing her mind, believes that we're sitting here waiting for me to get married. The day that was supposed to be the beginning of my life, but it's really a terrifically sad day that only recalls the end of Susie's life.

"I've seen Susie's dress." Mom leans over and smiles. "She's such a beautiful girl."

My heart cracks. I swallow and nod. I start to stand, but Mom grasps my arm and pulls me back down beside her. "I'm worried about her. She seems . . ."Mom sighs and weighs her words. "So fragile. So . . . so unable to cope with the world."

Mom's words freeze me to the spot.

"Betty says Susie is seeing a therapist"—Mom whispers the word—"about her problem and that Jake knows, but"—concern, perhaps even fear wander through Mom's eyes—"I don't know, Richard, life is so hard without layering an addiction on top of a marriage. Can you even call it that? I mean that's what Betty calls it, and Jake? What does Jake think? Have you spoken to him about it?"

I clear my throat. Dad never spoke to me, and I wonder if this conversation, the one that Mom is now having with me, ever did take place between her and Dad. She waits for my response. Her whole world right now hinges on what I, as my dead father, will say.

"Jake loves Susie very much." I squeeze Mom's arm. "Love goes a long way."

The fear slides from Mom's eyes and a peaceful smile lights her face. While my heart is breaking, I feel a bit of happiness at the idea that in my Mom's mind, all will be well. That later today, I will marry Susie, because I love her so deeply and together, because my dead father has said so, Susie and I will live happily ever after.

I love that this reality exists for someone, if only for an instant, in a misfiring mind.

"Oh my God, Mom!" Rachel meets us at the door with Sylvia and the two cops. The officers listen to what I tell them, mumble a few things to my sis, Judge Reynolds, and then both leave. Mom sits on the sofa near the sliders.

"Mom, you scared me to death." Rachel stands above our mother with her arms folded across her chest.

Mom looks past Rachel and leans toward me. "Who is this woman that keeps calling me Mom?"

"She doesn't know who I am, right?" Rachel, who is usually

MAGGIE MARR

so diplomatic and all about doing exactly what the doctors tell us to do for Mom, is at the end of her patience. This moment doesn't come often for big sis, but when it does, it comes for her hard.

Sylvia helps Mom to her feet and leads her toward the staircase. It seems we've both agreed to pretend we aren't irritated with each other and didn't argue before I left. Fine. She's my sister. I've played this game before.

"She was at The Bel Air Hotel? Where you and Susie were supposed to get married?"

"The entire thing is creepily weird, especially when you throw in today's date."

"Oh my God"—Rachel covers her mouth with her hand—"that's right. Do you think some part of her brain remembers?"

"Who knows? When I got there, she said she was afraid she'd be late for the wedding."

I walk through the house to the kitchen, hoping there's still coffee. Fatigue permeates my body. I haven't slept much. Last night was filled with things I prefer over sleep. I reach up into the cabinet and pull out a coffee mug. This one has a picture of my face from second grade on the side.

"You were such a cute kid," Rachel says. I'm uncertain if her comment is an attempt at an apology or if she's trying to soften me up for the conversation I know is coming. I pour coffee into my mug.

"This isn't working for me," Rachel begins. "And more importantly, it isn't working for Mom."

"This hasn't happened before." I face my sister who sits at the table. Dark rings beneath her eyes.

"But it could happen again."

"We'll childproof the front door. Put a different alarm on it."

"It's not just about her getting out, it's about her safety and her—"

"We'll hire another person."

180

"Jake, she's not getting the necessary mental stimulation."

"She can have two people here."

"You're not hearing me."

"Oh, I'm hearing you, I'm just surprised at what I'm hearing. You want to dump Mom in a nursing home so life is easier for you."

Rachel sits back in her chair and stares at the placemat on the table in front of her. She takes a deep breath, clasps her hands, and looks up at me. She's trying to remain calm, collect her thoughts, and lay out her evidence as to why Mom should be locked up in a facility.

But I'm the younger brother.

I know how to dig.

I let her start talking.

"No, Jake"—her voice sounds as though she's speaking to Lily's peer group—"what I want is a place that meets the specialized needs of Alzheimer's patients. A place that can give Mom the stimulation and protection that is necessary to enhance her life to the greatest degree while she remains alive. I want her to have a full life, on her terms, and I don't believe that's happening here."

I smirk. I cross my arms. I'm suddenly fifteen. "That's bullshit, Rachel, you're just tired of coming over here every damn day and you don't want to feel guilty anymore about the days you miss."

She swallows. I've struck a nerve and I know it. I'm her little brother, and I'm an asshole. Rachel couldn't be more dedicated to family if she were fucking Lassie. And I know how thin she's stretched and how hard she tries and how her biggest fear is she isn't doing enough for her family.

And what did I just do?

Told her she wasn't doing enough for Mom, that she was putting her own needs above Mom's. And I made her feel guilty for it.

"I . . ." She sighs, not an exasperated sigh, but the kind that comes before tears. "Jake," she nearly whispers, "I can't do any more than I'm doing now."

"Right? Like you believe that. Like I believe that."

Fuck or fight. Fuck or fight. These are the only ways I cope. My face is sullen. I direct my dead-eyed gaze toward Rachel, knowing that in this moment I'm killing her. Tearing her up on the inside. Knowing that I am a complete and utter asshole. Knowing that I'm the guy she turns to because there is no one else left, and now, I am being a bigger asshole to my big sis than any other guy has ever been.

"You're being a dick."

I have to give big sis credit, because when we were kids, she'd be up on her feet and screaming in my face by now. Instead she sits at the table, her face ashen, her hands clasped, and while she may want to scream, she may even want to beat the shit out of me, she's not. She's calm. She's cool. She's collected. And she's everything I don't want to be right now.

"And you're a selfish bitch."

"Mama?"

My heart drops to my toes. What the fuck did I just do? I turn to the doorway between the kitchen and the dining room.

Lily stands just inside the door, wearing her fuzzy unicorn pajamas, carrying Mr. Wooby Bear in one hand. Her round sleepy-eyed face stares at me.

Did she . . . oh my God . . . did she . . .?

"What is it doll-baby?" Rachel says with a pretend-lilt in her voice, as only mothers can do. I've just said the most unkind things to my sister, possibly in front of my niece, and there she is, my big sis, putting aside her own pain, her own fear, her own anger, anything that is her own feelings, so that she can help Lily. And she does it like every other woman, effortlessly, without thought. She does it for her daughter, even for me, and always for Mom.

She isn't a selfish bitch, I'm a selfish asshole. But that isn't a newsflash.

Rachel lifts Lily into her arms and cuddles her. Swings her gently from side to side in a way that comes encoded on that extra X chromosome. Lily's big blue eyes regard me almost as though I'm a stranger. Leery of who I am. She may not understand exactly what I said, but she can feel the charge in the air, the energy, the anger, the contempt, all the things I've directed at Rachel.

I start to reach out to place my fingers on Lily's cheek, but I pause. She turns her head away from me. Doesn't face me. Doesn't look at me.

A knife slams through my heart.

Fuck.

I turn, and without another word to Rachel or to Lily, through the house and out the door I go.

CHAPTER 30

I PULL into my parking space, turn off the car, and look across the garage. The parking spot that usually houses Tara's blue convertible is empty. I don't want to see her now. I don't want to answer questions about Mom. Discuss the imminent upheaval. I can resist and rage now, but finding Mom today makes this real for me. She'll need a safe place. I don't want the pain of moving Mom, the pain of sifting through my childhood, nor do I want the pain of thinking about or seeing Tara. I just don't want the pain. I don't want the inevitable pain that will course through my body and lodge in my chest the next time I see Tara. The ache because I'll want to touch her, and kiss her, and fuck her, but won't be able to.

Our time together is finished. Done.

I exit my car and climb onto the elevator. My Wonderfuck phone vibrates and I pull it from my pocket.

How's your mom?

I start to respond and then pause, second guessing myself. But I then realize that with the emergency I just faced, I would've left no matter which woman I was with. Any woman might've texted me this question.

Better.

I respond as Wonderfuck, not Jake. Concise. To the point. Because Wonderfuck is who I was when I was with Tara . . . wasn't it?

Actually no, but if I keep saying it to myself, maybe I'll start believing it. I take the elevator up, avoid looking toward Tara's door, and open the door to my condo. I look through the house to the balcony, the view, and like every time I enter, I see Susie. I see Susie as I did that night, that night six years and six weeks ago.

She stood on the balcony, but she wasn't facing the view. She faced the front door. She was waiting for me. Expecting me.

I smiled at her, like I always did when I saw her face, and she smiled back. It was the final time I saw her smile.

She stepped onto a table that used to be on the balcony, before I got rid of everything on the balcony, before I locked the door and never went out there again.

The moment lasted a lifetime. Slowly, so slowly, she stood on the table and looked at me. Our eyes locked and then . . . and then she leaned backward, her eyes, her blue eyes, still focused on me, and she was gone.

My throat tightens. My heartbeat is unbearably fast. Why am I reliving this memory now?

I . . . I was . . . unable to move, I . . . didn't know what had happened, was I awake? The thought, the idea, my mind couldn't process what my eyes had seen. Was I asleep? Was I trapped in some nightmare? A jolt of adrenaline and I was out onto the balcony, looking over the edge, hearing car alarms and, in the distance, sirens. I dropped to my knees. My breath stalled in my chest. I still don't know what prevented me from following her over the edge and onto the pavement below. I turn away from the view, the balcony, the past. I turn away, walk out of my front door, and leave my condo behind.

CHAPTER 31

I DRIVE. I drive without a destination. Without a purpose. Air whips through the open car windows. Suddenly I know where I'm headed.

The scent of salt. The Pacific Coast Highway. The wash of the sunset as the sun sinks into the ocean. One possible destination. The place I need to be.

I pull onto the drive, and the blue convertible is still parked where it was when I left. I knock. No answer. I turn the doorknob. I look straight through the house, like I can at my condo, but the view is impossibly different. Past the wall of windows is not a view of cityscape, but instead the ocean and the sun with violent magenta and orange slicing the sky, and Tara.

She stands on the deck in a white sweater, her arms wrapped around her torso for warmth. She watches the sun setting, because who passes up this kind of light show?

From a distance, I watch too, but the beautiful display I watch isn't the sinking of the sun, it's Tara. A gentle wind lifts her hair and the light accentuates her profile, the curve of her neck, her full lips. Tara's beauty eclipses the sunset.

When the sun slips into the sea, she turns to the sliders, and her eyes meet mine. Surprise in her gaze, followed by the type of smile you want to come home to, return to, see each and every day. The kind of smile that you can build a life around.

The type of smile I need to see.

"YOU CAME BACK."

I press my hand to her cheek. The pad of my thumb strokes her bottom lip and she tilts her head toward my touch.

"I did."

I came back as more than Wonderfuck, and she knows this. She knows, without me saying the words, that I'm here because I couldn't stay away from her. Because I needed more time with her. I needed her. I need tonight like I need air to breathe.

She knows this.

But what she doesn't know, the part that is unfair and that I won't tell her, is that I absolutely won't stay.

WE MAKE LOVE. WE DON'T SIMPLY FUCK, AND AFTER, as I lay with Tara in my arms, I realize that we've never just fucked. Not even the first time. I slip from her bed. The sun is rising. I put on my clothes.

"Leaving?"

"Not yet," I say. I lean down and press my lips to her lips.

She knows that there are unspoken words hanging in the air. I turn and walk to the kitchen and make coffee. It's not long before she enters with her hair wet. She wears an oversized white sweater, sweatpants, and fuzzy socks. She looks sexy because she isn't trying to look sexy. I pour her a cup of coffee and she follows me into the living room, where I've already started a fire.

We sit on a big white couch in front of the fireplace.

"Don't go." Her feet are curled under her. I fight the urge to pull her close and hold her in my arms. I want to stay with her for today and tomorrow and quite possibly forever.

"I can't stay."

"But you can." She sweeps her hand over her forehead. "Nothing prevents you from staying. From us being together, from us trying . . . why not?"

I look toward the wall of windows, at the deck, the ocean beyond, and the grey sky that hangs heavy with the clouds of June gloom. If the decision to stay were only that simple. But that decision, that risk, isn't easy for me, and won't ever be.

"Look"—she sighs and then takes a deep breath, as though steeling herself for the words she's about to say—"I know what happened." She closes her eyes and pulls in another deep breath, then opens them and peers at me. "Or I heard what happened, before I moved in . . . but . . . I trust you. I know even with this . . . this thing that you do . . . I know that you won't do that to me. That what happened between you and . . ."

I freeze. My heart stops beating for an instant. Her words have trailed away. She thinks she knows, but she has no idea.

"What do you *think* happened between me and Susie?"

Her jaw drops open, her gaze fixed onto me. She must feel this abyss that is opening in my chest, know the horrible feeling that she may have made the wrong assumption based on the look on my face and my tone. The most horrible error, and yet, the same error almost all people make. I don't disabuse them of what they believe to be true. Why bother?

"I . . . I mean . . ."—she swallows—"At first I didn't know . . . but then when I discovered this alter ego thing and all the women . . . and the way . . . how she died. I . . . I . . . I thought—"

"You thought that I was fucking around."

My voice is dead. Empty. I'm not angry. I'm not hurt. I'm not even surprised. Because this is what nearly everyone believes to be the truth about the tragedy of my life. Even Susie's family and friends believe that I must have been unfaithful. That I did something horrible, unforgivable, something that caused Susie's death.

But that's not what happened.

It's completely not.

"I didn't fuck around on Susie." My tone is devoid of feeling, because once your heart is ripped from your chest, how could you ever possibly feel?

Only Rachel knows the truth. Rachel and me and Mom—when her memory still fired—and Mom only because she overheard us. I've never had the heart to tell anyone else what happened between Susie and me. Never wanted to before now. Never felt the need. And even now, when I want to tell Tara the truth, somehow telling her, letting Tara know what happened, feels like a betrayal of the woman I loved.

"She . . . she had an addiction." My heart folds in on itself. "I found out. She went to see a therapist, because I loved her and she loved me and there'd been . . . there'd been over a hundred other men."

"Oh my God." Tara can barely breathe. She can barely understand the words I'm saying. In her eyes, the truth of what I'm saying fights with the fiction she's constructed in her mind and labeled as the truth.

"It's a disease. Like drug addiction, alcoholism, overeating—it's a disease and I wanted her to recover, but she relapsed. I was away on business, just before our wedding. I was in Japan and she relapsed and she told me. I was hurt and I was angry, but I never said we were over. But I think seeing how hurt I was, and knowing that I'd never let her go, that I'd always be there for her, that I loved her . . . with this fierce and undying love, knowing that . . . I think that's why she did what she did."

I stop speaking. Every word is true. I have Susie's letter. Part of me wants to burn the paper that has the words that Susie left me, another part can never let that letter go.

"I . . . I had no idea."

"You wouldn't," I say.

There was nothing I could've done to cure Susie, to fix her. I could no more stop her from being who she was than stop the waves from kissing the shore. This is the truth of my reality and the loneliness of my existence, and as close as Tara got to breaching the wall I've built around my life, I still can't let Tara into my heart, because that mind-numbing, soul-searing pain of loss and deception and impotence is beyond my capability to survive a second time.

"I'm sorry." I stand.

She stands beside me. She dips her head and then looks back up at me. She swallows. In her eyes is the reflection of my pain.

"I'm . . . I'm sorry . . . I—" I know she wouldn't intentionally hurt me. No, that's not in Tara's makeup. "Please . . . I just . . . my feelings for you are—"

"I know." I press my fingertips beneath her chin. "I have them too, for you."

The sadness in her eyes at my admission is nearly too much for me to endure. Instead of feeling the pain, I do what comes naturally for me now, I do what makes the pain go away. I lean forward and kiss her.

This is the time that will remain in my memory alongside my other times with Tara. This time has the sweet melancholy that whispers between two people when their love affair comes to an end.

"Please," she says, a whisper on her lips, and I comply. In this open living room with the waves dancing on the shore, I lower her back onto the couch and lift her sweater up and over her head. My hand grasps her breast and my mouth, hungry for the taste of her, pulls in her rosebud nipple.

A soft moan. I roll her nipple over my tongue, and my hand slides over her belly to yank at her sweatpants. Hot and sexual and bathed in a desire for each other, we are fierce and full of need. I pull her sweatpants over her hips. I release her nipple and run my lips down the hot flesh of her nearly naked body. I'm between her legs, and she's wet. Her desire is glorious and glistening. I spread her thighs with my hands and lean forward to pull her clit into my mouth.

Her hips tilt upward and her hands grasp my hair and pull. With my tongue I lick out the same letters I've spelled since the first time we were together, but this time, I add three more words.

"Please, please." She pulls me up to her. "I want you inside me."

I pull my pants down over my hips. This desire is a living thing deep inside me. This isn't wonderfucking anymore, this isn't a random woman I'll shuffle into my memory with all the rest. This is Tara. I'll remember her for the rest of my life. She'll be the redemption that I turned my back on, because in my soul I know I'm far too damaged for even love to redeem.

She grasps my cock and strokes down and back up along my shaft. The heat tightens and darkens. It curls through my feet and up over my calves and thighs. Desire thickens in my back. Her beautiful body is before me, her face, her eyes. I lean forward and press her to the couch. In one slow, strong, stroke, I am deep inside her sex.

Bliss. Complete and utter bliss.

Only Tara. Her mouth opens and a moan slips from her lips. She grasps my ass and pulls me deeper into her body. I thrust and pull back.

Yes, oh yes.

Her bottom lips pulls beneath her top teeth and I know she's close. I lean forward and kiss her. My mouth opening her mouth. My tongue sweeping and teasing and taunting.

"Please, Jake, please," she whispers, and I'm lost.

Consumed with my need and my pleasure, I slide in and out of her body. With each stroke, her sex tightens around my shaft. Pleasure erupts, and I come hard and fast.

A roar, deep and guttural, filled with loss and want and desire and need, rips through my throat and out of my body, and I know. I know in this instant that I've fallen in love.

Tara's body trembles beneath mine. Finally, after we've lain there for moments that seem like hours, and my heart has stilled, and my breath is caught, I look at her and I kiss her with a deep softness. I pull myself from her body. Then without another word, without looking back, I leave her alone in the afterglow of our sex.

Without even saying good-bye.

❧

I CAN'T GO HOME. I CAN'T GO ANYWHERE THAT belongs to my heart, because my heart is dead. Shredded. I thought my heart was ripped out of my chest when Susie died, but I was wrong.

My heart died on what was meant to be my six-year anniversary. My heart died when Lily looked at me with a mixture of sadness and fear. My heart disintegrated when I left Tara, alone, and in tears.

Jake is dead.

Only Wonderfuck remains.

So I go to Wonderfuck's favorite home.

I go to The London. I walk past Pierre, the concierge who knows me, knows the room that is mine. I haven't texted him details about a woman, I haven't made my usual requests, I haven't done any of the things I normally do when I'm wonderfucking.

I walk into my suite and faces flash through my mind. Faces with names that have been a balm on my wound for the last five and a half years. Six months of mourning Susie, and then the resurrection of me. Rebuilt as someone else entirely. Rebuilt into a man who only wants to give and receive pleasure.

There isn't anything left but Wonderfuck.

I stare out the window at Los Angeles, at the city that has forever been my home. Can I permanently say good-bye to Jake? Could I walk away from Mom, from Rachel, from Lily? Would their lives be better without me in them? Let Rachel do what she does best, which is lead the family and make plans, without my interference.

I can't see Tara again.

I text my realtor. I don't want to go back to the condo.

My Wonderfuck phone vibrates. I've been ignoring its beeps and buzzes for weeks now. I press the "off" button and lay it on the table beside the bed. I take off my clothes, I shower, I crawl between the covers, and I sleep. I sleep the sleep of the dead.

CHAPTER 32

"YOU ARE A COMPLETE ASSHOLE."

I rub my chopsticks together and place them on the soy sauce dish. Our server hands me a hot washcloth. I wipe my hands and hand it back.

"I said I was sorry."

"Don't be pedantic. You know this'll take more than one pathetic 'I'm sorry.'"

"How's Lily?"

"Confused. She wants to talk to you, but I told her you were away on business."

"That doesn't seem fair."

"What was I supposed to tell her? That you're an asshole who called me a bitch and then disappeared?"

Ouch. I deserved that. And more.

"I texted."

"Only because I threatened to call the police if you didn't respond." Rachel pours soy sauce into her dish. "She's my daughter, and if I'm too angry to talk to you then I'm not letting Lily talk to you. I'm not that good of an actor. Better we get past this and then when we're hunky-dory, you can come back from your business trip."

We order, and once our server leaves I look at Rachel. She's tired, but per her usual, looking as though she can hold everything together by sheer force of will.

"You're the only male role model in Lily's life. You don't get to act like an ass to me or to Mom in front of Lily. Is that rule clear?"

"It wasn't intentional."

"Being an asshole to me or doing it in front of Lily?"

"The second one."

"Right. Okay, fair enough. Adults disagree and I'm okay with that, but Jake, you really went in hard, and only because you didn't want to hear what I had to say."

She's right, and while I generally hate it when big-sister-Rachel is right and little- brother-me is wrong, in this case she is exceedingly right. I've had two weeks to cool off, and I've actually begun to miss my big sister and my niece. I don't tell her I've been to see Mom. Because I'm betting she knows.

"I'm sorry," I say again, making no excuses for my behavior. "I'll try to do better." It's the second sentence that thaws Rachel. I actually see the beginning of a smile laced with kindness.

"Thank you for the apology."

And I know I'm forgiven. She could make me pay for my mistake, but that's not who Rachel is as a human or as a judge. Not as a mother, a sister, or a daughter. She's all about trying to build kindness and being empathetic.

The server drops our drinks and edamame at the table.

"Now why is your place for sale?"

I pluck an edamame pod from the bowl between us. "Because I can't live there any longer."

"You didn't want to leave before."

"And now it's different."

"Is it your neighbor? The one you were dating?

"We weren't dating."

"Okay, fucking. The one you were fucking."

I toss the empty pod into the other bowl. "It's more than

that." I tell her about going home and reliving the moment Susie jumped from the balcony. "I haven't been back. I don't want to go back."

"Where've you been staying?"

I don't want to tell her, because telling her makes my other life seem too close.

"A hotel." I leave out the details and she doesn't ask.

Two platters of sushi arrive. I lift a piece of yellowtail with my chopsticks and place it on my plate.

"We need to discuss Mom." Rachel wears her serious I'm-a-judge face that tells people they better listen the fuck up. "Things aren't getting better, and her doctor wants her to go into an assisted living facility. She recommended a specific one for Mom."

I lean back in my chair. I'm not winning this battle, unless a miracle Alzheimer's cure appears on the scene.

"They don't have a spot for Mom right now, but they want us to come and look at it, and I want you to go with me."

"That sounds like hell."

"It's not what I want either. I can make all these decisions alone, but it's not fair, okay? I know part of you wants me to just do it, all of it, but then I'm the one who has to live with the decisions when you come and tell me I've made them all wrong. I'm not good with that. I'm not putting her in a place unless we both agree on it. It's simple as that."

Rachel is right. I'd absolutely prefer for her to make the decisions about Mom and where Mom goes, but she's also right that forcing her make all the decisions isn't fair.

"Set it up. I'll be there.'

Rachel nods and dips a piece of sushi into the soy sauce. "Now what's going on with the neighbor? Why is her place on the market too?"

My heart stalls. I look up from the piece of sashimi I just picked up. "What're you talking about?"

"You didn't know?"

"I haven't been back since that night . . . the night when . . ." I pause, because Rachel doesn't know everything about that night. About how I'd gone back to Malibu to see Tara and then left her crying on the couch. "I didn't know. Haven't talked to her."

"Are you okay?" She squints at me. "You look . . . I don't know, a little sick?"

I feel sick. My chest is tight and my stomach is sour. "Yeah. No. I don't know." The idea of not knowing where Tara lives . . . that throws me. I keep picturing her in her bedroom, with her laptop and Jango, and this fantasy I've created about what her life will continue to be, whether I'm in it or not, has just been smashed by the reality that soon I won't even know where Tara lives.

Rachel checks her phone. "Shit. I didn't realize how late it is. I have to get Lily from violin." She stands. "Next weekend. I'll send you the details. And call Lily. Later today. Come by tomorrow to see her."

I nod. Rachel waves and leaves. I pay for lunch, get in my car and drive to the place I used to call home.

"SHE PUT IT ON THE MARKET TWO DAYS AFTER YOURS," Dell says and hands me my mail. "I been forwarding this to your sister's like you asked, but these came yesterday."

"Thanks. You don't know where she's moving to?"

"No idea, but unlike you, she's still living here."

I turn to the elevator and ride up to the place I didn't want to ever see again, but now need to. I knock on Tara's door.

Jango doesn't bark.

They aren't here, Tara and Jango. Malibu? I don't know. She hasn't texted me and I haven't texted her. I've picked up my phone a million times to text or call, but each time I stop. Denial works until it doesn't, and based on the chasm in my chest, denial isn't working any longer.

My Wonderfuck phone vibrates. I pull it from my pocket.

Want to play?

Do I want to play? No, not really, not with any woman but Tara, but the text is from a number I haven't seen in weeks, one that makes me feel more normal than I've felt since the night I left Tara in Malibu. Yeah, this is what I need to get back on track. I need to wonderfuck and there isn't a better person to do it with, except Tara.

I shake that thought from my mind.

The woman on the other end of this text is just the woman to bring back Wonderfuck.

You know I do.

She sends back:

:) Tomorrow. 9 pm. My place. Be ready to Rock. My. World.

I'm not ready now, but my cock hasn't ever failed me, so I'll be ready to wonderfuck by then.

CHAPTER 33

"Darlin', did you think about my offer?"

Cheryl stands across the living room. She wears a light pink negligee beneath an open silk robe. I walk toward her. My cock stirs. A smile curls over my lips. Thank God. All I need is a wonderfuck. Good, hard, physical fucking. Sex can cure anything. It can definitely cure my need for Tara.

"I have." I stand in front of Cheryl now. Her lush lips will look good around my cock. I glance down at her firm round tits and her nipples grow hard beneath my gaze.

"And?" Her voice is a breathless purr. Desire rolls off of her. The scent of lust mixed with Chanel No. 5. She's just returned from Asia and I've just returned from my emotional abyss at The London. We're a perfect pair.

"And?"

"And I could be persuaded."

A smile simmers over her face. She reaches out and brushes her fingertips across the denim over my cock. I respond, like I always respond to Cheryl. My dick gets hard.

"Missed me?"

"Always."

"Ready to play?" she whispers.

Am I? I wasn't sure before now . . . I've never been unsure about wonderfucking Cheryl before. Her lush hair and curves are enough to send my cock into overdrive. She opens her robe and drops it to the floor.

Gorgeous.

Stunning.

Her curves are full, and desire rolls off her in an intoxicating mix. My cock responds. He's well trained and knows what's meant to come next.

"I've missed you." Her hand reaches up and the pad of her pointer finger presses to my lips. Then that long fingernail traces down over my chin and neck, down my chest, over my abs, making a long trail to my pants. She keeps going until her hand meets my hard maleness.

"Seems you've missed me too." Her hands unbutton and unzip my pants. I close my eyes, ready for the physical pleasure that will make my mind stop spinning thoughts of Tara. She strokes my sex, her touch strong and able. Up and down my shaft.

Pleasure. Pure physical pleasure.

Her lust-filled eyes look at me as she sinks to her knees before my cock. Every man's fantasy made real. I know what Cheryl likes. She wants me to be strong with her, to order her, to command her. She wants to be fucked hard and rough and fast. She likes to be dominated. I place my hand on top of her head and curl my fingers into her hair. I pull her forward to my cock. A long moan comes from her mouth.

"Fuck yes," she whispers.

I hold my cock in my hand. "Say it," I order, my voice a harsh command.

"I love to suck your huge cock." She licks her lips and opens her mouth.

For an instant, a millisecond, I see Tara's face. Gorgeous and smiling and looking at me with eyes that shine bright with more than physical want. Eyes that shine bright with love. I pause—I rip the image of Tara from my mind. I'm not that man. I am Wonderfuck. I grasp the back of Cheryl's head and shove my cock in her mouth.

Her lips surround my sex. Heat and suction and pleasure. My fingers tighten in her hair. Her lips stroke forward and back along my shaft. I close my eyes and sink into the pleasure of her mouth, but thoughts, images, Tara invades mind.

No. Fuck. No. I take a breath. I refocus. Heat. Wet. Suction.

Shit.

"Uh, darlin'?"

Fuck.

Cheryl holds my limp, lifeless cock.

Nothing.

This has never happened to Wonderfuck.

She slides her hand up and down my cock, working my limp flesh. I watch her mouth open and take me between her lips again. I will him to get hard. Cheryl's tits, her hot sex, the thrust, her mouth . . .

Nothing. Nada. No. Fucking. Way.

Cheryl continues for what feels like forever. Finally, she pulls away from me and leans back onto her heels.

"Happens to the best," she says, standing. She picks up her robe from the floor, wraps it around her body, and walks across the room to the bar. My head throbs. My chest is tight, and a feeling like shame thunders through me. I tuck my lifeless cock into my pants and sit on the couch. What the fuck. Cheryl returns and hands me a drink.

She settles onto the other end of the couch with a glass of scotch.

"Maybe it's time you retire."

"Don't stroke my ego." I sip my whiskey. "They shoot race-horses, don't they?"

We've wonderfucked enough to understand how the other one thinks. "You know that's not what I meant." She puts her glass on the table and leans closer to me. "Say yes to my offer. Come and be with me."

Come and be with her? I close my eyes, and I see the same face that's been in my dreams for weeks. I swallow. If I commit, shouldn't I commit to a woman I actually love? If I settle for this, for what's easy and safe, doesn't that just make me a fucking coward? I open my eyes and I look at Cheryl. If I wanted a relationship with continuity and without demand, Cheryl would be the perfect match.

"I can't."

"Why not?"

What to tell her? I'm not even sure of the answer. I just know that if I'm going to commit to one woman, it'll have to be a woman I love, even if that means the potential for heartbreak.

Cheryl smiles and grasps my hand. Her gaze is warm and she squeezes. "You'll never receive a better offer . . . Jake."

Frozen. My heart palpitates, and blood drains from my face.

"Darlin', don't look so surprised. You know a woman like me couldn't have a man into my home without knowing everything about him." She lifts her hands toward the ceiling. "I mean come on. Look around. This is simply too much unless I trust you, and how can I trust you unless I know you? Or about you."

I'm not surprised. Really. I guess.

"You're a smart man. I always assumed you knew that I knew everything about you, but wanted to keep up the charade." She rubs her fingertips across my jaw. "You know. To keep it hot."

I take a long drink of whiskey and fire slides down my throat. All kinds of surprises tonight. Perhaps too many.

"But please, Jake, don't tell me that you're giving me up for that little journalist of yours." She keeps her smile, but Cheryl's eyes narrow and her gaze hardens. "I just don't think that would be a very wise decision for a man like Wonderfuck to make." Almost as though she's giving me a warning.

"You know everything about me."

"I know enough." She takes a drink and eyes me over the rim of her glass. "I know about your sister the judge, and your mother and her challenges, and I know about Lily."

My chest tightens. This is much different than Tara knowing about me. This feels treacherous, maybe even deceitful.

"And I also know about poor dear Susie."

There is no kindness in Cheryl's eyes when she says Susie's name. "That wasn't your fault, Jake. Believe me, I know. When I found out that you'd been investigated for a potential homicide by the police? For the love of God, that the man I was fucking was possibly involved in a woman's death? My people investigated the hell out of that one." Cheryl twists her enormous diamond on her ring finger. "You couldn't save her. No one could've."

I stand. I can't sit. My brows pull tight and I scowl at the woman I thought I knew. "You've been lying to me."

"That's rich, darlin'." She smiles and actually laughs. "Because you've been lying to everyone you know, including yourself."

Jackpot.

Well, maybe not one person.

One person who has both Jake and Wonderfuck all figured out.

"You're right." I turn away from Cheryl and walk toward the foyer. "I have been lying to myself."

"Darlin'"—Cheryl calls after me as my hand reaches for the front door—"you're making a big mistake. Your sister's a criminal court judge, and as much as this is a 'vocation' for you and not a job, if this gets out? What you've been doing all these years? I don't know how she'll ever live it down. And an investigative journalist? Jake, I truly thought you were smarter than that."

I press my lips together. Every word she says makes sense. I've got too many loose ends. She stands and walks to me.

"Stay here. With me. Let me make you hard again." She reaches out. Her hand strokes the fabric over my cock.

And I know. I know that Wonderfuck is dead. Not just for Cheryl or any of the other hundreds of women I've pleasured. I know that Wonderfuck is dead for me.

"I can't," I say and walk out the door.

CHAPTER 34

I TEXT. I call. She doesn't respond. And why would she? After weeks of silence, and me leaving her crying on a couch, why would Tara answer me? She'd be a fucking idiot to respond, to take me back, to let me love her. But dammit, I'm going to do everything in my power to prove to her that she has no choice, that I'm the man for her, that I can love her in the way she deserves to be loved.

That Tara is meant to be mine.

I pull into the circle drive in front of my building and jump from my car. Who the fuck cares? Let them tow it. I need Tara and I need her now. A lightning bolt of need shoots through my brain. I must find Tara now. I was a fucking fool, but I'm a fool no more. I rush through the lobby. Inside the elevator, I circle the space like a jungle cat caught in a cage.

I'm down the hall and pounding on her door.

"Tara! Tara, let me in. I have to talk to you, Tara!"

I stop. I listen. Shit. Silence on the other side of her door. She's not here. I rub my hand through my hair and pull my real phone from my pocket. I dial her number again. There's no ringing on the other side of the door. Nothing. There's also no answer. My call goes to voicemail, and I leave what is my ninth message in less than an hour.

§

"WHERE IS TARA?"

"I tried to tell you, Mr. Reynolds, she's still living here, but she's not here right now."

I sigh and press my lips together. "Dell, it's important I find her. Do you know where she is?"

He shakes his head, but slides his eyes toward the office. "Mr. Reynolds," he lowers his voice, "you know that because of privacy issues, even if I did know where she was, I couldn't tell you."

"I do," I say. "I do know that." I lean over his desk and glance toward the office. Obviously someone else must be sitting there, for Dell to be so worried about telling me. "But I also know this is very very urgent and I need to know where Tara is."

Dell licks his lips.

"Okay, let's do it like this," I whisper. "Do you know where she is?"

Dell nods his head.

"Is she coming back, soon?"

Dell shakes his head.

"Is she at her parents'? In Malibu?" Dell raises both brows. "That's as close as an answer as I'm going to get?"

Dell nods.

I smile, thank him, and jet out the door.

§

TRAFFIC IS NEVER SLOWER IN LOS ANGELES THAN when you're in a hurry, and I'm in a hurry. I take the 10, race through the backstreets in Santa Monica to avoid a fender-bender on south PCH, and then hop back onto the PCH to get to

Malibu. By the time I arrive at the guard gate, it's late. Lucky for me, the same guard from two weeks ago is on duty. I manage to talk my way into the Colony even though I'm not on the list.

I pull onto the drive. Tara's car is parked beside a convertible Audi. Who the hell is here this late at night? Didn't Douchenugget drive an Audi?

My heart drops to my toes. I climb from my car. Fuck, please don't let her have gone back to Sir Douche-A-Lot. What if they're planning their wedding—part two? He's begged for her forgiveness and gotten it? I left her brokenhearted. Maybe he seemed like a real catch after me.

Fuck.

I don't care. I knock on the door. I wait. I knock again. This time more insistent.

"Tara! Tara, open the door!"

Finally I hear footsteps. The door swings open, and the man standing in front of me isn't who I expected.

"May I help you?" His hair is steel grey. His eyebrows pull tight together over the bridge of his nose. He wears a robe and looks as though he's been asleep for a while.

"I . . . I'm Jake and I'm looking for Tara."

He squints at me as though trying to process my words.

"Who is it, dear?" A woman calls from deeper in the house.

"Someone for Tara." He turns back to me. "Have you tried calling her?" he asks me, with a look on his face that says I might be slow and unable to process how civilized people attempt to find one another.

"She didn't answer and I need to speak to her."

"Well, she's not here."

I turn toward the driveway. "But her car—"

"She left it. She's been staying with a—" He stops speaking and eyes me again. "Who did you say you were?"

"Jake . . . we're . . . we're friends."

"Hmm. Right. Friends. Well, she's not here. I'll tell her you came by. Have a nice evening." He starts to shut the door.

I reach out and slam my hand to the flat surface to stop the door from closing. "But I need to see her now."

"Young man, I suggest you remove your hand." His tone is clipped and he puffs up. "Or I'm calling the police."

"I need to find her."

"She has her phone, and I'm quite sure she'll get in touch when she's ready to be found."

I drop my hand to my side. After a final stern look, he shuts the door. I stand in front of a closed door after meeting the person I suspect is Tara's dad.

I've made a great first impression, I'm sure.

❧

MY BEST OPTION TO FIND TARA IS TO WAIT. UNLIKE her bed, mine doesn't shake when she goes in and out of her condo. I lean against her front door—that way I can't miss her when she comes home. It doesn't matter if I'm awake or asleep, because I'll hear her, and she'll see me. The invincible Wonder-fuck, decimated by love, has turned into a stalker huddling at her front door.

I have no shame. I've left messages. I've driven to Malibu. I even attempted to bribe Dell when I returned to the building, but he didn't have any information worth buying. I settle onto the carpet in the hallway between our two homes, and I'm prepared to wait here for as long as it takes, prepared to wait until Tara comes home. Prepared to wait for her for the rest of my days.

"Jake?"

My eyes flutter open. A pain shoots through my neck as I lift my head. Something wet and warm slurps at my face.

Wagging tail.

Smelly breath.

Tiny whines.

I smile. "Jango." I've never been so happy to have a girl with bad breath licking my face before now. Her tail wags. I pet her and look upward over her head to the woman standing behind the dog.

She doesn't look nearly as enthusiastic to see me.

"What are you doing sleeping against my front door?"

I'm sure I look like shit. What time is it, anyway? I got here after midnight. Tara looks fresh and showered and has on clean clothes.

"I . . . I needed to see you." I jump to my feet. I do my best not to seem too needy or pathetic, but I've just spent hours sleeping in front of Tara's door, so I don't have firm grasp on appearing strong and detached.

"Excuse me." She comes toward the door with her key. I back away and stand beside her.

"Tara, please, come on, I need to talk to you. I have to talk to you."

Jango jumps up and plants her paws on my thighs. "See, even Jango knows how important this is."

She doesn't crack, doesn't waver. But she leaves the front door open when she turns and goes into her condo, which leads me to believe that I'm allowed to follow. I stop short in the living room because it's full of boxes in different stages of being packed.

"You're really moving."

"Yep. I really am." She unsnaps Jango's leash and lays it on the table. "Now what do you need?"

She's all ice princess on the exterior, but she still cares for me. I see it in her eyes. I don't deserve her feelings, but they're still there. I just have to convince her that it's okay to feel for me. That I won't disappoint her, that I won't let her down, that I finally know what I need in my life, and what I need is her.

"Tara," I step toward her. I swallow. All my Wonderfuck knowledge is gone. It feels useless, and I don't know what to say or how to read her or what's the best way to tell her what I'm thinking. So I don't look for an angle, I don't try to think of an approach. Instead, I simply start. "I'm sorry."

She crosses her arms over her chest and rips her gaze from me. Her cheeks flush red. I know that her emotions aren't going to stay hidden.

"I . . . you were right. I do need you. I want you. I want you more than anyone I've ever met. You were right, I was afraid, and now . . . now I'm not. Now I know that I have to be with you."

"Now? You know that now. After you left me in Malibu and then didn't call me for weeks. You show up here, and I'm just supposed to accept your apology and fall all over you and say 'Okay, Jake,' or Wonderfuck, or whatever name you're going by now?"

I stand there and I take it. I deserve it. I actually deserve more anger than that. "You're right," I say. "I have no defense, absolutely none. The only thing I have is a wing, a prayer, and the hope that you feel as though you can't live without me as much as I feel like I can't live without you."

Her mouth drops open and her eyelids flutter. Whatever she'd intended to say is lost to her now, so I keep going. "I love you," I say. "And that fucking terrifies me."

"Jake, you can't love me, okay? You can't."

"But I do. I . . . I don't want to be with anyone else . . . I . . ."

She looks at me. At first her gaze is harsh, as though she doesn't believe me, but then . . . then her eyes soften.

"Please, Tara." My eyes are hot and my throat is closing, but I don't fucking care, because I can't imagine a life without her. I grasp her hands, I look into her eyes. For a split second I see what I want, what I need. I step forward.

"I'm sorry, Jake," she says. "You have to go."

CHAPTER 35

"AND THIS IS THE COMMUNITY ROOM."

Rachel and I follow Julia, the Alzheimer's facility administrator, into a living room that doesn't look too much different than Mom's living room at home. Three older women sit at the center table with a woman in her twenties guiding them in a painting project.

"We have painting three times a week. Also three-dimensional art, light yoga, and community outings."

"They go out?" Rachel is thinking of Mom's escape.

"Our residents are in varying stages, and we keep a strict ratio of two residents per caregiver when we're on an outing. There are only eight residents here," Julia says.

"All women?"

Julia nods. "Let me show you two of the private rooms." Rachel follows Julia through the living room and into the hall. I walk behind them, but pause next to a woman who sits on the couch with an open book on her lap.

"You're awfully young to be considering a place like this," she says and lifts an eyebrow.

"Not for me," I say. I nod toward her book. "Any good?"

"Depends on who you ask." She flips it closed. "Let me guess, you're thinking about dumping your mom in this place?"

My chest tightens. I nod.

"That's what my kids did too." She rolls her eyes.

"Do you like it here?"

"The food's good. I have my own bedroom, but the woman who lives next door to me likes to sing 'Mary Had a Little Lamb' in the middle of the night." She shakes her head. "I'm not too keen on that tune at two a.m."

I smile. This lady seems to have her wits mostly together. "I'm Jake." I stretch out my hand.

"Rosalyn," she says and shakes my hand. "Rosalyn Harris." She leans forward and wiggles her eyebrows. "I bet you think you know me."

"I'm sorry, no, I don't think we've met—"

"Hmm. Really? You ever go to the movies?"

"Sometimes. You?"

"Not so much anymore. My husband, he used to make movies. Was a producer. He's dead."

"I'm sorry for your loss," I say.

"Don't be. He was an asshole."

"Oh, well—"

"Had a giant cock, though. Gave it to every actress he ever worked with. Marilyn Monroe, Jayne Mansfield, Elizabeth Taylor —he *really* gave it to Elizabeth Taylor."

"Wow, I—"

"But he loved me and I loved him. That's why we stayed together. Even while he was schtupping every actress in town. I left him for a while. Stopped him. Put that damn schmeckel away after I left for six months. It's always good for a man to realize what he has. They forget sometimes. Men forget."

"Jake." Julia stands beside me with Rachel. "I see you've met Rosalyn. Rosalyn, didn't you want to paint today?"

"Today? Not today. Today I'm meeting Paul Newman for lunch."

"Oh, right." Julia smiles. "Maybe you should head toward the dining room. I think they're going to begin serving soon."

Rosalyn stands and glances toward me. "Tell Mr. Redford I'll see him next Wednesday."

"Will do," I say and watch Rosalyn walk away.

"She does pretty well," Julia says. "In and out of reality. Not angry. And usually pretty content to be dating some of the biggest stars of the sixties and seventies."

Rachel sighs. Her face is ashen. The idea of putting Mom in a permanent place that both of us know she won't ever move out of, even in a place this small and this nice, is the pits. Plus, soon what's left of Mom's mind will be gone.

"It's very difficult for the family members," Julia says. "Have either of you gotten involved with any of the Alzheimer's support groups?"

"I have," Rachel says. "Just recently."

I look at Rachel. I had no idea that she'd started going to a group.

Julia smiles at Rachel. "I found it tremendously helpful when I went through this with my mom."

Rachel eyes are watery and she turns away.

"We were going to look at the bedrooms," Julia says and steers us both away from the couches and down the hall.

"I HATED IT."

Rachel doesn't look at me. She stands at the kitchen island with a glass of red wine and watches Mom and Lily play Go Fish at the dining room table. So far Mom has put down four mismatched pairs, but Lily is too sweet to say anything.

"Right, there's nothing to like about any of it." Rachel sips her wine. "But it was nice, right?"

"Yeah."

She takes a deep breath. "Julia said she'll call if a spot opens up. I put Mom's name on the wait list." Rachel bites her thumbnail. "This is our decision, right?"

"Right," I say. "We've decided together, and while it's not what we *want* for Mom, it's what we need."

"Richard?"

I look over at Mom and Lily. They both smile at me.

"Richard, is the nice lady with the dog coming over again tonight?"

"What dog?" I ask.

Mom looks at Lily. "Rachel, honey, what is the doggie's name? The one that comes over to visit?"

"Jango," Lily says as she puts down a pair of swordfish cards.

"Jango?" I ask and look toward Rachel. She has now stuck her nose into the refrigerator and is pretending like she can't hear what anyone is saying. "Jango comes to visit?"

"Jango and Tara," Lily continues. "Jango does tricks."

"It seems Mommy does tricks too." I walk to the refrigerator and stand just beside my big sis. "Have you seen Tara?"

She pulls her bottom lip beneath her top teeth. "There's no rule that I can't be friends with your neighbor."

"Nearly former neighbor, and when did you see her?"

"She came over the other night," Lily offers from across the room. "Jango can roll over now. She's been working on it."

"How long—"

"Not long," Rachel says in a way that seems to indicate I have no right to be irritated. "Look, I desperately needed a sitter one night and you were MIA, so I called Tara and—"

"She's babysitting for you now?"

"No, she came over that one time. And then we had her and Jango over for dinner the other night."

My heart jackknifes. I'm uncertain if I should feel happy about this or betrayed. Rachel doesn't know the depth of my feelings for Tara, so I'm thinking betrayal isn't part of the equation. "Did she . . . did she say anything about—"

"You?" Rachel asks.

I nod.

"No. Sorry. The only thing we talked about was her new job and her move."

"Where—"

"San Francisco." Rachel's lips thin. "And it's soon." She grabs the top of my arm.

Maybe she does know how I feel. Maybe I'm not nearly as stoic as I like to believe.

"How soon?"

"Next week."

"That doesn't give me much time."

MY PLACE DOESN'T FEEL LIKE MY PLACE ANYMORE. I'M tired of The London and I'm tired of hiding. I can't let the ghosts of my past determine the trajectory of my future any longer. I walk through the condo toward my bedroom. There've only been two women who've slept in this room; one is dead and the other wants nothing to do with me. I sit on my bed and glance toward the new Frederika on the wall.

The girl with the green eyes and the brown hair, facing the ocean. She's so similar to what I saw in Malibu when I stood watching Tara. A perfect moment that will stay seared in my memory until I die or I lose my mind. One is a definite. With my genetics, the other a real possibility.

Knock. Knock. Knock.

I walk through my place and open the front door.

My heart jolts in my chest.

"This is yours." Tara holds up a nondescript wine key. I don't know if it's mine or if it isn't mine, because I don't fucking care. What I do care about is that she's here, standing at my door, in front of me.

"Thank you." I take the wine key, and I fucking hope beyond hope that the wine key is only an excuse.

"You . . . uh . . . you went to my parents?"

I nod.

"My dad, he said you seemed . . . 'distraught' was the word he used."

I look into Tara's eyes. And the emotions are there, I see them, she can't hide them or even pretend that she doesn't have them, although I'm betting right now she wishes that she didn't.

"I'd say 'in love' is a better description."

Her mouth drops open but this time I don't hesitate, I don't pause, I don't let this instant of shock and surprise and whatever the fuck else she's feeling pass. This time I pull her close and press my lips to hers.

I kiss her. I kiss her with every emotion I've got. I don't hold anything back. I'm not Wonderfuck, I'm not even Jake, I'm just a guy who is madly in love with a woman who might leave him forever next week. A guy who didn't believe he could ever love again, so he did everything in his power to make damn sure that he wouldn't and that no one could love him.

But he did.

And he could.

And I do.

Tara kisses me back. I don't pause. I pull her into my place and kick the door closed. I don't know if this time is the last time we'll be together as what we were, or the first time we'll be together as what I want us to become, and I don't care. All I want is her right now. In my bed. In my arms. With me.

I sweep Tara up into my arms, and without letting her lips leave mine, I carry her down the hall to my bedroom. I set her on her feet beside my bed and pull her shirt over her head. My hands slide over her skin. I unhook he r bra and it drops to the floor. I lean forward and pull her nipple into my mouth.

"Oh Jake," she whispers.

All I want, for the rest of my life, is to hear her use that voice, filled with desire, and say those words. My hand slides down and slips her pants over her hips. I release her nipple and kiss down the front of her, down her belly to her panties. I pull them over her hips, down over her legs. Her sex is in front of me. I use my thumbs to gently spread the lips of her sex and my tongue strokes over her. She's wet for me. I press a finger into her as I suck.

Her breathing is short. She grasps my hair. Her panting turns me on.

"Jack, oh my God, Jake, I'm going to come."

I clasp one arm around her legs and keep sucking her sex. Her entire body is rocking now and tensing. I gently push her back to my bed and spread her thighs, and just as she's going over the edge, her entire sex is open to me, a gorgeous flower. I suck her clit and thrust two fingers deep into her sex.

"Fuck, yes." Her sex tightens around me and her hips buck up and push into my face even harder. I suck until the rolling of her hips stops and only tiny soft sounds come from her lips. I pull my face away from her sex. She lays on my bed, her eyes heavy-lidded.

"I want you," she says.

I reach into my bedside drawer and unroll a condom onto my cock. I pull her body so that she is laying on my bed with the covers beside us. I lean over her and she opens her legs for me. I press my lips to hers, the gorgeous taste of her still on my lips, and she tastes her own sex.

The tip of my cock presses forward against the muscles of her sex. I edge into her and she grasps my shoulders, her gaze on mine.

I want this for forever. I can do this. I know I can. I can be hers and she can be mine, because I am no longer afraid.

"Make me come, Jake," she whispers.

I thrust into her hard and pull back. Her mouth drops open with wild-eyed pleasure. She clasps her legs around me and we are one. My control doesn't exist. The tingle throbs up my legs and gathers in my back. My balls pull tight. She licks her lips, her body spasms and tightens around mine, and I am over the edge, taking her with me. Her nails dig into the flesh of my shoulders as come throbs from my cock. And every part of me belongs to every part of her and I want her to be mine.

§

I WAKE UP. TARA ISN'T IN MY BED.

My stomach tightens.

"Tara?"

No response. I bound from the mattress. Is she gone? Fuck. Why did I sleep? How could she leave? I didn't get a chance to tell her all the things I need to say. I run down the hallway of my condo naked, like a wild man, in search of the woman I need.

Not at the dining room table. Not in the kitchen. Not in the—

The front door opens.

She smiles. Her hands are full. Jango is at her side. Jango wags her tail and heads to me. I cover my cock with my hand, pretty certain I don't want any part of me mistaken for a chew toy.

"Afraid I left?" she asks with a wicked gleam in her eyes, part playful and part not. I deserve that.

"Yeah," I say. I pat Jango's head and take my hand from my cock when she goes and curls up on the couch.

"Go get dressed. I'll make breakfast. We should talk."

I pull my hand through my hair and try to determine if 'talk' sounds like a good thing or a good-bye thing. I can't decipher her intent. She's already got one frying pan full of bacon and is cracking eggs into a bowl. But I don't want to leave her, I want to talk to her now. I have things to say, and I need to know what is going to happen between us.

"Go put on some clothes," she says, without removing her gaze from the eggs she's whisking.

I turn back to my bedroom and get ready to face whatever this day will bring.

❧

"MY PLACE JUST SOLD."

I pour two coffees. This is how we're playing the morning, it would seem, as though we've not been separated for weeks, and I am not the former Wonderfuck, and that this is normal, her cooking eggs in my kitchen while I make coffee. But this isn't normal. I wish it were, and I'll do anything to make this the portrait for the rest of my life, but she hasn't committed, nor have we really talked about all we need to talk about.

"I have a new job reporting for the *San Francisco Post*. They want me up there next week." She's finished cooking the eggs and bacon and put them on plates. She turns to me and leans against the counter. "I leave in three days."

I swallow. I look at Tara and I know that her face is home. Being with her is what makes me feel solid and complete.

"Let me come with you."

"That's crazy. You've got your sister and your niece and your mom."

"I can come back here and help. I can fly back and forth. I don't have an office. I don't have to be anywhere specific. I have business in San Francisco." I walk to her and I slide my hands around her waist. "Please," I say. "I want to be with you. Let me go too."

Doubt in her eyes, but beside it, hope too. I understand those feelings, the idea that something you want couldn't possibly work out. Couldn't possibly end up just the way you wanted from the beginning.

"I meant it when I said it. I love you. You're my future, and I want that future to begin now."

"Jake, I . . ." She takes a step back from me. "I . . . there are some things that you need to know, that I should tell you, that—"

"Do you love me?" Because regardless of what she's going to tell me, that's the only fact I need to know. That's it. If she loves me, there isn't anything we can't get through. I know it. I believe it. Even with my past, maybe because of it, I'm certain that this, what I have with Tara, is strong enough to withstand anything life can throw our way.

"Yes." Her gaze is locked to mine. "I love you."

I kiss her. She kisses me. We're in each other's arms. I pull back and look into her eyes.

"Then I can go? Come to San Francisco with you and Jango?"

A smile cuts across her face and she nods.

"And we'll be together? Just you and me?"

She nods again and I pull her into my arms. This is what I want, what I need. My heart swells. I swallow and press my lips to hers.

"You've just made me the happiest man in the world. I love you, Tara."

"I love you too." Her hand reaches up around my neck and her lips are on mine.

"This is going to be amazing," I say. And I know it, I know that our life, this new life we'll build together, will be beyond anything I could have ever imagined.

"Still, I . . . there's something I have to tell you." Uncertainty flickers in her eyes.

My phone beeps and I flip it over and take a look. "You have a new story?" I smile at Tara, the woman I love. "It's a good day." I click the link. "And it's the landing page."

"Right . . . before you read it, I need to—"

Her words are gone. I hear nothing as my eyes skim the title, the words . . . the story.

My heart, the heart I've given her, is squeezed tight. I can barely breathe. My gaze flies up to Tara's.

"I . . . that's what I need to talk to you about."

I look past her to the balcony. Toward the past. Toward the first time my heart was ripped from my chest. Then I look back to my phone. I stare at my phone and the words she wrote that got her a move to San Francisco, a new job, a promotion, and . . .

"I'm sorry," she mumbles.

I read the title again, uncertain that I got it right the first time. I hope maybe I've made a mistake. But there it is—the words, the title, the story that could destroy my life and my family's: "Wonderf*cking His Way Through L.A."

PART II

CHAPTER 36

LOVE IS A VICIOUS BITCH. Twice I've fallen for her charms and twice she's shredded my heart. I won't be fooled a third time.

"Jake, this is a surprise."

Warren stands from behind his desk and rushes across his swank office with the million-dollar view that I paid for, with his hand outstretched to shake mine. He's surprised and yet deferential. He should be, because I own a huge piece of his ass in the form of a majority interest in the online news source known as the LA Post.

I stare into Warren's eyes. It's not bravado. My look is me letting Warren know that I'm here, and although he may run this place – a company that is successful and well into the black – I'm Warren's boss. I'm the money guy.

I've never thrown my weight around as the 800-pound gorilla before today, but I'm doing it now because I'm pissed, and heartbroken, and furious at a woman, that (no matter how hard I try not to be), I'm balls-to-the-wall in love with.

My gaze is a warning to Warren that he'd best prepare to take like a man what I'm about to dish out.

We sit perpendicular to each other. I'm on the couch and he's on a chair that every exec has in their office: the appearance of propriety and civility even though that is rarely the reality of what happens in a boss's office.

Surprise hovers around his mouth. His assistant comes in and sets a carafe of coffee and two cups on the small table in front of us. I don't bother with the niceties because I don't have the patience to be nice.

"I hear you're opening a San Francisco division."

"It was in the last quarterly report."

"Tara is being transferred."

Warren lifts an eyebrow. Surprise that I'm on a first name basis with a woman on his staff, and that I know about his employment decisions.

"She'll be a great addition to the group as they ramp up in San Fran."

He reaches for the carafe and pours a cup of coffee. "She broke that great story about that Wonderfuck guy. What a life right? He—"

"She's not going."

Warren stops mid-sentence, his cup hovers mid-air. He blinks.

I've never made any demand at the LA Post, but I am now, and I can because I'm the fucking 800-pound gorilla.

"But—"

I tilt my head. "But what?"

There is no response Warren can give me but 'Yes.' Warren has no options. This isn't a negotiation, this is an order. I own the LA Post and I own him. I own it all and in a way I own Tara. She diced what was left of my heart into tiny cubes and now...now I can't even find solace in the one thing that brings me pleasure, the one thing that saved me from the soul-sucking abyss after Susie died, the one things that keeps me from following Susie over the edge.

I can't even Wonderfuck.

"But I think she'd be a good addition in San Francisco and I'm eyeing her for managing editor position, so I think that—"

"Tara stays in Los Angeles."

This isn't a discussion or a democracy. This is a dictatorship and I'm a despot with revenge on my mind.

"Can I ask why?"

"You could." I stand. I walk toward Warren's office door and pull it open. I turn toward him. "But it doesn't matter because I own this place. The equation is simple. She stays in LA or you find another job. I've made my decision."

Warren swallows. Anger builds on his face.

Fuck his anger. I've lived on rage for years. Let him have a little discomfort with his coffee. Rage is an excellent sweetener. Let him be pissed, let him be enraged, let him say or do something stupid. I'm feeling angry enough to disembowel him with words. I'd prefer to beat the shit out of him, but that would be too much, wouldn't it?

"I own the Post. She stays."

Tara wanted to go to San Francisco, had her heart set on moving and taking her new job.

Too fucking bad.

I had my heart set on her loving me and me loving her and us being honest with each other, and that didn't work out. Guess we all learn to live with disappointment, and Tara is going to get a big lesson, because she absolutely fucked over the wrong man. Guess we both get to deal with heartache now.

LOVE IS A BITCH, BUT BETRAYAL IS A WHORE; A WELL maintained whore who teases you with her smile. You don't even know she's slit your throat and stolen your wallet until you're two pints down. I don't have good judgment when it comes to women, because that whore, Betrayal, has nearly killed me two times.

"*This* is the guy I'm talking about."

Rachel holds up her phone and twists the screen toward me. "This guy...this." She lowers her voice for the next word. "Wonderfuck." She flips the screen back toward her. "Have you read this?"

I nod. Every person in Los Angeles has read Tara's article.

"I mean, listen to what these women say: 'He made me multi-orgasmic.'"

Rachel lifts an eyebrow. "Isn't every woman multi-orgasmic? Her husband must've really sucked... Or not. Then this one. 'My husband told me for years that he thought I was attractive above the neck and below the ankles.'"

Rachel shakes her head and rolls her eyes toward the ceiling. "My god. How many women have been emotionally eviscerated by the men in their lives?"

She lays her phone on the kitchen counter and grabs a spatula. "I wouldn't believe all these quotes except every one of my married friends have told me something similar."

Her gaze comes up from the griddle. "Men are assholes."

I won't argue with Big Sis. Nope. I'm admittedly an asshole. I'll cop to that. We all are, the penis people. We are complete and utter assholes. What we get in muscle mass, gets taken away in empathy and emotional understanding. It's only the women in our lives that make us halfway bearable.

"I've never claimed to be perfect."

"Nope." Rachel flips the pancake. "You're one of the good ones. I've actually heard you cop to inherent male-assholeness." She leans against the kitchen counter and continues to read the Wonderfuck article, but this time out loud:

"*I expected a near sexual deviant, maybe a man in gold chains, almost past middle age, with a lascivious look and a sickening grin. Even while I'd been assured by the woman who referred me to Wonderfuck that what I was getting was a man on a mission. The James Bond of fucking. A man with a personal vocation to make every woman feel beautiful."*

Rachel's eyes light up. "My god, I want to meet this man."

She leans onto the kitchen island as though I have the inside track on meeting Mick Jagger.

"Did you know about Tara and this....this Wonderfuck?" She says the name with reverence, almost as though she's discussing Batman.

"I knew some of it," I say, because that's the truth. I know all about what the anonymous sources have to say. I could probably even figure out who the anonymous sources are. What I didn't know about was the article.

"So are you two...?"

I lock my gaze with Rachel's. "No."

And we're not. Not right now, and quite possibly not ever again. Not after this betrayal for her career.

"I wonder if there's more than one?" She flips two pancakes onto a plate. "Wonderfuck, that is."

I lift a shoulder and give a non-committal shrug. I know the answer. There is. I've seen more than one phone number scribbled on walls.

"This is beyond sexual." Rachel pours syrup onto the Minnie Mouse shaped pancake. "What he does is save women's souls." She puts the plate onto the kitchen table. "Do you think she actually had sex with him? For the article?" She licks a glop of maple syrup from her finger. "I guess I could call her. Ask her about Wonderfuck. Is that weird?"

I give Big Sis my evil eye. "I don't know. Is it?"

Rachel calling my former neighbor and secret-ex-lover to discuss whether she had sex for an article is weird. Even if Rachel and Tara seem to have a bit of a friendship on their own.

I must be successful in conveying my irritation over the idea of Rachel hanging out with Tara and discussing Wonderfuck, because she drops the Tara thing altogether. She turns to the refrigerator and pulls out the orange juice. My niece rounds the corner, still in her princess jammies, with some serious bed head. She totally has an internal radar for sugar. She must've smelled the syrup from the living room.

Lily smiles at me and climbs onto her chair and proceeds to destroy not one, but three pancakes. I decline a sugar-infused breakfast, and make another pot of coffee.

This kid owns me. I'm her slave, her servant, her uncle with a credit card, and no kids. Anything Lily wants from Uncle Jake she gets.

"Uncle Jake, you know it's almost my birthday."

I do the math in my head and this time the kid is kind of right. It's close-ish, although it seems as though we have this discussion every time I'm at her house. Okay. I'll play. I always do. She is, after all, my boss in nearly every way.

"And what is it you want for your birthday?"

She sighs and glances toward her mother. Rachel leans against the counter and watches Lily. My niece leans forward, her sticky syrup lips actually coating my ear with sugar.

"I want what I always want. I want a puppy."

"Lily, we are absolutely *not* getting a dog," Rachel says from across the kitchen.

Lily's Bambi-like eyes lock on mine. Her lips turn down as though her mother has just threatened to kill every puppy born between now and Lily's birthday.

"She doesn't want me to get one," Lily says softly and shakes her head with a solemnity that is more than grave in its demeanor. It's downright fucking heartbreaking.

If I still had a fucking heart.

"I'm sorry boo," I say.

I shoot big sis the side-eye. She's turned away from us toward the sink. I wink at Lily. I lean forward. "Let me see what I can do."

Her lips press tight and she looks as though she's fighting the urge to smile, to shout hurray, to do anything to alert her mom that Uncle Jakey is on her side and totally working all the angles to get Lily the dog she so desperately needs.

"I love you Uncle Jake."

"Don't think I'm not aware of what you two are up to," Rachel says. She now stands right beside us. "Dogs take time and energy and I have neither, okay?"

We both look at Rachel and nod our false agreement. Yeah, because Uncle Jakey is on the case.

Minnie Mouse pancakes finished, Lily slides from her spot at the table and grabs me with both arms and hugs me tight. This. These hugs. My god. They saved me before, made me whole, kept me sane, and they can save me again, because right now I have zero fucks left to give, and that includes even the ones involving the word Wonder. Yeah, the women in my life make me a better man. At least three of them do.

Lily skips from the kitchen and back toward the cartoons booming from the TV in the living room.

"They'll have a spot for Mom soon," Rachel says once Lily has exited the kitchen. "The place we looked at last month." Her voice contains far less excitement than when she discussed Wonderfuck.

"How can they know that?"

Rachel lifts a brow. "People don't generally move out of those places."

My throat tightens.

"One of their residents is ill and they really don't see a recovery happening."

My heart squeezes. I don't want a place for Mom other than our childhood home, but I do know that this is exactly what Mom needs.

"I thought we could start going through the things in the house."

"Or you could shove a sharp stick in my eye."

"Either one. Going through the house will mean less blood."

"Says you."

I'm uncertain that going through the familial detritus of our entire lives will cause less bloodletting than actually poking out my eye. Sifting through remnants of our childhood might be more painful. "Could we hire someone to do it?"

"Sure. Can you make an accurate list of all the pictures, trophies, yearbooks et. al that you'd like to keep?"

"Did you just use *et. al.* in a sentence?"

"I most certainly did. I'm a judge. Answer the question."

"Taking the fifth."

"You can't hire someone to do everything for you." She glances at her phone. "But according to Tara's article you can't even hire someone to give you the best sex of your life," Rachel says. "For that, you've got to find this guy, but hey, then it's free."

I put my coffee cup in the dishwasher. I can't discuss Tara, and I most certainly will not discuss Wonderfuck with my sister.

"Guess that'll make it hard for Vice to get any charges against this guy."

I can't quite swallow. I turn back toward Rachel. "Vice?"

Rachel nodes. "It's what I hear. This article is waaaay too much for our illustrious state's attorney. Seems like they're already coordinating a sting operation. Wouldn't want to be this guy."

"But his services are free," I say. "No money exchanges hands."

"Right. And I hope it's true, but they're concerned it's not. Just telling you the rumors I hear. They're looking for this guy." Rachel sighs. "Which means I won't get to." She smiles. "Unless he ends up in my courtroom."

My gut churns. God, no. Please don't let that happen. I round the corner to say goodbye to Lily, who is sucked into My Little Pony.

"I love you Uncle Jake."

"I love you too, bug."

She slides from my arms and plops back onto the couch with her soft mermaid blanket.

"Wednesday," Rachel says, and lifts an eyebrow. "You, me, and Mom at the house."

I nod, not nearly convinced that a stick wouldn't be better.

CHAPTER 37

THE ELEVATOR DOORS slide open on my floor and my phone beeps.

'We need to talk.'

The text isn't a surprise, but the fact that the words show up on my personal phone instead of my Wonderfuck phone is. The text is from a number that isn't connected to a name, but I've seen this number hundreds of times. I know exactly who wants to chat with me.

'Anytime.' I type back.

She sends me a time and a place. After all our time together we've never gone out to dinner. We may cause a scene. Her with the billion dollar business, and me, Mr. Wonderful-eligible bachelor-with-loads-of-cash, even if I do sport a tragic backstory. Hell, I'm more attractive to some women because of the tragic backstory.

I walk down the hall to my condo. I was determined to sell my place, but now? Now I'm unsure. I glance across the hallway. Tara's place appears abandoned. Now that she isn't moving, will she keep her condo?

I open my front door.

Woof. Woof.

Two paws land on my thighs and a slurpy wet smile greets me with a lick on my hand. I glance toward the balcony.

I always glance toward the balcony.

Tara paces in the living room. "You're an asshole."

I pat Jango, knowing that Tara's pup does not share her mistress's opinion of me. I curb my tongue because after Tara's betrayal I have some choice adjectives I'd like to hurl her way, but I don't do that. I don't hurl anything, adjectives or otherwise, at women.

My heart races. My hands clench and unclench. Tara's betrayed me and now she's in my home calling me an asshole.

I walk into the kitchen and set my keys on the counter. I open the refrigerator and grab a beer. I pop the top and turn toward the woman that I love and prepare to hear what she has to say, which apparently, from her demeanor, won't include the words 'I'm sorry.'

"You are an asshole," she says again.

"Yeah, I heard that part when I walked in."

I got nothing to add if that's all Tara has to say. I tilt my beer to my lips and head toward the back of my condo. I've got work and a computer and a ton of stuff to do that doesn't include Tara repeating the same four words all evening. She's behind me all the way down the hallway to my bedroom.

"Did you hear me?"

I glance at her. I nod.

"Well don't you care?"

I shake my head no. It's a lie. The calm, cool, nonchalance is the biggest fucking lie I'm telling myself because I do care. I love her. I hate her. I'm nearly destroyed by her.

My insides burn.

Heat pulses through me. The desire to throw this beer bottle against the wall tears through me. To get in Tara's face and tell her just exactly how she broke my fucking heart, how she used me, and betrayed me, and fucked me over. How my grip on sanity is tenuous at best, and she didn't have the right to throw me over the edge into this fucking shit show. Because not only did she betray me and cheapen what we have, she took away the thing that's been keeping me sane.

She took away Wonderfucking.

She's in my face now, all heat and anger and the scent of a woman that makes me hard.

"You ruined my promotion."

Her breath is hot against my face, her anger a living thing sliding supple over my skin. Fuck if I don't want to grab her and stick my hard cock into her.

"You have no loyalty. I have nothing to say to you."

The air between us crackles with anger, which fuels my desire.

"That's rich. You're fucking women all over Los Angeles because it's your *vocation*, and *I* betrayed *you*?"

"I didn't fuck other women. Not after you. Not....not after the hotel."

Her lips part into slack jawed surprise. Damn, shouldn't have said that. Tara's hold over me, my heart, my cock is absolute. Too much power for her to have. Fuck. Fuck. This is the worst.

"You loved *her*."

She points toward the balcony I don't ever walk onto.

"Enough to forgive *her*. She fucked hundreds of men, *hundreds* while you were engaged, and you forgave her. All I ever did was fuck *you* and you can't forgive me?"

I close my eyes. "You told the world."

What's left of my heart rips apart behind my ribs. Little bits of that muscle held together with the hope that there will be a lover that is kind and generous and honest and will make my heart sing with joy and not shred from pain. I did forgive Susie. A million and one times over a million and one betrayals.

"Maybe she used up all my forgiveness." I open my eyes. "Or maybe I just loved her more."

I know it's coming before her hand hits my face and I step into the slap because pain is my fucking salvation in this life.

Smack.

She lands a solid slap on my left cheek. That'll leave a mark.

"Feel better?"

Her fingertips fly to her lips and tears spring to her eyes. Her remorse is too late for me, for her, for us. She ruined what we could've had for a good story, a good click rate, a huge headline.

"You won. You got what you wanted. You're a big-time reporter with a big-time story."

"It's...it's not what I wanted."

Tears drip from her eyes and roll down her cheeks. She lifts her fingers from her lips and reaches toward my cheek. I grasp her wrist.

"No."

"Jake, please, I...I'm sorry."

And she is. She's sorry. It's in her eyes, her voice, I can feel it in my heart. I know she's sorrier than she's ever been and she'd do anything to make me whole. And I've been down this road before with a woman, and the story didn't end well. I point toward the front door. Because sorry doesn't fix this and I won't go down this road again. I can't. I tried.

"You need to leave."

Her bottom lip quivers, and I pretend that my heart isn't breaking. If she reaches out to me again, if she steps forward and kisses me, if she does anything other than walk out the door of my condo, I won't be able to watch her leave.

"You may not want to love me, but you do."

The sad fucking truth of the matter is that no matter how mad I am at her, what Tara said is abso-fucking-lutely true. She steps closer to me. I'm hard, and ready, and wanting no one but Tara.

"And I love you too."

I close my eyes. How fucked up is this? How fucked up am I? Pathetic, and infuriating, and the truth. And I want to fuck. I want to rip away her clothes and pull her to my room, and I want to fuck her into submission. Or maybe it's me who needs to surrender to the feelings I have and let go of the fury pounding through my heart.

She licks her lips. Inches from me, just inches away. The heat of her breath, and the warmth of her body, and the scent of lemons and lavender.

She leans forward and we are locked in a fury-filled soul-ending kiss. Heat flames through my body. Her mouth opens and my tongue slips deep into her mouth.

I want her. She's mine. Tara will always be mine even though I'm fucking furious. I don't want anything to do with her, and yet, all I want is her.

Her breasts press against my chest and her fingertips skim the soft fabric of my pants. She reaches beneath the waistband and she has my cock.

Hard. Long. Strong. She rubs me with her hand. I can't stop now. I won't stop now. I pull her shirt up and over her head and her pants down over her hips. My thumb strokes her nipple.

A moan comes from her lips and her grip tightens around my cock. I pull my lips from her, and dip down and pull her taut nipple into my mouth. Her fingertips weave through my hair and pull me closer. I roll her nipple in my mouth. I part her sex with my hand and gently circle her clit. Her hips roll forward and back in a rhythm my body knows, and I press two fingers deep into her sex. Again a moan, and I pull my lips from her nipple and kiss across her chest and pull her other nipple deep into my mouth. Yes. Yes. I want to fuck her. I love her. I hate her. But I will always want to fuck her.

It's been long for me. Too long. I can't go this long without the release of sex. I need to fuck. Fucking is what makes me feel alive. Fucking is what makes me feel whole.

I shove the dark thoughts away. Instead, I pulse in and out of her sex, and her body tightens around my fingers. Her hand still strokes up and down my cock. I turn her around and I walk her toward the wall of windows, the sliders by the balcony.

I press both of her hands to the glass.

"You want to fuck me," I hiss in her ear. "Fuck me here."

I spread her legs with my knee. I reach around to her front and my fingers slide through the curls of her sex. I circle her clit with the tip of my finger.

"Oh Jake, Jake," she says.

I look into the window. I see her reflection and it is enough. I don't want to see her face, I don't want her to know the rage and the pain and the love that fight for primacy across my features. I pull my hips back and I position my cock at her entrance. My arm snakes around her waist. With one hard, brutal, thrust I'm in her sex.

"Jake," she wails.

Her hips roll back and forth with each motion. I can see her reflection in the window. Her features wracked with physical pleasure and emotional pain. Will this be the final time we're together? The last time we fuck? The last time I touch her body, kiss her skin, smell her scent, feel the pounding sensation of my body slamming against hers? Tears roll down her cheeks. I bow my head and press my cock in and out of her body. She's given me so much pain, I'm nearly numb once again.

CHAPTER 38

Cheryl sits in a half-circle booth at the back of Dan Tana's. The lights are dim and the crowd sparkles with the glittering old money of Los Angeles. Her beauty strikes me. She's a breath-taking woman made even more beautiful by the way she carries her beauty. Strong. Aware. Powerful. She can be kind and loving, and with a southern gentility of a steel magnolia. Not a shred of weakness inhabits her existence.

There is nothing odd about the two of us meeting for dinner other than we've never been in public together before tonight. I've licked every inch of her skin, sucked on her sugar-sweet nipples, and caressed her clit, and yet we've never had a meal in a public place before this moment. I'm no long Wonderfuck for her. Now I'm Jake.

I approach the table and she tilts her head up toward me. While her lips smile, her blue eyes hold ice. Our last parting wasn't kind. I lean down and she presses her lips to my cheek. Chanel #5 whispers in the air.

"Jake," she purrs.

Her Southern accent embraces me like a warm stroke across the thigh. I wait for the jolt to my cock that comes with Cheryl's nearness. All the memories of her naked and us fucking, plow through my mind and yet, there is nothing. Not one hint of movement from my dick.

Fuck.

Fuck. Fuck. Fuck.

I sit beside Cheryl. No physical reaction to this woman means I am hung up on Tara. So hung up that the swell of Cheryl's breast that peeks out from the top of her silk shirt does nothing for me. She's been the most consistent sex in my life since Susie. My first Wonderfuck and my cock doesn't even twitch.

Fuck.

"I've missed you."

Beneath the table she rests her hand on my thigh.

I wish my cock had missed her too.

"I see you're still wearing my present. Guess that's a good sign."

I glance at my wrist where the watch she gave me, that is well north what any American family makes in two years, rests.

The server pours our wine and then quietly disappears into the background. The noises around us fade, and we are two people very much alone, discussing things that we never thought we'd discuss.

"Why here?"

"Well darlin' there's nothing to hide now anymore is there? I'm one of the wealthiest women in Los Angeles and you're one of the most prolific VC men, so I don't think there's any reason at all that people would be suspicious of us dining together. Makes perfect sense."

Her gaze softens. The ice in her eyes turns to the serenity of sky.

"I missed you," she says, her voice barely above a whisper. "I've missed us."

I know her words are true and I wish I could say the same words and mean them. I didn't miss her, not when I was with Tara and I believed there was a future between us. Then, I didn't miss anyone or anything but Tara. Even Susie had lost her grip on my throat. Not now. Now I can't have either Susie or Tara, and I don't want any other woman.

Like she can read my mind, Cheryl's gaze sharpens. "Please tell me you're not still seeing her? Not after what she did?"

Cheryl is correct. What kind of sadist would continue to see a woman who betrayed him the way Tara betrayed me? Maybe the same type of asshole who would remain engaged to a woman with a sex addiction she can't kick? So very fucking twisted and fucked up. My psyche is beyond damaged.

My silence tells my story, and Cheryl leans back into the booth.

"But why, sugar?" The remnants of her Southern accent hang in the air. "What good can come of seeing this woman? She betrayed your trust."

"I don't know." I swallow. "I'm not sure I *want* to see her anymore, but I may not have a choice."

"I'm not buying what you're selling. We all have choices."

Cheryl's hand strokes my thigh beneath the table. She strokes up and I wish for my cock to react, because then, yeah, then, I'd have a choice.

Nada.

"Darlin' you give everything you have where women are concerned, except your heart. That is like steel." Her hand drifts higher up my leg. "Except for that Susie of yours, I don't think you'll ever fall in love."

She's reached the front of my pants. Her hand drifts along my trousers. Her eyebrow lifts. She's not feeling what she expects to feel and neither am I. No strong, hard cock. No man who can Wonderfuck his cares away. No guy who could take Cheryl anywhere, anytime, and make her scream.

Cheryl's hand remains in the spot where my limp dick has replaced my hard cock. Her facial expression doesn't change, but her gaze tells a different story.

"I think I found my answer."

Sympathy. I see sympathy in her eyes. Fuck that. There's nothing worse than sympathy from a woman when your cock won't get hard.

I shift away from Cheryl's touch.

Heat burns a hole through my heart. Men are pretty fucking ego-driven where our dicks are concerned, and the idea that a woman I've pleasured hundreds of times has discovered that I can't get hard – when not long ago a glance at Cheryl could drive me to stone – is a blow I can barely fucking take. But it's true. This is the fact. The reality is that my dick is soft and the only woman who gets me off right now is the very one who betrayed me.

How fucked up am I?

"She's the only one right now, isn't she?"

My face doesn't move a muscle, not a slip of emotion, but Cheryl's known me too long not to read the response in my eyes. She realizes the fucking truth, that I am unfuckable, unless I am fucking the woman that I'm pissed at. The woman who betrayed me. The woman my heart and body wants but that my mind tells me is the worst decision I could possibly make.

"I always did enjoy a challenge."

My stomach sours. Not only does my dick fail to get hard for this woman but the idea of her trying, and me failing, makes me want to puke.

"We didn't come to this restaurant to fuck."

"Why the hell not?" she asks.

We could. Cheryl would let me try to take her in this booth or at the very least press my finger to her clit and get her off, right here, right now. I grasp her hand and pull my fingertips along her thigh to the edge of her skirt. Yes, she'd love it if I slipped my fingertip beneath her panties. I tease the edge of the cloth with my finger.

She gasps. A slight intake of breath.

Oh yeah, she loves this. I stare into her eyes and it's as though she's daring me, seeing if I'll actually do what I'm threatening. She wants me to push her to orgasm right here, right now, in this place. My finger trails along the soft skin and she slides her legs open. Hot wet heat is a millimeter away. I could make her come. I could press my fingertips against her clit and rub until she orgasms. I pull my fingers back from Cheryl's sex.

I stop.

Why? Who the fuck knows....because the desire is absent. I could get her off, right here in the circle booth at Dan Tana's but I don't want to. Instead, I want the one person I shouldn't want. I want Tara.

"I think you're making a big mistake."

Cheryl's voice is raspy, with hints of unfulfilled desire. She licks her bottom lip and takes a sip of wine. "That reporter of yours will only cause you a world of pain."

Cheryl's right. I *know* I'm making a huge mistake. I'm so fucking twisted and masochistic that the pain Tara can cause me is the only thing I want.

"She reached out to me."

My heart careens through my chest.

Cheryl continues. "How do you think she got all those quotes?"

"I didn't really think about it."

"Didn't think about it or didn't want to?"

"Didn't want to."

"You're hung up on this woman and you're ignoring her deceit. Why does that sound familiar?"

Heat cascades through my chest and I want to direct my rage at Cheryl, but I know the place my anger should be directed is Tara. Cheryl is the messenger of a story I want to pretend is untrue.

"She doesn't know about you. I've never mentioned you or anyone else."

"Well she found me. I don't how, but she did. I didn't respond to her request, but she's a reporter, she'll dig and dig and dig until she gets all the answers she wants."

Was Tara still digging? Was that what last night was? Not an attempt at forgiveness and starting over but another chance at deceit, a new story, a new angle, maybe even a—

"You know she's got a book contract."

Cheryl speaks my very fears.

"Next, she'll line up for the morning talk-circuit for this little article she's written. Seems like you've given her career quite the boost."

My guts twist.

"So darlin', I just wanted you to be aware of what you've gotten yourself into with this one. That's why we're meeting in public. Because what kind of woman would actually meet the Wonderfuck in public if she was actually sleeping with him?"

She sips her wine and her gaze caresses the diners in the restaurant. "My way of throwin' off the scent." Cheryl looks at me. "But darlin', you've got yourself a leak somewhere or maybe she's simply been riflin' through your things. Whatever it is, I don't know exactly what she knows or what she plans to do with what she knows, and that makes me pretty uncomfortable."

As it should.

"Any ideas about what she's up to now?"

I don't know what the fuck Tara is doing, and it's pretty obvious to me that I never did.

"I don't keep your number on my regular phone, or I didn't before you texted to set up tonight. I don't put names in my other phone. All that phone does is take texts and calls and—"

I stop. My heart burns in my chest. Fuck. Did she... Could she have...What the fuck..?

"Right." Cheryl's eyes register that I've discovered another fact that damns Tara even further. "I thought you should know what type of person you're dealin' with. It wasn't like she just sent out a notice on Craigslist asking for women who had visited Wonderfuck. She contacted us. Individually. Using our personal phone numbers."

I close my eyes. Tara didn't lie to me, she simply hadn't told

me the truth either. A lie by omission. I'm familiar with those....
Susie. Even last night. The fucking, and the emotion.

"I'm sorry darlin'." Cheryl squeezes my bicep. "A lot of people aren't what they seem, and I'm afraid this Tara is most definitely all about herself."

And I know that Cheryl is right.

CHAPTER 39

"WHY ARE THERE forty empty coffee cans in Mom's garage?"

I stand behind Rachel. She sits on the kitchen floor with all the cabinets open. She glances over her shoulder and up at me.

"Maybe for the same reason that there are thirty-seven empty butter tubs in the pantry?" Rachel sighs.

Going through Mom's house isn't easy. In fact, it sucks big time, and this is only day one. She stands and rubs her hands across the back of her jeans. "Lunch?"

I nod. We've been at this since 7 a.m., but it feels like a life-time. I follow her into the living room. Mom sits beside Lily who holds a doll on her lap and tries to braid the doll's hair. Mom gently combs the curls of a black-haired doll that sits on her lap.

My heart cracks. A faraway look inhabits Mom's eyes, as though her mind can't even latch onto anything or anyone in this room. She's fading, and some days that fade seems exponential.

Tatianna, Mom's nurse, touches Mom's shoulder. "It's time for a nap."

Mom smiles and nods, and without a word stands. Her eyes meet mine and she doesn't even bother to call me Richard, my father's name.

"You nice young people are so kind to come over and clean. Thank you."

She hands Lily the doll, then grasps Tatianna's hand. Together they walk toward the stairs.

"I didn't think anything could be worse than her thinking I was Dad, but this is."

"She doesn't even think I'm her version of Nurse Cratchett anymore."

Rachel picks up some crayons on the table where Lily and Mom were coloring before the dolls, and puts them in their box. "I'd rather she complained about me, than get that blank stare."

Rachel's voice is low and her gaze focused on the crayons and coloring books, but I hear the ache in my tough big sister's voice and know she's trying not to cry. Rachel is cleaning up, keeping busy, moving everything forward with a goal in mind, because that's what Rachel does, that is how she deals with tough issues and sadness and pain. Rachel digs in, puts her head down, and works.

Me? Well in the past I Wonderfucked my way through my emotion, but it seems that's no longer an option. Unless I fuck Tara.

Shit.

We leave Lily with both dolls and I follow Rachel into the kitchen where she pulls out deli meat, a tomato, mustard, and cheese from the fridge. She washes and slices the tomato.

"I had lunch with Tara last week."

My stomach tightens. I pause where I was pouring chips into a bowl for the three of us to share. These are not the words I expected, and Tara isn't a topic I want to discuss. I'd rather talk about Mom and the nursing home, scratch that, resident home, or even my inability to heal from my fiancée's death, than discuss Tara.

"She's not moving to San Francisco."

I say nothing because there's nothing to say.

Rachel stop slicing the tomato and turns to me. "Why did you do that?"

I can't answer. What can I say? She wrote an expose on the most intimate part of my life? We Wonderfucked, and then she wrote about it and I'm fucking pissed because she betrayed me on the most intimate level.

"Was it because of her article? The one about the Wonderfuck guy? Was she sleeping with you at the same time that she was—"

"Wonderfucking?"

I finish Rachel's sentence. Her face turns the same shade of red as the tomato she slices.

"She wasn't with me then," I say.

And it's true. Or a truth I've tried to maintain the entire time I've Wonderfucked. No blurring of lines. None of the women I sleep with know Jake, and no one who knows Jake knows of Wonderfuck.

Or so I thought. Until now. And Tara.

Yeah, Tara messed that up for me or I messed that up for me because I let myself care. I discovered there was a piece of my heart left even after Susie smashed it to smithereens. I made the mistake of giving that little bit to Tara, and she fucking chewed it up and spat it out.

"If you don't want to be with her, then why do you want her to stay in Los Angeles?"

"I have my reasons."

"Care to share?"

"Not with you. Not when you're lunching with Tara and talking about me. No, absolutely not."

My voice has an edge. I lean against the counter and look at Rachel. "How would you feel if I was lunching with your ex? You know, and discussing you and your life?"

"Not the same."

"Really? Because I imagine you'd feel like it was a betrayal, because you loved him, and he did something that broke your heart, and I'm you're brother and I'm supposed to be on your side. Not on the side of the dumbass that betrayed you."

Rachel's nostrils flare, and her gaze turns away from me and back to slicing the tomato. "Point taken." She slides the knife through the firm red flesh. "I...I don't think I realized how much...how emotionally involved you were with her."

"Right. Just because I don't talk about my feelings doesn't mean I don't feel them, okay?" I dump the rest of the potato chips into a bowl.

"You're right." Rachel's voice is softer. "I...I just always assume you're over something because you don't talk about it, but that's not fair and it's obviously not true. I'm sorry."

And I feel like an asshole. Because I know in my heart that if I would talk more to Rachel she'd understand, and she'd never intentionally betray me. She's always been on my side because that's the kind of sister she is, the kind of woman she is, the kind of person she is, and I'm simply a dick.

She would always pick me, her little brother, over anyone else because that's how Rachel rolls, but when I act all over it, and laissez faire, and as though things don't matter to me, well she does what adult people do. She accepts what my actions tell her and believes me.

"It feels a little raw," I say. "I...I cared for her. I still care for her. I can't talk about it yet, but I don't like the idea of you hanging out with her and talking about me because I don't think we....I....can trust her. She, well, she may not be who she appears to be."

Rachel's eyebrows pull tight. By even saying that little bit I've set her lawyer, now judge mind, to spin, and while Rachel may not consciously try to dig for answers like Tara does, Rachel will fucking dig, because that's what Rachel does too. She looks for answers where family is concerned.

What is it with these fucking women that I love? Why do they have to always look for the truth when I know that the truth is the one thing that will break their hearts?

I lean against the counter. "Are you ever loyal to me?"

"What kind of question is that?"

"Are you loyal to me? Do you fucking have my back? It seems any time I tell you anything you're off telling someone else about it. One of your girlfriends, one of my ex girlfriends. What the fuck, Rachel? If I talked about you as much as you talk about me, you'd be pissed."

Rachel's jaw drops open and my judge sister, who has an argument for every scenario, is actually silent.

"I mean, I get that you like my former neighbor, and I get that you and Jane were best friends, so you discussed me and Susie, but do you have to hang out with every woman I'm involved with?"

"I can't even—"

"What? Believe that you do that? Well you do. I mean what was it about Susie exactly that made you think you should have lunch with her every damn week to discuss me and her and our life, or the life that we were trying to build? And now Tara? I mean she came to your house once, got involved with me, and suddenly you two are besties? What the hell?"

"We're not...I mean...she called and—"

"Oh, so you're telling me that you didn't invite her to lunch?"

My sister sucks at poker, she sucks at lying, and she sure as hell sucks at basically anything but the truth, which is an awesome trait to have when you're a judge, but not so great when you're doing things that both you and your little brother know are pretty shitty.

"I always have your back, that's why I used to have lunch with Susie. That's why I have lunch with Tara, why I—"

"Bullshit. You're nosy and a control freak and intrusive, and you want to try and micro-manage my existence, and I've got one thing to say to that. Butt out. My life is mine."

Rachel's mouth closes so hard that the tiny muscle in her jaw flinches. I wait for the blowback that always comes from Rachel as to why she's right and why I'm wrong. This argument usually hinges on the idea that she's the oldest and I'm the baby and don't have any idea what I'm talking about.

But this time she's wrong and we both know it. Her silence proves it. I walk out to the dining room and put the bowl of chips on the table and hope it's a fast lunch so I can get back to my coffee cans.

❧

WHAT'S LEFT OF MY LIFE?

I pull open the drawer in the bedside table. My finger runs over the top of my Wonderfuck phone. My salvation for five years. The identity in which I sank my cock and buried my pain. Gone. Destroyed. Completely fucked by love.

Fuck.

I can't get hard except for the one woman who betrayed me. Freud would have a field day with my fucked up mind. How messed up is it that I only want the women who fuck me over?

What the hell?

The edges of my soul are fraying and my body is peeling away from my bones. I hold my Wonderfuck phone in my palm and pace the floor. Like a mother-fucking caged cat I have all this...this...pain and rage, and whatever else the fuck emotion I want to ignore, is bottled up and ready to explode. Fuck or fight. Fuck or fight.

I need relief. God, yes.

I refuse to fall inside a bottle again like after Susie. Where can I find relief? Where can I sink into what I want and what I need and who I have to be? I can't exist like this. The need eats away at my insides and I'm desperate for release.

I flip open the phone and punch in a number. A number that I know well. 'The London? Tonight?'

I wait. I stare at the screen. Want. Need. Rage. Desperation.

They careen through me, making me feel like a ship on an angry storm-soaked sea.

Finally, a reply.

'Yes.'

Desire pulses through me. Adrenalin floods my bloodstream. Fuck, yeah. My cock is hard.

When it was published, I read the fucking article. I read every damn word. The article that turned my carefully crafted existence into a freak show for every person in Los Angeles to see and judge and talk about.

Fuck the circus. I've never liked clowns.

I press the phone into my pocket and know that this, tonight, the London, is my first step back from the edge of the abyss, the beginning back to my Wonderfucking days.

CHAPTER 40

A FADED LIGHT slips through the crisp drapes. The sun stays in the sky. It's nearly summer, and dusk comes later to LA. The door opens behind me and I don't turn. I don't sit as I usually do when I wait for a woman to Wonderfuck. I'm not a stud or an alpha male in this moment as I stand with my back to the door staring out into the oncoming night.

I am a fucking captive.

The door closes and I hear her breath. That is how quiet the room is.

"Why are we here?" she finally asks.

I turn to her and just like every time I see her, the sight of her pummels the air from my lungs.

A tremor cascades through her body, but she keeps her chin at that full-on warrior-woman tilt, telling me that she doesn't really care. Letting me know without words that she's pissed at me, even while I'm pissed at her.

I walk toward her and I can see the pupils in her eyes grow bigger and her nipples grow hard. Her body betrays her arousal. That tilt? That anger? All of it is complete and utter bullshit. Something I've learned that she's good at selling, even to the people she claims to love. She wants me like I want her.

"Jake—"

"That's not who I am. Not here. Not to you."

Her gaze widens. Maybe not what she expected, not what she anticipated.

I stop in front of her. I'm bigger than her. Much bigger. She's seen what my fists can do to a man. She knows I have a hair-trigger temper that is backed by an abyss of rage that dwells in my soul. The energy in this room is different than the other day in my apartment. Much different.

I'm even angrier than I was before. Needier. More volatile.

My fingertips trace the edge of her jaw and her skin pebbles. Her breath shortens.

I'm angry at her, filled with this intermingling desire, but I'd never be rough with her....unless she wanted that.

"Why am I here?" Her voice is softer and her chin tilts down, more submissive now. The scent of her arousal fills my nose, and her heartbeat flickers fast in her neck.

I lean down, my lips close to her ear. "Because I need to fuck, and you're the only woman my cock seems to want."

Her eyes close with my words.

How do those words make her feel? Words of lust, but most definitely not words of love, because after what she did I can't give her those words, not anymore. She took my love and smashed it on the rocks for public display.

"What about you? Why are you here?"

Her tongue flicks over her lower lip. Heat rolls off her body. Desire. Want. She raises her eyes to me. "Because I want you. You're the only man I want."

Hard. As. Stone.

My cock is soft when Cheryl fondles me, and I can't get hard in my own hand, but now, standing next to Tara, without even touching her, I'm rock hard. Tara has emotionally castrated me. Until now. This moment.

My hands clench and unclench. Her nipples press against her shirt, pearls of pleasure that wait for my fingertips, my mouth, my tongue. Taut and sweet. Her lips are parted and her rosebud mouth is near my cheek.

"Jake," she whispers.

I don't want to hear her words. I don't want to know how sorry she is or feels. I don't want to hear about her guilt.

Anger mixed with carnal desire rushes through my body.

"No more words."

I grasp one of her shoulders and weave my hand into her hair. Her eyes are on me, and her desire for me to do whatever the fuck I want in this moment, is written across her face. I let loose of her shoulder, grasp the bottom of her shirt, and rip it open like a hot knife through butter.

"Oh my go—"

My lips end her sentence. A hard kiss. A kiss with power and control and command. I will take what I want because she is here to give it to me. Her mouth opens to mine. My right hand cups her breast and lifts it from her bra. The pad of my thumb strokes over the taut bud of flesh. A moan crosses her lips. Her hand shifts away from clutching the fabric of my shirt to my cock, where she grasps me.

Fuck, yes.

I pull my mouth from her lips, lean forward and pull the flesh of her breast, her nipple, between my lips. Tara's head falls back against my hand.

"Oh god, yes Jake," she moans in this high-pitched voice. "Please. Fuck me now."

No. I'm not going to fuck her now. I'm not going to satisfy her for a very long while.

No.

I'm going to make Tara writhe with pleasure. I am going to make her come and come and come again, until she's wrung out and can't come anymore.

My tongue slides around her nipple and I suck. My hand pulls up her skirt and my fingertip edges the lace of her panties. I press one finger over the fabric where her clit is. Warm and wet. Another gasp from her lips with the pressure of my fingertip.

I let loose of her breast and lift her into my arms. I walk from the sitting room, past the bar, and to the giant bed just through the French doors. I set her down in front of the bed. I reach around her, unhook her bra, slide my hands down the side of her body, and pull down the zipper of her skirt. Beautiful bare flesh, soft beneath my palms.

She's naked before me. Her figure full of curves. Her flesh prickled with desire, her lips red roughened from my kiss.

My cock could explode now. I remove every bit of my clothing while she stands at the edge of the bed.

There's a reason why Wonderfuck is an accurate name. Not just the motion of the ocean ladies, but the actual size is a Wonder.

Her gaze flits down to my engorged dick. She's taken all of me plenty of times, and she will again tonight, over and over and over, but it's been a couple of weeks and her eyes widen as she looks at my throbbing dick.

Women's eyes always widen when they see my cock.

Her fingers reach out to me and touch the tip of my cock. I close my eyes. Thank god, I'm hard. To lose your ability to jack off? To fuck? I don't think there is anything crueler on this planet.

A light stroke at first, then she grasps my shaft and slides her hand down all the way to the base. Her other hand massages the head of my cock, and then she is kneeling before me.

Those gorgeous rosebud lips open and her tongue flicks out over my flesh like she's licking an ice cream cone.

And I nearly come. Fuck, yeah. I've gone from Wonder-fucking all day to nothing, and I need this release. I'm an addict, and Tara's my only chance at a hit. I'm fucking thankful that I've got an erect cock, and the pleasure of her tongue on me is so immense I nearly come. She licks the pre-ejaculate off my cock, and now she does what every man in this entire fucking world wants – sometimes even more than to fuck – she slides my rock hard cock deep, deep, deep, into her mouth. So deep I'm nearly hip deep. Her hand is strong and chases the suction of her lips.

My hands are in her hair. I hold the side of her head. Eyes closed, I absorb every bit of this pleasure. Concentrating on controlling my slow, steady rhythm because I want to slam my cock hard into her mouth.

The muscles in my back tighten. Heat rolls up over the muscles in my legs and my balls draw close to my body.

She sucks harder and faster and the muscles in my belly quiver. I'm close. Her hand gently clutches my balls, and heat sears from inside me and shoots from my cock hard and fast, and the pleasure sprays from me deep into her mouth.

She swallows and sucks, taking every drop of me, and it is sexy as fuck. My body shudders and tightens. I bend forward, unable to stand with the force of my orgasm. Slowly, she slips my cock from her lips and her tongue flicks over the head of me.

Fuck. That felt good. Better than good. The first orgasm I've had since the last time I was with Tara. Now the edge is off. I step away from her and look down. Her gaze is on me and she has a slight smile on her lips. She should. She gives great head. She's beautiful, and she's just pleased me and made me come.

She glances at my cock and her eyes widen.

Because I'm hard again. Nearly erect. I can feel it. I know.

A quizzical expression passes over her face.

I haven't fucked in nearly two weeks and my body wants this, my body needs this, my body and my mind know that the only thing that keeps me even halfway sane is fucking. Wonderfucking. Right now, here with Tara, is my one chance to get my Wonderfucking quota in.

My smile is wicked. A smile that acknowledges Tara's about to have a night she will never forget. Panic in Tara's eyes. Not because of fear. She isn't afraid of me. She knows she can stand, dress, and leave whenever she likes. Ladies choice. Always. No matter how badly I may need or want to fuck her, everything is her decision. Those are the rules. The woman always gets to say yes or no. There are no other ways to play.

No. That panic is because my refractory time is infinitesimal and my hunger never-ending.

I take her hand and Tara stands. I press her back onto the plush bed, ready to give her the night of her life.

I don't feel generous. I don't feel giving. I don't feel what I normally feel when I Wonderfuck. A heavy thick mix of anger and want and need and love pounds through my body. A toxic mix of emotion that leads me to think only of my desires. I want to do to Tara whatever the fuck I want.

She will have pleasure, but Tara enjoying tonight will be a side effect, not my primary goal. My primary goal is to fuck away this pain, this anger, this sadness, my betrayal, and to fuck it away with the only woman my cock seems willing to fuck. I walk to the closet where I've unpacked a bag and some...toys.

I know what I want and it has very little to do with her desires and everything to do with my frustration. I pull out two ties. I packed belts too, but belts leave marks. Fuck it. I grab the whole damn bag and drop it at the edge of the bed.

"What's that?"

"I brought some—" I lift my eyebrow. I do not smile —"things."

"What kind of things."

Fuck the silk ties. Here come the leather belts. I grab two black beauties from the bag and stand beside the bed. I let the leather tip slide down the side of her body guided by my hand. She shivers.

"Spread eagle."

Not a word, and she does what I command.

Glorious. Her body is glorious in this position. Her legs down toward each corner of the bed and her arms above her head. A stunning X across the bed. Her sex has tight curls and they glisten for me. She is wet. I lift one of her arms and I fasten it to the bedpost. She closes her eyes and a flush climbs over her skin.

I place my body over hers and lift her other arm and fasten her wrist to the bedpost.

She wiggles both wrists and opens her eyes. A wicked gleam flashes in her eyes. "It's not very tight."

"I can make it tighter." My voice rasps out over my desire, over my barely-contained anger that covers my pain.

She leans up and nips at me, her teeth flashing and catching my bottom lip. I pull back. Surprised. A slight metal taste in my mouth. I lick my lip and feel a sting where my tongue worries a bit of torn flesh. Nothing much. Gone in an instant.

Fire flashes in her eyes.

"No need," she says. Her body is beneath me and I'm on my knees straddling her. In this position, I'm reminded of how physically imposing I am in comparison to her, how easily overpowered, how dominated, how vulnerable she is beneath me with her hands tied. How vulnerable, how trusting, and my heart starts to soften and ache, and a warmth akin to love courses through me.

Her hips shift and roll and I'm pulled back to the insistence of my cock.

"Safe word?" I ask.

"What's yours?"

I've had the same safe word since I became Wonderfuck. The one word that I've always known. No matter how deep I was into desire, how hard, how mindless things became, if I uttered this word while Wonderfucking, I was in too deep.

"Susie."

Her eyes go from excitement to pain. Sadness. Not the emotions that will help keep my cock hard. There is no jealousy in her gaze. Her gaze reflects back to me the permanent pain etched in my heart.

"And you?"

I slide my fingertip over her pubic bone, through her curls and rub her clit. Her hips hitch upward in response and I press two fingers of my other hand deep into her sex.

"What is your safe word?" I press in and out of her sex and lean forward, closer to her, the hugeness of my body hovering above her. "Because you may need it." An edge to me, an anger that is leashed, but pulling hard at the chain.

"Violet," she says.

I don't know what this means to her or why she's chosen it, and while this seems unfair for the slenderest of moments because she knows about Susie, honestly I don't fucking care.

That's a lie.

I don't *want* to care, but I do. I shift the thought from my mind, about what this word means to Tara, because I've got a hard cock, something I can't take for granted because it only happens when Tara is around. This cock desperately wants to sink hip deep into Tara while she's tied up and spread eagled on the bed, but instead I simply continue with my one finger stroking her clit, and two fingers on my other hand sliding through the warmth and wet of her sex.

Her hips roll up and down with each stroke. Her wild-eyed gaze latches onto me. Her face flushed with desire and her nipples tight. Her entire body a taut string seeking the release I can give.

"Please, oh my god, Jake. Please." Her sex tightens around my fingers and I slide my fingers from her sex and pull away just as she reaches the moment of release. My body stays between her spread eagled legs, but I don't touch her.

"No, no, no," she moans, her hips continuing to roll as though she can reach me and force me to provide her the pleasure she so obviously desires.

I don't want to simply provide her pleasure. I want to see her moan and wail and need. I want her to feel a deep-seated need that only I can satisfy. Much like me who has been emotionally castrated by this woman, I want her to know not only desire but need. She is the only woman I can get erect with. I can't even jack my own self off. I have to be with Tara. The one woman I loathe. The one woman I love.

I lower myself to just above her. A push-up above her flesh, a plank pose that causes my arm muscles to tighten and tremble. My mouth just above her mouth. The heat of desire between us. The live wire energy of pure lust sizzling between us.

"You want me to fuck you."

"God, yes."

"Too bad, sweetheart. I'm taking my own fucking time."

Her hips jut up and I feel the heat and wet of her sex so close to my cock, touching it and making my body fucking tighten, and my thoughts of taking it slow grow hazy with a wild lust overtaking and fogging my brain. I pull back from her. I'm between her legs and I press my lips to her and pull my tongue down over the curved flesh of her stomach and to her curls. Her body hitches upward. I cup my hand over her hip bone and still her rolling hips. I part her with my fingers and stroke my tongue over her clit. I start with the W that I edge out over her clit and keep spelling. I don't get to the U before she is moaning and writhing. I pull my face from her sex.

Another wail, another long moan, because I have again left her unfulfilled, unsatisfied, on the edge of her orgasm.

"Why? Jake, please."

Unfortunately for me, her moans do exactly what they are meant to do, they strip away my resolve to sexually taunt this woman for the rest of the night. I move up her body and pull her nipple deep into my mouth. I don't touch her sex because with one touch I'll send her over the edge into the pleasure she seeks. She's close and every touch, every taste, every bit of what I do to her can catapult her to orgasm.

Tonight, Tara will orgasm when I decide to make her orgasm, and not before.

Her body is mine for the taking and in her inability to move, I regain some bit of strength I've lost being unable to fuck. I enjoy that she can't move, she can't grab, she can't control or demand. This is not me Wonderfucking away her pain and giving her everything I have to give. I did that and she nearly destroyed me.

This is me taking.

This is me demanding.

This is me fucking in a carnal, wild way that is for me and my pleasure and my pleasure only.

I release her nipple and pull my lips across her chest to her other nipple, taut and erect and begging to be sucked. My body is above her and now I settle myself between her legs and let my cock, hard and long, rest in her cleft.

"Oh fuck I'm gong to—"

I pull my body off her. The pressure of my cock against her clit is enough to send her over the edge.

Fuck.

My balls pull up tight against my body and I know that I don't have long. That I too am going to fucking come all over her body if I don't fuck her soon. I reach past Tara to the nightstand and pull out a foil wrapper.

"I'm going to fuck you." Hard words. Hard tone. She writhes. My words, my tone, my command, my dominance makes her want me all the more.

"Yes, please, yes, yes," she says, her entire body thrumming. "Fuck me, please fuck me."

I plant my hand on either side of her head and the head of my cock rests at her entrance.

"You are mine." I thrust my cock deep into her sex.

A loud shriek of pleasure comes from Tara.

I pull back and thrust up again. She's so hot, so turned on, so ready for me, that two thrusts and her body tightens around me. My control is gone and I'm thrusting in and out of her and our skin is slapping. Hypnotized by the connection between our bodies, where my cock sinks into her body over and over and over again.

Heat flashes through me and down the shaft of my cock. I pull my head back, look into her eyes and let out a roar, releasing my rage, my pain, my pleasure, and surrender to that bitch named Love.

CHAPTER 41

"MR. REYNOLDS, it's my understanding that this altercation took place on the street, in front of a bar, after you'd been drinking."

I say nothing. I don't even nod.

Judge Williams peers over her glasses at me. I know she knows who I am, that I'm her colleague's little brother, but it feels as though instead of my being related to a Los Angeles County judge being a benefit to me, it may actually make this whole thing a lot worse.

"Your Honor, the police report fails to state that Mr. Reynolds came to the aid of a woman that had just been assaulted by her former fiancé." Cassidy glances toward the seats behind us and toward Tara. "She's here today to show her support for Mr. Reynolds."

The heat of Tara's gaze is on my back. I feel her presence as though it were her skin against mine.

"Mr. Reynolds, you're willing to take the offer presented by the City Attorney?"

"I am."

Judge Williams glances from me to my attorney, and then to the prosecutor standing behind her desk in the courtroom.

"Very well." She reads through a spate of legal mumbo jumbo, which my attorney has spent nearly an hour explaining to me before my court date.

"Your sentence will be deferred pending completion of your community service hours, as well as restitution and medical expenses." Judge Williams leans forward. "It would seem he lost a tooth."

I'm surprised it was only one. I don't say it, but I think it. McDouche-nugget got the benefit of my rage that night in front of Taggerts after he grabbed Tara and then knocked her to the ground. Douche-wad is a no-show today. Coward.

"Mr. Reynolds, I'm also adding on anger management therapy."

"What the fu—"

Cassidy grabs my upper arm. Her grasp is tight.

"Of course your honor, Mr. Reynolds will comply with all the court's orders."

"Therapist of his choosing to be approved by the court and paid for by Mr. Reynolds." She glances at the papers in front of her. "It would seem he has every financial advantage."

She's right. I do. I've worked for it, but I do have every advantage. I'm irritated and pissed at myself for losing my cool enough to end up in a courtroom in downtown LA. But after watching people in orange jumpsuits being led in and out of this courtroom for an hour this morning, I realize that the existence I lead is pretty fucking privileged.

I may have earned my money, but I didn't earn my privilege. That came for free. No way is justice blind or fair after what I saw in this courtroom today.

"Thank you, your honor," Cassidy says.

"Thank you, Judge Williams," I say, and I mean it. She could have thrown my ass in jail with the damage I did to Douche-muffin's face.

"Nothing, Mr. Reynolds. Nothing, for the next two years, are we clear?"

I nod. "Yes your honor."

I follow Cassidy through the gate toward the back of the courtroom. Tara isn't sitting in the cheap seats any longer. I'm good with that. I didn't ask her to come here, and really, I don't want to see her. Not now. Not here. Not as Jake. Not anymore.

"Find a therapist this week, send me the name and address. I'll get it to the court. Pay the money. Probation will contact you about your community service hours."

I nod.

I walk out of the courtroom and turn the corner.

Tara.

Still, even after fucking on multiple occasions, I haven't resolved my anger, her anger, our combined rage. My eyes glance over her body, the only place I can find solace anymore.

She's not alone.

Douchenozzle did show up today after all.

My jaw muscle twitches. They're talking. He's smiling. She smiles back. Now she's touching her hair in that very female 'I'm flirting with you' way that is completely un-Tara. What the actual fuck? Is she flirting with Sir Douche-a-lot?

How could that be?

She's smarter than that.

Isn't she?

What the actual hell?

Heat threads through my chest like an electrified wire hanger. I'm having a hard time believing what I'm seeing. That Tara is actually being friendly to the guy she caught banging his colleague on his desk.

Fuck.

Was the entire thing bullshit….from the beginning?

Her smile.

Her eyes.

The way she touches her hair.

Did she set me up from the first moment in the hall…did she know? Has she known since before that…

Sure the break up might have been real, but was anything else?

I turn. I walk. I don't look back.

Fuck or fight. Unfortunately for me, today, without Tara and because of Douchey, I can't do either one.

❦

"I can't remember, did you dye your hair or was this the actual color when you were in high school?"

Rachel stands beside me and tilts a faded picture in a frame toward me. Baseball circa 1999. Me with twelve other guys all in Pali High uniforms.

"Where'd you find that?" I reach for the photo and run through the faces of these guys. We were out getting high, drunk, and laid, when we absolutely should've been home locked in our rooms.

"Were we ever that young?"

"There's evidence that you were. So far I can't find any pictures of me while in high school." Rachel sighs. "Do you think she burned them? This one of you was in the time capsule that is Dad's office." She nods toward the far end of the downstairs where Dad's office is located.

"Seriously, it still smells like him. You know that Old Spice meets bourbon scent?"

I nod. I do know. I remember. Dad's sacred space. We didn't enter that room unless we were summoned, and the only time we were summoned was when we were in trouble.

"You know how we never went in there? Well it seems neither did anyone else. Even after he died."

I'm willing to continue in the garage if Rachel will go through Dad's study.

"Anything..." My words trail off because I don't want to ask but I have to.

"Incriminating?"

I nod.

"Not yet, but I haven't gotten to the locked drawers."

Deep breath. Who knows, we could have siblings in Sacramento. Not kidding. Not in the least.

"Speaking of incriminating, how did your court date go?"

Rachel uses the big sister voice she reserves for when she feels morally superior and I'm the younger brother fuck up. Like now.

"Okay." I stop there. My form of torture. I'm guessing that her buddy Judge Williams filled her in, off the record of course, on what happened in court, but now Big Sis wants to hear it from me and assess whether I'm repentant or on my way toward another fall.

"That's it?"

"You already know. Restitution. Fine. Community Service."

I pull out a garbage bag form the box and shake it open.

"And..."

I look over my shoulder.

"And a therapist of my choosing. Okay? Happy? A therapist. You've been angling for that for going on five years."

Rachel presses her lips together, which tells me that she knew about the therapist before I told her.

"Did you ask her to order therapy?"

"That would be completely inappropriate."

Great lawyer. Awesome judge. Again, bad fucking liar. I say nothing. I don't want to have this argument. Rachel has hounded me about going to therapy since Susie died.

"Let me know if you need a referral," she says, and walks toward the door between the house and the garage.

"Thanks." I open up the third giant box that's shoved into the half of the garage that doesn't house a car. So far I've found nothing but old newspapers, car parts, and tools. All of which now lie in their respective piles on the table I set up near the garage door.

"You only have a week, right? To find a therapist?"

"Thought you didn't discuss it."

She's incriminated herself.

"Did you see…" Rachel's words drift away. Great. Now there are two names she's uncertain she should say in front of me. Not doing so great with the women I choose to fall in love with.

"Tara? You can say her name. I know we argued about her, but I'm over it."

"Did you see her? In court?"

"We didn't speak, but yeah, she was there. And so was Mr. Douche."

"I'm guessing Mr. Douche is her ex-fiancé?"

"The guy I beat the shit out of because he knocked her on her ass? Yeah, he was there, and they were acting like long lost buds."

Rachel bites her bottom lip. Her face is tight as though debating whether to remain silent or tell me something that she thinks I don't want to know.

"Spill it."

Rachel sighs and glances toward the ceiling. "Look, I know you don't want me talking to Tara—"

"I don't care," I say, sounding more like a fourteen-year-old boy than a grown man. But ladies, no surprise. There are similarities. We are eternal man-children. "I'm over it."

"Not true. You lost your shit about me hanging out with Tara."

"Are you going to tell me or not?"

"*She* called *me*, okay, just so we're clear. We chatted. It would seem she's been talking to Greg."

"You mean Douchey? She's been talking to *Douchey*?"

Rachel nods.

"Is she a fucking idiot?"

"No, she's not an idiot. She's a woman who was in love with a man who made a mistake."

"Sticking your cock in another woman's vagina isn't a mistake. That's pretty intentional. A mistake is adding two plus two and getting five, which is actually more likely a mistake than fucking a woman other than your fiancé."

Rachel sighs. "While I agree with you 100 percent, I do understand what's going on in her mind. Okay. There were about two-and-a-half minutes when I talked to Dalton."

"You talked to Dalton? As in getting back together talked?"

"It was when Lily was hospitalized, for that fever? Right after he left and he had to come back and well..."

"You slept with him?"

My sister turns a shade of red reserved for fire engines and tomatoes.

"Are you kidding me?"

"I'm not proud of it, okay? But we were still married. I felt abandoned and Lily was in the damn hospital. Emotions were on high, okay? It was a rough time. So yes, we did. We slept together." Rachel takes a deep breath. "Then his girlfriend called from South America and I realized that he was a dumbass and I couldn't be married to a dumbass."

"Okay, I get it. You were still married. You'd been together for years, Lily was sick. Fine. But what's Tara's excuse?" I say it like I'm indifferent, but on the inside I am fucking enraged. Is she fucking him? Is she seeing him? What the fuck is going on? "They don't have a kid together, no one is in the hospital, and there's no reason she should be talking to him."

Rachel lifts an eyebrow and gives me 'the look', the one she's reserved for me, her little brother, since the beginning of time. The look that says not only are you stupid but you simply don't understand the female mind, which I don't...really, no man does.

"What? Why the look? What?"

"Okay, yes, you're right. They don't have children and no one is in the hospital, buuut, she did love him and they were engaged. The wedding was only six weeks away when she caught him and then she fell for this other guy who she found out has a bit of a problem with commitment...."

I say nothing. My sister knows less than half of what went down between me and Tara.

"Then she writes this amazeballs story about another guy who is perhaps the sexiest man in the universe."

I cringe. If Rachel knew who Wonderfuck was she definitely wouldn't think he was sexy.

"Then Greg calls her to tell her he misses her and he's gone to therapy, and that they should talk."

"Therapy? What the fuck is it with you women and therapy? As though therapy can erase every fucking sin?" I shake the trash bag and throw shit into it, disgusted by this entire conversation

"We believe in the power of change and redemption. We love a good redemption story. You know the bad boy who sees the error of his ways then goes through the long dark night of the soul, and because of the woman of his dreams, comes out the other side a better man able to love and care for the one woman he always loved."

Rachel stands with her hand clasped in front of her chest and her eyes wide.

"You read too many romance novels. You realize that we have dicks and if we're assholes who stick our dicks into other women when we're in a committed relationship that shit rarely changes...especially if it's a woman we've cheated on before."

"Whatever. We want to believe men can change. *We* change. We want to believe that you can too."

"We're a bunch of fourteen-year-old boys in grown up bodies. You really need to take the fucking keys to the world away from us."

"The future is female, brother."

"I'm down with that shit. Smash the patriarchy, sister. I am a-okay with female overlords."

Rachel smiles and shakes her head. "You're a smart man. One of the reasons I still love you."

I can't help but smile. Rachel is smart and amazing and has

always loved our family with a ferocious loyalty, even when our family was fucking nutbag crazy. Plus, she's bailed my ass out of jail on more than one occasion, which is really more than any person should ever ask of their big sister.

"Okay fine...I get it. But it doesn't mean I like it. Even if we're not going to be together, it doesn't mean she should be with Dochebucket."

"Then tell her."

I look away from Rachel. I don't want to have to tell Tara anything. I can barely talk to her. Of course she's the only woman I'm sleeping with, but we're really not talking. Not about anything important. I'm still too pissed about her article.

"Rachel?" The voice calls from inside the house.

"Oh my god, did Mom just say my name?" Mom hasn't used either of our names in nearly three weeks, plus she's stopped calling me Richard. We were both worried that the part of Mom's brain that remembers us was finished. We turn toward the door leading into the house.

"Mom?" Rachel scurries inside and I follow. Mom stands in the center of the living room in a white gown...is that...does she have on...

"Can you believe this still fits?"

Rachel's jaw drops open and her hand presses to her cheek. "Mom, is that...is that your wedding gown?"

"It was on the top shelf in my closest where I've always kept it, but then it was on the twin bed in the spare bedroom and I thought someone must have gotten it down. I don't know why I put it on. Guess I wanted to see if I could still get it on."

How the fuck is this my life? My sixty-seven-year-old mother stands in the middle of her living room wearing her wedding dress and for the first time in three weeks she remembers Rachel's name?

"Richard, do you remember this day?"

Oh fuck. Yep, she remembers Rachel but thinks I'm dear old Dad. When Mom thinks I'm Dad, I have this overwhelming need to not break Mom's heart. To at least say the things that she'd want Dad to say.

"You look as beautiful now as you did then."

Her smile could light up Los Angeles. Those are words that any woman would want to hear from their husband of forty-five years.

"Mom, let's go take this off and pack it up so it doesn't get ripped," Rachel says and walks toward mom. Mom pulls her gaze from me and gives Rachel a sharp look.

"Don't touch me, I don't even know who you are."

My sister's gaze shifts, and the corner of her mouth slips down. She recovers and pastes a smile onto her face. We've been through this before, this emotional whiplash that Mom causes because of this bullshit disease that shatters our hearts every time she's here. And then she's gone.

"No problem," Rachel says, her voice patient and filled with love. "I just wondered if I could help you with your dress."

Mom marches past Rachel toward the stairs. Her chin at a familiar angle, a slant we'd seen directed toward our father on many late nights when he returned home smelling of perfume, wearing lipstick on his collar that was a different shade than Mom's.

Rachel follows Mom up the stairs. She holds the train of the white gown, tinged yellow with age, my heart unsure it will ever recover from all the bullshit in my life.

CHAPTER 42

MY COCK IS LIMP. I grasp my dick and squeeze. Nope. Nothing. I've tried porn. I've obviously tried to jack off. Not a hint of wood. I close my eyes. I think of Tara.

Naked.

Her breasts full and round, and her mouth a gorgeous O shape. She kneels before me, such a gorgeous sight. Her mouth opens. She takes my cock into her hand and pulls my dick into her mouth...

I stroke up and down. Oh yeah. Getting harder. Firmer. Tara's mouth....yes, yes....Tara's mouth sucking my cock. From limp noodle to harder, not hard, but hard-ish. I stroke down and up. The wet suction of her mouth on my cock. Her slick lips on my flesh. Her mouth open and sliding over me. *This* is working. Finally, something other than Tara being in my bedroom is working. Granted, it's still her image, but oh yes, fuck yes, my cock is nearly hard. Faster and faster I stroke myself. Heat builds. Come on baby, come on. My body responds. I hold the vision of Tara in my mind. Fuck yes, I can jack off, I can masturbate, to Tara I can—

"What the Fuck!"

Gone. My erection is fucking gone! Like a snowflake in an oven, the motherfucker has gone limp again.

"Fuck!" I jump from my bed and force myself *not* to slam my fist into a wall. "Fuck!" I yank at my hair. Buck-ass naked and fucking pissed, I walk toward my bathroom. My phone buzzes.

Not my personal phone, but my Wonderfuck phone.

I grab the phone. I look at the number. My cock tightens. Tara. Fuck. It's Tara.

I don't want to see Tara. But I need to see Tara.

I need to fuck. I need to fuck her. I can only fuck her.

'Friday?'

I'm like a fucking addict. 'Where?'

'Malibu.'

Me going to Malibu on a Friday will mean me being with Tara for an entire weekend. Can I do that? Do I want to do that? The last time we were together in Malibu was when I walked out and left her crying on the couch. That was meant to be the end.

I thought it was the end.

I wanted it to be the end.

Didn't I?

I wish...I wish...what do I wish?

I pull my hands through my hair and shake my head. I wish I could go back. Back to when? Back to before Tara wrote that fucking article, to before Susie died, back to when—

'Yes.'

I type yes because yes is the only response that I can possibly give.

❧

"You're here because—"

"The Judge forced me to be here," I say. I shoot Vida my most charming smile. The smile that causes women to remove their panties.

She lifts an eyebrow and tilts her head. "Unwilling participants don't usually get much from therapy." Her tone is a study in non-judgment.

This'll be interesting if nothing else. I've hidden my true feelings for years. This woman – my therapist by court order – Vida, has to do the same thing every damn day. Hide her true feelings. What's it like being a waste can for other people's emotions? A place where they toss their emotional bullshit? If I ask that exact question, how pissed off will my new therapist be?

Instead I ask, "How many years have you practiced?" My gaze flits around her office. The colors are calming. Rich and deep jewels tones. Blue and green with some artwork on the walls that is meant to soothe. Her diploma is framed and hangs over her desk and books on shelves against the far wall. She sits opposite me on a chair while I inhabit a gray couch.

"Twenty-five years," she says. I feel her gaze on me. "Why don't you tell me what happened?"

I look into her grayish-blue eyes. "You don't get a file?"

"I fill out the forms you provide that indicate to the court you've participated, but no, they don't contact me and tell me what you did, nor do they inquire as to what we talk about."

A yellow pad for notes rests on her lap and a pen lays on the table beside her.

I take a deep breath. "Rage," I say. "Justified rage."

Again, with the lifted eyebrow, followed by silence. This is a technique, the silence. One that I've used in fact, as a businessman and as Wonderfuck. Silence is a key that unlocks the door to other people's thoughts, feelings, and needs. I wait. I wait longer than most people would wait to fill the silence. Can I make her uncomfortable with my silence? I'm pretty certain I can, eventually. Maybe not now, but soon enough.

"A woman. My neighbor was confronted by her ex fiancé and I beat the shit out of him."

"Why?"

"He knocked her down."

"He pushed her? Tried to harm her?"

I shift in my seat. "She grabbed his arm. He jerked it from her. She fell, and I hit him."

"Were you involved with her?"

"Not then."

"And now?"

Am I involved with Tara? Jake isn't, but Wonderfuck... "No."

"And in between then and now?"

She's got me. I can lie or I can be honest. Let's go with honest and see just how good Vida can dig. "Yes."

I go on to tell her parts of our short, sexual relationship. I leave out the sexy details and I omit the parts as Wonderfuck. I leave the story open-ended as to why this relationship failed.

"That sounds intense."

Lady, you have no idea. She doesn't have a motherfucking clue as to the intensity of my life, my feelings, my pain.

"Do you still have feelings for her?"

I glance at the clock. Smile at Vida. "Looks like our time is up?" I say with an obvious dodge.

She nods. She smiles. A knowing look flits through her eyes. My chest tightens with an uncomfortable rage.

"I have time for an answer," she says.

My smile drops from my face. Vida wants an answer? I'll give her one. I lean forward and drop my elbows to my knees, an intimate motion, as though I'm about to let her in on a secret, one that I haven't shared with anyone, maybe not ever.

"Vida." I look directly into her eyes waiting for her to blink, which she does. "I'm simply too fucking broken to care anymore."

Twenty-five years. For a millisecond, Vida's lips turn into a tiny O as though I may have penetrated that twenty-five years of therapeutic practice façade. Maybe I've thrown her for just a moment. Maybe.

"See you next week," I say, and pop up and walk out of her office. Let Vida chew on my fucked up psyche for a while.

❧

"RICHARD, ISN'T THIS WHERE RACHEL GOES TO school?"

There are so many wrong things about the sentence that just exited Mom's mouth. Instead of running through the mistakes, I pull into the parking spot next to the front door of Lily's school and turn off my car.

"Yes." I get out, walk around and open the car door for Mom. Getting Lily only takes five minutes, but I can't risk leaving Mom alone in my car for even that little bit of time. I'd come back and find my car on the front lawn, or Mom lost and wandering in the neighborhood surrounding Lily's school, or perhaps hanging upside down from the jungle gym in the play yard. I don't know. None of us do. Mom's become a complete and total wild card.

"Let's get Lily." I clasp her hand. Her smile crinkles the lines around her eyes. Is she smiling at me or is she smiling at Richard, my dad, and the guy she most often thinks I am?

Does it matter?

Not a fucking bit because she's smiling, and she's safe, and she loves the person she's with, and she's excited to see the person we're about to pick up from school.

We turn down the open-air walkway toward Lily's classroom. Today is music day in the summer enrichment program, and the strains of bongos and tambourines float toward us. Mom and I walk into Lily's classroom, a gaggle of parents line the wall near the door, all waiting for the last few minutes of music to end.

Lily sits between a red-haired girl and a boy with curly black hair. She pounds a cow bell with a stick.

Because, who doesn't need more cow bell?

The music teacher keeps the beat by slapping her hand against her thigh, and the kids shake their bodies and play their instruments. The tune? Who knows? But their joy and enthusiasm rocket this jamboree into the stratosphere. A smile curves over my face, reflecting back the look on fifteen kids' faces.

"Such a beautiful job!" the music teacher exclaims, and these kids absolutely believe her because their music is beautiful, their joy is magnetic. This moment for all the parents and aunts and uncles lining the back wall makes everyone forget about their bills, their mortgages, their jobs. All any of us are thinking about this second is how fucking-fantastic it is to watch these kids light up this fucking room.

I smile at Mom but her brow is furrowed and her lips are pulled down at the corner. Uh-oh. Storm clouds brewing, and there is likely no good reason why. I follow Mom's gaze toward the far side of the room.

"Mom, you okay?" I grasp her upper arm with my hand.

"Richard, I don't wish to cause a scene," she whispers, "but it's incredibly difficult for me to be here with that woman."

That woman? Fuck. That woman is the woman that Mom is convinced I've slept with, and while she's absolutely right, she thinks I am Richard and she's married to me and that I'm carrying on with another mother in Rachel's classroom.

My sanity careens just a smidge.

"Let's get Lily and go." I gently move Mom forward toward Lily, where she stands putting away the cowbell.

"Hey, doll, ready to go?"

"George wants to have a play date."

The boy standing beside Lily looks familiar. Discomfort edges around my belly. I glance from George to Lily. "Well, Lily, I'm sure your mom would be okay with a play date but I've got Grandma, and we're supposed to meet your mom for dinner tonight and—"

"Hi." Kendall's voice is smooth without evidence of the anger she felt the last time I saw her, but her eyes still have that hard-edged crazy. Mom stiffens. Kendall stands behind George and places her hands on his shoulders. "We'd like to have Lily over for a play date."

I know what kind of *play date* Kendall wants to have with me.

"I'm sure Rachel will be okay with it, but we're meeting her for dinner tonight. I'll have her call you."

"No." Mom's voice is low and coiled tight with rage. "You cannot have my daughter in your home." Her voice rises with each word, as though every syllable adds fuel to a fire. "You whore. You horrible slut! How can you do this? How can you sleep with my husband and then ask my daughter to come to your home?"

The classroom is silent.

"Mom," I say softly. "Mom, please, we need to go."

Confusion flickers in Lily's eyes.

"Mom, what's a slut?" George asks.

Kendall's jaw tightens. "We'll discuss this in the car." She turns George away from me, Mom, and Lily.

"Come Rachel, you have no business being around this type of woman." Mom sniffs and grabs Lily's hand. "Richard, if you wish to stay with that whore then please do. Lily and I will be in the car."

I turn to Kendal and mouth 'Sorry'.

Most of the parents in Lily's classroom know Mom has Alzheimer's. Lily's teacher flashes me an angry look as I trail Mom and Lily out the classroom door. Mrs. Bennett won't be allowing Mom in her classroom any more.

CHAPTER 43

"UNCLE JAKE, why was Grandma so confused?" Lily spoons mac-n-cheese into her mouth. The remnants of our take-out dinner litter Rachel's table.

Rachel answers Lily's question. "Honey, it's the Alzheimer's. Sometimes she doesn't know who she is or who she's with."

"That's why she always thinks I'm Mommy and calls me Rachel and Uncle Jake Richard?" Lily says.

Rachel nods.

"What does whore mean?"

Rachel coughs on her wine. "It's a grown up word that we'll discuss later." She gives me that bug-eyed mom look that asks 'what the hell happened' without saying the words. "Lily, honey, go get on your jammies and brush your teeth. It's almost time for bed."

Lily slides from her chair and heads toward the stairs. We both watch until her feet disappear from view.

"What happened?" Rachel carries the three plates to the sink. I stack containers and walk them to the trash can.

"Same as always. Mom thinks I'm Dad and that Dad had an affair with that mom in Lily's class, what's her name? Kendall. Don't you remember the music performance last spring?"

"I got a call from Mrs. Bennett on the way home."

"She looked pissed after Mom did her thing." I dump the bio-degradable containers into the trash.

"She doesn't think it's appropriate for Mom to come to the school if she's disruptive. It'll upset the children."

"Bullshit snobby private school," I mumble.

"You have no idea how hard that'll be if I can't take Mom into the classroom. I take Lily to summer enrichment and Mom to her day program before I go to work. I can't do that now. I can't swing by and pick up mom and then drop Lily, because I can't leave Mom in the car when I drop off Lily."

I cross my arms over my chest.

"We need to get her in a placement," Rachel says, scrubbing the plates in the sink before loading them into the dishwasher.

"Isn't she on the waiting list for—"

"Right, I know." Rachel's voice is sharp. "But that's a waiting list." She stops scrubbing and her shoulders drop. Her lips pucker tight and I see her shaking shoulders before I hear the tears in her voice. "I can't do this," she says, her voice quivering on each syllable. "I can't do all this on my own."

"Hey." I move in to hug my sister. It's part of keeping Rachel on the rails where her life is concerned. How she manages this juggling act I have no idea, but she does, and most of the time she makes the entire act look easy. She elbows me away.

"I don't need a hug, I need some help."

"Okay, want to hire a driver? Want me to—"

"No, I don't want you to hire a driver. I want you to drive Mom. I want you to take her in the morning and pick her up after her elder enrichment appointments. I want you to start looking for another place for her to live, in case we're on this wait-list for too long. Really, what I want, what I need, is to not worry about any of it for a while."

I get what Rachel is asking, but I'm not sure why she's asking it. "Rachel, there are people we can hire to help. People we've hired to help, why can't—"

"Because you've gotten a free pass for five years. Being generous about helping to pay for mom's care isn't the same as caring for Mom."

Her words sucker punch me in the gut. I want to disagree with her and argue that my money makes Mom's life easier, but what my money does is make my life easier for me.

"I want you to spend more time with Mom and not because I want to spend less time with her, but because I don't have any more time to give."

"Mommy, can you braid my hair?"

Lily stands in the doorway with a brush and two rubber bands. She wears her unicorn pajamas. The truth hits me, from five a.m. to eight p.m. every day of Rachel's life, she takes care of other people. Entirely and completely. While she's at work she cleans up societal messes in her courtroom. At home she takes care of Lily and Mom. She even takes care of me when I'm losing my shit.

When does anyone take care of Rachel?

Even now, after her long-ass day, Rachel smiles, dries her hands, and walks over to braid Lily's hair. She wants to hold Lily and hug her and put her to bed, but then what will Rachel get? Maybe thirty minutes of alone time before she collapses into bed and sets her alarm for 5 a.m. so she can get up and do it all over again?

I'm a little-brother slacker. Rachel takes care of everything and everyone and it's usually not until times like this, when she's completely overloaded between work and Mom and Lily, that I actually realize that maybe I should stop being a self-involved a-hole and offer to help.

Yeah. She takes care of our entire family over and over and over, day in and day out and I forget to notice until she's on the edge of collapse, because that's what you ladies do. That's who you are. You make all this self-sacrifice and continual quiet labor for the people you love seem so fucking effortless, all the while the weight of the world is on your shoulders. Sisyphus wasn't a man holding the weight of the world. Naw. Sisyphus was a woman.

"No problem. I'll take Mom in the morning and pick her up in the afternoon."

Gratitude washes over Rachel's face. I don't deserve her gratitude, because it's Rachel that keeps this entire family, or what's left of it, on the rails and out of jail, and somehow functioning in our own happy, yet dysfunctional way. "Monday, Wednesday, and Friday?"

Rachel nods. "Thank you."

And I feel grateful that I've done something for someone else simply because I love them, and I haven't done that in a long while.

CHAPTER 44

"Please, Jake. Wonderfuck me. Please."

She moans, and the head of my cock nudges the tight muscles of her sex. Her eyes fire with desire and want and need. Is that love? Fuck yes, it's love. Tara loves me. I press forward into her sex and her mouth drops open. Her face contorts with pleasure. This is heaven. Desire thrums through my body. I'm above her. I lean forward and press my lips to her eyes, her nose, and then her lips.

"Jake," she whispers. "Jake, I love you."

"I love you too, baby." My back muscles tighten and heat shatters through me. "Yes," I say, needing this release wanting this release—

Bzzz. Bzzz. Bzzz.

I open my eyes. My hand reaches for my cock, hopeful. Oh my god, please let me be hard.

My cock is soft.

Fuck.

Was it even hard when I was dreaming?

Bzzz. Bzzzz. Bzzzz.

The woman I'm furious with is the woman I need. There's a

thin line between love and hate. Even I don't need a therapist to know that I am hopping back and forth over that damn line where Tara is concerned.

I flip open my WF phone. It's a number I don't recognize.

'Need to see you.'

I've stopped answering. I'm no good to women right now. There's nothing I can do. Well, perhaps not nothing. I have lips and a tongue that still works, and I am good with my hands, but the level of frustration for me would be too high and eventually for them as well.

'Sorry. Can't,' I type back, unsure which of my pre-Tara women this is. Silence. The silence is so fucking deafening I could lose what's left of my mind. I'm up and out of my bed and packing for a weekend that I have no idea what it will bring.

Sex.

I'll get the relief of sex. I need that. But will I hate myself for needing it from the woman who fucked up my life?

I walk into the bathroom and look into the mirror. Unshaven. Tired. Rings beneath my eyes. Face it, man. Face it, and discuss it, and figure this shit out. The things I don't want to do.

The same things I avoided with Susie.

I knew. I had to know. I pretended not to know. At least that's what I believe now. All those nights she came home and showered. The afternoons I didn't know where she was. The phone calls when she whispered into the phone. All those times, I should've looked at Susie and asked, but instead, didn't, because I trusted her. I wanted to trust her. I wanted to give the very best of me that I had to give.

And I did.

I should've known.

I did know, didn't I?

My life is a mess. I turn away from the guy in the mirror because right now that guy is the last person I want to see.

❦

My blood boils. I need to fuck. I need to fuck in a way I can't possibly explain. The feeling is visceral and carnal and inexplicable. Fury rages through my chest because I'm unable to do what I need to do.

"I'm curious. What are some things you do for pleasure?" Vida asks.

Sitting in her office doesn't help my mood. In fact I'm even more pissed off than when I saw her last week.

"Fucking." I hold her gaze and plant my charming smile in my face. "I enjoy fucking for relaxation."

She's heard everything before, because the word, the thought, the idea of me having loads of sex doesn't break through her smiling patina.

"Sex is a primary enjoyment for you."

"Isn't it for everyone?"

"No, not always."

And I know that to be the truth. Sex wasn't a source of enjoyment for Susie. Sex for Susie was like whiskey to an alcoholic, or meth to an addict; a way to numb the pain and not feel.

"For some people there's little satisfaction in sex. What is it about the act that is satisfying for you?"

"Aside form the ejaculating part?"

"If that is the only satisfying part."

"The physical pleasure without emotional intimacy pleases me. I like to have lots of sex with lots of women so that I don't have to feel the emotions that come with intimacy. Emotions are inconvenient and uncontrollable. I don't like to feel them."

"Ah. Not always the wisest choice, to refuse to feel our emotions. You know they don't disappear just because we repress them."

"They become rage."

"Sometimes, yes. They can manifest in all kinds of ways. Physical illness. Rage. Sexual dysfunction."

I shift in my seat. Sexual dysfunction because I don't allow myself to feel?

"Could that include impotence?" I ask.

"It could," Vida says, with a practiced nonchalance that she's affected to appear non inquisitive and non judgmental. A way for therapists to gain their patients' trust.

I lean forward. "What would it mean if a man could only get hard for one woman?"

"Do you mean no ability to become aroused other than intercourse with one woman?"

I nod.

"Masturbation?"

"No."

"Pornography?"

"Tried it."

"Other women?"

"Not happening."

Vida sighs. "It could mean that there is a high level of anxiety or stress and that this person is the one place where you feel safe."

Bullshit. I don't feel safe with Tara, I feel completely turned on. Trust? Nope. I don't trust Tara.

"Or it could mean that there is a trauma either conscious or unconscious that prevents you from feeling relaxed enough about sex to have it with anyone other than that one person."

Maybe, possibly true. Maybe even unconsciously I feel safest with Tara because she knows about Wonderfuck. She is definitely the only person I trusted enough to tell about Wonderfuck.

"Jake, is this what's happening to you?" Vida's voice is soft. She's being extra gentle in asking, because men and their yam sack, nothing is more intimate to us than our erections.

"Maybe. I don't know for sure. Ever since I started seeing this woman I can't be with anyone else."

"Do you want to be with anyone else?"

"I don't know. What I do know is I want to be able to be with someone else if I want to."

Feeling stranded, isolated, and unable to fuck, isn't how I want my life to go.

CHAPTER 45

FOG SMOTHERS the sky above the Pacific. No bits of peek-a-boo blue welcome me to Malibu. I pull past the guard gate, down the narrow enclave road, and onto the drive at Tara's parents' place in Malibu. The wind whips the palms. The air is cool for a summer day. I park and walk up the steps. The front door is unlocked, just like the last time I was here.

Today, the house feels colder and grayer. Last time I was here, my cock knew what I wanted but my heart, my mind, the rest of me, raged against my need, my desire, my love for Tara.

And now?

My cock grows hard in spite of my doubts.

I walk through the house toward the back slider. Tara stands on the deck and stares out at the ragged surf. The choppy waves pound the shore. Her dark hair swirls on the wind and her fair skin appears porcelain in the gray light. She gazes toward the distance where the water fades into fog as though the world ends at that gray spot miles off shore.

"I betrayed you." Her words crash into me like glass breaking against tile. She doesn't look at me, her gaze fixed on the space of nothingness. No light, no water, no sky, no fog, just an impenetrable grayness. "You can't decide if you hate me or love me."

A tightening in my chest. My head and heart are in absolute agreement, but my cock wants her. I'm hard. For the first time since the last time I fucked Tara, I'm hard. My body thrums with desire, want, need. I'm furious with her, and yet I want her. Now. Here. My need is carnal and beyond my heart or my mind. This desire seeps deep into my bones.

For five years, Wonderfucking was my salvation, and now my ability to Wonderfuck away the pain is lost to me.

She took my identity, my secret, my solace as Wonderfuck, and gave my story to the world. She took my identity and she's taken my ability to fuck any woman but her.

I walk to her. My eyes lock on hers. No words. I have no words to explain my feelings. The fog thickens; a shroud between us and the world. I reach for her and pull her to me; my desire, my intentions on my face. My fingers weave through her hair. I bend forward and press my lips to hers.

Slow, hot, and full of need. My desire clear with my kiss. I slide my lips from hers and grasp her elbow. Her body presses against mine. Fingertips over the cotton of her dress sliding down the hem, to the flesh of her thighs. I slide my hands back up beneath the cloth. No panties. Ah, fuck yes, the warmth of her sex bare for me.

My fingertip slides between the lips of her sex and presses her clit.

"Oh Jake, yes," she moans beneath my kiss. Her hips press forward and my cock strains against my jeans. My fingertip circles her sex and her mouth parts, opening for me. Her hands grasp my zipper and she pulls it down. Hands grasp my cock and pull my sex from my jeans.

My finger slides from her clit into her sex. She clenches around me.

Fuck. I pull my lips from her mouth and turn her toward the ocean. Her hands grasp the rail in front of her and I lift her skirt above her bare ass. My hands slide around the roundness, caressing the soft flesh. I press my lips to the round, fleshy part of her ass. Soft. Smooth. Perfection.

Smack.

Her body tenses. She gasps.

"Jake, oh my god, I've missed you." She turns her head toward me and her face is in profile. The sharp cut of her jaw, the perfection of her cheekbones and nose. I'm so fucking angry with her and yet I need her, I want her, I can't get enough of her. I tighten my arm around her waist, my throbbing cock pressing upward. She bends forward and my cock presses up into her sex. I thrust. I'm deep into her sex.

Fuck, yes.

Heat rips through my body. I won't last long. I slide my hand to the front of her sex and circle her clit with my finger. Her head falls back toward me. I slide my finger over her clit and with my other hand reach up beneath her loose dress and pull the taut flesh of her nipple. Her tongue traces her lower lip. Pleasure shallows her breath.

"Oh, Jake." Her hips press back against me with each thrust.

Hard and fast we fuck. The fog, the darkness growing around us, the angry waves pounding the shore. I press my lips to the nape of her neck.

"Jake. Oh my god, Jake, I love you."

Her sex tightens around my cock. Heat curls my toes and my balls pull close to my body. Every muscle tightens and I explode into her. Sweet release shatters my brain. I see nothing. An explosion of pleasure with Tara in my arms.

❧

"CAN WE TALK NOW?" TARA SITS UP NEXT TO THE fireplace in the living room. "Are you worn out enough to have a conversation?"

"You didn't enjoy this evening?"

I roll to my side. We've fucked on the deck, in the kitchen, and twice in the living room. A fire warms the dark living room where we've just finished.

"You're avoiding the conversation."

Right. For so many good reasons, not least among them that I'm angry, and talking about what she's done isn't going to change my anger. Nope, instead of talking I've been engaging in this sort of drive-by fucking with Tara ever since her Wonderfuck story published.

"We need to figure this out."

"What's to figure out?" I roll onto my back and stare at the vaulted ceiling. "I fell in love with you and you used me for a headline." I'm pissed, and petulant, and my feelings for Tara have emotionally castrated me. What man wouldn't be filled with rage?

"I had a story to write—"

"You wrote about my private life without telling me."

"I didn't know it was you—"

"Bullshit." I turn my head toward her.

"Until ...." She looks away from me and toward the fireplace, takes a deep breath, and then looks back. "Do you remember the first night we were together? The night you ditched me at your place and took off?"

"Not my best moment, but yeah, I remember."

"You came back late that morning. You'd left me all alone at your place hoping that I'd leave before you got back. That was shitty."

For a split second I feel bad, because she's right. That was shitty, and my behavior got worse.

"I woke up before you left and there was a buzzing noise. I thought it was your alarm, but it wasn't."

I close my eyes. My Wonderfuck phone.

"I opened the drawer of your nightstand and there was a flip phone. Of course I opened it. I'm a journalist, and it's buzzing. I flip it open and there is this text, which simply says 'Want to play?' and me being me, I text back 'Play what?' And the response I got back was 'Wonderfuck'."

"You're not helping yourself with this story."

"I'm not trying to help myself. What good would lying be at this point? I'm trying to explain what happened. To see if you can understand my side and we can move forward after this or decide if we're over."

Over? If it wasn't for my cock we'd be so over, but so far the only person my dick'll get hard for is Tara.

"Then what?"

"Then you kicked me out of your apartment with the standard, 'it's not you, it's me' speech. I went home, ate a pint of Ben & Jerry's, and remembered a conversation."

"What conversation?"

"With my girlfriend. A couple months before she'd ended a long relationship with a man and she needed to rebound. One of her friends suggested she call this guy who had made her friend feel better. Not just better."

Tara breathes deep and her breasts move up and down.Fuck. I want her again.

"But he made her remember who she'd been before she let this asshole-guy destroy her. This guy brought back a part of her that she'd forgotten, and this guy had a name, a very strange name. A name that I'd now heard from her and seen on your phone. His name was *Wonderfuck*."

I pull my gaze from her breasts and again stare at the ceiling. I close my eyes.

"I start searching. I post on some message boards. I ask when I'm out with girlfriends. I even start to see this word, Wonderfuck in bathroom stalls and that's when...." She pauses.

I roll to my side. Her face glows in the firelight. Her voice fills with sadness and a heart wrenching realness in her words.

"I started not to care about the story. I didn't want the story. I didn't need the story. What I needed was what Wonderfuck could give me. What Wonderfuck could provide. I missed you and I missed that piece of me that I knew. God Jake, I knew what

Wonderfuck could give me back. You could awaken that part of me that I needed to go on with my life, to be whole, to be strong,.He could bring back the woman that I was before I lost her and traded her in for whatever Douchey-McDouche-Nugget wanted in a woman."

Tears drip down her cheeks and she wipes them away with the back of her hand. I fight the need to kiss them away, to sit up and hold her, to tell her it's okay, because as much as I want to comfort her, what she did, how she did it, wasn't okay then and isn't okay now.

I can't meet Tara's gaze any longer. I can't forgive her. Damn, but I understand what she wanted and what she was going through. Fuck, if I can understand, then I can empathize, and if I can empathize then I may forgive her. But I'm not ready to dole out forgiveness, not now, not yet, not in this moment. I'm still too justified in my rage and I want to keep my anger. Hang onto to it like a life preserver in a fucking storm.

"I got some women to talk before I met with you that first time, and because of what they said, I knew that I had to see you. I wanted you as Jake, but you wouldn't have me that way. You'd already told me that you wouldn't. So I made a decision. If you wouldn't be with me as Jake, maybe you'd be with me as Wonderfuck."

I tilt my head. I glance into her eyes. She lifts a brow. "You heard my voice on the phone message," she says softly. "You had to know."

"I knew."

My words come out raspy and thick with emotion, almost as though saying them makes my complicity more real. I don't want these facts to be true, but they are. I knew. When I texted Tara I knew who she was. I guessed what she wanted and I took the risk. Intentionally. For reasons that I'm not quite sure of now, I took the risk.

"I wanted you too...I just didn't know how...I didn't know if I could be with someone again. I..." I close my eyes and take a deep breath. Admission of introspection... vocalization of intro-spection is not easy for me. "I've used Wonderfuck to stay safe."

Tara nods and there's a look is in her eyes like she's figured all this out. Maybe she has. She's been with me as both Jake and Wonderfuck. She's written about me. Maybe she's analyzed me inside and out and nothing I say or do surprises her. Maybe she knows me better than I know myself. Maybe that's part of why I'm angry with her.

"When I got to the hotel I knew that you realized who I was and that I was coming to see you. I was terrified you'd throw me out or not be there. All I knew for certain was that I needed you, and if I couldn't have you as Jake, I'd take you as Wonderfuck."

Heat burns my eyes. The weight of her words exhausts me. "I don't know where to go with this...us....from here."

Sadness winds through my body. What we could've had together, what we lost, what Tara did, created this toxic mix of could-have-beens that I can't see a way past. "Why the story?" I search her face for the understanding and the forgiveness I so desperately want. I'm begging her to help me find a way past what she did to me, to us.

"I...I didn't have a choice where the story was concerned."

"We all have choices."

She glances away and her gaze drops to her hand, palm flat on the carpet. She shakes her head and says nothing more. In the silence after her words, even though I seek it, I still find no path to forgiveness.

"If I could take it back I would."

I don't believe her. I want to believe her words, but I don't because there are too many good things happening in her life for me to believe that she'd trade them for my love.

"Please, Jake, can't we at least try? I didn't want to hurt you. I just wanted women to know that they aren't alone. That they don't need to stay with the men that hurt them. That there are good men who are generous and kind and want to have sex with them no matter how ugly the men in their lives have made them feel."

I lie on my back and stare at the ceiling. My heart wants to try again with Tara, but my head tells a different story. The drama of being with her is almost too much for me to bear.

"I don't know how to trust you."

"I feel the same way."

My heart jolts. I turn and look at her.

"You're not the only one with doubts." She raises an eyebrow. "You spent the last five years sleeping with hundreds of women. Doesn't help that I walked in on my fiancé banging a woman in his office six weeks before our wedding."

It's easy and selfish of me to forget that Tara has her own demons to deal with. Each of us does. I'm asking her to trust a man who uses sex as his primary source of serotonin.

"If I can trust you not to sleep with ten women a week then I think you can at least try and trust me not to betray your confidence."

"It was never ten."

"More?" She lifts a corner of her mouth and smiles at me.

I roll toward her and drop my arm over her waist.

"Can we leave Wonderfuck behind?" Her eyes peer at me, a solemnity on her face. "Can I be Tara and you be Jake and we can be together? Just us. Not me looking for a story and not you fulfilling your vocation. Can we do that? Can we try?"

Every part of me longs to say yes to this woman, regardless of the betrayal, the past, my problems, her problems, our shared history. Every part of me wants to move forward with her by my side, and yet, there is flag tinged red, hovering in the distance, waving back and forth, because life is just not this easy. Not for me. And I don't know if what we've built is strong enough to withstand the problems that will inevitably shake each of us and this relationship we both want to have.

"We can try," I say. Her gaze has me. My body and heart is hers. To deny my desires and feelings is a lie.

I lift myself up and I'm above her now. Tara's bright blue eyes are joy and sunshine and all the goodness in the world.

"That's what I want. For us to try, and to be with you," she says.

I press my lips to her lips, and in this moment I know that while we both believe that we've agreed to leave the past behind and try to be together again, life has a way of shaking you to your core.

CHAPTER 46

I OPEN my eyes and the sky is blue. The gray is gone, the wind has ceased, and the surf is at peace. Outside the window, a vision of a calm and beautiful blue ocean. For the first time in what feels like forever I'm calm too. My rage is gone. Was it the sex or the conversation or the simple knowledge that I *want* to be with Tara and Tara wants to be with me and we've decided to be together?

My cock is hard. First time that I've woken with an erection in ...well since the last time I woke beside Tara. My erections have taken on a life of their own. Precious like gold, I look down at my hard cock. This morning wood shouldn't go to waste. Lucky for me I hear the thumping of footfalls on the stairs.

I'm ready. So fucking ready. I put my arm beneath my head, propped up on the pillow, ready to give Tara the full effect of my cock and my desire. The door opens and I shift forward.

"I brought you coffee." She holds two very full cups. She glances toward me.

I'm naked. Every fucking inch of me is buck naked and my cock is rock hard.

"I have something better than coffee."

"Yes you do."

I roll from the bed in all my naked, alpha-male -I'm-going -to -fuck -you -so -hard glory and take both cups of coffee from Tara. I set them on the dresser. I hope we spend enough time fucking that the coffee grows ice cold.

I turn back to Tara. She wears only a T-shirt and bedhead hair. She's sexy. Shockingly sexy. As much as I don't want it to, my heart pings.

I take her chin with a gentleness that escaped me since the article, but is now hitting me full in the chest. I've not felt kindness toward her since that fucking email on my phone telling me about her article. I pull her lips to mine and a soft gentle kiss comes from me. A kiss that says more than 'I want you'. This kiss says I still love you. I wish my kiss said I forgive you, but it doesn't. I don't have any forgiveness in my heart.

Her hand slides down over my cock and she grasps me in her hand. Fuck, yes. The pressure of her hand sliding up and down my sex, yes, this is what I want. I duck my head and my lips slip over her taut nipple. Like hot sugar. I roll the flesh in my mouth and suck.

"Jake." My name embossed with desire. My finger slides between the lips of her sex. She is hot and wet. I press my fingertip to her clit and stroke the bit of flesh. I slide two fingers deep inside her, and the muscles of her sex tighten around me.

Heat rushes through me. I release her nipple and my lips drift across her chest. Her hand grasps me tighter and she pulls away from me and backs toward the bed. She sits and I stand before her, my cock in her hand. My cock that can only get hard for her. My cock that doesn't desire any other woman but Tara.

She lays back and guides me up over her. I kneel on the bed above her and she pulls my cock into her mouth.

Fuck. I fight every urge I have to slam down into the heat of her mouth. She is beneath me and so vulnerable. Her hands grasp my ass and she presses me forward and I go with the rhythm she directs.

Heat. Liquid heat and pure suction. Pleasure pulses through

me. Locked on the place where my cock glides in and out of her lips. A tingle shoots up the back of my legs. Heat courses through my body. I won't last long. Her tongue circles the tip of my cock. Oh, fuck. My body throbs. Her hand clasps my ass and she slowly pulls me in and out of her mouth while her lips clamp around me. She presses me forward and sucks hard on my cock.

I pull my cock from her mouth and I turn my body. I can't continue. I want her flesh in my mouth. I need to taste her sweetness. She pulls my cock deep into her mouth and I spread her legs. Her hot sex is in front of me and I part her with my hand and stroke her with my tongue. Tara's hips roll up and I pull her clit deep into my mouth. Her sucking increases. She likes my measured stroke. I swirl my tongue over her clit. She pulls my cock deeper into her mouth and sucks harder.

I want her. I need to be in her.

Yes, god, yes.

I turn back around and my body is over her. She is hot and wet and her legs fall open for me. Her hips roll up and down and her breath pants from her lips. She grasps my cock and presses me toward her sex. I slide in and her legs clamp around me.

Her body is ready for me. I'm on the edge and need to come. I slowly slide my cock past the ring of her sex.

"Faster, harder, please, oh my god, fuck me," she says.

Flesh against flesh, my body slams into hers. Tara's eyes lock on mine and in her gaze I see a thousand questions and a thousands thoughts. We are one as I move in and out of her sex. Her body fits mine and heat barrels through me and through the base of my back.

"Yes, fuck me Jake. Fuck me harder."

I press in deeper and my body clenches.

"God yes, oh Jake, god yes."

I grab her and roll onto my back. She's above me, riding me. I cup both her breasts and pull her forward. This beautiful woman who is nearly maxed out on passion rides me. Ride my cock. Wonderfuck me.

"Fuck, this feels good." I'm lost again and I grind into her sex. She pushes back and leans forward, her hands planted on my shoulders. I hear a noise. I glance past her and toward the door.

What the fuck?

A woman stands in the doorway. An older version of Tara.

I watch her watching us. Her hand clasps her throat. She doesn't move. She makes no noise. She simply stands there and watches. I grasp Tara about to move her, when FUCK Tara shifts down on my cock and heat races through me.

I explode into Tara and she lets out a yell, her sex shivering and shaking and tightening around me. My entire body hardens. Tara collapses forward onto my chest. Both our hearts beat fast. I suck in air. Deep breaths. I pull my arm around Tara more tightly. She raises her head and looks into my eyes.

I glance past her. Empty. The doorway is empty.

"Uh, I think there was...I think someone is here." I press my lips to her forehead. "I think your mom saw us."

Tara's eyes widen, then narrow. Her face tightens. "What do you mean? Why do you think that?"

"Because I saw a woman in the doorway just as we were climaxing."

"Shit," Tara mutters under her breath. Her jaw muscle tightens. She slides from me and is off the bed and toward the bathroom. "I'll take care of it." She pulls on a pair of sweatpants and a shirt form the chair on the far side of the bedroom.

"Are you okay?"

She nods, walks out the bedroom door, and I hear her walk down the stairs.

I shower. I dress. I walk down the stairs. Voices in the kitchen. Is her mom still here?

"I wanted to see you, besides your father left his raincoat here. Why didn't you tell me you were using the condo this weekend, I never would've—"

"Wouldn't what?" Tara asks, her hand on her hips. "Watch us have sex?"

"I didn't watch you."

"You watched nearly the entire time."

I walk into the kitchen and am greeted by silence and irritable looks. My heart pounds and my throat tightens.

"Mom, this is Jake," Tara says by way of introduction.

Mrs. Jennings eyes me from top to toe and then back up. Her look seems disapproving and cold, which would make sense because she just caught me having sex with her daughter. But even while her face holds judgment, I see in her eyes that look. The look I've caught from women for the past five years. I know that look. She's hungry and wants what I can provide.

"Mrs. Jennings." I reach for her hand. She shakes mine, holding it just a millisecond too long. Her gaze is just a bit too intense.

"How did you two meet?" she asks. "Wait... are you the one who—"

"Came by late one night to find Tara? Yes, that's me."

"Oh yes, I remember that now. Tara's mentioned you before that even, and then after of course."

There go Mrs. Jennings's eyes again. Looking at me as though I'm a side of grade-A prime rib hanging from a rope in the center of the jungle cat exhibit at the zoo, and she's head lioness.

"I see you found her."

I glance at Tara who's moved on from making small talk with her mother to making fresh coffee. Her face flushes a bright shade of red.

"I did indeed. And you found Mr. Jennings's raincoat. That's why you were here, yes?"

"Yes." Again with the look in her eyes, but I ignore the look, and the tension, and the vibe of strange energy that bounces around this room. I know from experience that mother-daughter relationships are fraught with difficulty.

"You two enjoy the rest of your weekend together," she says, and walks down the hallway toward the front door.

I close my eyes. Let out a breath.

Fuck.

They've both been Wonderfucked.

CHAPTER 47

"RICHARD, how long has it been since we've gone to Carmel?"

I open the front door to Mom's house. We've just arrived home from her geriatric physical therapy session.

"I can't remember," I say. "Do you remember the last time we went?"

A smile curls over Mom's lips. "Oh yes darling, don't you?" She closes her eyes and a glorious smile takes over her face. "Don't you remember that lovely blue negligee that you brought me back from New York for the trip?"

Oh shit. TMI. Definitely do not want to talk about Mom and Dad's Carmel trip if it involves negligeé's.

"Hey Mom, want a snack?" I say, abruptly changing the subject. "Maybe some iced tea?"

We walk to the table in the kitchen and I help her sit in a chair. "Isn't Tatianna supposed to be here?" I pull out two glasses and a plate. "How about butter cookies?" I know these are her favorite and maybe it'll get her to think of something other than her trip to Carmel with Dad.

"Yes, please, and then I want you to tell me about Susie."

My chest tightens. My breath catches and I swallow. My head drops forward and I look at the plate on the counter that I've taken down from the cabinet. On the plate is my name, my five-year-old handprint, and hearts.

Deep breath.

It's emotional whiplash going from being my dead dad to the son with the dead fianceé that Mom can't remember is dead.

"How is everything going for the wedding?"

I grip the knob on the cabinet with an intensity I fear could pull the whole damn thing off the wall.

"Mom, I ...you know..." Times like these I struggle with the idea that I'm supposed to play along because playing along is just too damned painful. Luckily for me the phone rings, and I slip it from my pocket.

"It's me." Rachel is breathless as though she's rushing and she probably is because she rushes most places. "Listen, I've got a problem."

"Don't we all." I set the plate of cookies and the tea in front of Mom and walk out of the kitchen and into the dining room. "Isn't Tatianna supposed to be here?"

"All day. Isn't she there?"

"I haven't seen her yet." I walk to the sliders and look into the backyard. "So what's your problem?"

"Lily."

I stop. I pay attention, because nothing gets me to pay attention quite like the perfection that is my niece.

"I've been yanked into a meeting with the Chief Judge, an unscheduled meeting. Obviously he has a *wife* and childcare isn't an issue that he's ever had to deal with. I need a little help with Lily."

"That's not a problem. I can pick her up. Where is she?"

"She's at George's house for a play date."

My jaw muscle tightens. George, as in son of Kendall, who is the woman I've Wonderfucked, and recently tried to fellate me while I was sleeping. None of which is known to Big Sis.

"I can do that," I say, not wanting to at all. "But I've got Mom and I have no idea where Tatianna is—"

"I know Mom is wackadoo where Kendall is concerned, but I don't have a choice. Tatianna might be napping upstairs. Sometimes she does that. Go look before you drag Mom to Kendall's. Tatainna usually naps in your room."

"My room? Why my room?"

"I guess the bed's more comfortable than mine."

"Fine. Tell Kendall I'll be there in a half hour. I'll let you know if Mom is with me."

"Great. Thanks. You just saved my ass for sure."

I hang up the phone not feeling so great about saving anyone today.

⚜

THE HOUSE IN BRENTWOOD IS BIG BUT NOT monstrous, as though the wealthy people inside are at least attempting to not be obnoxious. I pull onto the drive and stop the car. Luckily for me, Tatianna was napping in my room so Mom isn't with me. Thank god for small mercies. I hop out of the car, walk to the door, and press the bell.

Last place I want to be.

Maybe second to last place.

Vida ranks number 1 on my list right now of places I don't want to be, then number 2 would be here—

"Hello?" The woman at the front door is not Kendall.

"I'm here for Lily."

"Mr. Reynolds, right?" She smiles. I nod. She leads me through the expansive house to the backyard where there is a ginormous rock pool equipped with a built-in waterslide. My gaze flicks across the pool to the woman lying on a lounge chair in a two-piece. A teeny-tiny two piece.

I check my cock. At this point I'm hopeful. I even envision the woman fellating me as she did not too long ago.

Fuck.

Nothing. Nada. Not even a twitch.

"Watch me Uncle Jake!" Lily calls from the top of the water-slide where she stands next to George. I wave and I watch. Out of the corner of my eye a flash of bikini as Kendall stands, slips on shoes, and walks around the pool toward me. Lily shrieks and plunges down the slide and into the water. George follows. They both break the surface and laugh.

Kendall sidles up beside me. This is the tiniest of two-pieces and to be fair the woman is a stone-cold fox. A MILF. Which I have.

"Hey, they're having fun. Why don't you stay awhile," she says, brushing her hair behind her ear. Her sunglasses hide the look in her eyes, but her body language says all I need to know. Breasts angled out, hips tilted to the side, hand touching her face. She wants me to grab her and take her to the pool house at the far end of the pool and Wonderfuck her.

I have sunglasses too. Thankfully. "We're meeting Rachel for dinner."

"That's not what Rachel said." Kendall juts out her chin. "She told me she'd be stuck downtown for a while."

Another shriek followed by giggles cuts through the air.

"Come on," Kendall says, and pushes a smile onto her face. "Besides, I *know* you're involved with someone now, so no worries."

My chest tightens. Involved? How would Kendall know that I'm involved?

"Come have some iced tea. Let them play a little bit longer."

Part of me doesn't want to, but another part does. I have...I have questions and Kendall might have answers.

"Uncle Jake, can we stay?"

"Fifteen minutes," I call back to Lily.

Both she and George clap and pull themselves out of the pool to go down the slide again. I turn and follow Kendall to the far side of the pool and sit on the lounge chair beside hers. She grabs her sunscreen and starts to slather it on her arm.

"You know that story about you?"

I say nothing, but lift an eyebrow.

"The reporter contacted me. The same woman you brought to the party." Kendall turns her back to me. "Would you? Please?" She hands me the sunscreen over her shoulder and unties the top of her bikini.

Normally, rubbing sunscreen on a woman's back would turn me on. I'd want her. I might even take her. Normally, I'd be more than willing to indulge her fantasy of me following her to the pool house and banging her against the wall. I squirt sunscreen onto the palms of my hands, rub them together, then glide my palms over her shoulders. But there is nothing normal anymore where my cock is concerned.

Nothing.

Fuck, my equipment is broken.

"Did you meet with her?" I ask.

Kendall holds her lush red hair up and out of the way of my hands. "I did. She seemed nice enough. Did you know she was a reporter?"

"I knew she was a journalist, but I didn't know she was doing a story on...." I don't say it. I can't say it. I've worked hard to keep my life as Jake and my life as Wonderfuck completely separate, and these breaches, these narrow connections, they make me uncomfortable.

"I guessed as much. I asked her, but she wouldn't tell me."

"So what'd you tell her?" I pull my hands from her skin. Her back is completely covered. I wipe my hands on a towel.

She ties her swimsuit top and turns to me. Her gaze is intense, her expression solemn. "I told her the truth. I told her that you saved my life."

My chest clamps tight.

"I don't know if that's true."

"It is." She picks up her wide-brimmed hat and fixes it to her head and leans back onto her lounge chair. "After you, I found myself again. And then after what happened at your mother's, well, I went and talked to someone." Her gaze tears from the kids in the pool and lands on me. "I went because of you and what you said that day."

"Is that a good thing?"

"It's a great thing," She crosses her ankles and smiles. "George's dad moved out last month."

"I'm sorry."

"Don't be. It's exactly what needed to happen. All of it, but I couldn't have seen it without you. Wouldn't have known it. There's something that happens when a woman gets married and has a child. I mean, don't get me wrong, I wanted all of it."

She turns her gaze toward Lily and George who are in the shallow end of the pool splashing and giggling. "I love George. I love being a mom, and I loved being a wife. But with all you gain, you also lose something. You give up some of yourself. I guess you have to, to do all those things for all those people."

She turns back toward me. "I'd almost forgotten that piece of myself and that piece is important; that part of me that is wild and free and brave and it makes all the other pieces fit together, it was the piece of myself that had heart."

She takes a deep breath and smiles. "I thought you should know. You brought that back to me, you made my heart beat again. That's what I told her when we met. It didn't make the article, but that's what I said."

"I don't know what to say....I'm...."

"Don't look so surprised. It might've just been sex to you, but I have a feeling for most of us women, being with you was much more than that."

"It wasn't just sex," I say. I know that, although I'd wanted it to be 'just sex' it never remained that way. I couldn't have cared this much about what I was doing if it was 'just sex.' "It was more than that for me too." I say. "You know how it started and why?"

She shakes her head and I wonder if I should share the specifics with her, but I decide not now, not here, with this beautiful sunshiny day and happy kids giggling in the pool. The details are too sad and they will remain for another day. Instead of telling her specifics, I look at her and say, "There'd been a loss in my life. A big loss and so I ....well, that's when I decided to do what I did. And it meant everything to me, the idea of it. It was something I needed to do to save myself and it was my—"

"—vocation," she says.

She smiles. I smile back, and we share this moment that is kind and warm and for an instant, all the fractures and damage in my soul feel mended and less obvious because she's fractured and damaged too. We all are. Every person has something that ripped them up, tore them apart, and shattered their world. We each rebuild from that place, that moment, that event that made us feel less than nothing. After that event, when we rebuild, we're the same person, and yet we're absolutely different.

"I thought you should know," she says. Her voice soft with kindness.

"Thank you."

"Mmhmm. You also asked how she contacted me? She phoned. At the time I thought you knew."

"I'm surprised you had good things to say about me after what happened at my mother's."

"I'm still so embarrassed about that." She presses her hand to her forehead. "I mean...she really played it off at the birthday party, didn't she? That's why I thought you knew about the article."

My heart picks up speed. I squint behind my sunglasses.

"Wait, what? But she contacted you *after* the birthday party?"

"Oh, no, no, no." Kendall shakes her head. "She contacted me before the birthday party. That's why I thought you'd given her permission to speak to me, to all of us, because you were there with her."

"I didn't give her permission or anyone's names or contact information. I didn't know she was writing the story." I smile and try to play the entire thing off as though this...this betrayal isn't killing me. "She didn't even tell me."

Tara knew who I was.

She knew who I was long before she said she did.

"Right, I thought maybe you gave her my name or my number...but then the weird thing was that she didn't know my name when she called me. She only knew my number. I don't think she was honest with you."

Heat sweeps through my body. What the fuck? I want to believe Tara, but every time I begin to believe her, another inconvenient fact knocks away the trust I start to build with her.

I wave to Lily and she climbs form the pool. It's time for us to go.

CHAPTER 48

"THERE SEEMS to be a great deal of stress in your life," Vida says.

I glance away from the large clock that sits behind her desk to my left. "Stress?"

"Well you mentioned your mother has Alzheimer's. Your sister is a Judge and a full-time single parent, and that you try to help. Your niece is only five, which is a challenging age as most of her needs are still met by the adults around her. Plus, your job seems very high risk. How do you manage all the stress?"

My inclination is to laugh, but I stuff that one deep into my chest because laughing seems like the exact wrong thing to do with Vida staring at me; her gaze intent and her question earnest.

I Wonderfuck...or I did, but I can't tell her that, can I? I can't tell her that I created an alter ego and that the woman that I'm in love with completely screwed me over by writing a salacious story about my alter ego while interviewing all the women I've wonderfucked. Oh, and by the way, I've also wonderfucked her mother.

Nope, no can do. Can't tell her any of that...

"I work out," I say.

Vida raises an eyebrow and makes a note on her pad of yellow paper. "You mentioned being engaged?"

Fuck. Did I? I don't remember saying anything about Susie. I need to keep better track of what I tell Vida because she's sharp and she takes notes and I've been trying to follow this rule of not telling her everything.

"I...she..." I swallow. I really don't want to talk about Susie. I still don't want to talk about Susie. "She died," I finally say.

Vida's face remains impassive, but sadness and empathy flicker in her eyes.

"I'm sorry for your loss."

I don't respond because how do you respond when someone apologizes for your loss? Nothing, nothing can be said to those words other than, "Thank you."

"That must've been incredibly difficult for you."

I don't answer because I don't want to talk about Susie. I don't want to think about her death or the aftermath, and the days and nights I lost, and how my life was empty until I figured out a way to save myself.

"How did you cope with that loss?"

I take a deep breath. Lying is exhausting. Maybe that's why I created Wonderfuck because Wonderfuck wasn't a lie, isn't a lie. Wonderfuck simply became my path to survival.

"I drank a lot and did some drugs. Lost myself in a bottle until my sister came and got me out."

"For how long?"

"About six months."

"Her death was unexpected?"

My heart is on a fishhook and Vida holds the other end of line, tugging and pulling and yanking with each word, every question, reeling me in through the fucking excruciating pain.

Fuck it.

"If jumping off a balcony is unexpected, then yeah, unexpected."

Vida's face isn't nearly as impassive. The skin around her

mouth tightens, and her empty hand fists as though she's forcing herself not to press her fingers to her lips and say, 'Oh my god, no. That explains so much.'

Does my fiancée taking a header off my balcony while I stood there and watched explain me and my life and my choices? Because I don't know. Seems to me like I was pretty fucked up before Susie decided to die, and I've been even more fucked up since her death.

"We grew up together. We were engaged. Our families were great friends and this was the perfect match. The perfect marriage. There would be big family holidays and grandkids and fabulous family ski trips and trips to the beach. Really, the whole thing looked grand. But here's the kicker. Susie was a sex addict. Hundreds and hundreds of men. Women too. I didn't know."

I pause and roll my eyes to the ceiling. "How the fuck didn't I know?"

My gaze lands on Vida again who is transfixed, her face frozen as though it takes all of her therapeutic prowess to simply listen to my tale.

"But I didn't, and she finally told me, and I told her I still loved her and that she could go to rehab. Work her program. That I'd love her through it, and I did. And she was working her program and in recovery."

I clasp my hands together. The muscle in my jaw tightens. "Six weeks before our wedding I took a business trip to Japan. I got back and Susie had relapsed. She was beyond upset. Wanted to call off the wedding, but I wouldn't let her. I told her no. I told her that I wanted her in my life no matter what, and I did. And that me wanting her to be my wife would never change. That I would always want her no matter who she was or what she did or...who she"—I swallow and take a deep breath—"fucked. I simply wanted her. I wouldn't let her go and I meant every word. She didn't want to agree with me but finally, after hours, she said okay. So I come home from work one evening and...."

I'm back. I'm in the exact moment. I'm standing just inside

my doorway. Susie stands on a table on my balcony. The night sky around her backlit by the high-rise lights. She looks like an angel, ethereal and gorgeous. She faces me and her blonde hair swirls around her face, caught by the wind. Her beautiful face. No fear. A smile. She takes one step back and...and...she's gone...

My stomach clenches and I stand. I bolt for the door and I'm out of Vida's office and down the hall. Bent over and unable to breathe. My guts twisting and pulling and knotting like my entire body will turn inside out.

&

"I'M SORRY."

I stand just inside the door to Vida's office. A cold sweat clings to my skin. That night. Susie. The memories overwhelm me. Vida's eyes harbor empathy. I've shaken loose her professional ability to remain distant.

I sit on the couch even though I don't want to. I want this whole damn session to be finished. Telling her about my life, my past, my present, is tiresome and obviously nearly too much for me.

"How long ago?" Her voice nearly shakes and she clears her throat. "When did this happen?"

"Six years ago." My voice is hoarse and high pitched. I clear my throat and lean back against the couch. We've got another twenty minutes. Fuck if I can make it. It would seem from Vida's demeanor that I don't get to go home just because I nearly puked my guts up discussing my dead fiancée.

"So this relationship with—"

"Tara."

"Was this the first relationship you'd entered since your fiancée?"

"The first emotional relationship." I reach for a glass of water and take a sip.

"So you've had other relationships?"

"Sexual ones."

"About how many?"

Too much reality for one day. Fuck it. I'm in. What the actual fuck. Let's see how much Vida can take.

"Since Susie's death?"

Vida nods.

"Different women?"

She nods again.

"I don't know maybe two or three—"

She nods, jots a note.

"Hundred."

Vida stops writing. She swallows. She glances up from her paper at me. "And before Susie?"

"None. I mean Just her."

"From?"

"From the time I was fifteen until the time she died."

She lifts an eyebrow. From her look, I know I'm an unusual case. I fall outside the norms of human sexual behavior.

No shit.

I haven't even told her the best part yet. I haven't even told her about Wonderfuck and I'm uncertain I ever will.

"So sex is how you handle stress."

"It was."

"And now?"

"And now I can't get hard unless I'm with Tara."

"Can't—"

"—get hard. My cock, my dick. It won't work."

"Unless you're with Tara."

I nod.

"And this started?"

"Around the same time she wrote her article about Wonderfuck."

Vida's eyes widen. Oh yeah, she's read the story. She knows. Every woman in Los Angeles knows. The way my phone's been blowing up, they all want a piece of what that story offered. She taps her pen against her pad of paper and her tongue brushes her bottom lip. "Are you saying that you're—"

"I'm saying that the woman I'm involved with, the first woman I've been emotionally involved with since the death of my fiancée, wrote the story about Wonderfuck. I'm also saying that I've slept with several hundred women since the death of my fiancée, and until that story, I could sleep with any woman I wanted. And now, I can no longer fuck. I can't masturbate. This"—I hold my hands in front of my crotch—"no longer functions unless I'm with Tara."

"The woman who wrote the article."

I nod.

"She knows about your lifestyle and she knows about Susie?"

I nod.

"Does she know?"

"About my malfunctioning cock?"

Vida nods.

"Yeah, she knows."

"Anything else?"

"Well, what Tara doesn't know is that I slept with her mother."

CHAPTER 49

EACH TIME I VISIT MOM, the house Rachel and I grew up in looks less like a home and more like an empty shell. I plant Lily in the living room with Mom and two dolls.

"Rach?" I call. I don't hear any response but when we left for ice cream she was headed to Dad's study, one of the final places with loads of remnants of our childhood. Fading sunlight makes the hallway lonely. I turn into Dad's office. Paneled wood, floor to ceiling book cases, huge dark-pained windows, and a giant mahogany desk create a very heavy,masculine look. Being called to enter this room used to scare the hell out of me. Still does.

I shiver.

Sitting at Dad's desk, Rachel looks like a little girl playing grown up. She's holding what looks like a photo in her hand. A shoebox is open on the desk.

"You okay?" She glances up.

Our gazes meet. Her eyes are red-rimmed and giant tears fill her eyes. What is in that photo? I walk around the desk and stand beside her. I press my hand to her shoulder and look down at the picture she holds.

My heart catches and skips a beat. There we are. All of us. Before. The happy before. I do the math in my head and this is…five, six, seven years ago? Rachel is pregnant, just barely showing, her hand beneath her belly and Dalton stands beside her smiling, with his arm around Rachel's shoulder. Mom and Dad stand in the center. Mom's eyes are so bright, so clear, so wickedly sharp, I'd forgotten how they looked when her mind worked. Dad, alive, and laughing and beside Mom is … My heart tightens and I have to remind myself to breathe.

Susie. My beautiful Susie. She is laughing and her whole face is absolutely lit up. I'm beside her with this giant stupid grin on my face, like someone – whoever is taking the picture – just told us a hilarious joke and they might've. This picture is alive, and there is joy and happiness and love and just so fucking much.

Rachel sniffles and drags the back of her hand beneath her nose. "What the fuck happened?" A tear drops from her eye. "And how did we not realize how good it was that day? I didn't, did you? Did you have any idea how this…What was it? A Sunday maybe? A cookout in the backyard? I'm pregnant and Susie's over and Dad's grilling and it's just a normal Sunday. How did we not know how lucky we were? How brilliant that day was?"

I put my hand on Rachel's shoulder and I bend down and press my lips to her head. She's right. She's so fucking right. The people we desperately loved were all alive,and healthy, and happy, and filled with joy. It's just a normal day and we didn't even think about what we had, and who we were, and how good we had it. Or how lucky and blessed we were to experience that exact moment and how fucking quickly – with one foot over the edge into space – with the blink of an eye, so many of us would be gone.

Abso-fucking-lutely gone.

I don't say it but I think it. Just Rachel and me. We're still here, and we've got Lily. On a good day we have Mom too. But in the photo that Rachel holds we were the luckiest people in the world and we didn't even know it at that time.

"We still have each other," I say, and Rachel smiles. She

places the photo on the top of the desk and looks back at the box. "This was in the bottom drawer of his desk."

"The drawer that's always locked?"

Rachel nods. She pulls out more pictures from the box. One of Mom and Dad, which looks to be when they were on their honeymoon. "Wow, you do look just like Dad, no wonder Mom gets confused."

I take the picture from Rachel's hand. Yep, we do look really similar.

"Except for the smile," I say. "I definitely have Mom's smile."

Rachel glances at me. "Yep you do. Lucky bastard."

I put the photo back onto the desk. "Anything interesting?"

Rachel shakes her head, no. And then she stops. "Unless you count this." She lifts a picture from the bottom of the box.

Dad and another woman stand in front of the Eiffel tower. They're kissing

"That isn't Mom."

Rachel shakes her head. "Nope, not Mom."

"Looks like he has on a wedding ring. What color is her hair?"

Red.

"And there we understand Mom's fixation with Kendall. That's the woman that he left her for. Didn't ever know they went to Paris together," Rachel says.

"Not much is known about that time," I say. "Other than Dad was out of town a lot."

"Right," Rachel says. She tosses the photo back in the box and pops on the lid "I think I'm finished for today." She stands and walks over to the bookshelf where she plucks a tissue from a box. "Mom and Lily?"

"Had ice cream and are playing dolls."

Rachel looks out the window. Daylight fades to night. "Think we'll go home and relax."

"No hot date?"

She rolls her eyes toward the ceiling, "Never."

"Do you want me to come over and watch Lily? I mean, do you need some time to yourself?"

"You're kidding? You're *offering* to watch your niece?"

"I'm always here to watch Lily."

"Right, I know that I can always *ask* you and you'll usually say yes, but I still have to ask."

"That's what most people do when they want things."

"No, that's what men do when they want things. Women like it when other people offer. It's a kink in our DNA, and in the nearly six years that Lily has been alive I don't remember you ever offering to watch her before today."

Is that right? Quite possibly. I can be that self-involved. I know I can.

"I'm offering now."

Rachel lifts an eyebrow and slips her phone from her pocket. "Okay. I can find some friends to do something with." She glances up from her phone. "I'd love that."

"Done. I'll hang out here with Mom for a little bit. Be at your place in about an hour?"

"Perfect." A smile slips onto her face. "Thank you. I could use the break." She presses a kiss to my cheek.

"No problem." Thankfully, I feel less like a self-involved asshole and more like a human being.

⚜

I CLOSE THE BOOK AND PLACE IT ON THE NIGHTSTAND beside Lily's bed.

"Uncle Jake, I know what kind of puppy I want."

"What kind?" I sit on the bed beside her. Her expression is serious, as though she's pondered this important question for a long while.

"You know the dog that your friend Tara has?"

"Jango?"

"I want a puppy like Jango."

"Hmmm. I'm not sure what that is, because I think Jango is a rescue dog. Tara adopted her from a shelter so we wouldn't know for sure what kind of dog her mommy or daddy was."

"That's what I want to do," Lily says, her gaze serious. "Mommy says that Jango looks like she's part lab and part shepherd."

"That sounds good."

"So I want one of those."

I lift the blanket and pull it up higher over her body.

"Has Mommy said yes yet?" she asks, a hopeful lilt in her voice. "You know my birthday is very soon."

"Leave it to me," I say. Knowing full well that convincing Rachel to let Lily have a dog will be harder than convincing a vegan to eat a cow.

"I love you Uncle Jake," Lily mumbles, her eyes already closed and the sound of her voice indicting she's drifting to dreamland.

"I love you too." I lean forward and kiss her cheek. She's an angel. An absolute and total angel. And if my angel wants a dog then I've got to find a way to get her one, even if that includes hiring a dog walker to come to Rachel's two times a day. Scratch that. Big Sis seems irritable about me hiring people to take care of family. OK. Even if I have to come over here myself? Hmm..that changes the dynamic. Nope. Not doing that, but then I can't expect Rachel to take on the responsibility either.

Damn. Like a light bulb moment, I see what's up with Rachel and why she doesn't want a dog. Yessirree, another creature in the house to take care of. Damn. Rachel does need more help.

I stand and walk out of Lily's room. My phone buzzes and I pull it from my pocket.

'How's Lily?'

'Asleep', I text back.

'Thank you!'

'Have fun', I text, and I hope she does. I hope that maybe for a couple of hours tonight she forgets all the responsibility that she has, the shit-ton of work she does, and how she takes care of Mom, Lily, and even me. I walk down the stairs to the family room and grab the remote. I turn on the TV and the doorbell rings.

Standing in the doorway is Kendall with her red hair and her 'crazy-eyes' as Tara calls them, but they don't look so crazy. She carries a glass dish.

"Came by to drop this off to Rachel. Had no idea she wasn't here."

"She's out to dinner."

"I know where it goes. I'll put it away."

Before I can say no, she slides past me into the house and down the hall to the kitchen. She opens up the cabinet beside the stove and puts the glass Pyrex dish onto another one that is nearly identical. "So she left you here with Lily tonight?" she asks, all smiles. "It's nice of you to babysit."

She stands and puts both her hand into the back pockets of her jeans, which causes her very nicely-shaped breasts to pop out in front. She surveys the kitchen and the family room. "Want some company?" She steps forward. She's near me now and her intent, her desire, what she wants from me, is pretty clear. Her breasts so close to my chest, her upper teeth tugging on her bottom lip, and her eyes half-lidded with that you-can-have-me-if-you-want-me look. I'm clear on what she's after.

And nothing. My cock doesn't even respond. I might as well be standing in my shower with ice-cold water dumping on my head.

"I uh....I can't." I take a step back.

That irritable look, like the one she gave first in the bathroom at the birthday party and then in my bedroom when she fellated me, crosses her face.

"Still seeing the reporter?"

"That's not it. Ever since the article came out I can't...well things don't work they way they once did."

She glances down at my crotch. "Are you kidding?

I shake my head, no. "I wish I were."

"You can't...you're not...."

I nod. No need to fill her in on the detail of Tara. "I've tried, and well, there's nothing going on."

"Have you been to a doctor?"

"Not yet. But I am seeing a therapist."

"My god." Her fingertips press her lips. "That's...that's horrible."

Are those fucking tears I see in her eyes?

"I mean you have such a gift, what you do to help women, how you helped me. My god." She backs away from me like I've told her I have leprosy and it's contagious.

"I uh..I hope it works out for you."

"Me too," I say, and follow her to the front door where she slips out and shuts the door behind her.

Until now, I've never been grateful that I couldn't get hard.

CHAPTER 50

"WE'RE DOING THIS?" I pant out the words and throw my arm onto my forehead.

A giant grin pulls across Tara's face. "Looks like we are."

I suck in air trying to regain my breath. For nearly three weeks we've been back and forth between our two places with Jango trailing behind. Take out and movies and dinners and even a play at the Geffen. This, our thing, has become a relationship. A real relationship.

She turns toward me and lies on her side. Her hair mussed from our exertions this morning. My gaze lingers over the perfection that is her body. My wonderland. I take a deep breath and know that I am happier now than I've been in what feels like forever. I sigh and press a kiss to her nose. Fear creeps along my spine because there are still conversations to be had, things that need to be said, a past that needs to be dealt with, but I don't want to believe anything can come between us.

"So my mom wants us to come for dinner."

The past roars at me and I flop onto my back.

"Come on, she's been asking since that day in Malibu, now that she knows we're spending so much time together."

I press my hand to my forehead. This. Now. This moment

would be the perfect time to tell Tara about Wonderfuck and her mom. I have to tell her, don't I? Is it possible that this could remain a little secret between Mrs. Jennings and myself? A part of my past that remains in my past? No. She has to know. Needs to know. I roll to my side and gaze into her eyes. They are a brilliant blue and filled with joy.

My stomach squeezes. I've seen this kind of joy before. This is a joy that includes love, and visions of a future that we both want.

Susie. Susie's eyes held this joy when she was in recovery, and we'd discuss our house, our future kids, and everything we wanted to accomplish together. I never though I'd get to see that kind of joy in another woman's gaze, especially a gaze directed at me. "Tara, I..." I start speaking with the intention of telling her what happened between her mother and me. I sigh. Shit. I shake my head a little and surrender to the fact that I'm not strong enough in this moment to ruin that look of joy. I press my lips to her forehead, then pull away and look into her eyes.

"Of course I'll go. Just tell me when."

"Thank you." She presses her lips to mine. The warmth in her kiss makes me hard but it also makes my heart warm.

Is it possible to re-grow a heart because in the last three weeks it felt as though mine was nearly whole.

"Thank you. You know I love you."

She says it with such an earnestness and a truth, that I know her words are real. And my heart that I've been re-building and stitching back together over time, and really if I'm fucking honest probably since the night in the hall when she was holding that damn wedding dress and I knew something was wrong even though she didn't tell me. I've been piecing my heart back together and working through my past for this very moment.

I look at Tara and I think it. I know it. And I say it, too. "I love you, too."

Her smiles widens. Her hand is on the side of my face and her lips press to mine. Now this heat between us isn't just about feeling happy with the other person. No. This heat between us is more, much more, and my cock is hard and pressed against her.

That sigh, with a little moan that I've heard over and over again, comes from her lips. That tiny little sound makes my belly clench tight because it's that very sound that tells me each time that she's pleased and I'm wanted. Her desire ripples through her body like desire ripples through mine.

And it's more than desire. So now, here, when we fuck, it's not just fucking. It's become more than fucking, more than wonderfucking. It's become this beautiful, passionate event between the two of us that has taken on more than this physical act has meant to me in the past. What happens between me and Tara is more than a vocation, it's a dominion. She has dominion over my body and my soul. A duet of two lives. A desire that is intertwining and brilliant and magical and can only be called making love.

Her hand slips down over my belly and her fingertips trail along my flesh until she has my cock in her hand. She strokes down and my breath flows from my body. Her mouth opens to mine and our tongues tangle and tease.

I rise up above her knowing that the need I feel she feels too. My lips pull from hers and our eyes latch onto each other. She is here, beneath me, with her blue eyes that mesmerize me, and her mouth open in this beautiful pleasure.

"I want you so much."

And my cock glides into her heat, her warm, sensuous heat. I am enveloped by her silky, velvet warmth that surrounds my cock and I lose my self in the wet hot heat that is her. I slide in and out of her, both of us reveling in the pleasure of skin-to-skin contact. My cock in her sex.

Fuck. My body can't contain this pleasure and my body is stone.

"Oh Jake." Her muscles clench around me and pull me tight and deeper into her sex. I press forward and with one final thrust my body stiffens and heat rips through me. Heat jets from my body rip into hers.

"Tara!" I yell her name. A prayer and a plea on my lips as I come.

"THE BEACH TODAY?"

"That's the plan," I say, and continue filling the cooler with ice.

"Could we ask Lily and Rachel?"

I stop. I take a breath. Asking Lily and Rachel to join us at the beach makes what Tara and I are doing, real. Bringing my family into the mix makes everything we're doing real.

"The Malibu house is empty. What if we have them meet us there and then we play, grill, hang out? They could even spend the night if they wanted."

This is a huge gift, in fact this is one of the first things I thought of the very first time I visited Tara in Malibu: What a great place for a family to hang out and spend time together. What Mom and Dad's house was to Rachel and me before all the ghosts that now inhabit our life and our childhood home.

"If you don't want to ask the—"

"Of course I do." I walk from the kitchen to the dining room table and grab my phone. I punch in the speed dial for Rachel, smile at Tara, and ignore the panic clutching my insides.

"THIS HOUSE IS AMAZING!" RACHEL SAYS. SHE DROPS her overnight bag on the floor just inside the open sliders that lead to the deck and the ocean that is steps beyond. "Seriously, if I had this, I don't think I'd ever leave."

She turns toward me and Tara. We unload groceries we picked up for today and tonight. In Rachel's smile I see a question. Because of course she has questions. She hasn't seen Tara and me together, and yet here we are functioning like a couple. Tara turns toward the fridge to load in the cheese, and Rachel raises her palms in the universal 'what the hell is going on' symbol.

I smile and fight back a laugh. Walk closer to Tara and nuzzle my face into her hair. "Rachel's confused, shall we let her in on us?" I'm getting hard and realize that I won't be able to do a damn thing about it, which is highly unusual, because Tara and I have gotten into this amazing habit of simply having sex whenever we want.

Tara shuts the refrigerator door, smiles at me, and together we turn to Rachel, who is back to pretending nothing is going on by staring out the open sliders at Lily who is on the deck brushing Jango.

I wind my fingers through Tara's fingers and walk toward Rachel.

"We're dating," I say.

"I guessed as much," Rachel says, and smiles. "I'm happy for you because I really think the two of you make a good couple."

She pulls Tara in for a hug.

"We've kind of been seeing how it works, the last few weeks," Tara adds.

"And it does? Work?" Rachel asks.

"Really well," I say.

This knot in my chest slips apart. I feel it almost as though it's a real entity. Suddenly, this tightness is gone, and I glance out to the deck where Lily sits beside Jango. I squeeze Tara's hand and look at Rachel, who has a real smile on her face, and I wonder and hope and pray that all the pain of the last six years is finally behind us. Yes, there will be sadness and hiccups and bumps but maybe, just maybe, we're all ready to have some simple joy and peace and this day, this night, is the start of all of that for us.

"Mommy can I go into the water?"

"Bean, I'll take you," I say. I walk to the sliders and bend down and grab one of Jango's balls. "Guess who loves to swim?" I ask Lily and point toward Jango.

"Oooh!" Lily claps and jumps up and down with the excitement of having Jango and me in the ocean with her.

"My god, I'm going to end up with a fucking dog," I hear Rachel mutter under her breath. Quietly enough so that Lily who is already back on the deck with Jango can't hear her.

"That was always my plan, sister, dear." I scoot out of the house before she can find anything hard to hit me with.

CHAPTER 51

THE SUN HOVERS just above the ocean. Orange, gold, and pink streak across the sky. I open the top of the grill and set the cedar plank that carries a side of salmon inside.

"Here you go." Tara walks up and hands me a glass of white wine. There is a peace winding through me that I haven't felt in maybe forever. I sip my wine and place my arm around Tara's waist. This is how I want life to feel; smooth and soft and silky with beauty and love and a slow joy that permeates the air around me.

"Good day?" Tara asks.

I don't even know how to quantify this day. This very simple day of throwing a ball into the waves and running into the surf with Lily by my side while Rachel and Tara sit on beach chairs talking and reading. Today is the best day I've had in what feels like a lifetime. I look into her blue eyes that I'm starting to call home.

"The best day." I kiss her. "I love you." I say, and I know that this moment is seared into my memory. Could a lifetime possibly be made up of moments like this one and all the brilliant moments strung together during this day?

"Do you think Rachel will mind? I invited our neighbor over for dinner."

"Naw, she won't mind." I turn away, lift the lid and give the salmon a peek. "Is he single?"

Tara nods. "Very. Well-adjusted. Widowed. And has a good job."

"She may end up thanking you."

Tara's gaze drifts to the house and I follow her gaze. Rachel brushes Lily's wet hair. She's fresh out of the bath and wears summer pajamas. "I don't know. I think she's pretty determined to get Lily raised before she gets involved with anyone."

I understand that determination to stay un-involved, but I also now understand that sometimes it's not a choice. Sometimes the person you're meant to be with doesn't wait for the perfect moment, they simply arrive, unrequested and unwelcome, and their presence requires you to do the work you need to do to share your life with them.

"She's focused on Lily," I say. "But sometimes being in love isn't a choice, it simply is."

She turns her face to me and presses her lips to mine.

Warmth flows through my body because I want a lifetime of this. What today and tonight is, this is what I want. Tara's stomach growls.

"You're hungry."

"Starved," she says. "And that smells amazing."

I lift the top and peek in. "Five more minutes."

"I'll go pull the potatoes," she says.

I watch the woman I love walk into the house. I turn toward the surf. The sun slips into the calm ocean. The waves caress the shore and I know that everything is right in my world.

"HOW HAVE WE NEVER MET?" I ASK. ALEX IS THE TYPE

of man that in my business I feel I would've run into at some point.

"You do VC, I make movies. Your kind isn't exactly pounding down the doors to invest in films."

"Fair enough." I take another sip of my wine and squeeze Tara's hand. Lily's eyes are heavy and she looks like she may fall asleep at the table.

"Rach," I whisper, and nod my chin toward my niece.

"Excuse me, I'm going to put my little one down."

I'm up before the words are out of Rachel's mouth. "I've got it," I say. I lift Lily from her seat and without a peep, she snuggles her head onto my shoulder. Her hair smells fresh and of sun and wind and strawberries. I smile at Tara who stands.

"I'll help."

I walk up the stairs and down the hall to the room with a double bed. Tara pulls back the blanket and I gently put Lily in the bed.

"That's the good kind of sleep," I whisper. "The kind that comes after a day of sun, family, and fun." Lily is so deeply asleep her eyelids don't even flutter.

"There's nothing sexier than seeing a man carry an adorable child and tuck her into bed," Tara says. She tilts her head toward mine and we kiss. A soft and gentle kiss, the kind that comes with love.

We walk out of Lily's room and I shut the door but leave the tiniest crack. Rachel's laugh comes up the stairs. Big Sis sounds happy.

"He's a nice guy," I say.

Tara wiggles her eyebrows. "I know. I was kind of hoping that Rachel would think so too."

Another laugh from downstairs followed by a deeper, masculine laugh.

"It sounds like they're having a good time. Well done. You think you can fix up both the damaged Reynolds' kids in one month?"

"I can try," she says.

"That would be quite an accomplishment when you consider our failure in love."

"Not really a failure on either of your parts was it?"

I pull her into my arms and close my eyes. "It felt like a failure." The warmth of Tara's body feels good pressed against me. Almost as though failure isn't possible when she's this close and my feelings are this good.

"No failure," Tara whispers. "Sadness, but no failure. You tried to do everything for the woman you loved. How is that a failure?"

A breath shudders through my lungs. Heat builds in my eyes but the weight of guilt that compresses my chest when the topic of Susie comes up isn't present. The loss is still there and I guess the loss of Susie will be with me for the rest of my life, but the guilt over not being able to save her seems to have gone.

"Her death wasn't your fault."

I open my eyes and nod. And while I know that Susie's death wasn't my fault, I'm still not ready to let go of the belief that if I'd only let her go, she'd still be alive and living her life.

"There you two are." Rachel stands at the far end of the hallway at the top of the stairs. "Lily okay?" Rachel brushes by me and peeks into the room. I stand behind Big Sis and peer into the room too.

"She's the best thing I've ever done," Rachel says.

"She's perfect," I say.

Rachel turns back to me and Tara, "I started the coffee and Alex is breaking out the dessert he made."

"He bakes?" I ask.

Tara nods.

"He's perfect for Rachel," I whisper in Tara's ear.

We follow Rachel down the stairs. The table and kitchen have already been cleaned and the dishwasher loaded. Big Sis may be the best house guest ever.

We head to the living room where Alex has built a fire in the fireplace. Tara brings over a tray with coffee cups, plates, a carafe and silverware, and Alex follows behind her with the chocolate torte. Rachel starts to cut pieces while Alex tells me about the next film his company is putting into production. Rachel hands me my piece and I cut into the torte and take my first bite.

"Hey," Alex says, and nods toward Tara. "How's that new book of yours going?"

"You're writing a book?" Rachel asks.

I glance toward Tara. A book? She hasn't mentioned a book to me... My gaze is locked to hers but she won't meet my eyes.

"It's nothing, just this idea that I have and I'm thinking—"

"Nothing? Ha, it's not nothing," Alex continues. "Every publishing house in New York has made her an offer. I've even made her an offer for the film rights for this yet to be written book."

My belly squeezes and suddenly the untangled knot in my chest is tangled and tightened again.

Because I know. I know before anyone asks.

"What's it about?" Rachel balances her plate with a piece of torte on her knee and takes a sip of her coffee.

"It's uhhh—"

"It's that brilliant article she wrote for the LA Post," Alex breaks in. "Everyone wants a piece of that. The click rate was off the charts and if they can't find the guy then they definitely want his story."

I put my plate on the table beside my chair. I can't eat another bite. I swallow. I look at Tara but she doesn't look at me. Instead, she gazes at her plate and scoops some of the torte onto her fork.

"You never mentioned a book deal," I say. I try to keep my voice thoughtful and light as though simply surprised by the idea that the woman I'm seeing has a book deal when on the inside I'm screaming, What. The. FUCK?!

"I've gotten some offers based on the article but I haven't

taken any of them." She finally meets my gaze. "I'm not sure I want to write it."

I nod. Her response makes me feel a bit better, if not entirely. She's lied by omission. She should've told me that people wanted her to write a book, that she'd been approached. I feel lied to with her decision not to say anything.

"I loved that article," Rachel says. "It resonated with every woman I know."

"You don't think he's a little creepy?" Alex asks. "I mean a guy just wanting to fuck a boatload of women and claiming it was his vocation? Doesn't that sound like the world's worst pick up line to you?"

"No, it seemed like he never had to pick them up. That they were always reaching out to him."

"They were"—Tara's eyes flick to me—"He's legit. According to all the women I spoke to and when I met him, he truly believes that this is his vocation and he does it because he loves women and he wants them to feel good about themselves."

"Was he gorgeous?" Rachel nearly pants.

I stand with my plate. I can't sit here and listen to my sister pant over a man that she believes is distant when actually it's me. That is simply too strange.

"Come on ladies, really?" Alex smiles and shakes his head. "Tara, you didn't embellish any of what the women had to say?"

I stand in front of her and reach out for her now empty dessert plate. Her gaze meets mine and I can't hide my disappointment, my discomfort, or the sadness that radiates from my heart. Her gaze screams, 'I'm sorry', but my mental state in this moment won't allow me to accept her apology.

"No, they all felt as though he'd saved them," Tara says, and her gaze locks with mine. I break away from her, unwilling to give her the acceptance she seeks.

"If you heard the stories that my women friends tell, you'd understand why," Rachel says, and hands me her empty dessert plate.

"It's that bad?" Alex asks.

"It's that bad." Rachel says. They look at each other and there is this moment between them. I feel the spark.

Rachel takes a breath and looks away from Alex. "My goodness, I ate too much," she says, and lets out a nervous laugh.

"Go for a walk with me," Alex says.

Rachel glances at him. The invitation is for her and her alone, and in his tone, his words, is more than simply a walk. Rachel glances at me and Tara. "You guys mind?"

"Not at all," I say.

Alex stands. Rachel is on her feet and grabs her jacket from the closet.

"Have fun," Tara says, and Rachel and Alex are out the sliders and across the deck and onto the beach.

Silence.

Uncomfortable silence.

I take the plates into the kitchen and turn on the water to rinse them off.

"I didn't tell you because..."

Her words drift away as though she's waiting for me to break in, waiting to see my reaction to her lie.

I turn off the water and turn to her. "Because why?"

"Because I thought you'd be upset."

"I am upset."

"I haven't taken any of the offers."

"Do you want to?"

"Of course I want to. They're offering me sick money, and what writer doesn't want a huge book deal?"

I step to the island that separates us. "If it's only about the money, I can match any offer you've received."

She sighs and crosses her arms over her chest. Her gaze slips toward the window and the ocean beyond. "It's not just about the money."

"Of course it's not. It's the prestige. You want the prestige of a big book deal with a super-sexy topic." I wipe my hands on a towel and toss it onto the counter.

"I can't do it anyway. I'd need your permission and you won't give it to me."

"You didn't ask for my permission before."

She closes her eyes and takes a big breath. "I want us more than I want that. I don't want this between us, I want—"

"You want everything for yourself is what you want. You want me and you want the book deal and you want the film and your ego wants the prestige that comes with having that big thing that everyone is talking about."

"Do you know how many interviews I've turned down?"

"What does that have to do with anything?"

"I've turned them down so we could have a chance at this, and now you want me to feel badly for the success I have?"

"No. I want you to admit that the success you're having comes at the expense of the trust we need to build a relationship."

"I don't see it that way."

"You don't see how not telling me that you got offers for this story, my life story, which includes my private decisions and my pain and how I've managed to cope, is lying to me?"

Rage thrums through my body. My voice tightly restrained. This is nearly the exact same argument we had a month ago, only this time it's over a book deal. I'm an idiot. I'm a fucking idiot who is lead around through life by my cock.

"I didn't agree to do the book because I want to have a relationship with you."

"But you didn't tell me."

"Why do I have to? We were barely speaking until three weeks ago. Sure we were *fucking*, but that is all we were doing. You wouldn't talk to me about anything and certainly not this. If I'd brought this up when it happened? The first time I told them no—"

"The first time? They keep asking?"

"Of course they do. It's a great story, Jake. I'm sorry, but you're crazy fucking life makes a great story. Must be horrible to be you." She tosses that last line at me with loads of sarcasm. I don't know what to do with her words.

"Yeah, well, it's much harder to live the story than it is to rip it off."

Her mouth drops open and I brush by her because my anger is too deep and running too fast. If I stay in this room with Tara I'll say things that she might not be able to forgive, and part of me still holds out hope for her. For me. For us.

CHAPTER 52

DAYLIGHT EDGES THE DARKNESS. The sound of waves crashing against the shore is my only companion at 4 a.m. I lie on the couch in the living room. Tara and I have a fierce détente, one that included me saying I wanted to watch some TV downstairs, but ended up with me falling asleep on the couch and never going upstairs to bed.

The shhhh of the back slider opening. I look over the side of the couch. Rachel slipping in with her curls disheveled and her shoes in her hands. She turns toward the window and waves and then turns back toward the couch, which contains me.

"Oh, hey, you're up," she says. And stops. That fire engine red that decorates her face when she's embarrassed arrives on scene. "I uh..."

"No explanation needed. You're a grown woman and Lily was with her Uncle Jake. It's all good."

She smiles. "Why are you down here?" She puts her shoes on the floor next to the door. "Fight?"

"Argument. Plus I fell asleep down here and my sister woke me up sneaking into the house."

"One thing led to another..."

"You like him?"

Rachel walks to the kitchen and pulls a glass from a cabinet. "He's a nice guy and I'd go out with him again if he called but I don't think he will."

"Why not?"

"I'm not his type."

"What do you mean, you're not his type?"

"Well, I'm over twenty, have a graduate degree, a job, and a child. From what I can tell, his type includes being younger than twenty-five, jobless, vapid, and definitely child-free." She sips her water. "I'm kind of his walk on the wild side."

"Must be kind of cool to be exotic."

"Ha, I didn't think of it quite that way but I'm going with that instead of feeling like a worn out shoe. I'm holding onto the words, 'collector's item'."

"His loss."

"How'd Lily do?"

"Great. I checked on her a couple of hours ago."

"And you?"

I wave my hand.

Rachel walks to the couch, lifts my feet, sits, and puts my feet on her lap. "Listen, this is only your second real relationship."

Which is true. While I've slept with a load of women I've never been emotionally involved with anyone but Susie.

"I mean, I know that there must've been women, but you don't talk about them and you've never brought one around, so I gather this is the first time you've felt deeply for a woman since then."

Rachel takes a deep breath and looks at me. "Plus, and I'm only guessing here, and you do have a therapist who could prob-ably help you with all this, but here's the thing. After Susie's betrayal, I can't imagine that it's easy for you to be vulnerable with a woman."

Susie's betrayal? The words hit me square in the chest. I stare at Rachel, letting her words sink into my brain.

"It's hard enough to let yourself love someone, but then when the person you love is fucking like a hundred people all while you're engaged?" Rachel shakes her head. "Plus, Tara has her own baggage, what with what Douchey-pants did to her."

"Right." My mind spins. I'm a guy, so I only see things from my angle until someone smarter, more insightful, and almost always female, points out to me the other side of the situation. Face it ladies. The penis-people, we aren't inclined to see anything but our own side. You always help us see the other person's point of view because we're not wired to do it on our own.

"There are things," I start. I look at Rachel sitting on the far end of the sofa. "Things that have happened that you don't know about"

I'm edging close to this place that I've never gone with Rachel, not just because she's a judge, but also because she's my big sis, and as much as I play like her opinion of me and my life and my decisions don't matter, they do. Her opinion matters a whole lot. "Things that I've done, people I've been with..."

My gaze remains on hers eyes. I'm trying to read her reaction, to see how much I can tell her without her flipping out.

"We've all got shit in our past that we wish had never happened, okay? As long as you haven't killed anyone, we're good."

Then there is silence. Because while I didn't push Susie off the balcony, her family thinks I killed her. Most people that were Susie's and my friends think I must've done something really horrible for Susie to have jumped off the balcony, so while I didn't push her, according to them, I'm the cause of her suicide. I've bought into it. I don't tell them the truth, and Rachel doesn't tell them the truth, and Jane, Susie's sister, doesn't tell anyone the truth about Susie's life and her addiction out of respect for her, and her parents that hate me. So yeah, some people do think of me as a person who caused Susie's death, which would only make it even worse if the truth about Wonder-fuck got out.

I close my mouth. Unloading my alter identity onto Rachel would only be a selfish release for me and I know what selfish gets you. Selfish gets you a dead fiancée. If I told Rachel about Wonderfuck, she'd worry that she should help me or that she was doing something wrong by knowing. I'd put her in a horrible position. If I don't tell her, then if my identity ever gets out, she can honestly say she had no idea. And I want that for her, more than I want to tell her my secret.

"She's got her stuff to deal with from her douche-a-lot and then you've got your stuff to deal with from Susie, so this isn't necessarily going to be an easy road for either one of you."

Then throw in Wonderfuck, and the article and the book, and we've got a bumpy-ass ride. But I don't say that part.

Rachel stands and drops my feet to the floor. "I'm rooting for you two, little brother. I like her. She's smart and nice." Rachel's eyes dance around the living room. "Plus, this would be a kick ass place to have Thanksgiving and Christmas."

I smile, because her thoughts are nearly identical to mine as far as the Malibu pad.

I stand and toss the blanket I've been snuggled beneath onto the couch. I'm being a dick or kind of a dick. I follow Rachel up the stairs and she turns right.

"Goodnight," she whispers. "Or good morning. I'll see you in a few hours."

She enters the bedroom where Lily sleeps and closes the door. I turn left and open the bedroom door.

The giant bed faces the amazing view, and Tara is scrunched on her side with the plush white duvet covering her. I pull off my clothes and slip beneath the blankets. Her body is warm with sleep and I slide up behind her and spoon her.

I'm hard. One hundred percent hard. I put my arm around her and nudge my cock toward her ass.

"Babe," I whisper in her ear. "Tara, babe." She turns her head and her ass presses back toward my cock.

"Babe, I'm sorry." My voice trembles. "I'm sorry, and I do want this to work, and I do believe you."

My ego is bruised and battered, but Tara's not the person who caused the wounds or built the walls around them. That came later. She's the woman loving me in spite of all the pain that is part of who I am.

She rolls toward me and looks into my eyes. "I'm sorry too," she says.

I press my lips to hers and that tiny little sigh with a moan escapes her lips.

Fuck, yes. I want her.

My hand cups her breast and twirls the taut flesh of her nipple. Her hips rock forward and back, her ass pressing against my cock. I slide my hand down over her belly and to her sex and slip my fingertip to her clit where I press.

"Yes, Jake, oh yes." Her hips press back toward me and I circle her clit with my fingertip. The pressure of her ass against my cock intensifies.

My lips press to the back of Tara's neck. Heat sizzles through my body. I press my leg between her thighs and lift her thigh. I scoot down and nudge the head of my cock to her sex. I press her legs open and slip forward into her. Fuck, I want her. I want her with an unqualified intensity. I press the head of my cock into her sex.

"All I want is you. All I'll ever want is you." I press upward and she gasps. The moan crosses her lips again.

She turns to me as we rock together, forward and back. I kiss the edge of her mouth and continue to circle her clit. I stroke in and out of her and her body tightens around me. Our desire is so hot it won't be long. She whispers my name and I'm gone. The sun brightens the room and the light bathes us both as we fall over the edge into our orgasm together.

CHAPTER 53

I PULL to a stop in front of Tara's parents' home. Not on my list of things I want to do. How the hell will I get through tonight? Maybe Tara's mom doesn't remember me. Perhaps she's forgotten about our night together? We met once, three years ago, if memory serves.

I don't want that memory.

I press thoughts of Tara's mother to the back of my mind and follow Tara up the steps of her parent's Bel Air home. The entrance is gigantic and is an attempt at a statement.

"Mom? Dad?" Tara's voice echoes off the marble floor.

"Back here," her father calls out.

We walk down a long hallway and into the TV room where her father lounges in one of a dozen recliners. He watches a baseball game on a projection TV. The announcer blares out the latest score.

"Jake, good to see you again."

He stands and shakes my hand. His smile doesn't reach his eyes. "Beer?"

He walks toward the bar at the far side of the room and I follow. On top of the marble cabinet is a silver bucket with ice and beers. I pull out a Stella and he opens the bottle. He watches the game while he talks.

'"Sorry, have some bucks riding on this game. You a baseball fan?"

"I like the Dodgers."

"Daddy grew up in Chicago," Tara says. "He loves his Cubs."

A player hits a grounder toward first for an easy out.

"One more inning to go," Dennis says, and slaps me on the back. "See you found Tara." He winks as though we've got our own private joke because of the night I came to Malibu looking for Tara and stumbled across her parents.

Yeah, that's not the only thing we've shared.

"Where's Mom?"

"Upstairs. Getting dressed. She's having a hell'uva time deciding what to wear."

"Aren't we eating here?"

"We are." Dennis tilts his watch and looks at the time. "And hopefully soon. I have a meeting at 9."

"Tonight, Daddy?" Tara glances past her father toward me. "Couldn't you have waited until tomorrow?"

"Sweetie, money never sleeps. Who do you think pays for this place?"

Tara's face crumples. Right. I've met more Dennis's than I can count. He's correct that money never sleeps, but what he forgets is time marches on, and while you can always make more money you can't create more time. After losing Dad and Susie, and Mom losing her memory, I know that time with family is more precious than any of the dollars Dennis might make at his meeting tonight. But I'm the guest in this house, and I'm dating his daughter. I don't say anything to Dennis about his business meeting.

If business is really what his meeting is about.

Because if memory serves, according to Tara's mom, Dennis has a penchant for sex clubs and twenty-somethings.

"Tara tells me you make loads of money," Dennis says.

His crass words rattle me. They rattle Tara, too. The color drains from her cheeks and she pulls a beer from the bucket. I lift the corner of my mouth and shoot her a glance, which is my attempt to tell her that I understand this is the only language her father speaks. According to Dennis, every person's value is determined by the money they make.

"Wish our girl did the same," Dennis continues. "Has the best education money can buy and what does she want to do? Write. Ha! Won't make a living on that, will she?" He smiles while he says the words, as though they're a joke, but they're not a joke to Tara. She flushes red and takes a long drink of her beer.

"She seems to do pretty well."

"Right, if you call middle-class well. Damn waste if you ask me. To take those fancy degrees she has and not make some real money. Why be poor when you can be rich?"

To Dennis, wealth only comes in the shade of green. Tara stands beside me and I grasp her hand and squeeze. Money is great, makes life easier, but what about love, and family, and children? Tara's face is a shade of gray. This isn't the first time her father has derided her for her job and her income. Even though he's Tara's dad, he's an asshole who has no idea who his daughter is or how accomplished or respected in her field she's become. I want to say all these things but I don't. I say nothing, because no matter what I say, this man will only see her value based on how big her salary is.

"Hello." Tara's mom breezes into the room, her black hair falling in loose curls around her face. She wears a bright blue dress and heels.

"Jake, it's good to see you again." She reaches for my hand and pulls me in and places a peck on my cheek.

She remembers me.

Her lips remain on my skin just a little too long, and she grasps my upper arm and squeezes. Our eyes meet and in them I see a plea. Is she as worried as I am? Does she wish, like I do, that this wasn't happening, that we simply had the awkwardness of her accidentally walking in on me and Tara and not the embarrassment of actually having sex with each other?

"Dennis. Did you offer Tara and Jake drinks?"

"Don't they have them in their hands?" Dennis barks. He slides his gaze away from the game and toward his wife. There is no love in his look, no compassion, no joy over seeing his wife enter the room. He doesn't love her. It's obvious in his words, his tone, his stance. This man does not love this woman.

The crowd on the giant TV cheers.

"Could you turn that off and we'll go into the living room and chat with Tara and Jake until dinner is ready?" Lorraine asks.

"You three go," Dennis says. "I want to finish watching the game. What time is dinner? I have to leave in an hour."

The muscle in Lorraine's jaw twitches, but her expression doesn't change. Her smile, a tight false smile, remains on her face. "Let me go ask." She looks at Tara and then me. "Why don't we head to the dining room and I'll ask chef when dinner will be served. Dennis?"

"What the hell, Lorraine? I told you I'm going to finish watching this game. There's one inning left. It's my damn house and my damn cook and my damn food. I'll be in when I'm damn well ready."

Tara ducks her head as though each word is a smack. I squeeze her hand. She swallows and I see she's holding back tears. She's sad for her family. Her parents are completely unhappy with each other and it's obvious. I know from experience that the things you ignore as a family become apparent when there's someone new in the room. Fresh eyes make it impossible to ignore what we often choose not to see.

"I'm sorry," she whispers.

"Don't be." I walk with her out of the TV room and down another long hallway. "You've met my family, right? You know we're nuts."

She smiles. I stop and look at her. I press my fingers beneath her chin and tilt her head toward mine. We kiss, and this kiss is meant to reassure her and make her feel loved and cherished. I want to give her the love she needs, the attention she craves, and the reassurance that I will never judge her simply on the amount of money she makes. She steps away and I glance past her.

Lorraine watches us again, this time from a doorway at the end of the hall.

"Come into the dining room,. Chef says dinner is ready. I've let Dennis know."

The table is long and imposing and meant to be just that way. The three of us sit at one end, leaving the head of the table open for whenever Dennis cars to dine.

"I'm sure your father will join us when he can."

Dennis doesn't join us. An hour later we are completing our meal when he pops into the dining room to tell us the baseball game has ended and he's heading out to his meeting.

"Good to see you again, John. Don't get up."

"Daddy, it's Jake," Tara says softly.

I stand and shake his hand.

"I'm sure we'll see you again. You know, as long as our girl doesn't walk in on you banging your assistant against your office wall."

He slaps me on the shoulder as though he's just told the best joke, but he hasn't. He's just told the story of the worst thing that has ever happened to his daughter and used it like a punch line to a pathetic joke.

"Thank you for dinner." I sit down, because in this moment those words are the only polite thing I can think to say. What I really want to do is tell this guy that he's a complete and utter asshole and that he's done nothing but embarrass his wife and daughter since I arrived. I don't say any of that because I'm Tara's guest and I don't want to rock the world that she and, more so, her mother, inhabit.

I flash Tara a look. I want her to know that I see her, that I love her, and that I know what a jerk her father is. That her father's inability to be polite, kind, or loving, doesn't impact my feelings for her. If anything, Dennis's behavior makes me more protective of Tara.

"Bye, peaches." Dennis bends down and plants a kiss on Tara's cheek. She forces a smile to her face and pushes her chicken around her plate.

"Bye, Daddy."

In that moment, I see the little girl Tara was once upon a time. The child that was ignored by her father as he dashed off to his business 'meetings'. How he never noticed her growing, or praised her for anything. How he pointed out her flaws over and over and over again. I see that little girl and I understand why Tara fights for the truth and to be heard and why she needs to be seen. I also suddenly understand why she dated McDouchey for so fucking long.

"I'll be back late." Dennis's spits these words toward Lorraine. No good bye, no term of endearment, no kiss on the cheek. Just a quick bark and a fast exit.

Tara's mom doesn't cover her emotions quite so easily this time. Pain lives in her eyes.

A memory floods my mind. The story of her and her marriage. Why three years ago she met with me. She'd not slept with her husband in nearly a decade. They shared a giant home, a daughter, and nothing more. She didn't leave him. She still loves him. While that love may be weathered, and bitter, and filled with a recalcitrant rage, it's still there on her face, in her eyes, as she watches her husband leave for what could be the millionth time in her life.

"Coffee?" she asks, and being the perfect hostess covers her sadness with a smile.

I nod, as does Tara.

"Excellent, let's have it in the blue room."

"You never lived here."

Tara shakes her head. "We had a much smaller place in Calabasas when I was growing up, but then one of Daddy's deals took off and he wanted this as an investment." We walk down a third hallway toward the blue living room, this one more intimate, according to Tara's mom.

"The house seems so big."

"It is. Mom hates it. Dad travels all the time."

"It would seem so—"

"Lonely?"

I nod.

"I asked Mom about that once. Right after they moved in."

"And what'd she say?"

"She asked me if I wanted to get a mani-pedi." Tara smiles. "Our family isn't big on discussing emotional issues."

"Maybe that's why you need to."

"I'm certain that's why I need to discuss things and find the truth," she says. "They've taught me a lot about what it means to have a good marriage and a good relationship by showing me what I don't want to have. I thought I'd learned all that, but then with Greg?" She shakes her head and sighs. "He taught me that I don't know nearly as much as I think I do, and that I need to always listen to my little voice. When it feels like something is off, it usually is." Her brilliant blue eyes stare into mine. "I can't pretend everything is okay when it isn't."

Her words hold so much meaning not just for her, but for me, and for us.

"They both seem so...so sad." Her voice is soft.

"You can't fix them."

A tiny smile curves over her lips. "Your fancy therapist tell you that?"

I return Tara's gentle smile with my own. "Just one of the things my fancy therapist has told me."

We enter the blue living room. And while it may be more intimate than the yellow living room, I wouldn't say it's cozy.

Plaid. Lots and lots of plaid, with dark wood and paintings of people on horses, with hounds and red jackets.

"I don't think I've actually ever sat in this room," Tara says, sitting on the couch.

A tray with coffee and cups is already on the table in front of the couch.

"We don't have to stay if you don't want to. We can go back to my place and eat ice cream out of the carton. I'll even make you coffee."

Tara smiles at my suggestion and whispers in my ear. "As different as I want my life to be from this one and as different as I am from my mom, and as much as I don't understand, she's still my mom. I want her to be happy. I wish she'd just take the leap and leave. I think she'd be much happier on her own."

I can't tell Tara that Lorraine thinks that too, and that she stays simply because she's scared that Tara won't love her if she leaves.

Tara's phone buzzes and she slips it from her pocket. "I'll be right back." She jumps up, presses her phone to her ear, and darts out of the room.

"You find my life pathetic?"

I turn to my left and Lorraine stands by my side.

"No, I...I think Tara worries about you."

Her eyes narrow. "I worry about her."

She sits on the couch beside me and pours herself a cup of coffee.

"She told me you had no idea about the article, that you didn't participate."

"She told you it was me?"

"No, but I know you, so I knew who she was writing about before she did." She lifts an eyebrow. "Don't worry, I didn't say a word. I can't really, now can I?"

Relief floods through me, but I can't keep this secret forever, can I?

"You can't tell her," Lorraine says. "It would ruin my relationship with her and that's all I have left in my life. My marriage—" she glances into her cup of coffee, pauses and her gaze darts back up to me—"well you've seen what my marriage is like."

She leans closer to me, and her gaze locks to mine. "You've given up your Wonderfuck ways?"

Her eyes penetrate me and I'm not certain she's asking for herself or for Tara's well-being. "Or could you be convinced, that Wonderfucking is something you should resume?"

My stomach lurches. The thought of Lorraine, now, as Tara's mother. My teeth grind together.

"I..no...no, that isn't a part of my life any longer."

"That's good to know." She sips her coffee. "Although I did enjoy our time together."

"Jake, are you ready to go?" Tara stands near the doorway.

"Tara, come have some coffee before you leave," Lorraine says.

"Can't. Just got a call from work. Warren needs me for a story."

Lorraine rises and walks to Tara. She pulls her into a hug. I stand on the other side and watch. Her mother shoots me a look, one that seems to say, 'don't make me tell her the truth.'

"I love you, Mom. Thank you for dinner."

We walk to the front door. Lorraine pulls me into a hug. "Be good to my girl," she whispers into my ear.

I glance at Tara, who is on the far side of the entryway pulling on her jacket. She hitches her purse over her shoulder.

"Thank you for dinner," I say.

I open the door for Tara and suck in the night time air. We walk down the stairs holding hands, finally free from her parent's unhappy home.

CHAPTER 54

"THIS PUPPY THING has gotten a little out of control."

Rachel pulls a sheet of paper that has been folded into a perfect square from her purse. "Take a look at this." She unfolds the paper and hands it to me.

A hand-drawn picture under the words, 'perfect puppy meets your perfect girl'.

"Smart kid," I say.

Rachel plucks the picture from my fingers. "I think someone's giving her instructional tips on how to emotionally blackmail her mother."

Rachel narrows her eyes at me and I give her my I'm-totally-innocent-face.

"How many times do I have to say this, I cannot handle a dog."

"What if I hired a trainer and someone to walk the dog twice a day?"

Rachel closes her eyes and sighs. "That would be helpful, but what about the middle of the night when she's whining, or vomits, or needs to be let out? Jake, we're not home enough for a dog. I'm gone from 7 a.m. to 5 p.m. almost every day. Some days even longer than that because Lily and I come over here to hang out with Mom. If anyone should have a dog it's you."

Rachel glances toward the backyard where Lily throws a tennis ball and Jango bolts across the yard to retrieve it. "But seems like you may already have one."

"Every kid needs a pet."

"A goldfish would be easier."

"You can't snuggle a goldfish."

"Says the guy who tried to cuddle mine when he was three years old."

"Cleopatra looked lonely, I thought she would like it if I petted her."

"So much trauma where pets are concerned."

Rachel stuffs the note in her purse. "The guest room is finished. How did the garage go today?" she asks, changing the subject.

"Still have three boxes, but I'm nearly done."

I glance around the living room. Rachel has packed up everything but three family pictures on the walls. All the knick knacks have been removed from the furniture and the built in book case. "Has Mom said anything to you about the house looking different?"

"Only how clean it is."

"I didn't realize how cluttered this place was. It actually looks really good without all the stuff."

"Which brings me to my next question," Rachel says. "What are we going to do with this place?"

"I thought you and Lily would move in."

"Here? You want me and Lily to live here?"

"It's perfect."

"Uh, not perfect. She'd have to change schools. It's completely inconvenient for my work. No, not moving in here."

"Well we can't sell it."

"Why not?"

"Because it's the house we grew up in."

"Jane's parents just sold their house."

My heart squeezes. I glance at Rachel and she looks up from her purse at me. "Sorry," she mumbles. "I thought you knew."

I didn't know and somehow the idea of Susie's childhood home not being her family's feels both like a kick in the chest and a release.

"It's okay. They always wanted to move out to the desert."

"That's what Jane said." Rachel lifts her purse and glances around the living room. "This place can't sit here empty and Mom won't be moving back in so—"

"Okay now you just sound mean." I walk toward the back sliders.

"Not mean, just realistic. There's a difference you know," Rachel calls toward my back.

I say nothing. This isn't a decision we have to make today. We haven't even heard from the residential facility where Mom is wait-listed. There's really no reason to discuss what to do with the house.

"Hey." Tara wraps her arm around my waist and smiles. I brush a kiss over her lips. Lily lifts the tennis ball and throws it into the pool, and Jango runs and jumps into the deep end.

"Not quite the beach," Tara says. "But she seems to love it."

Jango swims to the stairs in the shallow end and climbs out. She holds onto the ball, and Rachel steps out the back door just as Jango gives a giant shake. Water bullets at Rachel and she sputters.

"Reason 347 why I don't want a dog!"

She covers her face with her arm. Too late. She is pretty sopped with smelly dog water. Tara does her best not to laugh, but I don't even try to pretend.

"Mommy, don't say that," Lily wails. Her gaze goes from Rachel to me. "Please Mommy, please, a dog is all I want for my birthday."

Lily drops to her knees and wraps her arms around Jango's wet neck.

"Great," Rachel mumbles. "Now we both smell like wet dog."

Rachel wipes water from her face and shakes her arms. "No way, Lily. Not this year."

Lily turns her head toward me, still hanging on to Jango. "Uncle Jake, you promised."

"You promised?" Rachel turns to me and creases her eyebrows. "You *promised* you'd get her a dog?"

"No, I promised I'd convince you that she should have a dog."

"Giant fail Uncle Jake, giant fail." Rachel turns to Lily. "Come on bean, we have to get home. There's summer class in the morning."

"Can't we wait until Grandma gets up from her nap?"

"Go on and check, she might be up." Rachel says.

Lily scoots by her and into the house.

"Plus grab a towel from the hall closet and wipe your face and arms."

I'm way too familiar with the look Rachel shoots me when Lily goes into the house. She walks toward me, droplets of water still glistening on her forehead and cheeks. She lowers her voice to a threatening tone. "So listen, buddy, you're getting Lily a dog because I refuse to be the evil mommy who never let this kid have a pet, but here is the deal. You are going to take this dog during the day, got it? Except for weekends. We get weekends."

"We have a dog with a visitation schedule?" I tease.

My annoyed sister ignores me and keeps talking. "You will take and keep the dog any time we're not around, basically any time I tell you to. You will hire a dog walker and a trainer. Got it? I am not going to rain on Lily's parade, but you're going to be responsible for this circus, like the guy who walks behind the elephants at the end of the parade."

"Done." I smile. I know a good deal when I hear one, and any deal that gets Rachel to agree to a dog for Lily is a good one, no matter how much work it involves for me.

Rachel doesn't smile back because she knows this is a win for me. I have no problem hiring an army of dog service people to get Lily what she wants because I'll do nearly anything to make my niece happy.

"Good to see you, Tara."

Rachel leans closer to her. "I don't know how you put up with this guy but it's always good to see you."

"Sorry about Jango," Tara says.

"No worries." Rachel hitches her thumb my direction. "I blame him."

She finally shoots me a grin to let me know she's not completely pissed at me. "I'll see you later this week?"

"Of course."

"Don't forget next Saturday. Party starts at two but—"

"You need me by noon. Eleven if possible."

"Absolutely right."

"When can she get the dog?" I ask.

"After the party. I can't watch twenty kids, forty adults, and a dog. You can take her to the shelter on Sunday after the party."

"I won," I whisper to Tara as Rachel walks away.

"I heard that," Rachel calls from the doors. "And you didn't win by the way. I got everything I wanted when it comes to this dog."

I frown. This is true. She probably even got more. Rachel waves at us and heads up the stairs toward Mom's room to see if she's awake, and to collect Lily.

"Having fun?" I pull Tara in for a kiss.

"I always do with your family. Was it nice growing up with so much love?"

I tilt my head. Love? Was there a lot of love? I guess there was. Aside from Dad having his affairs and Mom throwing him out. Until he came back. And before it got really bad, yeah, there was a lot of love.

"Yeah," I say, and let my gaze skim the backyard with the pool and the trees, and the clubhouse in one of the trees. "Yeah, it actually was."

❦

"RICHARD, DID YOU BRING THE PRETTY LADY WHO IS going to help with Rachel?"

Mom walks down the stairs from her bedroom with Tatianna behind her. Jango waits patiently at the bottom of the stairs, her tail wagging. She's a big fan of Mom's and the feeling is mutual.

"Such a good doggie!" Tara hands Mom a biscuit for Jango. "Sit."

Jango complies and Mom feeds her the biscuit.

"I just love it when she comes to visit. Don't you?"

I nod. Mom has decided that Tara is meant to be the nanny for Rachel, which is okay, because she likes Tara and I like that she likes Tara, and that Mom likes the idea of Tara taking care of children in our family.

"Oh, did the cleaning people come again today?" She glances around the living room. Nothing has been moved today, but maybe it's the first time she's noticing the changes.

I grasp Mom's arm and steer her out to the patio. It is late afternoon and a warm breeze ruffles the yard. Not too hot and not too cool, but still Mom wears a sweater.

"The yard looks so nice. I really must get some flowers potted." I sit Mom on the rocking chair near the slider, knowing it's always been her favorite. She looks at me and creases her eyebrows. "I know that I know you, but I'm sorry, I simply can't place you."

My heart cracks. I've heard this a few times from Mom, but these words seems to be coming more and more frequently. I can't help but wonder how much longer before she's forgotten all of her existence, all of her memories, all of us.

Tara squeezes my hand and then sits next to Mom. Jango lays down at Mom's feet.

"I think Rachel would like a dog, don't you Richard?"

I'm thankful that she's back, even if I have to pretend to be Dad.

"I do. I think we'll get her one for her next birthday," I say, grateful to have something to talk to her about.

"When is that?"

"The party is next weekend."

"Oh my, I need to get started on the cake." She starts to stand and I reach out toward her.

"No, Mom, I mean....Mom, we'll order one from the bakery."

Her gaze appears perplexed, as though she's processing the words I'm using and not quite understanding what I'm saying. Slowly she sits back down.

"Oh yes, the bakery. She likes chocolate. You know Rachel prefers chocolate to yellow cake."

I nod. I also fight the tears burning the backs of my eyes, and the knot tied in the center of my throat.

"What does she want on it?"

"A dog."

"Aren't we getting her a dog?"

"Right, but the picture she wants on her cake is a dog too."

Mom laughs, "Smart girl, making certain we remember what she wants by putting it on the top of her cake too."

I smile. I am grasping this moment, holding onto it, because as much as I don't want to believe it or admit it, I know that these moments are the best moments that are left and that they are slipping away like soap bubbles on a breeze. They're rising upwards and quietly bursting, leaving nothing but the memory of their iridescence behind.

"That party should be fun," Mom says.

Her voice is drifting, and I see that while she's spent the afternoon upstairs in her room napping, her chin is nodding, her eyes are closing, and she is going to sleep again. Tatianna is by her side and she has a blanket she pulls over Mom.

"The fresh air is good for her."

I stand and so does Tara.

"I will bring her inside in just a little while. She likes to nap out here. She talks about how you and your sister and your friends used to play in the pool."

I nod. I close my eyes. I hear the birds chirping in the trees. The breeze tickles my skin. And, finally, through the melancholy, the happy memories of my childhood float through my mind.

CHAPTER 55

"HOW MANY BALLOONS does one six-year-old need?"

"Keep blowing," Rachel says, and spins by me with a tray of cookies.

"What about a helium tank?"

"They can't all be helium, what do we do when they all float away?" Rachel says, and is out the door.

I turn to Tara who gamely agreed to volunteer for Lily's party. She ties another bow around another stuffed puppy.

"What's the theme again?"

"Puppies," Tara says, and pats the stuffed animal on the head.

"There are twenty five-year -olds descending on this house and they each get a stuffed puppy."

"And ears." Tara picks up a headband that has puppy ears sporting glitter. She puts them on.

My heart seems to be contradicting modern science and is actually regenerating. "You're too cute for words."

Tara blushes and smiles at me. "Think this pair can be mine?"

"I know that pair can be yours." I walk around the table and pull her into my arms. The kiss is warm and gentle and filled with a different kind of need. The need of wanting her in my life on a more permanent basis.

"Knock it off you two, there are children coming in the back gate." Rachel sweeps back into the kitchen. She leans toward Tara, "Again, I blame him." She smiles.

"He gets a lot of blame."

"Ah yes, well he's the youngest and a boy, so from me he gets all the blame. Now, from our parents, he got all the adoration and attention. And me? I simply got responsibility."

There is a kernel of truth in big sis's words, but there is also simply some playful teasing.

"You also got to torture me and tell on me," I say.

"The good old days." Rachel continues toward the sink. "I think I'm ready."

Lily flounces into the room wearing pants and a big shirt with a dog on the front.

"The theme continues," I say. "What you wearing Lily?"

"My new favorite shirt, Alex gave it to me."

I look at Rachel and raise an eyebrow. "Alex? As in lives in Malibu Alex?"

"Yes," Rachel says in a kind of don't mess with me tone. "He's out of town this weekend, but we saw him recently—"

"Oh? *We* saw him, did *we*?" I smile.

"And he knew Lily's birthday was coming up," Rachel continues, ignoring my playful but insinuating tone. "So he brought her the shirt."

"I see."

I flash Tara a look and she feigns like she doesn't know anything but I see a look exchanged between these two women that I love. And it's good. It's good that my sister likes Tara and Tara likes my sister and that they're friends, because them getting along makes life easier and pleasant and happy. And for the first time, maybe ever, I am down with easy and happy. Not only down with it, but actually cultivating it, and realizing that I can choose the happiness. I look at Tara and smile.

I choose Tara.

"Uncle Jake?"

I pull my gaze from Tara, one of the few times I've ever considered looking at anyone other than my niece when she's talking to me.

"Yes, my love?" I bend down and scoop her into my arms because she is six today and soon I won't be able to lift her.

She dips her head and raises her beautiful eyes up to me. "Uncle Jake," she says, in the softest, most gut-wrenching voice. "What did you get me for my birthday?"

I smile, I can't help it. This kid has my number and she pulls that thing out and twists my heart whenever she feels like it.

"I can't tell you."

She sighs. Oh the sigh that could end all sighs. "I want a puppy," she says and lays her head on my shoulder.

I glance at Tara whose eyes have widened. She has her hand over her heart as though she's seeing the most spectacular show of familial love.

"Don't be fooled," Rachel stage whispers in Tara's ear. "She pulled that same move last night for a chocolate chip cookie."

Rachel is again out the door, this time with a tray filled with sandwiches.

"Sweetie, I know what you want, but I can't tell you what I got you," I say.

"Please?"

"Lily." Rachel calls from the backyard. "Mathilda is here."

"Mathilda!" Lily yells and wiggles out of my arms. With a smile she is off like a shot, the thoughts of her love for me and her need for her puppy an evaporated memory.

"She's gonna' be so surprised," I say.

"You think you can hold out until tomorrow and not tell her?" Tara asks.

It's a legitimate questions. With all the presents she gets today she won't even notice that mine is missing, but there will be so much disappointment about no puppy.

"Maybe we don't have to wait for tomorrow." I wiggle my eyebrows.

"Oh my God, did you get her a dog?"

"I can neither confirm nor deny the possibility of a recently adopted puppy showing up at this house, after, of course, I've cleaned up and poured the wine for Rachel."

Tara claps her hands together beneath her chin. "Ooo! I love puppies and I can't *wait* to see Lily's face! I can stay, can't I? To see the puppy?"

I move back in close and put my arms around Tara.

"Absolutely." I duck my head and kiss her. "I mean you're practically family." I kiss her again.

She is. Even with the challenges, or perhaps in spite of the challenges, I have reached a place where I can't imagine a life without Tara. Does that scare me? Hell yes. Is it worth it?

Yeah. Absolutely worth it.

How do I know? I feel it. I feel this need for her to be in my life deep in my core, and regardless of what pops up at us, I know we can overcome it.

"Hello." Kendall stands on the far side of the kitchen, holding a gift wrapped in birthday paper decorated with puppies.

I step away from Tara and take a quick breath.

"Kendall, this is Tara."

Kendall squints, but puts a smile on her face and reaches out her hand. "We met, a couple of months ago, at the Barrett's party."

A flush starts in Tara's neck and rolls up into her cheeks.

"Right," Tara says. "The...uh...the Ferris wheel party."

Kendall nods. She waits and looks at Tara, almost like she's waiting for something more, another statement, more words.

"Well," Kendall finally says. "George is outside and I better get this present to Lily. Good to see you, Jake."

She slips by me, and gives my upper arm a tight squeeze, as if to say, 'be careful.'

I turn back to Tara and certainly hope that I am.

❧

"RICHARD, THAT WOMAN IS HERE."

I look around Mom toward the pool and the group of parents. Where is Tatianna? Mom's agitation is palpable and I don't want a scene at Lily's party. Rachel is inside with Tara and all the children are crammed around the table waiting for the cake. I know she's speaking about Kendall, but I don't know where she is.

"Did you hear me Richard? That...that....whore is here!"

"Mom." I grasp her hand. "Want to go inside? Maybe help me find Tatian—"

"No Richard." She rips her hand from mine, "I absolutely do not want to go inside. I want to know why that whore is here for Lily's birthday?"

I glance at the crowd again. Two women from the flock of parents glance toward Mom and me. Most of the adults at the party know about Mom's Alzheimers. An uncomfortable silence grows in the crowd.

"Mom—"

"Stop calling me that," Mom yells. "I am not your mother, I'm your damn wife, and I refuse to have that whore here for my daughter's birthday."

The entire backyard is silent. Even the kids surrounding the table are quiet. Lily's eyes grow wide, like she can't quite understand what Grandma is saying, but she does understand that Grandma is confused.

"Mom, please. It's Lily's party."

"I hate it when you call me Mom, Richard. I can't stand it. I can't stand this. How could you possibly let that woman come to our daughter's birthday?"

She stomps into the house just as Rachel and Tara emerge with Rachel holding the cake, candles blazing. Everyone starts singing. I'm thankful for the song instead of the awkward silence.

To the guests' credit, they fake it and quickly recover. The parents rally and surround Lily with smiles and sympathetic glances toward me and Rachel. Every parent at the party seems to understand that they must make up for those moments; that Lily must remember the happy parts of the party, not the strange things that her Grandmother yelled at her uncle.

I wait until the cake cutting is finished and then I go inside and upstairs. I peek into the guest room where Mom now lies on a bed fast asleep. Tatiana sits on a chair by the bed.

"She's better now," she says, and goes back to reading her book.

I shut the door and sigh. I walk down the hallway and stop at the top of the stairs.

Kendall.

She's stepped out of the upstairs bathroom and is now just in front of me.

"I needed the bathroom," she says

"Right," I say and pause.

"I uh, I was surprised to see her here."

"We...we seem to have worked it out."

"Really?" Kendal shakes her head. "You worked out that the woman you're supposed to trust wrote a secret article about you telling the world about your secret identity?" She raises her eyebrows. "Wow."

My heart tugs in my chest when she says it like that. None of this seems very workable, but I trust Tara. Don't I?

"Did you ask her about who she called and when?"

"I did."

"And?"

"And she disputes it, says it didn't happen that way, says it was after the party."

"And you believe her? The woman with so much to lose?"

Kendall walks toward me and is close to me now.

"She says your version of the timeline is off. That she started the story before and she hadn't put together who I was until after the party."

"Then how did she get all the numbers?" Kendall asks.

My heart drops. Too many unanswered questions that I don't want to ask. "I...we haven't gotten into the details."

"I understand," Kendall says. "I just hope she doesn't betray you again."

She glances toward the bottom of the stairs. "Someone discovering that you're Wonderfuck is the type of thing that could destroy your family. Especially Rachel." Kendall brushes past me and down the stairs.

"Jake!" Rachel's voice comes from the landing.

I didn't know she was there. Much closer than I want. I walk down the steps to meet her at the bottom.

"What the hell is going on?" Her face is ashen.

My heart pounds. Shit. She must have overheard, but then I follow her gaze to the front room, where the dog trainer has arrived and twenty five-year-olds screech with delight. Lily's best gift of all wiggles in her arms.

"We decided on tomorrow," Rachel hisses.

"No, *you* decided on tomorrow. Besides, I waited until the end of the party. These kids are all on the way out the door."

"You lied to me." Rachel's eyes hold ice. Her tone is different and I wonder if it's the puppy she's discussing right now, or did she overhear Kendall and me on the stairs? "You've been lying to me for a long while now."

Those words tell me all I need to know.

"Uncle Jake! Uncle Jake! Did you see my new puppy?"

Lily races toward me holding the adorable lab-shepherd mix while Rachel forces a smile to her face but shoots me daggers from her eyes.

I squat down. "What will you name her?" I ask, pretending everything is well.

My gaze zips over the crowd, and in the far corner of the dining room I see Tara speaking to...Kendall. And neither of them look happy. They're hidden in plain sight by the chaos of the moment. The puppy, the kids, and most parents trying to gather up their young and head out the door.

"Daisy," Lily says, and gives the furry floppy puppy a kiss on the head and then puts her on the floor.

I glance back up in time to see Tara shrug and shake her head, and Kendall raise her hands in an 'I don't know what to tell you' way. They both look disgusted with each other.

Lily pulls me in for a hug. "Thank you Uncle Jake, I love you."

And I realize that after today, my niece may be the only woman left who does.

UNAVOIDABLE CONVERSATIONS AREN'T USUALLY HAPPY conversations. No, they're the conversations that are required because something has gone wrong. Events force the topic. The discussion becomes mandatory.

I'm in my condo and the fading light streams through the sliders that lead to my balcony. The front door opens and closes and Jango's nails tippity-tap across my floor. She stops in front of me and sniffs me. Her tail wags furiously. She can smell Daisy.

"You're gonna' love her," I say, patting her on the head. If you ever get to meet her. I don't say that part because my hope is that yes, all of my suspicions, all of my fears, can be cleared up in a conversation.

My heart knows otherwise.

Tara has changed into her comfy clothes. She wears leggings. Her hair is up in a ponytail and she wears an over-sized flannel shirt. Relaxation flows through her. I fight my urge to walk to her and kiss her, touch her, sweep her into my arms and carry her to my bedroom. To ignore the unpleasant things. To pretend that nothing uncomfortable has happened. To be with Tara no matter what she's done. But I can't because the unavoidable conversation has to start now.

I turn to Tara and I don't smile. I've decided on the point-blank approach. "How did you find the women that I slept with?"

She curls up on the sofa with her feet tucked beneath her.

"We already discussed this."

"Humor me."

"I started with the conversation with my girlfriends."

"Before the end of your engagement?"

She nods. "Right before that. And then I remembered that conversation and I started looking for the name in bathrooms and chat rooms and I asked around and—"

"Right, I get that part. But how did you find them all?"

"They lead to each other over time. Conversations, questions."

She looks away from me toward the balcony as though she doesn't want to have this conversation. Neither do I.

"And my phone?"

"And your phone. That was the way I knew it was you."

"You didn't take numbers from my phone?"

The flush of red starts on her chest, rolls up her neck and into her cheeks, and I know the truth before she says a word. I only hope, I pray, that she says the right words, because while I can't forgive her now for lying to me and betraying me a second time, I can possibly not hate her if she tells the truth now. Not hating the woman that I love, that would be good for now.

Tara looks me in the eye. She doesn't say anything at first. Then her gaze goes to the balcony, that fucking balcony that haunts my life. She looks at it and then back at me. "Yeah," she says softly. "I took the numbers from your phone."

My heart plummets. This is the end. There is no coming back from the hit because there've been too many hits from which this relationship can recover.

"You know about your mother?"

"I do."

My brow creases. She knows. She knows everything.

"Why now? Why are you telling me now?"

"Because crazy Kendall said she'd out your identity to the world if I didn't tell you the truth."

Tara looks away from me. She crosses her arms in front of her and rubs her upper arms with her palms.

"I...Jake, I did it then for a story, but I wouldn't do it again. I love you. I'm in love with you." Her gaze locks to mine. "I gave up my book deal for you. Even told Weston I wouldn't do another article on you. I've—"

Her gaze is locked with mine. There is a plea in her eyes.

"Please," she says. "I can't imagine my life without you."

"I feel the same way," I say, my heart pumping out equal parts love and anger. "But you still have to go."

CHAPTER 56

THE SILENCE after losing Tara is deafening.

Before, with Susie, there was chaos after her death. Chaos and tragedy and family and friends, and a funeral. Out of that chaos came a need for silence, which was granted to me. Losing Tara, saying goodbye to the relationship we tried to build, despite the lies and omissions, was not externally chaotic. It wasn't loud, but it was deafening in its silence.

I walk into Mom's new residential facility. The air is cool and slams against my face. I pull off my sunglasses and my gaze sweeps the front entrance, which is determined to look like the front room of a home.

"Hey, I'm Mrs. Reynold's son," I say.

The man sitting at the front desk nods and pushes a button so I can enter the home. The lock is a precaution so that the residents don't wander away, and after Mom went missing a few months ago. I understand the precaution, but my heart hates that my mother is in a locked facility.

I walk through the living room, past the dining room and kitchen toward the hallway. Three doors down on the left I stop and knock. The place is small and each resident's room is a mini-suite with a front room, bedroom, and bathroom.

"Come in," Mom calls.

I open the door.

"Uncle Jake!"

Lily runs toward me. Daisy bounds after her. I bend down and hug Lily and give Daisy a pat on the head. Lily wraps her arms around me.

"I miss you Uncle Jake. When are you coming over to see me?"

I glance at Rachel. Her lips form a severe line and the muscle in her jaw flinches. Her gaze darts from me and Lily back to Mom.

"We were just going," Rachel says. Her tone icy. She bends down and kisses Mom on the cheek.

"Thank you for watching Rachel," Mom says. "I should be feeling better soon." Rachel presses her hand to Mom's shoulder and squeezes. "No problem." Big sis fights back tears.

"Hi Mom." I set a box of See's truffles on the table by the front door and walk to her.

"Richard, how do you get handsomer every time I see you?"

I smile and kiss her cheek. I look at Rachel. "Don't go on my account."

She pulls at the collar of her shirt. "We're not, Lily has a music lesson tonight."

"No I don't," Lily yells from the far corner.

"Yes you do," Rachel snaps.

"You can't avoid me forever," I say quietly, so only Rachel can hear.

"Why not? Weren't you going to keep this a secret forever?"

"That's different."

"Right about that," Rachel says. "One is good for my mental health and Lily's, the other puts my entire career in jeopardy." She leans forward. "And makes me question your mental stability."

Rachel's eyes flash with anger and concern.

"We need to discuss this," I say. "I think that you'll understand if I can just explain what I was doing and why I—"

"No. I don't want to know." Rachel holds up her hand. "The less I know the better." She turns toward the front of Mom's room where Mom and Lily are playing with Daisy. "I need you to get anything you want out of Mom's house. I'm putting it on the market."

"No you're not," I say.

Her gaze cuts me like a hot knife through butter. "Yes, I am. I don't want that place. I don't want the memories of the past, especially since our future is going to be so different."

The words she says, combined with her tone, shock me.

"What do you mean?"

"I mean that if you have that much disregard for me and my job, and potentially even Lily's safety, then I don't know you at all and I have no intention of letting a person that selfish and...and....wanton be a part of my life."

"I'm sorry," I say

"For what?" Rachel shoots back. "For fucking that many women, or for putting me in charge?" Rachel's gaze glances from me to Mom. Her bottom lip quivers and she fights back tears.

"Rachel you three are the only things I have in my life. Can't we...can't we get together tomorrow to discuss this? Please, let me tell you what happened. Let me tell you why—"

"I can't jeopardize my career and Lily's future while you get your shit show in order, OK? So no, we can't get together tomorrow, and to be fair, it may be a long while before I feel differently."

A knot the size of a melon forms in my throat. These are the women I love. These three are my life and I've disappointed the one woman that our entire family looks to for love and guidance. Rachel is our touchstone, our matriarch, the foundation of our family ever since Mom's mind fled the jurisdiction. I've disappointed her and the idea that I might be banished from the warmth of this family saddens me.

My chest tightens. I fight the tears that press into my eyes.

I walk to Lily. I scoop her into my arms and press my face into her curls. I love her. I love Lily with the kind of love that is amazing and pure and heals me in more ways than I ever could have imagined. She saved my life when she was born. She saved our family. I will not cry. I will not give her a bad memory because she doesn't know...she doesn't know that I've fucked up in what could be an unforgiveable fashion, and that quite possibly, her mother, my sister, may not let me see her again for a very long time.

I look at Rachel and Mom and Daisy and Lily, who plants a kiss on my face, smiles, and wiggles out of my arms so that she can play with Daisy. I pet Daisy and look into Lily's eyes.

"Call me whenever you want and if Mommy says it's okay. Bye, Lily." I force myself not to cry. "I'll see you and Daisy soon."

The tears are about to win and I don't want that. I turn to the door because an exit is the only way. My niece will never know how badly my heart is breaking.

❧

"YOU'VE BROKEN UP WITH TARA, THE ONLY WOMAN YOU can sleep with?"

I nod.

"You aren't speaking with your sister or seeing your niece?"

I nod again.

"Your mother was just put in an assisted living facility."

"Residential care."

Vida raises an eyebrow. "Excuse me, residential care."

"Yes."

She taps her pen onto her pad of paper. "How long before your head explodes?"

"That's why I come to you."

"Right, but Jake, you have to work with me a little. I mean these are all some major changes."

"I don't know how to fix any of them or if I want to fix the thing with Tara."

I do. I desperately want to fix the thing with Tara.

"Are you being honest with yourself?"

"Honest with myself? Yes. With you? No. Look, here's the thing, I want Tara. I love Tara, I know that. But I can't trust Tara. I know that too."

Vida nods and scribbles a note on her pad of paper. Looks up at me.

"Okay, but then how were you able to trust Susie?"

I sigh.

"I don't know. Maybe I didn't? Maybe I couldn't trust her either, but I was just so fucking obsessed with getting what I wanted that I was willing to be with her no matter what she did. Maybe I thought eventually I could love her through it, maybe I thought...." The light clicks on in my head. "Maybe I thought I could save her."

Vida's gaze is locked onto me as though she's willing a child to take his first step.

"And Tara doesn't need to be saved."

"That sounds plausible," Vida says.

"Still doesn't solve my problem because I absolutely do not trust her and I don't know if I ever will." I shift on the couch. "Or if I can."

"Is that a fair assessment?"

"She lied about writing the article and stole the numbers from my phone."

"They are egregious offenses," Vida says. "What about your side of this? Are your hands clean?"

I lean back against the couch. Are they? No, not really. I slept with Tara, ditched her, didn't tell her that she'd slept with a man who slept with hundreds of women as his vocation, then invited to be one of those women, left her crying on a couch....

I lean forward and put my elbows on my knees. "I...I can't see a way to bridge that gap."

"Okay, what about Rachel and Lily?"

My heart yanks and twists.

"She won't speak to me."

"She feels betrayed."

"By the person she trusted."

Vida nods.

"You may need to give Rachel time. She loves you and you love her, which is obvious based on the relationship you've built. She simply may need time to work through her feelings."

"Right. Patience isn't my strong suite."

"And yet often, patience and time are the only things that can get us to where we need to be both emotionally and in our inter-personal relationships."

Vida's words resonate with me but still don't fix the fucking pain traveling through my chest. All I have left is Mom. And reports from Fletcher, the dog trainer once every couple of days on how Lily is doing with Daisy. Yes, Rachel lets me Facetime with Lily and Daisy, but she doesn't invite me over, nor does she talk to me.

And Tara.

My heart twists tighter. Tara seems to have disappeared again. That is her MO when things aren't working between us. This time I won't chase her. This time I won't go to Malibu and look for her, nor will I go to Warren and tell him not to transfer her. This time she can go. In fact, maybe that would be the best thing that could happen. Maybe I should tell Warren that Tara needs to go and work in the San Francisco office.

"Our time is up today. You know your six months is up today," Vida says.

"What are you talking about?" I stand and turn to Vida.

"The court only requires six months of anger-management therapy. You've completed that requirement."

A tiny smile pulls over my face. "So I'm well. Like mentally, one hundred percent?" I ask in a teasing voice.

"You've done good work here. I'm not sure any human is ever

'well' when it comes to mental health because I don't know that we're ever broken. I can say you've confronted a number of problems and the requirement is complete."

She smiles and she pushes a strand of silver-gray hair behind her ear.

"I'll see you next week," I say, and turn toward the door. "I've still got a whole lot of stuff to work through."

"No problem," Vida says. "Next week then."

I walk through the door, confident that there is at least one woman in my life that thinks I'm making progress, still speaking to me, and that I'm not completely insane.

CHAPTER 57

"RICHARD, come and feed the birds with me."

A breeze ruffles Mom's hair and she walks out the back door of her residential facility into the giant backyard. The sun streams down. It's nearly fall in Southern California. The backyard is filled with shade and this place is located closer to the ocean than Mom's place, so it is cooler too.

She walks toward a tree and sprinkles bird seed on the ground. I follow behind.

"Do you remember the hummingbird feeders you used to put out every spring in the backyard?"

I remember Dad doing that.

"I loved those." Mom smiles. She sits beside me on a wooden bench in the shade. We watch the birds swoop and dive and then peck at the bird feed she's sprinkled by the tree.

"How is it going with Tara?"

I whip my gaze toward Mom and in this moment there is lucidity. A wicked-sharp gleam in her eyes, like the picture from Dad's desk drawer, as though Mom is completely present. I want to weep because we're getting nearer to the end of her lucidity. The other day she held her toothbrush in her hand and had no idea what she was supposed to do with it.

"We...we broke up."

"Ah," Mom says. "But it was different than Susie, yes? I mean she didn't have..."Mom glances away from me. "She didn't have that same type of problem, did she?"

"No."

Irony strikes me dead in the face, because in this scenario, it is me who had the problem, not Tara. The need to subvert my emotions by fucking every woman I possibly could. By fulfilling my vocation.

"I...she did something I can't forgive."

"Can't or won't?" Mom tilts her head and that sharp-eyed gaze that I desperately miss, focuses on me.

"Can I take your picture, Mom?"

I slip my phone from my pocket and point it in her direction.

"Jake, this is silly," she says, but pats her hair, tilts her head, and smiles.

I know as I press the button this will be the final picture of my mother with her sharp-eyed gaze knowing everything about where she is and who she is with. I feel this to my core. In fact, if I can let my heart believe it, this will be our final conversation.

"I love you, Mom."

Wanting her to take that with her on the journey I know she will leave for soon, the journey, that while her body will remain here with us, her mind will be unreachable by me and Rachel and Lily.

"Hey, want to see the picture of you with Lily, Rachel, and Daisy?"

Mom smiles and nods and I turn my phone to her. Again with the damn. fucking knot in my throat and the tears threatening to careen down my cheeks. I pinch my nose.

"Darn allergies," I say and smile. "Lily looks so much like you Mom."

I try hard to keep my voice from cracking. "She loves you so much. We all do."

"I love all of you too."

She looks at me and squeezes my arm. For a second, I see it. I see that she knows that she's missing giant chunks of time from her memory, but can't bear to speak about it, not in this moment, not in what could be her final moments with me.

"Jake, you deserve to be happy. We all deserve to be happy in life. There was a time that I was unhappy with your father—"

"Mom you don't—"

"No, please, let me. It's...it's important to me."

She looks into my eyes and I know she must say these words to me.

"I didn't think I could ever forgive him, or trust him, or even if I'm completely honest, if I would ever love him again. Especially after what happened between us. But Jake...I let him back into our home and into my heart because he said I could trust him, and I could love him, and that he would do anything he could to prove that to me"

Mom smiles and leans forward.

"I took that leap of faith and I've spent the rest of my life grateful that I could be that brave, and some would say foolish. But life is full of risks and sometimes those risks are worth the fear."

I turn away from Mom and look across the yard toward the sun setting. A deep breath fills my lungs.

"Mom I do love her. I'm afraid. I just..."

I turn back and the sharp gleam in Mom's eyes is gone, replaced with a blank look of child-like happiness.

I don't cry. I fight that urge. Instead, I reach my hand out to my mom, or the woman that looks just like her but has no memory of her life or me. I grasp her hand and smile at her, even while I want to cry.

"Thank you, Mom."

She smiles and turns toward the birds, and I don't even know if she remembers my name.

I walk into Rachel's house because the door is unlocked.

"Hey, I'm here."

Lily tears down the stairs with Daisy hot on her heels. All big puppy paws, she tumbles after Lily, the two of them an adorable pair. Rachel walks out of the kitchen and looks at me.

"Lily and Daisy have puppy school."

"I know."

I bend down and scratch Daisy's head. She's so happy her entire backside wiggles. "Fletcher's already in the backyard."

"See you when we're finished Uncle Jake." Lily bolts through the house to the yard.

"Why are you here?" Big Sis says to me, her arms crossed.

"We have to talk."

She sighs and even though she's tough, she knows I'm right.

She turns toward the kitchen and I follow her. From this spot we can watch Lily, Daisy, and Fletcher in the backyard.

"So talk," she says.

She opens a cabinet and pulls out a glass, uncorks the wine bottle on the counter, and pours herself a drink.

"It started about a year after Susie died. It was consensual, word of mouth, and never commercial, in any way."

"No money. Not ever."

I shake my head. "Not ever."

"Perks. Gifts. Meals. Travel?"

"No, not generally. But if there were take-out meals I paid. Hotel rooms all paid for by me. I did receive one gift from a woman I saw for nearly five years."

Rachel swirls her wine and takes a sip. "But that was the anomaly, not the rule."

I nod.

"Fine. So you're a sex addict like Susie. I wish I'd known sooner. Maybe I would've judged her less harshly."

"This wasn't about the sex."

"It wasn't about the sex for Susie either."

I scrub my hand through my hair and look at Rachel. "This was because of what happened to Susie. I never wanted any woman to feel like she did. Like there was nowhere to turn. And I....I needed the physical intimacy and even the emotional connection, but in a way that I could control. A way that didn't put me at risk. A way that allowed me to feel safe. That what happened between me and Susie, that I would never fall in love again, and it worked—"

"Until Tara."

I nod. "Until Tara."

"Did you know about the article?"

"Not until it was posted."

"Shut. Up." Rachel places her wine glass on the counter and leans toward me. "That bitch didn't even tell you before it posted?"

And like that, in an instant, she is my big sister again. Still angry at me, probably disappointed, and definitely worried, but right now she is angry because in her mind, regardless of all of the above, I'm still her baby brother, and nobody gets to wrong her little brother, except maybe her.

I shake my head.

"And you forgave her?"

"I love her."

"Oh, Jake. We don't choose very well do we?"

She lifts her glass and takes a long sip of her wine.

"Fuck," she says. "So why now? Why are you two broken up now if you'd forgiven her about the article?"

"There was more. At first she said she figured it out after we started seeing each other and she copped to putting it together when she saw my phone."

"Fuck." Rachel's eyes grow wide. "The flip phone! And here I was worried you were dealing drugs when actually you were simply peddling flesh to the entire Westside."

"She found it and at first she said that she just saw the name, but actually she downloaded all the numbers and contacted all the women."

"Wowza!"

Big Sis goes to a cabinet and lifts out a couple of Pyrex dishes. She opens the refrigerator and pulls out a container of cheese and mashed potatoes.

"How'd you figure all that out?" She turns back to the counter. "Hmm, that's an extra dish." She lifts a Pyrex and puts it aside.

"An extra dish?"

"Yeah, that one's not mine."

"Right."

It's the one Kendall brought back to Rachel.

"How did you find out about the phone numbers?"

"There's a woman that she reached out to, that figured out my real identity, because I bumped into her as Jake."

Rachel sprays one of the Pyrex dishes with oil. She sets down the spray can and looks at me.

"This is all fucked up. Why did she tell you that? Why did Tara tell you the truth, finally?"

"I guess someone threatened to out me if she didn't come clean.".

"Now what?"

I glance through the window toward Lily. Daisy races across the yard between Fletcher and Lily. Lily throws her head back and laughs.

"I don't know."

I pull my phone from my pocket. "I saw Mom yesterday," I say, and flip the phone around to Rachel so she can see the picture I took.

"Oh, Jakey. It's her." A tone filled with longing. Rachel presses her fingers to the corners of her eyes. "I...I don't think we'll see her much anymore. I mean the Mom who remembers our name."

"No, I don't either. It's almost like she clawed her way to me."

I look into Rachel's eyes. "She told me why she took Dad back. How it was maybe the most foolish things she ever did and definitely one of the bravest. How thankful she was that she'd been that brave." I press my lips together. "Love requires bravery."

Rachel looks at me. "Be brave."

CHAPTER 58

I KNOCK on Tara's door. I hear Jango's nose pressed up against the bottom edge and I picture her entire furry body shaking with joy that I've stopped here to see them.

My belly tightens. I've been thinking about this moment, wondering what words I should or can say that will let us move forward, help us to get past the events that divide us, and I don't know what those words are. I don't know what exactly to say because I'm still angry and hurt and a little pissed off. But I know that none of that matters because I love Tara and she loves me.

"Jake?"

The door opens. Jango is out the door and her paws are on my legs and she hops a little on her two hind feet she's so excited to see me.

I pat Jango and stroke her soft fur. I look back at Tara. "Can we talk?"

Tara nods, suprise on her face, and I don't blamer her. In the past month I've given her no indication that I'd ever speak to her again. I've done a pretty good job with my avoidance system and managed not to see her nearly the entire time, with one slip up in the parking garage because I stopped and got groceries.

I walk into her place that I've been in a million times. This time feels a different, as though something is ending and maybe, I hope, beginning too.

"Can I get you anything?" she asks.

I shake my head and she moves to the couch.

"Sit," she says, and reaches out toward the blue chair in the living room.

"I...I need to talk to you," I say. "I need to put some of these things behind me."

The color leaves Tara's face as though she's completely aware that this moment, this conversation with me is most likely our last conversation.

"Jake, I....I have so much I want to say to you, need to say to you, but even when I say all these things you'll still—"

"Please let me say what I need to say."

She surrenders to the couch and Jango lies down at her feet.

"Tara, I love you."

Tara presses her hand to her mouth.

"I will love you for the rest of my life. I know that, and that's part of why I was so upset. Because I felt as though you traded on that love, but I traded on it too. I believe you when you say that you wouldn't do this again and I know that we both have baggage to unpack and put away in this relationship. But I know I want to do this work with you."

Absolute shock, I see it in her eyes.

"You...you...want us to be together?"

"I ... this has been hard on me. I, I am still trying to work through my anger at you going through my phone. Actually lifting the numbers so that you could get a story."

She nods and her face looks grim.

"But where love is concerned, I need to be brave, and I want to be brave with you." I walk to her and I pull her to standing. She is right in front of me and the scent of fresh soap and hints of lavender come with her.

"I love you. You love me. We aren't perfect people, but we

only get so many trips around the sun and I don't want to spend any more of them without you by my side," I say.

"Are you sure?"

"I've never been so sure of anything in my life."

She looks up at me and I know in this moment that this is the woman for me, that there will never be a Wonderfuck again, that there will only be me, Jake, and her Tara, and together we will get through the bad and cherish the good and be a couple that weathers it all.

I know this because I trust that this love I feel pulsing through what was once a heart deadened by pain, has come back to feel and love a woman that I'm ready to build a lifetime of memories with.

A smile slips to her face and she weaves her hand through my hair and kisses me. I know that there is nothing more in this world that I will ever want or need. I only want to be her Mister Wonderful.

The End

Thank you for reading *Wonderful Love*. If you enjoyed this book, please take a moment to leave a review on Goodreads or your favorite online retailer. Reviews help readers discover new authors, and I am grateful for all reviews.

BOOKS BY MAGGIE MARR

The Hollywood Girls Club Series

Hollywood Girls Club

Secrets of the Hollywood Girls Club

Hollywood Hit

Hollywood Girls Club, the Series

The Eligible Billionaires Series

Can't Buy Me Love

One Night for Love

A Christmas Billionaire

Last Call for Love

Running from Love

Eligible Billionaires Books 1–5

Eligible Billionaires: The Travati Brothers

A Forever Love

A Billionaire for Christmas

A Convenient Arrangement

A Forbidden Love

Eligible Billionaires Books 6-9

The Powder Springs Series

Courting Trouble

The Christmas Wish

Candy Cane Lane

ACKNOWLEDGMENTS

With every book there are many people to thank. First, thank you to my readers. I love writing and I love that you read my writing. Thank you.

Thank you to the Maggie Marr SUPERSTARS!
Thank you to Kristin Nelson, Maria Connor, Jennifer Brown, Kelley Jefferson, Kiki Chatfield, Kelly Hartog, Cami Brite, and Michael Canales.

Thank you to RWA, LARA, & OCC.
Thank you Margaret A. Marr, Lauren Harrison, Nealie White, Gayle Leftwich, Dixie Marr, Linda & Bill Henderson, Lindsy & Mark Henderson, Paula & David Glasscock, Amy & Brent Zacky, Garrett Marr, Victoria & Karl Makinen, Maria Seager, Peggy Cafferty, Molly Ware, Ally Carter, Pamela DuMond, Cassie Hayes, Sylvie Fox, Theodora Taylor, Allie K. Adams, Beth Yarnall, Jenn LeBlanc, Tameri Etherton, Kelly Hartog, Let It Rain, Catherine Bybee, Debra Holland, Debbie Decker, Sydney Holmes, and Bob.

Thank you to Chad and the kidlets; to the moon and back--
everything is for you.

ABOUT THE AUTHOR

USA Today Bestselling Author Maggie Marr is a hopeless romantic with a dirty mind. She writes strong women and the men they love. Maggie got her start in entertainment slinging boxes in the mailroom and eventually became a motion picture agent. Over twenty books later, Maggie still works in entertainment and makes her home in Los Angeles.

Please join her mailing list to get a FREE Maggie Marr starter library and keep up with all things Maggie!

Website: www.maggiemarr.net
    Newsletter: http://eepurl.com/c050yz
    Facebook: Maggie Marr Books
    Twitter: @maggiemarr
    Pinterest: Maggie Marr
    Instagram: Maggie_Marr_Author